THE

BY

To Allens,

David W. Walker

David W. Walker

— I hope you enjoy this read —

WINPUBLISH

WINPUBLISH

LONDON . NEW ORLEANS. NEW YORK

A Division of Wincustomers, LLC
New Orleans & Mississippi Office
PO Box 1374
Hattiesburg, MS 39403 U.S.A.

None of the characters in THE TRAITORS is an actual
person nor are the historical figures presented as factual
portrayals. The entire action and plot of the book is
fiction, based on intriguing study of period commando
operations and projected weaponry of the Luftwaffe and
Japanese Army. Any resemblance to any actual person or
persons is purely coincidental.

For information address:
Winpublish
New Orleans & Mississippi Office
 PO Box 1374
Hattiesburg, MS 39403 U.S.A.
+1-601-450-4445
www.winpublish.com

ISBN – 1449985629
EAN-13 9781449985622

Dedication

This book is dedicated to my father, Leon "Red" Walker who served as a radar technician on destroyers in the North Atlantic in World War II and who will remain an inspiration for me always.

Acknowledgements

Among those who have made this book possible are my wonderful wife Kim who has always encouraged and supported my writing efforts and my brother Lee whose enthusiasm is a vital spark to my creative endeavors.

I'd like to acknowledge the incredible effort Ray Sharpe has put forward in shepherding this book into production. No list of acknowledgements would be complete without my thanking the 365th Writers Avoidance Support Group and its noble captain, Bill Kirby for their invaluable critique and encouragement.

CHAPTER 1

February 13th, 1945

Lieutenant Marcus Johnson caught it in the periphery of his vision—a small shadow far below, grazing over the treetops, hardly moving. Making sure the rest of the sky was empty, Marcus banked the silver-winged P-51 to starboard, fed power to the Merlin V-12, and began his attack like a hunting falcon steeping for a dove. In seconds he realized the target was no fighter but only an unarmed Storch, maybe on a reconnaissance mission, or maybe lost. Unarmed or not, it was German and his mission was to blast it out of the sky, something the 100th fighter squadron had been doing a good job of over the last few months. Encountering enemy planes of any description was becoming a rare event on his patrols. His gloved fingers closed over the trigger button as the target swelled in his sights.

The first burst knocked holes through the port wing of the Storch and the squarish monoplane began to waggle back and forth. Marcus figured the thrashing was probably caused by damage to a control surface, but the movements continued in a more deliberate manner as he shot past. He just had time to glance across to the cockpit and see the beleaguered young pilot waving frantically.

The red-tailed Mustang with black trim tabs, pulled up to a higher altitude and Johnson took another precautionary look around before circling back to draw alongside the defenseless spotter. There was no satisfaction in flaming non-combatants, though it was an accepted part of his job. He made a quick decision. If this German wanted to surrender, fine, but if he were up to something odd, he'd find out quick what the Mustang's cannons could do to a box kite.

The P-51 didn't like loafing along with the slow Storch, but Johnson managed it like the twenty-two-year-old professional he was. He had three kills on fighters and had blown two tanks to hell along with a pair of locomotives. Marcus didn't fancy painting a German "Piper Cub" alongside those markings on the *Shady Lady's* cowl. This scared kid wasn't the kind of superman he'd been training to fight back at Tuskegee field in Alabama. Steadying the Merlin, he peered across to the glassed-in canopy below the angular wing of the Storch.

The German pilot was having trouble with the controls, but clearly signaling his wish to land and surrender. Johnson doubted the small plane would have enough fuel to make his home field but could probably make a landing near a forward army position he'd crossed about thirty miles back. The Kraut would have to take his chances. He'd do him the favor of leading him in. Marcus just hoped he didn't foul his plugs doing this slow tow job. He motioned for the Storch pilot to bank right. The German waved back with obvious relief. Johnson chuckled. He'd never taken a prisoner.

Oberstleutnant Gerhard Kessler grunted and handed the coffee back to the orderly. Kessler cast an angry eye out the window of the metal hut to scan the concrete runways of the aerodrome. A fuel truck lumbered past spraying icy water up in an oily sheet. Beyond the truck, a pair of Me 109 fighter planes sat, their crews loading ammunition belts into their guns. A lone figure bicycled between the fighters making directly for Kessler's hut. The gasping private leaped from the bike and hurried up the steps, his breath steaming before him in short white puffs.

"Where is my plane and pilot?" Kessler snapped. He was tired of delays.

The private, out of breath, swallowed and gasped his reply, "Gone, Oberstleutnant!"

"What do you mean?"

The airman straightened. "Your Storch is missing, sir. The mechanics say your pilot came for it thirty minutes ago and took off. He said he was under your orders. He had signed papers, Oberstleutnant."

Kessler stared at the airman. "You are certain of this?"

"Javol, Oberstleutnant."

Kessler rubbed a hand across his face. "Bring me the telephone," he barked to the orderly. Kessler walked across the room to study a wall map near the wood stove. The orderly scrambled to bring him the phone with its long cord from the desk.

Kessler ran a finger across the measured lines of the map. "Poor, foolish Rudi," he whispered. "You will never make Switzerland, my lad. Another fifteen minutes perhaps." Kessler took the phone to order up a pursuit.

February 16th

As he waited for the aide to return from the Colonel's office, Chris Clancey stuck his dress cap under his left arm and straightened his tie. He'd always felt uncomfortable in dress uniform. The medals and trim meant nothing to him—especially after he'd shot the woman. That had done it really, more than any of the other jobs. Blowing up bridges, fuel dumps, killing with guns and knives; it had seemed like a war. It made a kind of sense. He could still pretend to see a right and wrong in it. But shooting the woman, even a bad woman, was too personal. It had been cold and quiet, too much like murder. He hadn't even been angry. Chris studied the new skin on his hand. It had taken months to grow the borrowed flesh over the burns. He wondered if they could graft some self-esteem onto his soul as easily.

The aide returned beaming. "The Colonel will see you now, Captain Clancey. Congratulations on your recovery."

Clancey walked through the door the aide held open. The room seemed smaller than he remembered. The English sun, shining through the tall window behind the desk, cast the standing figure of his superior in a dark profile. Chris only thought of him as the Colonel. A rank, not a man. The Colonel was the one who had handed him the choices he had taken. Older, ingratiating, even affectionate, Chris had never allowed himself to accept his commander in those human terms. He had promised himself from the beginning that what he did must always come from within with no hint of personal loyalty or the false comfort of affected camaraderie. The orders he followed came only after he had made the choices for himself. Now, staring at the Colonel's silhouette, he considered the scale with which he had come to measure him. The Colonel cast a shadow, but Chris wasn't sure it shouldn't have horns and a barbed tail.

"Clancey, my boy, it's great to see you. You look fit, son. Guess it's all that good food in the hospital, right?" The Colonel stepped forward to extend his right hand but paused. His eyes moved to Clancey's other hand. "Here, let me get a look at McAndoe's work."

Chris set his cap on a chair and held up his left hand. The Colonel studied it carefully, absorbed in his inspection.

"My God, but that man does a hell of a job. Don't tell me where he borrowed the new skin from. I've seen lots worse mitts on his RAF boys that are back flying. Of course, I'm not suggesting you don't punch your ticket home. God knows you've more than earned it." The Colonel nodded, agreeing with himself, "Chris, I feel really inadequate trying to thank you for all you've done for us these last two years. I've had a lot of fine men working under me, son, but I've never been prouder of a one of them than you, and that's the God's truth."

Clancey bit his lip. Don't say anything. Don't fill in the gaps. That's what the old bastard's waiting for. He's waiting for a chance to get you to talk yourself into something. Chris had promised himself this was the end of it. No more missions behind enemy lines. No more. They'd made him dirty, but they hadn't damned him yet, not while he could still be sick about it maybe. He had seen what more of it did to a man. He'd seen what he could become, and he wasn't going to do that for them, no matter what flag they waved.

After a pause, the Colonel broke the awkward silence between them. "Jesus, boy. They really took it out of you, didn't they? I'm sorry, Chris, I know they got their hands on you good the last time. I read the full report. But that doesn't tell you everything. Pretty rough, huh?"

Clancey nodded.

The Colonel gestured to a plush chair and leaned back on the desk, lifting the lid on a wooden cigar box. When Clancey declined the offered tobacco, the Colonel took one for himself. Pausing to scrape up the flame, he snapped the silver Ronson shut with a click before crossing his arms and looked down at the young captain. "You don't have to talk about it if you don't want to, Chris." The Colonel flashed a quick smile. "I can't give you a medal, but I can sure give you your papers home and I guess that's worth a lot more than a handful of ribbons in this bitch of a war."

Clancey waited.

"I wish like hell I could give one to every kid I've sent behind the lines." The Colonel rubbed his neck. There was another long silence.

At last, Clancey took a deep breath. "You want me to do another job, don't you, Colonel?"

The Colonel rolled his cigar in his fingers, studying it before answering. "Nope. I don't want you to do it, Chris. I admit I was thinking that way until you came in here. Hell, you know me, son. But I think they skinned you a little too deep last time. I'm not going to throw you away. I have to believe some of my boys finally do get away with it. Remember, when I recruited you for that first mission, I told you you'd probably not live to see the end of this war. Well, I think you will. I'm not usually happy to be wrong. No, we'll call the hand now and you get to carry home your chips. I want at least a few good memories when I have to sit by the fire remembering this stinking job."

Chris Clancey was surprised. This was not what he had expected. He could usually read the Colonel pretty well, knew when he wanted something, knew when he was holding something back. He was holding something back this time, all right. But maybe it was because he genuinely cared about Clancey. And, maybe it was because he thought something was wrong with him, that whatever this mission was, it was too big and important to risk on him. Too important to risk on a cripple. Curiosity and suspicion were conditioned reflexes with Clancey. They had kept him alert and alive for the last two years and were too strong to ignore now. He knew he couldn't walk out of this office not knowing what was too big for him to face. He hated himself for asking, but he hadn't been able to forget that what went on in this room could make a difference, a real difference, in the world that was ending and the one that was coming.

"All right, Colonel. What is it?" Chris asked. "What's the mission you won't send your 'favorite son' on?"

"Nothing, Clancey. I'm filling out your papers, there's no catch. See, they're right here on my desk." The Colonel had turned to indicate a few sheets of stationery with various stamps lying beside them.

Chris shook his head. "You haven't stamped them yet. You need me for something, or you thought you did ten minutes ago. What is it, Colonel? I deserve to know what I'm turning my back on before I try to forget it."

The Colonel walked around the desk and sat down, picking up the papers. "Sorry, Chris, I can't do that. Not even for you. This one is—"

"Big? They're all big."

The Colonel grinned. "Right. That's right. They're all big." He picked up one of the stamps. He flipped open an ink pad and began to knead the rubber back and forth on the wet surface.

Clancey bit his lip and stood up. "Do you have anybody you think is better than me?"

The Colonel leaned back. "That's an interesting question, Chris. It's all in how you look at it. Do I have a better pilot? No. A better man with explosives? No. A man who operates better under pressure?" He stopped. "Not like you did."

"That's changed?"

"Maybe."

There it was. If he was going home, he'd have to live with that answer. Clancey took a breath. "Maybe I am used up, and maybe I'm not. I can still kill, if that's what bothers you. I don't like it, but then I never did."

The Colonel pursed his lips and took another drag on the cigar. "That was one reason I kept using you. When a man starts enjoying the killing, he's not far from killing himself. That kind of man isn't any good to me. I've had to develop a sense of when a man might cross over that line, Chris."

"And you think I'm about to?"

"I didn't say that. Intelligent people react to violence in different ways. But, invariably they have to accommodate the fact of their actions into their own moral balance. I think I know you, son. I don't think you're going to be able to keep coming back to dead center. I don't like to take a chance on that kind of unresolved business going on with my boys when they're out in the field."

"So now you're a damned psychiatrist?"

"Son, in this job, I have to be God Almighty Himself."

Chris looked out the window. "I hate this war, Colonel. I hate everything about what's going on right now. I mean, you and I know it's over. Hell, everybody above the rank of private knows it's over. Everybody but Hitler. And a lot of boys are going to be killed just to please the fantasies of that diseased bastard and the sons of bitches running the war for him. And that fucking bunch is not going to quit as long as they can kill a few more of us, or some Jews, or Russians, or anyone else they can get a claw into. It's an endgame now. I don't aim to die in a stinking, no-purpose endgame." He paused again and turned to look the Colonel in the eye. "I came in here to turn you down on whatever you were going to sell me, Colonel."

"Everything you've said is right, Chris. It's a bloody endgame and it's going to be a beaten, broken Germany no matter what that idiot does or doesn't do. But if this mission fails there'll be a lot more losers. A lot more. And they're going to be Americans."

Clancey closed his eyes. This wasn't what he'd come here for. Or was it? To ask more would be to volunteer. He knew that. He also knew the Colonel was right about him. He had reached the point of no return. He'd never be the same man who'd taken that first mission. Whatever meaning his life had now wasn't going to be waiting for him at home in Iowa. That Chris Clancey didn't exist anymore. He opened his eyes and looked across at the Colonel. "I'm in, sir. If it really is for all the chips."

The Colonel set down the rubber stamp. "Do you remember the Me-264?"

Clancey was surprised. "Sure, big-assed, long-range bomber the Germans tested but never put in production, other than a handful. Two or three, I think. Big bomb load, or lots of fuel, I guess. Hitler had one standing by at Leechfield to fly him to Japan if the coup had come off. We nailed it and the other ones never got finished, as far as I know. You're not trying to tell me they've been producing the things in secret. Even the Germans couldn't hide an operation that big."

"Of course not," the Colonel agreed, taking another draw on his cigar. "But, they do have three we didn't know about. They've hidden them pretty well."

"So what? Three airplanes don't mean anything, even if they were the best in the world. They've got a lot more than three of those jet fighters and they're not doing them much good. Too little, too late, thank God."

The Colonel was watching him closely as he spoke. "The planes are only a part of it, Chris. They don't need many. It's what they'll be carrying and where they'll be going that concerns us."

Clancey felt a cold chill flooding his chest. "What is it? What are they carrying?"

The Colonel stood up again. "We didn't think even that madman would resort to this. We've fought a whole war with these bastards and it's never come up. Until now." He studied his cigar tip. "Chris, have you ever been a hunter?"

"No."

The Colonel laughed. "Not until you met me, anyway! Well, the most dangerous animal is a wounded animal that's crazy with pain and fear. That's when they'll do the desperate thing no rational creature would risk as long as there was hope. That's the most dangerous time. When you go in to finish the job. That's what this mission is about."

Clancey waited.

The Colonel turned to stare into Clancey's eyes and Chris could see fear in his face for the first time. "Germs, Chris. Biological warfare. Plague death. It killed a third of Europe in the Middle Ages. And that was when people didn't travel. That's what's in those bombs. Enough plague to turn New York, or Boston, or Washington into a withered, dying wasteland. And those planes can hit anything from Maine to Miami. Not waves of bombers, just three planes slipping over the Atlantic one sunny morning next week and it starts. Who knows where it would end, thousands, maybe millions." The Colonel stopped. "That's it."

Clancey sat still. That was it all right. "When do we start?"

"Right now. There's someone I want you to meet." The Colonel leaned down and flipped the switch on his intercom. "Lieutenant, get my driver." He turned back to Clancey. "Sorry I had to drag you back into this, Chris."

Clancey shook his head. "I won't lose any sleep over this one, Colonel. Three planes out of the blue, no warning, and thousands of women and children die in agony. No sir, anybody that would have anything to do with that needs killing. This is one I can live with."

Clancey swayed against the seat cushions of the olive-drab Ford as the driver negotiated the roadway at the rapid pace preferred by the Colonel. Clancey turned his eyes from the road. He never felt comfortable with anyone but himself at the controls of an automobile or an airplane. "So, how do we know about this business, Colonel? I wasn't aware we had a network in Germany."

"Not much of one, anyway," the Colonel replied. "No, this was a slip-up. One of their boys found out about it, grabbed a Storch, and headed west."

"What? Is he a scientist or some general looking for a deal? 'I'll tell you my secret if you'll save my ass'." Clancey began to wonder how much credence to give this frightening tale.

"I wish you were right, Chris. I wish it were just a tall tale, and maybe it is, but the guy you're going to see is a nobody, a simple Luftwaffe pilot, not even a combat flier, just a Storch chauffeur. He was flying an Oberstleutnant Kessler to Berlin when he slipped away and made a dash for our lines. Konnings is his name, and all he wants in return for what he knows is for us to go and help him get his sister out. Not asking much, is he?"

Clancey closed his eyes. "You mean he really believes we might do that? Send him back with a team?"

"He's eighteen, Chris. And pretty naive for a superman."

Chris leaned to steady himself against a long curve. "This is starting to get complicated. You haven't gotten everything out of him yet?"

"Jesus, boy. We just got him in here yesterday. They dumped him on me when the field desk couldn't decide what to do with him. At first, he wouldn't talk to anyone but intelligence, and then he talked too much for the French desk to handle. They figure he's just a scared kid trying to come up with a story to buy himself some kind of deal, but they're too busy to sort it out. God, I hope they're right, but he's said enough to scare the hell out of me. We could sweat the rest out with a little time, but time is about gone, if he's telling the truth. I'm hoping he's changed his mind about this going back business, or maybe you can charm it out of him. You speak German better than anybody in the department."

Clancey frowned. "It sounds like a lie. A set up."

"For what purpose? To scare us? Besides, if the Nazis wanted to trick us into believing this business, they'd be making some overture for a truce or something. No such luck. If they wanted to tie up a few of our intelligence officers, they'd be wasting a lot of effort. O.S.S. is more useful spying against the Russians now than against the Wehrmacht. Hell, Hitler's so screwy even his own people don't know what he's going to do from breakfast to lunch. We sure can't make much sense out of eavesdropping on them, which is what we're doing most of the time anyway."

Chris sighed. "Okay, so how does a taxi pilot know the truth about what's probably the most important secret of the High Command? Come on, Colonel. I don't want to get killed for a pack of desperate lies by a deserter. He just figures we'll treat him better if he's got secret information."

"You're not telling me anything I haven't already told myself, Chris. But frankly, I talk to this kid and I get cold from my crotch to my crown."

"He could be a set-up himself. Maybe he thinks what they want him to think. We did a few numbers like that before 'Overlord', or so I've heard."

"It's possible, I admit. But we can't afford to take the risk."

"You mean you can't afford for *me* not to take the risk."

The Colonel tapped the cigar on the ashtray mounted in the back of the front seat. "No, Chris. You see this kid and then you decide. If you think it's smoke, I'll stamp those papers. That's a promise." The Colonel's somber gaze trailed into a reluctant smile. "You might want to 'pray about it a mite,' as my mother used to say."

"Well, I lose my bet," Clancey said without enthusiasm. "You did have a mother."

Private Rudi Konnings woke to the sound of a heavy lock being turned and forced himself up from the bed to face whoever was about to enter the room. He had been surprised to be in a room and not a cell. Except for the bed, a small table, and a single straight-backed chair, it was bare, but the wooden floor was clean and the freshly plastered walls and plush curtains almost gave the illusion of a guest room. Still, he had known there were bars in the windows even before he had bothered to look. Through these, he had looked down on the stone wall of the estate and the deep forest just beyond the barrier patrolled by soldiers with dogs. It was funny, Rudi had thought; he had never seen an American until two days ago, and now he was surrounded by them. Even his scant English let him enjoy a mild amusement at their turn of speech. It was as if the English language was perhaps a second tongue for the Americans as well. His amusement had not lasted long. The relief at being captured alive and achieving contact with Allied Intelligence had receded quickly to the gnawing fear that had spurred him into deliberately betraying his government. This fear's grim companion was the growing suspicion that he had deserted his sister to an even more horrible fate which would be of little consequence to his captors once they had what they wanted from him. He resolved again to hold out for Reisa's rescue, no matter what they threatened him with. He was not naive. He knew what the Gestapo did to men to get them to talk. And he knew that all nations at war had men who would seize on any method to further their ends when it was expedient. He prayed he was wrong about these men.

The colonel he had met that morning was back and with him was a tall, gaunt officer. This one looked more somber than the colonel. Strong and sinewy, yet somehow unsettled. An injury perhaps? Yes; the left hand was bright pink, new skin. Had it been a wound of battle, or perhaps the Gestapo? As he rose to greet them, Rudi wondered if he, too, were in for 'new skin'.

The colonel ordered the guard to close the door and then motioned Rudi to sit back down on the bed. The colonel pulled up the wooden chair from the small writing table and sat. The other officer continued to stand, looking at Rudi in an introspective manner. He felt his pulse quicken. Rudi knew what he said in the next few moments could make a great difference, not only in the lives of countless strangers, but also in his sister's fate and his own.

"Rudi, this is Captain Clancey. The captain has spent a lot of time working for me. He's concerned about your story and I'm afraid I have not been telling it very well. He'd like a few more facts. We don't turn our people loose on such scant evidence every day. The captain here doesn't risk his life without making damn sure it's worth it, either. I'm sure you can understand his position."

Rudi could hardly believe the words. "You believe me? You will get my sister out of Germany?"

The Colonel took a drag on his cigar and shot a glance at Clancey. "Not without a lot more information, son. Right now you've told us a scary story, but that's all. We need to know more. Just tell us the whole thing, from the beginning,

Rudi swallowed. Maybe, they did believe him. Maybe, his prayers had been answered. He took another deep breath and looked up at the still, silent captain.

The man finally nodded to Rudi and said, "Sprich Deutsch, bitte."

"Sie sprechen Deutsch?" Rudi was relieved, though not surprised, that the captain spoke his language. It would make this much easier than using the interpreter they'd brought in before. The captain indicated he should begin and extended him a cigarette which he lit for him. The match illuminated the baby pink skin of the captain's hand as he held the flame to the cigarette. Rudi took a long drag on the luxurious tobacco, and after exhaling the warm, reassuring smoke, began his story.

CHAPTER 2

"I am a private in the Luftwaffe, an aide to Oberstleutnant Gerhard Kessler. He was a friend of our family and, from flight school, he claimed me for his personal pilot. He had promised to watch after me before my father was killed in an air raid last year. My family's home is near the village of Halburg in the southwest, near Ulm. It is not so far from the Swiss border. My sister lives there still.

"In the months I have served Herr Kessler, I have come to see with my own eyes that Germany's days are ending. I have come to see that many horrors have been done by our leaders—our nation. I only hope that your countrymen reach the Fatherland before the barbarous Russians who hate us as no others. Now there is a *final* horror, for which we could never be forgiven."

Rudi paused. "This is my fear, not that we lose, for we have already lost, but that we will be torn apart by the nations who will see us as monsters." Clancey saw the desperation in Konnings' eyes. "You must understand, my sister is the one thing of value I have in all this world. All I can think of is what becomes of her when this war is ended. What becomes of all of us?"

He shook his head. An ironic smile flickered for an instant at the corner of his mouth. "Reisa, my sister, she says if we allow this thing—it is not what becomes of us, but what *we* become."

Konnings took a nervous drag on his cigarette. He knew he was rambling, but the captain seemed very patient and showed no sign of hurrying him.

"I was home for short leave last week as Herr Kessler did not require me and it had been long since my last time home. I was excited to see Reisa for the first time since my training. She is seventeen now and lives in our home with Gretchen and Hugo Borgman, our servants. When I arrived at our house, I was surprised to find another Luftwaffe officer there visiting her. Hauptman Klaus Reichmann, a famous bomber pilot. When I was a kid in the youth corps, I had been introduced to him. He had flown many missions both over England and Russia. And here he was visiting my baby sister. Reichmann seemed most uncomfortable discussing anything to do with his unit or the planes. I gathered he was involved with something unusual. I did not think much of this. You know that good soldiers do not speak much of such things. Being quite tired, I went up to my old bed and left my sister and Reichmann alone.

"I awoke later to the sound of motors overhead, and thinking it might be British bombers, I went quickly to my window. I could not make out the type of airplane above, but I saw my sister and Reichmann walking in the garden below. They were in hard conversation. They seemed very much distressed. I was curious and watched Reichmann leave for his car. I wondered if my sister was perhaps breaking the heart of the great flyer.

"I met her on the porch as she returned from the drive. Reisa was surprised to see me waiting for her and, even in the moonlight, I could see she was shaken; not at all, the cheerful, charming hostess who had pampered me and Reichmann at dinner. To my questions, she was silent for a long time and I saw her face streaked with tears. I asked her what was wrong and she said she had promised Klaus she would tell no one, but that we were different. We never had secrets, ever since we were children and I could see Reisa was afraid. Finally, she told me everything there on the steps of the house as we sat huddled together against the cold."

Rudi took a nervous drag on the cigarette before continuing. He looked up at the captain again but could detect no emotion on the American's face.

"It was Klaus. He was being commanded to do something—to fly a mission he could not fly. Reisa had asked if it were too dangerous and he had laughed bitterly. No, it was not dangerous for him, but it was wrong. Very wrong. The worst thing of all. He said he had always felt the Luftwaffe was superior to those S.S. pigs—that they would never be tolerated after the war. He had ignored them; first, because they made him sick, and then, because they scared him. Now they were telling him what to do. Now they were going to make him one of them—a murderer."

Konnings glanced up at the captain. "You understand, it is not the same to be a murderer as to be a soldier?"

The captain nodded. "Yes. Go on."

Rudi took a breath and resumed his story. "So I said, 'What is it, Reisa? What is the thing Klaus Reichmann will not do? Is it a secret weapon? A rocket plane?' I guessed maybe it was a new bomb, maybe a special rocket. I was amazed at the incredible weapons our scientists have made. I wondered what was so much greater that even a pilot like Reichmann would not dare to use it.

"Reisa stared at me and her eyes were wide with fear. 'Oh Rudi,' she said, 'you have heard of the poison in the great war? The gas Father talked about?' I swallowed as I remembered the stories. She began to cry. 'It is worse. Much worse. It is a thing that falls upon a man and goes into him and cannot be stopped. It is sickness and death, always death. Nothing can stop it. It blows on the wind. It is plague. Black Death from the air. The terrible plague of long ago.'"

Konnings looked down at his cigarette which was a stub of bright ashes. He looked up to find a new one being held out to him by his interrogator. His hands were shaking as he thanked Clancey and took the new light.

"So, then, I asked, 'Where is he taking this terrible weapon? What is he to bomb?' She looked at me and whispered, 'America.' 'The American *army*?' I asked her, but she said no. It was to America the poison would go. That Klaus was to fly across the world to release the Black Death on America."

Konnings shuddered as if he were cold. "I shook my head. It cannot be. There is no airplane that can do this in all the Luftwaffe. But, then I remembered the plane that had wakened me. A bomber, a very large bomber, and they were not the motors of the British Stirlings or Lancasters. There had been no bombs or anti-aircraft fire. Large bombers. German bombers. I had heard rumors of the secret planes before. Messerschmitt 264. You know of it?"

"Yes, we know of this plane," Clancey nodded again, his arms crossed, his hands tucked under his elbows.

"That was it, of course, but it was too fantastic, too crazy. Why America? I asked, why so far? Reisa shook her head at me and kept crying. Because Roosevelt was a coward who would only fight a war from half around the world. If an American city were stricken with such a plague, then he would stop his army. He would leave us in peace to fight the Communists. Like Moses and the plagues of Egypt, when the babies of the Egyptians died, then the pharaoh let Moses go. But this time, it will be American babies and wives and old men and children. Everyone."

Rudi took a shaky breath. "Reisa said Klaus will not do it. He will not fly the mission. They may shoot him, but he will not be a murderer like that. He said the Fuhrer is mad to think like this, that it will bring the whole world down on us forever. It will make us like Cain. It will be the end for us all. Germany will be ground under like a nest of snakes."

Konnings looked up at Clancey and asked, "She was right, was she not?"

Clancey stared into the boy's blue eyes. "Yes, your sister was right. Now tell me the rest. All of it. I have to know everything you know and more."

Rudi blinked, comprehending. There seemed to be no surprising this one. He had the look of a man who has seen everything and perhaps done it.

"Reisa asked me what we could do. What could *we* do? I said I only knew what she knew and Klaus Reichmann was a German hero. I was nothing, a mere chauffeur for Kessler. Did she think I should go complain about the secret plans of the S.S. to the High Command when I flew Kessler to Berlin on Monday? I was scared and angry. Angry, because I knew we must do something. To know a thing like this—it put it into your hands. When I woke the next morning, it was as if I had never slept. Reisa asked me to go to Mass with her, but I could not. I was thinking I could do nothing, so I would do nothing. And I did not wish to think of this in a house of God."

Rudi leaned forward, bracing his arms on his knees as he sat on the bed, looking ahead of him now. There was a change in his voice, a more positive note, no longer hesitant, as he began to recount a memory of his actions.

"I had breakfast in my room. Gretchen brought it up to me as she had whenever I was home on holiday as a schoolboy. I remember pulling out the maps from my satchel as I drank my tea to start planning our flight to Berlin the next day, just to have something to do, something else to think about, and then I realized I was much closer to the American lines than I was to Berlin. If I could just warn them. Could I somehow drop a note or letter of some kind? No, that was crazy, not a chance in millions, and how to explain a little error in navigation when I got back? No, that was stupid. Besides, I was not going to be alone and I would never speak of such matters with Herr Kessler. 'A German soldier does what he is commanded, Rudi. He does not question.'" Konnings laughed and rubbed his neck.

"It was clear to me, I must go all the way when I go, and I must go alone. There. I had said it. I was going to do it. I was going to fly the Storch into France and give myself up. When I knew I would do this, I was scared, but I was happy. I could not wait to tell Reisa of my idea. I sat and studied the maps again and again. Finally, I figured out how I should get away from Herr Kessler. 'A little trouble with the motor, Oberstleutnant. If we could stop in Ulm, I am sure I could fix it in no time whatever. Yes, I am certain. Here are the work forms, if you would sign one before you go to the officer's hut, it would greatly speed matters. Here, this one on this line, please sir. Thank you, I shall have her ready in half an hour. You will not miss your dinner in Berlin.' A little paper I have inserted in the work order and I have permission to fly to the next base for a document pick up." Rudi Konnings grinned. "I would have made you the very good spy."

He looked down, the moment of humor gone. "Reisa was frightened for me, but proud; I could tell. She said she would tell Reichmann of my plans when he came again, which he had promised to do whenever he could. I told her she must not speak of it, for if anyone learned she had knowledge of my plans, then she would be in terrible danger. No, Reisa must say only that I had seemed very frightened of the war and drank much, talking only of the American bombers and how hopeless it was to continue. She must call me the coward. We argued over the matter of Reichmann. I only pray she has cursed me for a traitor and reminded them of my father, the war hero."

Finishing his story, Konnings' face was somber. The moment of pride at his courage had passed.

Clancey walked to the window to peer down at the guards. He spoke in a calm voice. "Do you know where the bombers are hidden?"

Konnings looked up. "Yes. Reichmann told Reisa and Reisa told me."

"Then tell me now."

"That I will not do, not until we are in Germany, you and I."

Clancey turned around to stare into the face of the eighteen-year-old. "Don't be a fool, Konnings. You know we can't let you go without that information."

"You will not let me go *with* that information, I think. Either way, you will only have it from me when we are in Germany. I must get my sister."

Clancey narrowed his eyes. "You know that we can get it out of you if we have to." It was not a question.

The young pilot tightened his lips. "You can try. Someone tried to get something from you once, I think, maybe. Did you tell them?"

Clancey held his gaze. "I have been trained to take pain. Have you?"

Konnings swallowed. "They have my sister. I will take the pain. You may get it from me, but it will be hard and it will take you time. And maybe it is already too late. It is for you to say."

Chris turned to look at the Colonel who nodded. He turned to face Konnings. "All right, Rudi. We'll do it your way, but I'm the

boss. Everything I say goes with no questions asked. You get out
of line just once and you'll like the Gestapo a lot better than me. I
leave my God at home when I go on a mission like this, so don't
think for one moment you will be pulling me around when we get
on the ground again. You'll give me what I want or I'll make you
look so bad your sister wouldn't know you from a raw steak."

Rudi Konnings swallowed with fear at the captain's threat but
a boyish smile spread across his face as he realized he was going to
go on the mission. "Thank you, Captain. God bless you." Though
he fought against it, his body shook as he choked back tears of
relief.

Clancey looked across at the Colonel who was studying the
boy. He drew a tired breath. This was definitely going to be a bitch
of a job.

"Achtung, old thing." Wilmett was at his cheerful best. He
clapped Chris Clancey on the arm and extended a hand to a curious
Rudi Konnings. "Good to have you with us, lad. Allow me to
introduce you to Joan Eleanor."

Rudi turned around to meet the indicated female, but, at
Wilmett's good-natured laugh, looked again at the grinning
sergeant who gestured to an open canvas tool apron on a work
bench. In a pocket rested a small metal rectangle with a pair of
knobs and what appeared to be a speaker guard as on a telephone.
A radio of some type, but a very small model.

"*This* is Joan Eleanor." Wilmett beamed. "She's quite a good
little sister to our old W/T. You see, the wireless was such a bother
to set up and operate without attracting attention. It was tons
heavier and just as likely as not to go bonkers when pitched out in
a parachute."

Clancey was incredulous. "Come on, Roger, you can't mean
this is a new wireless? It can't be five pounds," he said lifting the
small device up in one hand. Ear plugs trailed from one end of the
radio while an antenna was in another pouch.

"Four, actually." Sergeant Wilmett crossed his arms with an
air of satisfaction that bespoke his pride in the compact device.
"She works on a wee set of batteries right inside. Now she'll not
reach London, of course, but she'll beam up to a plane overhead

and you can talk all you like until the petrol runs low or some bright Kraut—excuse me, lad—some bright *boy* notices there's a Mosquito buzzing about at 40,000 feet and decides to go have a pop at it. There's just no way to trace her down, no power surges or signals spreading out all over creation. A proper jewel, she is."

Chris tapped his lower lip. "How do we let you know when we want to transmit? You can't keep a plane waiting all the time."

Wilmett wagged a finger at Rudi Konnings. "Ahhh, there's the rub. Now lad, the Captain here always sees the two sides of everything, a good habit for them that lives by their wits." He grinned back at Clancey. "Right you are, my captain. We cannot keep a plane overhead waiting for your lovely voice, so we have to have a prearranged time and a prearranged place pinpointed for your transmissions. I grant you it's not perfect, but then, what is in this lovely war? I'll still take Joan Eleanor here over the W/T ten for ten. You'd be surprised at the number of complaints we get from the old sets; that is, we would get, if they could manage to call in over them. I just hope a few of those lads get to come back to complain some day in person."

Clancey nodded. "Well, show us how to work your girl here."

Chris Clancey fired the six rounds rapidly, but methodically; his arm extended, his body sideways to the target. At the end of the long room, the man-shaped dummy puffed small bits of stuffing as the shots buried themselves in the chest of the dark silhouette. The bulbous silencer had softened the noise of the escaping gases to a lethal hissing. Clancey turned to Rudi Konnings and reloaded the gun, still self-conscious of the feel of his new skin stretching over his knuckles as he forced in the new clip.

"Have you ever fired a silencer before?" he asked in German.

Rudi shook his head. "I have not fired a weapon since my training. I am not such a good shot."

"Come with me." Clancey walked down to stand within ten feet of the target. "The sound will fool you. The gun is not loud but it bucks very hard. You must stiffen your arm and wrist, yet keep your fingers nimble. You should fire several times, until your target goes down, and if he is not dead, you should keep shooting. You should not aim for the face; that is too hard. The heart is great, the gut is safe. But don't wait to see it happening. When you start to shoot, do not think of anything but killing your target. None of that cowboy shooting in the movies, that is all crap."

Rudi swallowed and grinned. "You like the cowboy movies? They are my favorite, your American West. You have been there?"

Clancey handed him the gun. "Put the whole clip into the stomach. Keep firing until the gun is empty. Keep the gun out in front of you." He stepped back and to the side as Rudi lifted the gun hesitantly. "Schieben!" he commanded.

Rudi Konnings threw up his arm and began firing. The first three shots were wild but he hit the target on the fourth. Gritting his teeth and squinting, his head tucked tight to his shoulder, he put the last two shots solidly into the target. He turned to face Clancey who quickly grabbed the gun.

"Idiot. Never point a gun at me. Here, you load like this." He loaded the gun carefully.

Rudi watched Clancey silently a moment before speaking. "It was not so good."

"You had better shoot first and last and you had better be close. Think of sticking it into him like a spear. That will line it up better."

Konnings grinned as he took the gun back. "I have not had much practice with spears either, Captain."

Clancey frowned. He did not want to like this boy. He did not want to know him at all.

"And this deserter, Konnings, I understand his father was something of a hero in the last war, is that right, Colonel?" The little man in the black leather overcoat pulled his glasses off as he sank back in the swivel chair of Colonel Shaeffer's office.

Shaeffer, who had just returned to his office to be warned he had a visitor, eyed the Gestapo agent warily. For half a deutschmark, he would have thrown the greasy little bird out of his chair, but he knew that weasels like this were having men like himself shot on a regular basis these days, so he was inclined to sit on his anger until the self-important little bastard chose to leave.

"His father was General Victor Konnings, a pilot under Von Richtofen. He was an ace and decorated with the Blue Max. A true hero of the Luftwaffe. He once dined with Generalfeldmarschall Goering himself in our quarters here. It was an occasion of honor. General Konnings was an inspiration to our pilots."

"A great pity he could not have served as a better one for his own son. Oh, well, in some the blood runs thin. Perhaps his mother was not so Aryan?"

Shaeffer coughed. "I would not know about that, Herr Geltman."

The Gestapo officer crossed his legs with deliberation, letting a doubtful silence build on the end of Shaeffer's statement. "But it is the duty of a commanding officer to know everything about the pilots under his command, is it not? Come, Shaeffer, we know that Judith Konnings was a Jew."

Shaeffer's face was red. "The mother converted long ago I understand. The boy is Catholic. That, I know. I have seen him at Mass."

Geltman grunted. "A change of 'superstitions' hardly changes the blood, Colonel. How a Jewish boy could ever have come to pilot a plane in the Luftwaffe is a crime for which there must be an answer."

"As for his piloting, well, he was Oberstleutnant Kessler's personal choice for his own pilot. A Storch is hardly a Luftwaffe weapon." Shaeffer despised the inside-out game he must always play when dealing with Gestapo fanatics and S.S. officers. This Geltman was the worst he had known. A colonel in the Gestapo who preferred to be addressed as *Herr* Geltman no doubt disdained the military title as an affront to officers of the regular forces; a defiant reminder of the superiority of his own position. Of course, it would be easy to say only what the fool wanted to hear, grant all power, as if Shaeffer still had any, but something inside him still was not ready to capitulate, would not let him turn entirely from his own reality yet. No, he must continue to play the game. "I did not know the boy well, sir, but I ask you if you are saying that the mother's Jewish blood was stronger than the father's Aryan blood? I thought it was the other way around."

Geltman grinned, then stood, lifting his gloves from the desk. "Thank you for reminding me of this, Colonel. I am always interested in the nature of blood. Perhaps one day we shall be able to examine yours. In the meanwhile, I suggest you let me know if any of these men had contact with the traitor or his sister." Geltman reached into his coat and tossed a sheet of typing paper onto the desk.

Colonel Shaeffer picked up the list and scanned it quickly. "These men are all members of the special squadron flight crews. The Me264 crews."

"There is something special about anyone who associates with a traitor, Colonel." The agent picked up the model of a Heinkel 111 from the edge of Shaeffer's desk. "Tell me, Colonel, have you wondered just what these special crews are doing here, hidden away like this? Wondered what all these secret plans are about?"

"I don't wonder about my orders, I carry them out. When these men arrived, I took every measure concerning them that I was told to effect. They train at night. They are watched. They are all perfectly good airmen, as far as I can tell."

"And what do you think of the science crews? The special underground installations? Surely you speculate on these strange, secretive elements? The trucks and tanks? The rumors? No thoughts on all of these?"

Shaeffer was careful. "I, of course, have wondered at the peculiar nature of this installation since I was brought in to set up the aircrews here. As you are certainly aware, I was told that these special arrangements were top secret and not to be questioned. I was told that the S.S. troops were here to enforce that secrecy. As I have said, I have always followed my orders."

Geltman nodded and carefully set the model back on the desk before continuing. "Yes, it is good that you follow your orders well, for these papers contain your latest ones." He handed Shaeffer a sealed packet which bore the stamp of the High Command. "You will see, Colonel, that I am no longer only concerned with the security of the area, but am officially to take command of the security of this base, as well. I have been fully briefed on the mission by Himmler himself. It is so important that he has seen fit to have it administered, not by the Luftwaffe, but by the one arm of the Reich that is completely incorruptible. His own Gestapo. The Fuhrer has seen the wisdom of this." Geltman smiled and shook his head with mock self-reproach. "But enough of that.

Though only one must rule, we are to be partners and partners must share. So, before I inform you of the full meaning of this secret base and its mission, I ask you to inform me of any man you suspect of less patriotic devotion to duty than yourself."

Shaeffer stared into the unblinking eyes behind the round lenses. "Our crewmen hold their duty to Germany in the highest possible esteem, Herr Geltman."

Geltman began to open the packet. "That is good to hear, Colonel Shaeffer. And I must remind you that I hear everything."

"Tell him to tuck and roll, Captain," the burly parachute instructor said to Clancey as he eyed the young German private.

Private Rudi Konnings nodded to the paratroop sergeant as Clancey conveyed the command in German and bent quickly into a fetal tuck, dropping and rolling over onto his back.

"Not so good." The big sergeant shook his head. "If he stiffens up like that, he's going to take a terrible pounding on hard ground. He's got to take the momentum with him, like this." The sergeant dropped gracefully into a rolling action as naturally as a cat finding its feet. He looked up into the face of his pupil as Rudi nodded his appreciation. "If he drops into trees," he continued, "tell him to try and meet them with his back and be certain to tuck for the impact. Let the chute grab the branches, don't try to stop himself. Lots of broken legs that way."

Rudi nodded again as Clancey translated for clarity.

The sergeant turned to Clancey. "How long have we got to train him?"

Clancey shook his head. "This is it. There is no more time. You won't see him again after today."

"Christ! Well, he seems a nice kid, maybe someone upstairs will be watching out for him for once."

Clancey grunted. "That's only for fools and drunks. Better get him up the tower."

"Right."

Clancey turned to look at Konnings who was waiting for him to translate. He pointed up to the jump tower overhead and watched the German swallow as he followed the line of his up-stretched arm. The young private looked back at him and sighed.

"Kann ich auf dem Autobus fahren?"

Clancey frowned. "I wish." The boy was smart enough to be afraid. Maybe that would keep him alive. Clancey caught himself. He'd better watch out. Caring too much about another agent was a liability. It was the way he'd been caught before, and it was the reason he'd spent the long months with Dr. McAndoe stealing skin from one place to graft onto another.

Reisa Konnings hadn't heard anything yet. It was Thursday and nothing had been said. She wondered if Rudi had been able to carry out his desperate plan. She polished the concert piano in the great room again as she tried not to think of all the terrible possibilities. Gretchen had gone to the village and Hugo was pottering in the potato garden. The house was very still, as if it, too, were waiting for what must happen next. Suddenly, there was the sound of a motorcar crunching to a stop on the drive and a metal door closing. She listened for the sounds of footsteps on the walk to the house. Was it Klaus? She heard the other doors closing and rose from the piano bench to greet her visitors.

CHAPTER 3

The Colonel sat back and listened as Chris recounted the plan for him. The young German sat in a chair watching him as he listened. If this boy was a plant, he was a damn good one, the Colonel decided.

"...so, the three of us, Heidigger, me, and Konnings, jump ten miles west of Halburg and make for a deserted barn approximately here, by Konnings' estimate." Chris fingered a point on an aerial photograph taken by reconnaissance planes searching for camouflaged industries. "We will use this coordinate for our Joan Eleanor which we will call in at twenty-three hundred hours Saturday. If there is no contact, we will try again at that time every day for three days. If this does not work, we will expect possible contact from another agent at the barn using the code word, 'Horseman.' Having established ourselves at our safe point, we will observe the Konnings house to see if there is any indication of Gestapo activity. If this proves to be so, we will avoid contact until the time is right for a rescue attempt on Reisa Konnings."

Chris Clancey did not pause here though he was tempted to. It was still unpalatable to lie, especially to a trusting youth, but he knew that if the Gestapo had their hands on Reisa Konnings, there was nothing to be done about that. You didn't make a plan about a thing like that. He realized that Heidigger knew all this in advance of their briefing for he had not even raised an eye at the unorthodox instructions. Clancey continued his recital as if the whole plan were a simple routine of proven procedures that, if followed, could lead to nothing less than certain success.

"Should there prove to be no Gestapo interference, we shall establish contact and then, aided by the Konnings, determine the direct location of the Me-264s and their crews. This done, we will contact through Joan Eleanor at our earliest opportunity and determine whether a bomber strike or sabotage will best meet the needs of the mission. We shall remain in the area to determine and evaluate the results of the strike or sabotage before proceeding toward the Swiss border or other point of recovery indicated through Joan Eleanor contact."

The Colonel nodded. "He understands all that?"

Clancey looked at Rudi Konnings. "Yes. Just like I told it."

"Good. And you understand all of it?" The Colonel studied his eyes as he lifted his cigar.

Clancey said nothing.

"Well, I guess we need to pack our bags then." Heidigger grunted from across the room. "The Tommies'll be taking off for their nightly bombing run in no time. If we want our cover for the fly-over, we'd better get moving."

Rudi Konnings studied the new member of the team. He seemed eager to be going. Rudi wasn't sure he liked this man. It seemed strange to look forward to anything so dangerous. He had his reasons, but he could not imagine anyone, who really had a choice, choosing such a way to fight a war.

Chris Clancey bent over to rest a hand on the back of the co-pilot's chair as he peered out the split windscreen of the twin-engined C-47. This part of the mission was, perhaps, the most consistent, he thought; the drumming vibration of the big airplane as its airscrews pulled through the enemy dark was always the same. This was the last step-off from the safe, solid world of rank and order. Everything from here on was a dealt hand to be played for ultimate stakes. The cards might be stacked against you but they were the only cards and must be played.

The co-pilot looked up at Clancey.

"It won't be much longer, sir. Ten minutes. The Lancasters are turning for their run on Stuttgart."

Clancey watched the silhouettes of the English bombers veering away to portside and glanced down at his watch. Everything seemed to be running on schedule. No night fighters had intercepted them, no unanticipated flak. That, at least, was good. He worked his way back down the fuselage where Rudi Konnings and Edward Heidigger were sitting on opposite sides of the plane.

Heidigger was rubbing his eyes and talking in German, loudly, to be heard over the motors. Rudi seemed barely aware of the monologue though he would answer Heidigger's occasional questions with short, distracted replies.

"You are certain this barn is still standing?"

Konnings looked up again. He nodded but said nothing.

Clancey moved up carefully and lowered himself down beside the young German. "Once you are out the door, your decisions are made," he said with a grin.

Konnings responded with a smaller grin. "I suppose that is so."

Heidigger laughed. "The fall is not so bad, Rudi. It is the landing that hurts."

Clancey ignored Heidigger, who he did not like, and wished there were, at least, some other agent available who knew German well enough for this mission. It would take much more than a fluent knowledge of the language to keep them alive down there and the team was disjointed enough as it was. He turned to Rudi Konnings. "Your sister is a very pretty girl. Would you mind showing me her picture again?"

Konnings seemed grateful for the happy distraction. Searching out his wallet from inside his flight-suit and civilian garb beneath, he offered a small black and white picture. The photograph was a grainy snapshot of both Rudi and Reisa Konnings sitting on the steps of a house, holding a dachshund with his ears outstretched between them. Rudi laughed, then seemed slightly embarrassed. "It is not so good a picture of Reisa but it is a better picture of who she is for me." He continued, pointing to the dachshund, "Reisa had just said that Wolfgang should be the one going to the Luftwaffe since he already had his wings." Rudi looked up to Chris who was studying the tiny vignette of normal family life so alien to their surroundings.

Clancey nodded. "He certainly looks as if he might create enough lift. He is an old dog?"

"Yes. We got Wolfgang for my tenth birthday. Reisa named him after Mozart. He would sit and howl along with her as she played the piano. I used to kid her that he was really Mozart's spirit and his purgatory was to listen to her playing his music. She would chase me about the house."

Heidigger laughed. "Sounds like a nice life. Germany, before the war. Country houses and pets. Then you people got bored and decided to declare war on the human race."

Rudi's head shot up, his face red. "Yes, I am the son of a rich man, a man who tried to hide his children from what was happening in the world because he had seen what the world can do to children. I am not ashamed of my family, Herr Heidigger."

Heidigger leaned back, grinning. "Take no offense, Rudi. I just wondered if you had ever known any Jews personally, or ever read any books that needed burning."

Clancey eyed Heidigger, but said nothing. This was standard Heidigger; always working the needle, the fastest way to know the man you were working with, he had said. Clancey didn't care for the idea, but Heidigger was still alive and that was pretty good data for any hypothesis he cared to put forward. Besides, if Rudi rose to the bait this easily, he wouldn't be very useful under the kind of pressure missions like this produced. Better to let the boy work out his own position on the team, he decided.

Rudi Konnings' face was calm now as was his voice. "My mother was Jewish. She loved my father very much. I never knew her. She died when I was very young. As to burning books, I would not know, but I once read a copy of the Treaty of Versailles. *It* should have been burned."

Heidigger whistled. "Jewish mother? Sorry, boy, your old man must have known how to grease the skids. Maybe his reputation will be enough to keep the bad boys away from baby sister altogether." He turned his attention to his kit but his sarcasm was not lost on Konnings.

It occurred to Clancey that Rudi Konnings was perhaps the bravest man he had ever met. To be going back to Germany as a known traitor in order to secure the safety of his sister; Konnings was certainly naive, but also very brave. Clancey did not choose to think of this as a matter of personal virtue or moral achievement; but only as a quality. A quality a man might have as some other man might possess a skill with knives, like Heidigger; or alacrity with explosives, as Clancey had. It was unwise to ponder one's companions' moral qualities at all in a war. That led to judgments based on abstractions, and actions foreign and unnatural and, ultimately, unwise. It was only a fact to understand about him. So long as it was truly understood, it could be useful.

Clancey looked up as the red light of the fuselage blinked. He stood, bracing himself against the airframe. The co-pilot entered their cabin and made his way to the side door and held up his thumb. "Two minutes to jump, sir. Opening the door."

The sudden blast of air sucked loose grit around in a short whirlwind as Clancey clipped his static line to the wire cable that ran above their heads down the center of the plane. The two others followed his example.

The cabin light turned green and Heidigger braced his gloved hands on the sides of the door, looked over his shoulder and mouthed a silent obscenity before leaping out of the airplane. Rudi Konnings moved up into position at the door and braced himself as he had practiced that morning. He was still trying to remember everything when Clancey pushed him out. Clancey followed after Konnings, diving outward and downward, his feet together, bracing for the slinging snap of the static line ripping open the big, silk parachute that would set him pivoting slowly downward into the dark ocean of air. He was always amazed how fast the plane would be gone, and with it, the roar of the motors. Now, the only sound was the air rushing around him in the night. He looked down to see the other two chutes, but at first, could see only one. He was nearing the ground before he spotted the other chute traveling beyond the moonlit clearing he was trying to side-slip into.

As he anticipated the shock of the rising earth below him, Clancey realized that his questions were gone. He was no longer looking into himself and there was a brief moment of relief at this reprieve of the soul; for now his life and every moment ahead of him would demand the clarity of thought and purpose that would leave no place for conscience, concern, or even fear. This was the place of war, the kingdom of power and fate. He saw, now, what he had always known. He had never been free of this fate; that the Colonel had known it also, had only pretended, perhaps for himself as much as for Clancey. It did not matter. Nothing mattered now but doing what he was doing until it was done or he was dead.

Now he hit the ground and rolled, distributing the shock throughout his body. He quickly unclipped the harness and began retrieving the parachute, collapsing the air from the large, green dome that had spread above his descent like a signboard proclaiming his arrival to anyone who might be gazing into the sky. Always, he half expected a large crowd to be gathered, waiting for him by the end of his seemingly endless flight until he was reassured by the vastness of the landscape which rose dark and empty to receive him. Now, crouched low on the light slope of a hill, he surveyed the open ground he had fallen into on the odd chance he might have been sighted and, indeed, drawn an unwanted reception.

There was a noise. Clancey froze. His muscles tightened as he strained to determine the nature and direction of the source. He could see no movement but rather sensed it. Again, a faint noise, a step on grass, and Clancey had his pistol out and ready. He waited, and again it came, soft but distinct. He stood slowly. It was faster now, hurried. He moved uphill, bending with the slope, ready to drop. Nearing the crest of the hill, he edged his head to peer over the top. He held his pistol out before him in his right hand and raised his signal clicker outward in his left. If it was Heidigger or Konnings, he would be answered. If it were a true enemy, it would warn them.

He clicked twice and waited. There was no answer, but the soft sound was back. Then, he saw his phantom.

The cow wanted no part of the sky-borne intruder and moved away in a short gallop that quickly settled into a walk again as she receded into the distance of the pasture. Clancey grinned after her. A cow. It was only a cow, not a Nazi cow or a Nazi meadow or even a Nazi forest. It was easy to forget that Germany was still a large span of forests and fields, rivers and streams, the people populating it as sparsely as a single can of paint spattered over a football stadium. There was much more space than paint. Even a stain as evil as Hitler's war machine formed only the tiniest fraction of this world. The work of any spy was to move in those spaces, to move among the enemy as a particle repelled by like polarity.

Clancey, assured of his privacy, turned to the task at hand. He draped his loosely rolled parachute over his shoulder, pulled his pack strap over his other shoulder and began to move in the direction of the parachute he had seen drifting ahead of him before he landed. He hoped it had come down before reaching the tree line. He climbed over a fence composed of a pair of rusted barbed wire strands and paused frequently to sound his clicker, yet had no response. He reached the tree line. This was not good.

He found Rudi Konnings twenty minutes later. The young German's harness hung almost motionless, suspending its occupant some eight feet from the ground. Chris Clancey had almost passed him when the shadow of the gently spiraling corpse had blocked a patch of moonlit forest floor in front of him. Clancey had spun around to look directly up into the face of the dead man. He had immediately set about releasing the German's harness and took the heavy weight of the body on his shoulders. Even before he had laid the German on the ground to check his pulse and breath, Chris knew he was dead. He gently probed inside the collar of Rudi's jumpsuit and grimaced at the irregular firmness against the skin.

Clancey looked around then drew his clicker up and sounded it. Still no response. He began to pull down the chute caught in the tree and had to climb it part way to finally dislodge it. As he worked, he listened carefully for any hint of approach. Still no Heidigger. Resigning himself to his task, he unzipped Rudi's jumpsuit and searched for his wallet and papers and any other materials he thought might give away his identity or prove useful on the mission. Then, he pulled off his own jumpsuit and, reaching into the pack he had left at the base of the tree, pulled out the small collapsible shovel. It was slow, hot work and he paused occasionally to sound his clicker, hoping Heidigger would respond, but determined that he must make his way to the barn alone and hope Heidigger would be waiting when he arrived. Of course, Heidigger might be dead also, or worse, captured and even now being interrogated; in which case, this was an awful lot of wasted work. He looked over at the pale face, illuminated by a chance patch of moonlight. No, Rudi Konnings deserved a burial at least. Courage ought to count for something. Yes, Chris thought, here, he would bury courage.

Clancey was tempted by a slow anger that surprised him. Was he mad at Konnings for reminding him of something he had lost? No, that was not it, because there were plenty of brave young men dying every day. That part of Clancey was still there, he decided, just better educated and not so easily drawn out. Was it God he was angry with? Chris laughed quietly to himself. If there was a God, then indeed he would be mad at Him. No, Chris thought, it was death he was mad at, death he had accepted for himself and felt no dread of. It was the stupidity of death. Not of it coming, for that was a given, but in its fakes and feints which hinted at the idea of a secret to survival, the thought that one could become charmed by work or virtue or even luck. Chris unscrewed the cap of his canteen and took a cooling drink. He chided himself. He had better stop thinking like this or he would find himself wondering if he were being punished for his lack of respect for Fate. We are never far from the pagan gods, he thought with a grim grin, remembering a snatch of an Oxford Don's radio broadcast he'd heard back in London one evening.

Chris was finishing the grave now and mopped his brow with a handkerchief from the leather jacket he had hung on a nearby branch. He had better watch himself, he thought. Here he was about to bury a man and had worked through enough theology to write a cynic's sermon. He knew what the Colonel would think if he knew of the sinister thoughts that flocked so easily in his mind. The Colonel was right, there was a fine line between efficiency and madness, he could sense it, but would you even know if you had crossed it? He paused to pull and lower the body of Rudi Konnings into the hole he had prepared. It was not wide enough to lay the body perfectly flat and Chris had to turn the German sideways to fit him in. He then forced the two parachutes down around and on top of the body and proceeded to pack as much earth as he could to cover the contents of the hole. As he packed in the loose dirt, he remembered burying Bullet.

Bullet had been his favorite pet. The cat his sister had given him when he was younger he hardly remembered and had never cared for. The countless amphibians didn't know they belonged to him and he had never considered them particularly worthy of any personal devotion on his part, either. But Bullet was powerful and alive to the world around him; a perpetually grinning Labrador Retriever that cared more for Chris than anything else in the world. Chris had enjoyed the unalloyed affection of the big dog who he alone could admonish or delight. He had felt a responsibility to Bullet and, indeed, it was in the service of the big animal that he had first come to extend himself beyond the bounds of selfish gratification. He had worked to feed the Lab by delivering newspapers and had seen to the dog's needs even when it was inconvenient for him. His parents had been very fond of Bullet and he could easily understand why. The animal had turned their son into a better animal.

He would never forget burying Bullet. He had been summoned by a pair of his friends after returning home from school. The boys had quietly led him to a ditch by the road and shown him Bullet, dead. Later that day, he had placed the hard, furry body in the hole he had dug out behind the orchard. His father had left him to dig it alone. He remembered packing the earth around the body of the dog. He remembered his sisters wanting to have a prayer and a hymn. He hadn't cared about any of that. The one thing he remembered clearly, even after all these years, was his father talking to his mother in the kitchen when he was in the den. He could hear the voice as clearly as a recording, just as audible in this German forest as any other voice could be. "Bullet taught him more today than he has since we got him." Just like that. Bullet taught me the secret that day all right, Dad. If you love something, no matter how healthy and happy it is, it is going to die. Everything dies. Good for the boy. Hell of a lesson. The lesson of the dog. Well, move over Bullet, here comes another poor dead son of a bitch.

Chris finished his job by brushing the earth with a branch to cover over his hand and boot prints and then looked down at the radium dial of his watch. He had a long way to go and not a lot of time left to get there. He checked his pocket compass, re-shouldered the pack of plastic explosive, and set out through the trees toward the dirt road he knew intersected these woods within the next three kilometers.

Clancey had only seen one vehicle on his march along the hard-packed dirt road and had easily hidden before it neared him. An ancient truck, running very roughly with terminally grinding gears, had staggered up a hill he was ascending. The lights had been taped into the usual black-out slits, but the truck bore no army markings and appeared to be civilian. Whatever it was, it was obviously running on very poor quality fuel. This was quite understandable in light of the severe rationing of petroleum. The Allied wings had been pinpoint-bombing the German oil reserves for ages now. Whatever the truck was carrying, it must be pretty important to someone, Chris decided. He had been tempted to run up and try climbing into the back for a free ride, but decided this was more from laziness than true need. He was already within four or five kilometers of his rendezvous at the farm and it would be foolish to risk a confrontation unnecessarily in order to rest his legs and save a few minutes.

The barn was indeed dilapidated, Chris surmised from his vantage point on the ridge of a hill that ran diagonally southwest of the structure. The farm, by contrast, was well kept, the grass obviously cropped by goats he encountered after moving off the roadway as he sighted the wooden bridge which served as a reference to him. The barn was, in fact, almost gone. The backside had given way and the roof sagged close to the ground while many boards from the front were missing. Several of these lay in a rotting stack to the side of the structure, probably left from early attempts to salvage some of the better lumber. According to Konnings, the farmhouse was not visible from here and it seemed that, if they were cautious at all, there would be little danger of discovery during the short time they would need to occupy the crumbling ruin.

Chris held his clicker up and used it. He doubted it would be heard this far from the barn but sound often traveled farther than you suspected in the open. He was surprised to be answered by a click just to his right. He repeated the signal and waited. He turned to see Heidigger emerging from a copse that bordered the ridge. Heidigger clicked, waiting, then came forward after Chris answered.

"Have you seen Konnings?" Heidigger asked.

"Konnings is dead. Broke his neck in the trees."

Heidigger shook his head and spat. "What a bitch. That puts a screw in it for sure."

"You just get here?" Clancey asked.

"No. I've been here about an hour. I decided to wait out here and watch for you. I had a bad feeling about that kid—too damn virtuous. Almost made you forget he was a Nazi. Still, you never know."

Clancey ignored Heidigger's comment. "Well, we may as well go in and get some rest. The sun will be up soon. We've got to make some plans."

Heidigger said nothing but went back to the copse to retrieve his pack. After checking the radio to make certain it had survived the drop, they stored their gear under debris inside the barn. Heidigger took the first guard shift and Clancey lay down on his sleeping bag and tried not to think about Rudi Konnings or his sister or Bullet.

CHAPTER 4

Captain Klaus Reichmann sat on the edge of his bunk and slowly began to take his boots off. His mind was still reeling from the conversation he had just had with the base commandant, Colonel Shaeffer. He did not know if he should be sitting there on the bed or trying to make a mad dash away from the base, perhaps even from Germany. He had been informed that the base was closed and all passes withdrawn, including his own. There were no messages or letters permitted. The other men had nodded their heads when the new restrictions had been announced, privately acknowledging that whatever it was, they were now going to begin their great secret mission.

To Klaus, it was secret no more. He, alone, had learned the truth. For Klaus, it was the waking from a dream to a living nightmare. As much as the dreaded coming event, he now had new agonies to lay beside his fear. Did they know about Rudi? About Reisa? About him? He had tried to look into Shaeffer's face for any clue to his fate, but had seen nothing there. Shaeffer might not know anyway. He stopped. He couldn't blind himself to reality. They knew all right. They always knew about things like that. The Gestapo didn't require proof. They could kill you for a rumor.

He began to wonder how he could have let himself sink into this mess; how he could have told Reisa something so horrible that

to even know of it could be death. He had been weak. And hadn't
he really wanted someone to do something about it? Had he
thought his *girlfriend* could do something about it? God. What an
idiot. Didn't her stupid brother know they would make a
connection? They could prove nothing, but that didn't matter.
Didn't the fool realize what he was risking? No, of course not, no
one realizes anything until it is too late. Then it doesn't matter.
That's how wars are fought. Oh, philosophizing is a great step
forward, Klaus. Brave Klaus. You sit and stew and worry about the
great criminal act but it is the silly little brother of the girl that
takes his life in his hands for you. And you wonder what you can
do. At last, you are willing to do something, but you have nothing
left to do. Klaus Reichmann, hero of the Luftwaffe. Well, if they
come for your balls, it will serve you right. You can't hide,
Klaus—not in a uniform, not in a nightmare. You will have to do
something.

He looked around him. Most of the boys appeared eager
enough now that it was obvious that they would soon be in action.
They seemed relieved that their waiting was ending. Waiting was
the constant enemy in war, his old squadron commander had told
him back in the days of the Blitz on England. It gave a fellow too
much time to think, and thinking poisoned the heart. Tension had
risen as the crews had waited and waited for some word or signal.
They knew only the obvious, that the mission was to be very, very
dangerous, involving a long flight since the Me264's were
designed for long range. In fact, the planes had been called the
"New York Bombers." The bomb loads must be either a newly
developed bomb of vast power; or else, the target must be one of
equally great importance. There had been much speculation as the
days passed.

"I think we will blow up maybe Churchill or Roosevelt,"
Reichmann's radioman, Willy Frankl had volunteered. "Only
something strategic like that could account for this much attention
to three airplanes. Even big birds like these."

One of Reichmann's gunners, Paul Hoffman, shook his head.
"Don't be silly. Such small targets. How would we ever find them
if we did get to Washington or London?"

The navigator, Lt. Heinrich Lauda, snorted. "It could be something like that. If we knew in advance where they were going to be. Maybe one of those conferences, with Stalin also, huh? You think not, Paul? Did you read about the Americans shooting down the Japanese Admiral Yamamoto a couple of years ago? A squadron of P-38's flew hundreds of miles to meet his plane at the precise moment before it was to land. Pow. They blew his yellow ass to bits. Japan lost their war that day."

Reichmann shook his head. "No, they lost their war on December 7th, 1941, and ours too."

"Shhhh," Hoffman cautioned looking around. "Don't talk like that even in jest, Klaus. This may be a Luftwaffe base, but I've seen too many black overcoats around for my taste."

Frankl grunted. "Don't you think if we got Churchill, Roosevelt, and Stalin, we could stop the war? Surely it would freeze the Allies at least for a time. Maybe it would be time enough maybe for us to build more jets, or rockets, or a few more of these Big Geese?"

Lauda shook his head. "Maybe in '42, before it was all over in the desert, or before Stalingrad." There was an uncomfortable silence as he uttered the still cold name of the great disaster. Lauda looked around at the other airmen with an ironic smile. "So, it's all spit in a basket, really. Some of us are going to live a few more months, maybe that's all it will take, and some of us won't. It's just a question of when the generals have finished the game, really."

Frankl put his hands on his hips. "I may not have been around as long as the rest of you fellows. But I can't believe you are as hopeless as you seem. You take pride in talking like the war is already lost and Germany defeated. Maybe so, but *anything* can happen. It's not like the old days. Our scientists might be ready to give us something we can turn this world on its head with. I won't give up just because it's dark now. Remember, it's always darkest before the dawn."

Heinrich Lauda chuckled and slapped young Frankl on the back. "Yes, Grandmother. Thank you for reminding me to keep a stiff upper lip. Oh, well, at least we get to play with the new toys."

Paul Hoffman nodded. "That's right, my boys. We may be few but we are wondrous. Jets. Rockets. And, finally, we are flying the great bomber we have begged for since '38—"

"I understand they've redesigned these 264s over completely, even the cockpit's been moved around for the bombardier to have room at the nose and the forward gun. Even radar for you, Lauda," Frankl said.

"Only a half-dozen years too late," Hoffman finished. "Maybe we'll win the next war."

Klaus Reichmann leaned back on the bed and stared at the ceiling. "No point in wondering about the future. It will be handed to us soon enough."

"You know something, Captain?" Frankl was always eager. "You've talked with the commandant? You know the mission?"

Klaus' co-pilot, Reinhardt Von Tripps, stepped out of the toilet with a copy of a sexy movie magazine in his hand and a towel around his neck. "You're worse than a woman, Frankl. You'd never have made it through the Russian raids. If Klaus has something to tell you, he'll tell me first and then I'll tell you. Don't worry, when it's time for you to really be scared shitless, I'll let you know. Meantime, you might take up the study of Eastern meditation."

Reichmann frowned. "Where is Braun?"

Lauda grunted. "Still over at the hanger. He's with the other bombardiers. It's one of their special meetings. You know, I still don't see why we couldn't keep Reinhaus for this business. It's bad luck to break up a crew."

Dieter Kroft, the other gunner, sat down on his bunk. "Strictly speaking, I don't think Braun is really a bombardier at all. And where the hell are the bombsights? For that matter, when are the bomb racks going to be installed? We keep flying these practice hops with all that water in those special slab tanks. We must be going to carry the biggest bastard bombs that ever existed."

Von Tripps hung his towel over the edge of his upper bunk. "I think that is to simulate the fuel load for the flight. No sense lugging that kind of petrol around until we are ready for the long run, eh? We've got to be able to take off with that kind of load, so we practice with the weight, right? But I will say one thing,

Klaus," he turned to face Reichmann. "I don't like these rocket take-offs. It's not how an airplane should go up. I feel like my ass is going to fry every damn time we set them off. The whole damn plane has been cobbled up more than a cheap whore's girdle with the extra equipment that's been hung onto it, but this rocket shit— damn. Let us just say I am officially wetting my hero's underwear."

Reichmann wasn't listening, he'd shut his eyes to think. He had been as curious as any of them, wondering just what they were doing in a hidden base in the middle of nowhere, flying experimental planes around in the dark, firing wing rockets to drag the massive payloads off the ground. It did not take a genius to know something very different lay ahead. Klaus had not stayed alive for six years in the Luftwaffe by not trying to find out everything there was to know about his situation. This base had been a complete blank. Total secrecy ruled. Then, just as simply as things often happen, he had followed his intuition and it all rolled out for him.

When the group had started back from a conditioning run around the perimeter of the field, Klaus had stopped to empty a rock out of his boot. He'd fallen behind and was walking around a parked truck next to an innocuous domed bunker with an S.S. sentry standing by its camouflaged entrance. He heard the sound of glass breaking and an expletive and stopped to glance into the rear of the truck. A technician in a full-length white lab coat struggled to lift a wooden crate from the bed of the truck. The man had pulled off his heavy gloves to re-grip the box. It was obvious that he was not a part of the standard Luftwaffe unit. He instantly fitted into the part of the mission that Reichmann knew must be its true heart. Instinctively, Klaus moved to give aid and to gain what knowledge could be gathered for his own purposes. If that involved a little play-acting, well, it would not be the first time.

"Let me help you with that," he'd said, climbing up onto the bed of the truck, being careful to keep the sentry just out of sight.

"Ah, the Luftwaffe to the rescue." The man laughed gratefully, his breath puffing small clouds of condensation. "Thank you. They ought to have some soldiers out here to carry things about, but these S.S. guards don't seem inclined to move much from their guns."

Klaus nodded agreement. It was obvious this man was not used to working around the S.S. It was also obvious he was a talker, exactly the man Klaus needed. He decided to play his long card as casually as possible. He didn't know how much time he would have before someone joined them.

"Here, let me get the other side of this. We should slide it over to the rear. We could carry it better if we were on the ground to lift it down to the cart, you think?"

"Save our backs, yes," the man agreed appreciatively.

As they dragged the crate to the rear, Klaus kept his voice calm as he asked, "You fellows in the special team amaze me. I imagine it's nerve-wracking working with the bombs like that."

Without looking up, the technician shook his head as he climbed down to the ground. "At least we don't have to fly the damn things over the enemy. You fellows are the heroes. All those fighters and anti-aircraft fire. Now, that is danger."

Reichmann dropped to the ground and pulling out a pack of cigarettes, offered one to his new friend. "You get used to it. I flew over London in '41 and you could have walked on the flak."

The other man took the cigarette, leaning forward for Reichmann's match and puffing the tip red before keeping up his side of the conversation. "That's something else, certainly. I would lose my nerve in a week."

Klaus blew out his match. "I tell you, I might lose my nerve on this mission. These secret tanks—if something cracked them—how much chance would we have of getting away safely?"

The technician shook his head. "Don't worry. They designed these things to be absolutely unbreakable until the fuse charge breaks them up. They have to be sealed perfectly. Of course, if something did screw up and you got a broken seal in flight…" he whistled. "In one hour, you're feverish. A couple more and you're out of your head. Dead after that. It's ugly. Scary as hell. No stopping it, either. Just like the Middle Ages, only worse. You'd do better to pull out your pistol and shoot yourself. That's my advice." He laughed as he added, "We do well to imitate Nature when we

look for ultimate weapons, don't we? Just be sure you drop the
damned things a long way from home."

Klaus' smile was the hardest bit of acting he'd ever done.
"Hell, yes. So, you just breathe the stuff in, that's it? Looks like
masks would be all we'd need."

The technician shook his head. "No. Vermin. Fleas infected
with it. The thing is looking for warm bodies, you see? It's alive.
Not like the old gas. Plague bites you. It only stops when there
aren't any bodies to get onto. Of course, keeping the little buggers
alive in the bombs is a difficult bit of timing."

"Kostner!" A voice called from behind the truck.

"Coming!" The technician shouted back and turned to grip the
crate. "Come on, let's set this bitch down on the cart."

"Huh?" Reichmann's mind was still working at the enormity
of the secret he had just unearthed. "Oh, yeah. Get a grip. The
weight's more on your side."

As they carefully lifted the crate over the back of the truck and
lowered it onto the wheeled cart, Reichmann's new friend added,
"Hey, don't tell anyone I filled in any blanks, will you? But since
you already knew about the plague bombs anyway—"

Klaus shrugged his shoulders as he stood up from the crate
rubbing his hands together in the cold. "Ja. Don't worry. I'll keep
my mouth shut. Thanks for the warning about the containers." He
turned and walked back around the truck toward the hidden
barracks, mindful to keep his body out of the sentry's line of sight.
He heard the technician talking to another science team member
and the slight squeak of cart wheels turning as he walked away. He
fought to keep his legs from shaking. From that moment, he had
lived with fear like a spider's egg inside his heart.

That's when he'd told Reisa about the plague bombs—the
hellbrew. And he'd guessed about the target, after all, they'd built
these 'big geese' for the Atlantic all along. But he'd been wrong
about that. That's what Shaeffer had told him. No, it wasn't the
Americans or the English. Not this time. He remembered the God-
awful winter of '42, the brutal cold, the frozen motors, the burning
planes, bodies littering the snow. He'd lost Fritz after a crack-up
when they'd been sighted out on the open by the enemy. They'd
nearly got him, also. They were like wolves—swirling, relentless;

their hunger for vengeance insatiable. The bombs for the first missions were for them. The Russians.

The house matched the description Rudi Konnings had given. It was big, though not domineering or especially grand. It was out of sight of the village, which was only evidenced by the tip of a church steeple that Chris picked out with the binoculars far to the South. The wooden fence and gate now stood where once iron had bordered the grounds; the barbed sentinels lost to a metal drive some years before as Rudi had told him. Clancey swiveled the binoculars around to view the garage which also housed the servants' quarters. The corner of what appeared to be a small potato garden was just behind the house. There was no activity visible with only a bicycle laid against the side of the house to indicate that it was occupied. He glanced at his watch. Nine forty-three. No one had entered or left the house in the half-hour that the two agents had been watching it. He rubbed his eyes with his left hand and twisted around on his side to look over at Heidigger who sat in the shadow of a tree just down the slope of the small hill the two men rested on.

"Well, how about it, Chris?" Heidigger said around a match he was nibbling. "Is the little girl home?"

"I don't know. But I can't see any indication of Gestapo anywhere, either. In fact, it's almost too clear. I'd feel better if I saw some sort of activity."

Heidigger nodded. "If the bait wiggles too much, it gives the hook away. You a fisherman, Chris?" Heidigger hardly paused on Chris' shrug. "Well, I am. Love it. It's the game, son. You've got to enjoy the game. Hell, this is something you'll remember all your life. You'll either be a hero or dead."

"Most heroes are dead," Clancey mumbled as he scanned the estate. "And if this is fishing, then I'd hate fishing, too."

Heidigger laughed. "You're too tight. You got to let the line out. Too tight and snap. You've lost the whole outfit; hook, line, and sinker."

Clancey rolled over on his back. It was too bad Rudi hadn't made it. He'd know. He'd be able to see quickly if it were all right or not. But, Chris just couldn't be sure. He looked up into the barren branches above him. "If I knew that the brother of the girlfriend of one of my pilots for a secret mission had suddenly defected or turned traitor. If I knew they'd met just beforehand and I knew the pilot didn't believe in the mission, I wouldn't just be sitting on my hands."

Heidigger grunted. "If, if, if. If you were God, you'd know everything. The Gestapo isn't God, or better not be. We knew this wasn't going to be a piece of cake, Clancey."

Chris shook his head. "And, if I thought he'd defected, maybe I'd think they'd send over a team to look around. And where would they start? Where would be the one friendly place they might count on?"

Heidigger yawned. "Sure. It's simple. Heydrich's in there with a division of S.S. troopers waiting for us. Only they're real quiet and—" He raised his head. "Here comes company."

Chris picked up the binoculars again. Yes, it was the maid as Konnings had described her. Her bicycle was working slowly over a hill in the road that led from the village. In the wicker basket was a large paper parcel. Meat from the butcher. The woman was in her sixties and, though obviously wrinkled, her frame was sturdy and her attitude quite determined as she pedaled.

"That would be Gretchen," Heidigger commented and pulled out his hunting knife with the carved horse head hilt; a favorite memento from his days as a hunting guide in Wyoming. "We can question her."

Clancey nodded, but added, "We'd better keep things informal. She could be a part of a trap. We'll do the friend of the family routine. You wait for my signal to announce your presence. If I go in, don't come out unless I say 'Horseman'. If I say, 'Perfectly safe'—"

"Then it isn't, of course." Heidigger licked his lips. "I'll be careful, old son. Just don't be too jumpy. I wouldn't want to shoot the goose that lays the golden eggs."

Clancey and Heidigger scrambled down the slope keeping the road out of sight until they could crouch against the bracken bordering the shoulder. Heidigger disappeared from Chris' view as Clancey straightened up and stepped into the road just a moment before the tiring cyclist labored around the bend of the hedge-bordered path. He held his hat up in greeting and smiled widely, placing himself in position to arrest her progress if needed.

"Guten morgan, meine Frau. Entschuldigen Sie mich, bitte." He held his hat in his hands and smiled as he implored her aid. "Komme ich auf diesem wege nach Halburg?"

The woman coasted to a stop eyeing him skeptically and stepped to the opposite side of her bike some feet from him. She considered him for a moment before finally smiling with forced courtesy and asking what address he sought.

Clancey smiled wider, dipping his hat again before replacing it cheerfully on his head. "Dank. If you could be so kind, I am searching for the home of a friend from the Luftwaffe. I was released a few days ago. My health is not what it was since the Russian campaign."

The woman smiled with kinder eyes. "You poor lad. Perhaps I may know the way to your friend's house. What is his name?"

"Rudi. Rudi Konnings. We met a few months ago at an airfield near Paris. Alas, we were busy then. Rudi told me if I were ever in hard times, his family would be happy to give me a hand. They must be fine people, the Konnings. Do you perhaps know of them?"

With smiling eyes, Chris Clancey watched the woman carefully and knew only the simplest signal would have Heidigger with his blade at her throat inside a half-second. He rubbed his brow and pretended to stagger slightly.

"Are you quite all right?" Gretchen Borgman leaned forward instinctively reaching out in support of him.

Clancey caught himself and grinned. "I… I am so sorry. It's just I get dizzy… The injury, you see. I get dizzy a little bit."

Gretchen smiled sadly. "Yes, of course. I am afraid Rudi is not home, but I am the family's maid, Frau Borgman, and I am sure Rudi's father would have been proud to have you come and share a meal with us if nothing more. You know, he was a wonderful flyer in the Great War."

"Yes. Rudi is very proud about it. That was how we got to be friends. When Rudi got the letter about his father's death, well, I saw he was sad and we talked about it. He mentioned you as well. I should have known you from his description. Is his sister well?"

Frau Borgman was silent again for just a moment and Chris wondered if he had gone too far, tried to draw out too much. He imagined he heard Heidigger shifting his weight in the brush just to the left of the woman. He was relieved when she spoke again.

"Excuse me, it is just that, well, we have had some bad news about Rudi."

"No. Is he dead?" Chris took a stricken half step forward.

The woman shook her head. "I do not know. He is missing. Reisa is quite distressed. We are all much concerned. But please, come with me. You should meet Reisa. We will be happy to share our table, though it is much humbler than in other days, I am afraid."

Chris bowed slightly. "I am honored."

Without a glance over his shoulder, Chris escorted the woman along the road and up the drive. He laughed at the nearness of the destination and made some joke to which the woman responded good-naturedly. Heidigger kept pace slightly behind them along the hedges that boarded the road.

He had played it carefully with Frau Borgman, no more leading questions for a time. Just be the discharged airman, Clancey told himself. Let the fish eat before you set the hook; he remembered Heidigger cynically echoing his grandfather's advice. Chris was ushered into the kitchen of the big house where Gretchen Borgman set the wet packet of veal on the counter before wiping her hands on a towel and leaving him to go and find Reisa Konnings. He looked around the kitchen and out the back window at the servants' quarters over the garage. A hollow-cheeked elderly man in farm clothes was working the garden with a hoe and taking no mind of him. The doors of the garage were shut. It was very quiet in the house except for a sudden spattering of loud clicks and Clancey turned to face a dark-skinned dachshund rushing eagerly into the room on the hard wood floor; its nails rattling on the polished surface. The animal was white-throated with the grey whiskers of age and the long, drooping ears he'd remembered from the photograph. Well, Mozart was here, anyway. Have they taken your mistress, Wolfgang? Are these kindly old men and women

Nazi spies? Well, you look genuine enough. Yes, I wish you could talk.

"Hello, I am Reisa Konnings."

Chris Clancey's eyes rose quickly to observe the trim, young brunette who entered the room trailed closely by Frau Borgman. She was about five foot three, almost alabaster-white with shocking grey-blue eyes. He sought out the mole just to the right of her wide, lush lips. It was there all right--but, of course, that was easy to fake. The photo was black and white and he couldn't very well take it out to compare. The hair seemed right. Nothing stood out to him. Of course, it wouldn't. He had to ask himself one question and answer it before he could give himself away. Was this woman the sister of Rudi Konnings?

He bowed slightly from the waist. "Ah, fraulein, my name is Fritz Molder. I am a friend of your brother's. Rudi told me to look in on you if I was ever in Halburg, so here I am. I fear this is an inconvenient time."

"Call me Reisa, please!" The girl indicated a chair at the kitchen table for him and took the opposite one as she continued. "A friend of my brother is always welcome here. Gretchen, cut Herr Moler some bread and cheese. He must be famished. Now, tell me what I may do for you, Fritz?"

Chris nodded appreciatively, eyeing the large loaf of bread that the maid was slicing. His hunger was genuine and helped to mask his careful inquisition. As he waited anxiously for the food, he smiled and remarked that he was given to understand by Frau Borgman that there was some bad news concerning Rudi and he wished to know what manner of misfortune this would be.

Reisa Konnings sighed. "Rudi is gone."

"But he is not dead?"

"We are not certain."

"He was shot down? Over enemy territory? I understand him to be a pilot for some officer. Rudi joked that he would never see the front now. I wish his joke had been true."

Fraulein Konnings was quiet, introspective and eyed him silently for a few moments before speaking. "It may be that... that Rudi flew to the enemy on purpose."

"I do not understand."

"You were his friend, Fritz… Did he ever say anything to you about the army? You know, about not liking it?"

"Oh, all soldiers talk of that."

"Yes, but Rudi said some things to others that could have gotten him into real trouble if the wrong people had heard them… about our leaders."

Chris couldn't be sure. She was either good or real. If she was really Reisa Konnings, she might be concerned about an old friend of her brother's or possibly imagining that somehow he had gotten through and that this man was connected to him. The alternative was just as likely, and he knew he was nearing the point of no return. He hoped Heidigger wouldn't have to finish this mission alone. He looked up at the girl and nodded quietly, his eyes flicking to the maid who was wiping out some cups at the sink with her back to them.

Reisa's eyes followed his and she nodded quietly. "Gretchen dear, will you go out to the garage and find that old kit of Rudi's? I imagine there'll be a memento of Rudi that Fritz might like to have."

The woman turned and bowed, "Certainly, fraulein." She opened the rear door and stepped out of the house in the direction of the garage.

Reisa turned to face him silently as the door closed. "You are not German, are you?" she asked.

Clancey frowned as if puzzled.

Reisa Konnings closed her eyes. "Your accent is very good, but it is not quite as good as it needs to be. I think Gretchen knows, too."

Chris decided to chance everything. "Rudi got through."

"What?"

"Your brother got through to the Americans."

She opened her mouth to speak but no words would come.

"We don't have much time. Will you help me?"

She swallowed. "Please, are you—"

"It doesn't matter who I am. I am here to find those planes and stop them. I need your help to find them. Rudi said you would help. Will you?"

She closed her eyes and rocked her head up and down. "Thank God. He is alive."

Chris felt a cold wave roll over his heart. "He landed in American territory. That's why I am here. I've got to know exactly where those planes are. Can you show me on a map?"

She brought a hand to her chest, steadying herself. "I think so. I've only been near it, but Rudi has landed there with Kessler. He told me how it is hidden."

"Camouflaged?"

"Yes. That is it. They are very clever at it."

"Do you have a car?"

"I can get one."

"How close can we get?"

"Within perhaps two kilometers. I am not certain. Is Rudi here? Aren't there others?"

"How will you get a car?"

She grinned. "My boyfriend is a pilot. Perhaps Rudi spoke of him?"

Chris nodded. "Captain Reinfeldt, wasn't it?"

She stared at him. "No. Klaus Reichmann. Captain Klaus Reichmann. He will help us. He is the one who told me—of the bombs."

Chris looked out the window of the kitchen. "Who is here with you?"

Reisa smiled gratefully. "Just the servants. Gretchen and Hugo Borgman. But I am holding my breath every time an automobile passes. I was certain you were the Gestapo trying to catch me up. Gretchen is suspicious, too. You were right to be worried about her. That butcher knife would have killed a Gestapo spy."

Chris stood. "You don't mind if I look around, do you? I never take unnecessary risks."

Reisa Konnings stood. "Certainly, I only wish there was more I could do. We are not much of a force here, I am afraid, but whatever we have is yours and your men's."

Clancey smiled at her. He dreaded telling her about her brother's death. What would it serve? There was no sense in making the next few days more miserable. There was always plenty of time for misery later. Plenty of it to go around.

He followed his hostess through the house, cautiously examining any room or furniture that might conceal hidden Gestapo agents. His eyes carefully marked family portraits for discrepancies. As they returned to the kitchen, he flattened himself against the wall at the sound of the screen door opening. He was relieved to see Frau Borgman enter with a large, dusty leather suitcase in her arms and lowered the pistol which had appeared instinctively in his hand. The woman gasped at his weapon and dropped the case.

"It's all right, Gretchen." Reisa Konnings reassured the woman, stepping forward to take her arm in a calming manner. "Herr Molder is not Gestapo. He is from Rudi. He has come to help." She bent down to pick up the scattered memorabilia.

Gretchen Borgman stared at Chris Clancey. "You are… Inglander?" she asked, phrasing her words as if she had not heard him speaking perfect German only minutes before.

Chris frowned. "The less you know about me, the better it is for everyone." He looked out the window at the approaching figure of the gardener. "What about Hugo? How does he feel about Rudi's treason?"

Reisa Konnings bristled. "Please. It is the Nazi monsters who have committed treason against the German people! What Rudi is doing is trying to save us from becoming the Judas of humanity. There will not be a country on the face of the Earth who will spare us if the horror bombs are dropped."

Chris nodded. "Very well, then." He walked to the door and stood waiting for the gardener to reach the foot of the steps.

The old man paused and settled the end of the hoe on the ground. "Who are you?" he squinted.

"What did Rudi Konnings call you when he was a child?" Chris held out the gun but his attention was focused on the woman behind him. He was braced for any sudden movement.

The old man's mouth fell open. "Are you mad? Rudi called me nothing. Hugo. Just Hugo. I swear it."

Chris lowered the gun. "That's right." He turned to face Reisa Konnings. "You understand. I had to make certain."

She nodded. The color was flooding back into Frau Borgman's face as Chris stepped into the yard and held up his hand to wave at the hedge.

"Horseman!"

A portion of the hedge moved and Heidigger calmly walked into the open as casually as a man taking a stroll. A man who strolled with an automatic pistol at his side.

Chris turned back to look up at Reisa Konnings. "Now, let's have that call to your boyfriend."

CHAPTER 5

The Colonel chewed his cigar as he watched the twin-engined Mosquito drop its wheels onto the long runway. The plane looked small and insignificant compared to the big Lancasters parked along the sides of the strip. It was the only tenuous link to Clancey, Konnings and Heidigger. He hoped nothing had gone wrong with the transmitter in Clancey's jump. It would be a crime to lose touch with the team at a time like this. Though the only men dropped into Germany that had been able to make contact had been equipped with Joan Eleanor, it was still virtually an experimental device and being in the right place for a contact could go wrong a dozen ways. He felt a twinge of guilt for pulling Clancey into this one, but then, who could he send? He remembered how he had recruited Clancey in the first place.

It had been two years now. The Colonel had just gotten his desk when he'd heard about a downed B-26 crew that had escaped from the continent. It had been a beauty of a report. The pilot spoke French and German like a native; had been a pilot in Europe for a French airline just before the war. When the Germans had started up, he had flown reconnaissance with the French until they were beaten, and then, made it out at Dunkirk and volunteered for the RAF. He'd flown British bombers until the United States entered the war and reeled him in. He'd been among the first to prove the 'Widow Maker' could be a devastating combat weapon in the hands of a gifted pilot, not just an overcomplicated way of killing off their own crews. Clancey had led some smokestack level raids over Germany before he'd been boxed in by a pair of Focke-Wulf 190's.

The Colonel shook his head in remembrance. Yes, a man who can cut his way out of prison camp and lead a bunch of Yanks out of Germany and occupied France was just the man for a job like this. The usual pattern for getting an agent for Germany was recruiting German prisoners that might be anti-Nazi from P.O.W. camps. It was next to impossible to get an American who could not only speak the language well enough, but knew the thousand and one details that living in a country alone could provide. The difference in being able to blend in or be shot as a spy could hang on knowing the name of a school in a supposed home town, or the color of the town hall. If it could go wrong, it often did. Chris had been the best possible case; German grandmother and a year with apartments in Paris and Berlin. You couldn't train that.

Chris had not been interested when first approached. The Colonel admired that about him. Eager beavers scared him. But then, Clancey's girlfriend had got herself blown up during an air raid and he'd wanted to make it more personal. The Colonel had been able to provide that. The trouble was, it wasn't really personal after a while. If you kill enough people up close, even bad people, you quit being a person—at least, the one you thought you were. The Colonel felt bad about that. He genuinely liked Chris. He liked all the men he picked before he sent them out.

The Colonel broke from his reverie as the Mosquito taxied in. There had been a stop-over for fuel in France and then on to the designated target. The British plane's speed and altitude abilities more than made up for its more limited range. It was a natural for these missions. His only misgiving was the 'hand-in-glove' business necessitated by using too many English personnel. Donovan didn't like it and neither did he. He'd had to put together a little fiction to cover this mission from the Brits; he'd even kept it secret from the next desk. It was too chancy to let too many hats cover it. Besides, if it turned out to be true, it could end up being technology they might not want to be sharing with the partners.

The damned Russians were always looking over their shoulders, anyway, licking their chops for a bigger piece of the pie. Well, they might get the damned jets and rockets, but this was sure as hell not something they should get a smell of. And hadn't even Donovan himself said he'd recruit Stalin if he thought he could win the war a minute sooner? The Colonel frowned. They were all smelling the end of the war and losing their perspective. They were forgetting the big picture. Well, as long as he brought it all in, sealed and tight, it would be the best of all worlds. That wasn't easy. Too many teams were dying. Another mistake would not go well with Donovan. No, the Colonel would wait until the cards were really on the table before he opened the door to the partners, or even Donovan. Not until he had it pinned down perfectly. He chuckled to himself, *"If the Brits don't come onto me about it, it's damned sure the Germans don't know we've tumbled to them."*

"Yes, Klaus, please... I will have Gretchen cook for you. I know Colonel Shaeffer will let you come... Tell him I said it would be an affront to the memory of my father if he does not give you a pass. Come on, I need a ride in the country. One gets tired of a bicycle. Yes... yes." Reisa Konnings laughed and looked up at Chris Clancey as she hung up the telephone receiver. Her voice was grave again as she spoke to him.

"Klaus will come. He has a car. I could not tell him anything over the line, of course."

"And he'll be willing to cooperate with us?" Heidigger sat across the table with his gun lying in front of him while he rubbed the dachshund's chin. The dog looked over at Chris and, seeing his attention, jumped down to come around and paw at his knee.

"Yes. I think—yes." The girl nodded emphatically as if she had resolved the matter for herself with little doubt. Chris hoped she knew her boyfriend. A pilot spilling his guts about an unpalatable mission was a long way from a man ready to commit treason against his country.

Chris watched her eyes. "If he does not, what will we do?"

She stared at him silently for a moment. "Are you asking me?"

He nodded. "I have to know who you feel more loyalty to, Reisa. Reichmann, or your brother?"

The girl swallowed. "We have to stop the bombs," she said, looking down at her hands in her lap.

He nodded. "Good. You have to make your mind up to these things beforehand. If you wait, sometimes—"

"I understand," she nodded.

Chris looked down at the dog straining to lick his fingers. "How is old Wolfgang?" he asked absently to take her mind off the subject.

There was a slight pause, and then the girl answered, "I have not seen him recently."

Chris brought a hand to his face as if to rub his eyes. He would give her another chance. "Rudi's Wolfgang is not around?" he asked, peering in the kitchen at the maid cutting up the veal. He knew that Hugo was working the garden furrows just beyond the back door. He could hear the hoe scratching slightly and gently stood up to stretch.

"No," Reisa sighed, "No, I don't think he has had any leave lately." She grinned and looking over at the dog, snapped her fingers and called, "Come here, Otto. Come here, old boy."

Clancey looked at the dog and then at the girl.

"But he is the best pilot I've got." Colonel Shaeffer gripped the edge of his chair, repressing himself again. "You've no proof he had anything to do with the deserter. And, what possible evidence is there that Konnings' desertion had anything to do with this mission?"

In response, Herr Geltman lifted his dark, wide-brimmed hat and ran a hand through his hair as if determining whether the colonel was worthy of a reply. He smiled a short, tight-lipped smile and tossed his hat on Shaeffer's desk before answering in an indifferent voice. The lack of passion made the message seem even more menacing. "I will tell you this, Colonel. This is a war. And we are soldiers, not lawyers. Captain Reichmann does not belong to you. He belongs to me. Proof is something you need to settle an argument. We, of the Gestapo, no longer have arguments, Colonel. *This* is not an argument. Do I make myself clear to you?"

Shaeffer felt his rage pacing inside him like a trapped tiger. Who was this little insect of a man to order a Luftwaffe colonel around? Had this man ever faced danger from the enemy? Did he know how it felt to have every searchlight in London lighting you up like a Christmas tree for the anti-aircraft batteries? Did he know what it felt like to fly home with your fingers plugging the bullet holes in your arteries? No. He was just one of the Fuhrer's nasty little peasant gods, the kind one found everywhere now, little men telling real men what to do and what to think. Small wonder they were losing the war, with so many congenital defectives given free reign. Shaeffer thought this very clearly but he did not say it. When he spoke, he was the very voice of reason itself.

"Of course he is not *my* pilot, but he is a hero to the men. A real leader. He has flown more missions than any bomber pilot in my group. He can deliver your weapon on the exact target in a snowstorm. You can't throw that kind of talent away because of a silly boy running scared."

"Ah, but where did the scared little boy run? That is the question, "the Gestapo man wagged a finger back and forth in front of him. "A squadron of fighters was sent to block his try for Switzerland. But he did not show up. There are ground reports of a small plane overhead in an almost straight line from the aerodrome where the plane was taken to the enemy occupied country. Why would he do this? I will tell you why. Because his sister talked him into it."

"She's a fine girl. How could she have known of a thing as secret as our mission? And why would she make such a plea?" Shaeffer knew if the war ended and he were near Geltman, he would use the first minute of armistice to kill this man.

"She is a little Jewish bitch as I told you, Colonel—ah, a half-Jewish bitch. I stand corrected," the Gestapo officer smiled. "And she has told us everything. I had her brought in two days ago. Oh, she wasn't too cooperative at first, but, the servant couple was quite commendable. In fact, we would still be in the dark if they had not called us on the telephone about Reichmann's visit. Apparently, he is not too careful about where he talks his treason."

"You have the girl?" Shaeffer had met Reisa Konnings at a dinner before the war when she was no more than a child. He felt a tightening in his stomach but tried not to show his emotion to his visitor.

"Yes, in a safe place, not on your pathetic little airbase. Don't worry, the Konnings girl is quite comfortable. She may even have time to wake from the drugs before we shoot her. It is wonderful what modern medicine has offered us. Fear and modern medicine are such a civilized way to get what we want. You'd be amazed, Shaeffer, what we can fetch up out of almost anyone. There are no secrets anymore."

"And Reichmann? What are your plans for him?" Even as he fought the bile is in his throat, Shaeffer felt himself letting go of his old friend. 'Wolf bait' they used to call it when a traveler threw meat on the trail to slow the wolves. He wondered just who or what he would not throw to the wolves to escape them now.

Geltman stroked a finger over the model He 111 bomber on the desk. "Oh, we are handling that very carefully, my Colonel. Do not think I am so stupid as to drag off the hero of the squadron. We have him where we want him for now. But he will never fly the mission. Rest assured of that."

Chris Clancey stretched his arms and yawned. "It has been a busy morning, fraulein. With your permission, I would like to sample the hospitality of one of your beds."

His young hostess smiled. "Certainly. It will be some time before Klaus will be able to drive out here and I may need to answer the phone; so you will excuse me if I let Gretchen show you to the guest room?"

"Thank you."

She stood. "Excuse me, but do you need to make contact with anyone? I had always heard you spies carried radios around with you. I suppose it is only so in the adventure stories?"

Heidigger grinned. "Oh, we have our ways, fraulein. Don't you worry. I'll be running along soon enough to pop a line in the post."

Chris looked at Heidigger. "Yes, but we do need to let London know we are *perfectly safe*," he said calmly and saw the twitch at the corner of Heidigger's eye. "We needn't keep them waiting for confirmation. Why don't you go out and get our radio?"

Heidigger nodded and stood up, taking a final sip of tea before setting it down and strolling toward the kitchen. One would hardly notice that he had picked up the gun with his other hand.

The girl turned to call Frau Borgman for more tea as Clancey brought his gun out and moved around the table. His left hand darted around the girl's neck and pulled her off balance against him, his hand clamped over her mouth as he brought the barrel of the gun up against the base of her spine sharply.

"Don't think I won't kill you because you are a pretty girl. The only hope in hell you have is to tell me everything you know. You'll tell it to me, anyway. Your people taught me a lot about that."

He felt her bucking against him and he jammed the gun in tighter until she froze. He watched Frau Borgman turn to view his seizure of the girl and, before she could scream, Heidigger had dropped her with a chop to the neck. She fell down fast, banging against the wooden floor like a load of wood, cracking her head on the hard surface. He was out the back door in two strides and Chris heard the hoeing stop.

Clancey forced the girl back and pulled out a chair for her to sit in. Heidigger returned with Hugo before him, trembling and uttering a short cry when he saw his wife on the floor with the blood beside her head. The girl's eyes never left Clancey's. She was perfectly still.

Heidigger's voice was flat. "What gave them away?"

Chris nodded to the dachshund. "The dog."

Heidigger laughed. "He forget his cover?"

"She called him Otto. He's Wolfgang."

Hugo moaned. "Why? Why did you call him Otto?" He looked to the girl as if stricken, pleading for a reason.

The false Reisa glared back. "Shut up, old fool! The little bitch lied about the dog."

Clancey could imagine it. They'd have broken her; pain—drugs—something. They'd have gotten the important things; she couldn't have known how to hide them. When they had that, they'd have gone after details in a hurry to put together the impostor. They wouldn't really have needed her to tell them these things. They had the servants, but it would be easy now. They'd won. Except, she still wanted to fight—to resist. It would have been the effort of a sister who had nothing left, but maybe one little thing. The last thing. Just a prayer, probably. Or maybe a little victory for herself; a lie they could not break. Because it wasn't a lie *they* would have imagined. Why bother to hide a friend's nickname? A favorite dish? The name of a dog? He wondered if they'd killed her when they were through and if it had been quick.

Clancey sat down facing the girl. "Where is Reisa Konnings?"

"You expect me to tell you that?"

"You are going to tell me that."

"She's dead."

"Then, so are you, bitch." He put the gun to her knee. "But you're going to find out about pain first. Just in case there really isn't a hell waiting for you."

The girl flinched. "That won't help you find her."

"Now we're getting somewhere," Heidigger said and turned to the old man. "How about Hugo? Hey, old man, I'll cut your balls off and feed them to you if you don't tell me what you know."

Hugo began to shake and cry. "We—we were afraid. They would have killed us if we hadn't helped them. She would not talk. They would have killed her."

The girl glared at the man. "She told us everything, old fool. And you turned her in."

"No. No! It's not true!"

"Take it easy," Clancey said, shoving the girl back. "If Hugo has enough to say, I may not need to trouble you after all."

Hugo was crying, whimpering. "We did not know. We were afraid. We heard Rudi planning to fly to the Americans. We knew we would all be in trouble. We decided that if we told them what we knew of Rudi, then they would leave us alone. We told them it was Reichmann and Rudi, not Reisa, but they would not believe us—"

"Where is she now?" Clancey said without taking his eyes from the girl.

Hugo shivered as he answered, "I don't know. They took her from here. They asked so many questions. If we did not do as they asked, they would kill her."

Heidigger whistled. "Looks like it's back to our Lilli Marlene here. How about it, Lilli? Your memory returning?"

The girl did not look away from Clancey. "Your mission is ruined. We have the girl. We know you are here. This house is surrounded by our men. If you surrender—"

Clancey smiled very slowly. His mouth drew wide.

"Why are you smiling? You have nothing to smile for. You are in terrible danger." The girl was looking older as she spoke, the mask of innocence long dissolved. Her eyes were darting from Clancey to Heidigger and back.

Clancey shook his head. He held up his left hand. "Look at this hand, fraulein. The last time I 'surrendered,' one of your sisters burned the skin off my hand with a blowtorch. It wasn't as painful as the operations I had to have to replace it. I'm not going to lie to you. I'm probably going to kill you, because you are probably going to do something foolish. You will stay alive just as long as you help me. When you stop helping me, then you are going to die. If I get the girl, I promise you, I will let you go. You'll be tied up and hidden somewhere, but you'll be alive. If you lie to me or quit helping me, then I will shoot you, because you will just be a problem. Do you believe me? It's important to know if you believe me. If you do not, then I will have to do something to you to convince you."

The girl said nothing but nodded slowly, her eyes fixed on the pink flesh of his rebuilt hand.

Heidigger turned Hugo toward him. "You're a long way from out of the woods, old man. See to the old woman if you want to, but be careful not to do anything foolish. Nobody ever burned my hands because I never let anybody live who even smelled like trouble."

Hugo nodded and moved carefully to kneel over the stricken woman on the floor.

Chris Clancey sat back in his chair. "Who will be driving the car? What is the plan?"

The girl bit her lip. "It will be one of our men, of course, dressed as Reichmann. He will drive you to a point in the woods where our men will be waiting to seize you. He will be here soon."

Chris nodded. "Where is Reisa being held?"

The girl hesitated and Clancey said nothing but stared into her eyes. "In the hotel in the town," she replied at last. "Geltman has set up his operations there on the upper floor."

"You're going to walk us in. We're going to get the girl."

"I can't do that."

"You can walk me in. I have great papers. Hell, I'll out-rank you. All I want from you are directions. If you want to try a break when we get inside, you may try. But, I promise you, I will put a bullet in your spine. You might live, but you'll never walk again or enjoy a lover. Something tells me that's very important to you." He turned to Heidigger. "Tie her up."

Clancey stood and walked to where Hugo was trying to soothe his wife's pain. He helped the old man lift the woman and they carried her to a bed. He checked the room over as he began to figure the course of action they would take in the next hour. Finally, he sat down in a corner chair and wished he had a cigarette.

Chris looked out the window on the crisp winter afternoon, the wind rustled the tops of the pine trees like the quickening blush of a boat's sail as the morning breeze comes up—an adolescent memory slipping free of its niche. He felt old. Twenty-eight shouldn't be old, but it was. It was old if you've already used up your life, he thought, old if everything you've cared about dies. God, he could barely remember anything from before the war and the parts he did were distorted, separate; some of them seemed like pictures from an album someone else owned. Maybe something someone had said would come back. But it was like a bell without a clapper. There was no point of contact.

Now he just had this one thing he did. This nasty job he tried to believe in. They all laughed at the idea of the shining knight, the hero rescuer, but that was the true hope behind it all. If you didn't want to save the world, what the hell were you doing in this? Well, it was too late to save the prince and princess this time. The prince and princess were both cooked. One dead of a broken neck and the other a Gestapo captive. He wasn't doing so well either, sitting around waiting for a Nazi chauffeur to drive them off to prison. He rubbed his eyes. So, why was he here? Was he trying to save the world or was the Colonel right? Was it the only thing left in him that was alive? Life reduced to the thinnest edge. He'd enjoyed playing with the Nazi woman, showing her his power, his control. That was the kind of power he hated in Heidigger, and he used to think the fact that he hated it set him apart from the bastards. It didn't seem to, anymore. Well, no time for this kind of mental masochism now, he thought. There was a car to catch and people to kill.

Geltman set down the phone. His smile was wide and he blinked his eyes with excitement as he turned to Colonel Shaeffer. "Thank you for the use of your telephone, Colonel. That was my headquarters. It seems the Americans have taken the bait. I will now go on a little walk in the woods. Would you care to see what an American O.S.S. spy looks like? The American hero has come to rescue Rapunzel in her tower." He laughed. "Sadly, we have switched Rapunzels."

Shaeffer said nothing but wondered how long it would be before this creature would be after him for treason of some sort. Of course, there was no treason to be found. Only the treason of not being as diseased as Geltman, and that was becoming a crime. He stood and took his cap from Geltman who held it out to him in a parody of politeness. The very touch of the man's gloved hands made Shaeffer feel violated. He had not had a drink since his last visit to Berlin. He resolved now to become very drunk as soon as he could arrange it.

Michael Kitchens took the cigar the Colonel offered and sank back into his seat. He shook his head and took out the notepad he had used to record the information from the contact.

"It's pretty bad, sir."

The Colonel waited.

"One of the team was killed in the jump. Broken neck."

"Which one?"

"Konnings."

The Colonel sighed. "Go on."

"The contact point is good. They are pursuing the house of Konnings' sister. The equipment is secure. They will advise soon."

Kitchens looked up from his notes. "That's all. It's all on the tape recording."

"Thank you, Mike. I'll hear it later. Any trouble getting in?"

"Not really, sir. We saw a patrol but they were so far below us I don't think they knew we were there. Those little wooden kites can really get up there."

"The, uh, Mosquito crew quiz you much on this one?"

"No, sir. They're all business."

"Hmm."

Mike smiled. "You thinking of sending in another team, sir? I'd like to go."

The Colonel waved his cigar. "Not yet, Mike. This looks to be a delicate job, and for that I'll take Chris Clancey over a division. Unless we lose all contact, we'll play the worried mother and let Clancey and Heidigger work it. Remember, this one is absolutely our baby. We stay with the pure intelligence angle as far as our *Partners* are concerned. You up to going back tomorrow or do I need to send another man?"

Mike shook his head. "No, sir. It's crowded in that little crawl space they hollowed out, but I'll be ready. And remember, I'm in line if you need someone to go in after Clancey."

The little black BMW coupe drew up to the side of the house. Clancey watched as the smartly-dressed Luftwaffe captain climbed out and adjusted his cap. He looked the part all right, rod straight and totally at ease. He looked like a good Nazi's idea of a crack pilot, right out of a newsreel. Clancey's experience with fliers, however, especially those who'd been shot down a few times, was that they tended to look a lot more human; not quite so invincible. He waited until this false Reichmann was inside the house, ushered in by the woman agent before stepping up behind him and sticking his gun in his back. In a few moments, the new man was undressed and securely tied to a brass bedstead on the second floor, his mouth gagged. Heidigger sat in a corner chair, his gun in his lap.

"The way I see it, "Clancey said, "We have about three choices."

Heidigger nodded. "We force the base location out of the bitch, recon in the car, and get our asses out to the barn to call a strike. We either both go, or one of us goes and one stays back. But what's the third plan?"

Clancey looked out the window. "They may be onto us pretty damn soon. They may be on to us now. And I wouldn't trust that woman to bleed if she was cut. We need the Konnings girl. Maybe she can get us to the boyfriend—and that's a pass to the base. Maybe she knows all we need to know. We get the girl and we've got the key. We can get the hell out of here, too."

Heidigger shook his head. "That's too complicated. You want to save the girl, Clancey. You're still the fucking hero."

Clancey turned to look at Heidigger. "I'm still the fucking boss."

"You've got the balls, Clancey, but you've still got no brains."

"Right. Now, that we've voted, you get the keys from Fritz in there and I'll change into his uniform. I'll ride in the back with my gun on the girl who'll sit beside you in the front passenger seat. If we're seen, it'll look like the right kind of business is going on."

Heidigger raised an eyebrow. "And the old couple and Fritz?"

Clancey thought for a moment. "Put the old people in the root cellar. Let the girl see you shoot the man."

"I could save us the bullet."

"Damn you, Heidigger. Use the gun."

"The old boy might get out of that cellar."

"Not until someone comes to let him out. We'll let them overhear a few things first. Give 'em a wrong location on our camp and let drop we've got a back-up team. Too much won't help, but that might set them off in wrong directions and tie up a few extra men."

Heidigger laughed. "Shit, Clancey. You're just a sentimental old fool."

Clancey walked over to his briefcase and flipped up the lid. He traced a finger over the plastique cubes and sat down to start kneading the charges. He knew he had to hurry. The Gestapo wouldn't want to be kept waiting.

The BMW whined down the asphalt roadway, the exhaust leaving a frosty wake in the cold. There was no traffic and the girl leaned forward and pointed at an approaching turn off. "It's in there. The secret base is hidden beyond that hill. You are going to miss it."

"Nice try, sister," Heidigger replied cheerfully.

"Sit back," Clancey said leaning forward over the back of the seat. "As I said, we're going to the hotel in the town."

"You can not be serious."

Heidigger nodded. "We thought we'd go check your papers at the local Gestapo headquarters. We'd hate to be kidnapping a non-official spy."

"You are mad." The woman stared at them both.

"I'm turning in the American spy," Clancey said. "Here's what you're going to do and if you don't do exactly what I say or do anything I don't say, then I will kill you—just the way I said."

Geltman tapped his fingers on the seat of the parked Mercedes and frowned. "I do not like this, Shaeffer," he said.

Shaeffer tried not to smile. Even enemy espionage seemed preferable to Geltman's priggish arrogance. "Your men are ready. The road is covered by three machine guns and the gate looks to be a reasonable barrier for a hidden airfield. Surely you have planned for everything, Herr Geltman—unless your agent has been found out."

Geltman glared at Shaeffer. "There is always a risk, Shaeffer. The Gestapo asks much of her agents; but where there is no risk, there can be no glory."

Shaeffer nodded. "Soon perhaps you will have your glory."

Geltman looked again at his watch. "I should call in to the hotel. Perhaps there has been more communication with Agent Brandt." He took the radio phone from Shaeffer and attempted to ring the set at the Gestapo headquarters in the town. There was no answer.

"The swine. Someone is asleep at the radio. I will have an answer for this." Just then the radio phone buzzed but it was not the hotel calling. It was a Luftwaffe sergeant calling for Shaeffer. Geltman angrily handed the device to the Colonel.

"Shaeffer here. What? What?"

Geltman was staring at Shaeffer's incredulous face. "What is it, Shaeffer?"

The colonel looked up; his face a picture of stunned surprise. "We had best drive to the town, Herr Geltman. Something has happened."

CHAPTER 6

Clancey nodded slightly to the guards on the street as the girl braked the BMW to a stop in front of the village's one hotel. He was surprised at how long it had taken the adrenaline to come up for him. They'd changed drivers outside the town and Clancey had wondered if the girl might not try something with the car, but she hadn't. He wondered if he would have. No, the odds were too wrong. If she were going to do something, it would be inside. The question was when. Now things were moving slowly as the girl spoke to the guards and he walked Heidigger around the car with his gun in the man's back. The guards had responded by bringing up their guns, but the girl's credentials and his rank were enough and they were inside now. Reisa Konnings' room was supposed to be on the second floor if the girl hadn't lied or Konnings hadn't been moved.

There was a woman at the desk, a rather tired, older lady who watched them with little interest. Two officers sat in chairs at a table near the front window. A guard was stationed outside a door at the top of the stairs.

It could hardly have been better. Apparently, most of the men were engaged in the ambush planned for them. The two officers had risen curiously as Clancey's party entered and looked briefly to each other before moving toward them. One of them called to the guard on the upper balcony who unslung his machine gun and jolted down the stairs to join them.

Clancey eyed the first officer, an S.S. Oberleutnant, with cold disdain. "I must speak with Colonel Geltman at once. I have a prisoner for him."

The young officer was attempting to look unimpressed. "That is very interesting, mein Captain. We will take charge of your prisoner. As it happens, Herr Geltman is out at the moment but should return soon. If you wish, you may wait here. I will be happy to take down your name and unit for the record."

"That is unsatisfactory," Clancey snarled. "If Geltman is not here, then I must speak with Berlin immediately. Take me to your radio—and, I am afraid I cannot trust this prisoner free of my sight."

The Oberleutnant shook his head. "I must see some proper identification before I consider your requests," he smiled. He turned to face the girl, "And yours as well, fraulein."

Clancey sensed the moment was here. He knew the girl was edging away and quickly reached out and jerked her forward and indicated her face with his pistol. "Fool. I have uncovered a plot. This is a double-agent your stupid Geltman sent to catch this man. I have them both. Now, if you value your miserable skin, you will take me to your radio. If you do so immediately, I will grant you the chance to occupy yourself elsewhere when I make my report."

The younger officer eyed Clancey sternly, but Chris could see the man's throat tighten. The other officer had drawn back somewhat and the guard was now looking to the Oberleutnant as much as at Heidigger who groaned as if he were recovering from a beating. A blob of rouge made an angry welt along his temple.

Clancey unbuttoned his pocket, pulled out a wallet and handed it to the officer. He looked directly into the girl's eyes as he did so, letting go of her to use the bad hand. She started to move, but the guard moved the barrel of his gun toward her sharply and she stopped.

The officer opened the wallet and pulled out an official paper bearing the stamp of the Waffen S.S. His eyes stopped at the signature on the bottom. The best forgers in the unit had not been allowed to issue this signature yet. It had been saved for a desperate moment. The Colonel had managed to get it for him, just in case, and only in the most extreme conditions. This seemed to fit those parameters to a T. The officer's head sprang up reflexively and he snapped to attention.

"I am sorry, mein Captain. We must be always wary here, you understand. I will lead the way to the radio." They marched up the stairs with the officer leading; Clancey still holding the girl's arm, Heidigger being followed by the guard with the machine gun and the second officer who asked the clerk to bring up some tea.

At the door of number six, the Oberleutnant knocked and waited for a challenge to which he replied with the countersign. The lock bolt was drawn and the door opened. Clancey felt the light energy which flowed through him as he adjusted his strategy from moment to moment. Each step into the unknown demanded lightning-quick thinking. A chess match with a half-second clock. The slightest hesitation—the one wrong move or unguarded moment—meant death or worse. There were six variables now, he determined as he stepped into the room; the guard who answered the door, the radio operator who sat at the set (apparently waiting for contact with Geltman as the girl had said), the two officers, the guard with Heidigger, and the girl. Six to two. This was the girl's moment. If she was going to do anything, she would do it now, he knew. He did not wait but turned to her, suddenly gripping her throat with both hands and then, as she tried to shout, he hit her with the gun, knocking her unconscious. The Germans all started forward, but Heidigger held his ground, waiting the word.

"She was trying to swallow poison," Clancey said as he bent over and pried open her wet lips. "It must have been in a tooth. I checked her for pills when I caught them."

The officers stared at each other. "Place her on the bed," the Oberleutnant said to the second guard who stooped to do as he was ordered.

Clancey was unhappy to see that Reisa Konnings was not in the room. That changed the plan. He turned to the radio operator. "Call Gestapo headquarters in Berlin. Let me know when you establish contact."

The radio man bent forward holding a microphone in one hand and a headphone against one ear.

As they waited, Clancey holstered the Luger. The officers seemed to relax as he snapped the flap over the hilt. Chris sighed and absently opened a button on the blouse of his uniform to reach a hand inside and scratch. His fingers trailed against the pommel of his own gun with the silencer. Now the radio operator spoke into the microphone and turned to face them. "They ask your code name, Captain."

Clancey angrily reached forward and grabbed the headphone and microphone from the startled soldier. "Give it to me," he ordered and spoke into the phone in a clipped, impatient voice. As he spoke, he patently ignored the operator on the other end of the connection.

"Ja! Ja! This is 'Dagger'! Now, put me through to Klemkeit. Ja." He paused, then turned casually to face the others and leaned against the wall. Arrogantly eyeing Heidigger, he mocked, "The Americans must be desperate to send such examples of their intelligence service, no?"

The others laughed politely. Clancey straightened up from the wall. "Javol! Yes, I have them both. No. I do not know… but surely… Ja." He placed the microphone against his chest and spoke in a commanding voice to the young officer, "They demand to know if the prisoner Reisa Konnings is still alive."

"Yes, of course," the officer replied. "Though perhaps she wishes it were not so."

"You must bring her here at once."

"But I have told you she is alive."

"I must report that I have seen her alive with my own eyes. I do not question my orders, Oberleutnant. Do you?"

The officer snapped his heels together and left the room.

As they waited, Clancey could barely stand to hold the earpiece against his head but he had to muffle the growing shouts of the official on the Berlin end of the line. He spoke calmly into the microphone, "They have sent for her. If it is as I suspect, Geltman is in it, also." To this last remark, there were gasps and turned heads around the room, not to mention a furious shout over the headset. He made his plan as the door handle turned.

It was Reisa Konnings—upright and moving slowly before the officer. She was small and dark, and were she not so frightened, perhaps quite pretty, Clancey observed. Her eyes darted about the room and came to rest on his. A shudder seemed to pass through her body and Clancey realized that, to this innocent creature, he appeared the very embodiment of evil. Though it was a pose he had worked to achieve, to see its effect on one so young and vulnerable made a part of him both ashamed and afraid. He quickly turned to the officer. "This is Reisa Konnings?"

The Oberleutnant nodded. "A mousy little thing—you would be surprised how long it took to get her to talk to us. We had some good ideas for her, but Geltman likes to use the drugs first before the real pain. Perhaps later the little mouse will spout some Hebrew for us if we ask her the right way."

Clancey grunted and lifted the microphone to his mouth. He was stalling. There were too many and the girl was partially between him and the officer. The guard with the gun was not distracted by the girl now; he'd have to be target one if Heidigger was going to get a chance. It was time, but it wasn't right yet. He needed a distraction; something to buy the half-second he would need to have the gun.

And then it came. There was a timid knock at the door and the muffled call for tea from outside it. The Oberleutnant who had just brought in Reisa Konnings turned to open the door, his right hand crossing his body to the knob. At that instant, Clancey handed the microphone to the operator who grasped it and the headphone which was suddenly loud and livid. In the same movement, he brought his good hand to his holster and shouted to Heidigger. "Now!"

His first shot hissed solidly into the turning face of the guard. The other guard was too slow for Heidigger, whose knots were suddenly gone and was driving his boot dagger up under the guard's sternum as the radio operator tried to rise. Clancey slammed the soldier across the neck with the pistol and before the man landed on the floor, turned back to take careful aim at the Oberleutnant who had opened the door for tea and had only now spun back to stare into the barrel of Clancey's gun. The silencer hissed and the shells rocked the startled German backwards, knocking the tea tray out of the desk clerk's hands. The other officer, who had been sitting in a chair watching, had started to claw at his holster but never cleared the leather pouch as Heidigger had again used a boot kick to drive the cartilage of his victim's nose up into his skull. The man was jerking in unconscious spasms on the floor as Clancey moved through the door way and grabbed the clerk, pulling her into the room.

Reisa Konnings sat on the floor where she'd fallen, staring wild-eyed at the mad action that had exploded around her. In less than seven seconds, five men had died. Her journey in hell had taken a fast corner, Clancey decided.

Heidigger was free now and held the guard's submachine gun on the clerk who was quivering against the wall. Clancey bent down and took hold of Reisa Konnings' hand.

"Fraulein Konnings, we are not German soldiers. We have come to get you out of here."

Her eyes were wide though still very tired and her voice was strained. "My... my brother?"

"He came for us. We've come to stop the bombers. You must come now, we haven't got much time."

"Are you... Americans?"

Heidigger laughed. "Tell her we're the good guys."

Clancey shook his head; shooting people up close never made him feel like a good guy. Still... anyone, who enjoyed hurting girls like Reisa Konnings, wasn't really human... not by Clancey's definition. He tried not to wonder if he was still one.

He lifted the girl to her feet. "Can you walk? We have to get to a car."

She nodded.

"What about the bitch?" Heidigger motioned to the false Reisa still unconscious on the bed.

"I guess she's done us all the favors she can," Clancey said quietly.

Heidigger reached over and pulled a pistol off one of the dead officers and turned to aim it at the temple of the unconscious S.S. agent. As he placed the barrel against her skin, Reisa Konnings shouted and moved forward, reaching to restrain the methodical Heidigger.

"No! You cannot!"

Heidigger looked up, irritated. "She'd do the same for us only not so quick. Be sure of that."

Clancey pulled the girl back. "Fraulein, we are leaving. We can't allow her to get away, and taking her with us creates problems. I am sorry."

"You are not Nazis. You don't kill because it is easy."

She was desperate, frantic. Clancey didn't like the way this was starting. He made a decision. He looked up to Heidigger.

"We'll take her with us. Maybe we can use her to cut another corner."

Heidigger shook his head. "You're crazy. You don't keep a cobra in your pocket. If it makes you squeamish, I'll do her when you're out the door."

Clancey looked at the girl on the bed and the clerk. He spoke to the clerk first.

"The war is over, Madame. In a few weeks, the Russians and Americans will be here. It is time to get ready to hide. If you wish to see the Americans arrive and peace come, you will do exactly as I tell you to do. Do you understand me? I have just killed these men. I will kill you just as quickly if you refuse me. It is your choice."

The woman's face was absolute parchment. She nodded slightly.

"Good. You will now go down to the entrance of your hotel and call the two guards inside. Tell them they are needed upstairs. Tell them there is a problem with the prisoners. Lead them up the stairs and into this room. Open it for them. Carry this tea pot. You will not be too hurried."

The clerk looked back and forth between them.

Heidigger smiled and leaned closer. "I will have a gun aimed at you the entire time, Madame. If you attempt to run away, you will die in that moment."

Heidigger's gleeful expression seemed to mesmerize the woman for a moment and then she nodded. Smoothing her dress, she reached for the tea pot which Clancey held out for her.

"You will live, Madame. That is my promise as a soldier. And, later, you may tell as much as you wish to anyone who asks, but you must do this thing now."

Heidigger followed the woman down the stairs with his gun and silencer.

"You're certain the front is solid for two more days?" The Colonel asked, his eyes working over the meteorologist's charts. "The Atlantic is socked in, huh?"

The young R.A.F. officer nodded. "Yes, sir. It's a pretty dismal picture. If you need something flown in from the States, you'll have to wait a few days, I'm afraid. Perhaps, in forty-eight hours, there'll be a break."

The Colonel frowned. "Never mind what I need, sergeant. I just need accurate information, and that's always critical."

The meteorologist straightened. "Yes, sir. You have it, sir."

The Colonel leaned back in the chair. "Very good. You're dismissed."

The sergeant gathered up his charts and moved to the door.

The Colonel looked out the window and puffed his cigar. "Well, Chris, let's hope that cover lasts long enough and those Mosquito boys can keep finding our needle in the haystack."

When Heidigger and the clerk returned from the lobby alone, Chris turned to the false Reisa Konnings who he had just revived with a sip of water from a carafe in the radio room. "You will live as long as you can help us. Tell me now how you will help us."

She stared back at him, but the hate in her eyes was gone; his own tiredness seemed to have moved into her. Maybe all the players felt this way when they saw it was ending.

She nodded. "I… know where the field is."

Heidigger frowned and looked around the room. "What about this place?" he asked Clancey.

Chris didn't look away from the girl. "We'll blow it. I've got my things. It'll take me about ten minutes to do it the way I want."

Heidigger grinned. "That would be satisfying. Hey, no sense in not opening the little safe over there while we're here, is there? That's one of my old specialties. Looks like they borrowed the local strongbox. I've seen tougher cookie jars. Probably a good idea to truss up Mata Hari here first."

Clancey glanced at his watch. "How long to open it? We don't want more company."

Heidigger laughed. "I bet you a drink at the Criterion I beat you."

As the Mercedes pulled into the village, Gestapo Colonel Geltman gripped the windshield brace and raised himself in reaction to the scene in the street. Smoke billowed from the crackling pile of debris that had been his headquarters. Several men were rushing about the wreckage dumping buckets of water on the burning remains that had spilled out into the thoroughfare. The Gestapo man dropped back onto his seat in disbelief, his eyes transfixed on the destruction.

Colonel Shaeffer tried not to be amused by the shocked despair of his fellow passenger. He reminded himself that this might hold tragic consequences for himself as well as the Gestapo man's career. As his chauffeur braked to a halt, Shaeffer shook his head. "Amazing," he offered, "these spies must have enormous guile to effect such an attack. There must be a full squad of them."

Geltman stepped out of the car before speaking. "I will have every one of them before me. I will castrate each bastard involved—American and German alike. *Nothing* will stop me or the mission."

Shaeffer nodded. "The mission will proceed, Herr Geltman. My crews are ready. We wait only on the final word from the science team."

Geltman leaned in against the car so that his words were clearly understood. "Yes, Colonel, you will carry out your part of the mission. Be certain of that. And your planes are the bait I will use to catch these jackals. Your planes—and your traitor."

An S.S. captain approached them, gave the Nazi salute, and asked what orders Geltman had.

Geltman stroked his chin and wiped his glasses on his sleeve. "Search the ruins, Captain. Look for everything—especially the body of a young woman. Send a squad to the Konnings' house and search it completely. The rest of the men must move to the base. We are to be the guests of our good friends, the Luftwaffe."

Shaeffer winced. God, was Geltman destined to be his own personal demon? "Our facilities are limited, Herr Geltman. We have no hotels in our hidden base. Our quarters are not much better than rat holes. The better to hide, of course."

Geltman laughed. "Where better to hunt for rats, then? Perhaps the sight of a few more Gestapo and S.S. uniforms around will help the courage of any other *worried* aviators like young Konnings, and keep them on the dutiful path of honor."

Shaeffer did not reply but slid back in his seat, mentally praying the planes would be flying soon. Perhaps, when the 'Big Geese' had gone, the vultures would leave with them. For an instant, he wished he'd been on that flight with Rudi Konnings; but no, he was a German officer in the Luftwaffe and whatever happened, as long as anyone remembered that vaunted service, he wanted his name to be one held in honor. Duty to the last if to the last it must be.

CHAPTER 7

The car crunched through the brush off the side of the dirt road. Heidigger switched off the ignition and turned to grin at his fellow passengers. "Well, whatever else happens now, we've at least shoved a rather large cob up the local Gestapo anus."

Clancey looked across at the quiet imposter beside him in the back seat. He wondered again whether keeping the woman alive had been worth the risk. That Reisa Konnings had quickly emerged from her earlier stunned state to active participation in their speedy escape, he attributed in large part to his decision to let the Gestapo agent live. It was important that this young girl trust them. Clancey instinctively knew that, for that critical allegiance, Reisa Konnings must view her rescuers as morally superior to her captors and not merely as a change of guards.

Reisa turned to face Clancey over the back of her seat. "Do you think we have escaped?"

"Fraulein, there will be no real escape until we are out of Germany."

"When will that be?" she asked. "How will you do that?"

The girl was still on the verge of shock, Clancey observed and he must be very careful of how he phrased everything.

"We will leave when we have completed our mission. Without that, it would have been useless for your brother to have risked so much." He smiled, trying to cushion the reality with a human touch. To smile was human. To Clancey, it was the easiest lie to use.

The girl nodded. "Yes. Yes, that is right. You have risked much also... For your...courage, I thank you. I will do what I can." A smile flickered at the edge of her mouth and Clancey realized it was an effort on her part to assure him of her loyalty.

Heidigger grunted. "Well, if you're certain we're not too near the barn, we'd better cover our trail and try to hide the car. Not much fuel left, anyway, and I'm certain there would be a little curiosity over strangers hunting for Benzin about now."

Reisa nodded. "From what you tell me of it, Rudi must have meant the old Rossman stables. They have not been used for many years. We often played there as children. It is just over those hills," she said pointing through the trees beyond the hood of the car. "We can walk there in less than an hour through the wald."

Clancey looked the waiting Gestapo woman in the eye, his pistol still held resting in his lap. "We need to verify a few things before we make our report," he said. "How far is it to the airfield?"

The woman looked across to Heidigger who was watching her in a mildly amused manner. "I am not certain. I do not know this area well. If I had a map, it wouldn't be difficult—"

Reisa Konnings interrupted. "I know how far. At least to an entrance. I have not been there, but I have been told."

"Your traitor brother no doubt." the Gestapo agent snapped.

Reisa turned to stare at the woman and Clancey was glad to see that a spark of anger could still rise to her eyes. "A true German hero told me. Not all those who wear the uniform of the country are blood-hungry butchers like your Geltman."

"Ah, but you talked to him, didn't you, my pretty girl? You told him all about your brother, didn't you?"

Heidigger grinned. "She didn't tell him the name of her dog."

The woman glared at Heidigger but she turned back to Reisa as the girl answered her.

There was blood in Reisa's face now. "I told him only what he already knew. I knew little else. But I did not tell—"

"What? Who is the spy in the base?" The woman laughed. "You think you have hidden your boyfriend from danger? You stupid little tramp. Do you imagine your little friendship with the great Reichmann is such a secret? Perhaps at this moment his leash has been tightened."

Heidigger laughed. "Well, you're just a bundle of fun, old girl. I'm just as much a psychopath as your friend, Geltman; and, if you're all out of helpful hints, I'd as soon start a little game of tit for tat, if you understand me, fraulein?"

The woman stared defiance at Heidigger but his alarmingly boyish smile as he mouthed the threat chilled her, Clancey could see. God, how he hated this. Playing the devils against each other and placating the saint while he had to think of a plan. No transportation, no surprise left. The enemy had all the cards. The book for survival said to get the hell out now. They'd gotten close, as close as they could, but the little voice in his head—the one that belonged to all martyrs—said there was only one move to make. Move in. *The cobra can't bite you when you're on his back.* Riki-Tiki-Tavi. Clancey smiled without mirth at the memory of the childhood favorite his mother had read him at bedtime. Yes, move in, Riki, and strike. Never run when running only delays the inevitable.

His leg brushed against the briefcase and he thought of it for the first time since throwing it into the car. Probably not much use, but as Heidigger had said, no sense blowing the building without opening the safe in the little radio room. The briefcase would not likely have much of value to their immediate needs, but you looked at all your cards. Sometimes, you got lucky.

It was dark now and the two men sat a little apart from the women, as they rested inside the ruined barn. Clancey was moving his small flashlight over the papers spread out on the brittle hay. Heidigger was smoking a cigarette and rubbing his toes.

"The way I see it, Clancey, we're about ten kilometers from the main gate of this secret Kraut carnival and that's if the Konnings girl is right. I mean, this is third-hand and under a bit of stress. Mata Hari doesn't seem to be putting up much of a fuss and that doesn't feel right, either. You know our map doesn't exactly match up to their descriptions—which isn't too surprising since it was published over a decade ago. We order a bomber strike and miss, by even a mile or two, and it's wasted. They'll start moving everything, if they haven't already. So, what's the master plan?"

Clancey considered Heidigger's points in silence before finally answering. "They aren't going to move anything. Not yet. They may hurry things up, but chemicals, bacteria… the kind of thing Rudi Konnings told us Reichmann was talking about will take special tanks, technicians, a support system that won't be just sitting around anywhere. And it's all hidden so well our best recon planes haven't been able to spot it yet. There's no way they could make that kind of move in a hurry. No, they'll try to nail us, and they'll fly those bombs as soon as they can. That could be any time now."

Heidigger grunted but only nodded.

"Even if we know where to bomb," Clancey continued, "it might be too late. We've got to get it all plotted as soon as possible." His eyes had been scanning the papers before him as he talked to Heidigger. Nothing out of the ordinary, nothing he hadn't expected: ledgers, lists of personnel, a large cache of banknotes, various correspondences. There was a photograph of their Gestapo agent prisoner, whose name was Carla Brandt, and a photograph of Reisa Konnings. A large manila folder, tied with string, had his attention at the moment, though his curiosity was hardly moved with this dull task. Then, as he slid its contents out on the hay, his eyes widened, his focus contracted to the maps showing what could only be the mission. Broad, red lines vectored from Halburg. A coldly whispered "Damn." issued from his lips as Clancey ran his fingers over the colored paper, as if to assure himself with touch that his eyes did not deceive him.

Heidigger glanced up at Clancey's exclamation. "What? What is it?"

Clancey turned the colored map again and brought the flashlight over the red lines. "This is the mission, for God's sake."

Heidigger was staring over his shoulder now. "Hey. We know the routes, we might intercept before they hit the States."

Clancey shook his head. "Wrong direction. They're not aiming at us. They're headed for the Eastern Front. They're going to hit the Russians."

The two men were silent. Then, Heidigger whispered, "Well, that takes some of the air out of it, doesn't it?"

Clancey looked at the agent. "What do you mean?"

"I mean, what if we let it go? Look, the Reds aren't exactly going to turn around and march home when this party's over. Ten or twelve years from now when they've caught their breath, they'll just pick up on the Nazi job themselves. Only they'll already be halfway home."

Clancey stared at Heidigger. "Are you suggesting we not report this? You think we should let these bastards dump this hellfire on our allies because we don't need their help anymore?"

Heidigger groaned. "Jesus, Clancey, this is not baseball. Can't you see it? The Russians get kicked in the face and stop to think about it. They'll slow down or stop and Germany will surrender to us. We'll get everything these fucking Kraut geniuses have been cooking up for the last ten years. Good God, Clancey. You've seen the reports. Look at those rocket bombs and fucking jets. If we got our hands on those babies intact—hell, if we get all the brains behind them, we'll rule the fucking world. For once, the right people will have the right weapons."

"He's right, you know."

Clancey turned the flashlight up to shine on the face of Carla Brandt. She was grinning as she sat with her back against a wooden stall, her hands still tied behind her. Reisa Konnings sat beyond her, watching quietly.

"It would be the best of all things if the Russians were stricken. Then you Americans could join with us. You know yourselves that you have much Aryan stock in your population."

Heidigger laughed. "Ahhh, she's full of it, Clancey, she's just Gestapo gas. But *listen* to me, I'm telling you, nobody wants the Russians to beat us to Berlin. You've got the big picture to consider. What about your little friend over there, huh? How do you think those Cossack boys will treat her and the women like her? We're not talking about the Boy Scouts here. Think of the favor you'd be doing the world."

Clancey swallowed. He didn't want to think about the *big picture*, not the way Heidigger would paint it. "We've got a mission to do. We're not supposed to determine policy. We were sent to destroy those planes before they can drop that stuff. That's still our mission."

Heidigger snorted. "Maybe they'll change the mission when we send them the facts."

Clancey bit his lip. "It's not that simple, Heidigger."

"Well, what do you plan to do about it?"

"I'm going to locate that base. I'm going to get the right coordinates. You stay here with the woman. Make the contact when it's time. Tell them what we know. I'll get back before dawn if I can." He turned to the girl. "Will you come with me?"

Reisa Konnings nodded. "Yes. We can get bicycles from the house. It's not too far."

Heidigger pulled a drag on his cigarette, the tip glowing bright in the dark. "There may be someone watching it."

Clancey smiled. "I think our friend Geltman is a little too busy to be closing the barn door after the horses are gone."

Outside, walking over the hillside in the cold moonlight, Clancey felt a sense of relief he hadn't had in the last two days. Reisa Konnings was silent, walking beside him, small and thin, just a child really, he thought. Only no one who'd been interrogated by the Gestapo could be considered that again. The contrast in being alone with this girl and the tension of being with Heidigger and the Gestapo woman was incredible. Clancey remembered how close he'd come to walking away from all of it, how he longed for real isolation, a place in his life that could just be silent. No plans, no traps, no fears. Just quiet like this countryside and the girl walking beside him. Drawn to her innocence, he felt repelled by his own nature. His hands were bloody, instruments of war, tools of death, just like the killers in the barn.

"It would not be like that?" the girl asked, her voice still quiet in the open air. "It would not really stop the Russians, would it? It would not save us? What you said. It's not simple like that, is it?"

He took a deep breath as he continued walking beside her. She hadn't turned as she had spoken, but she glanced over at him now, to see if he was going to answer her.

"Nothing is ever simple or easy. No one has used the poison gas in this war, yet. Do you wonder why, fraulein?"

She nodded. "Yes, I have wondered. I have heard the stories from my father's war. The mustard gas. The things it did to men. It is horrible, but many horrible things are done."

"Neither side has used the gas," he continued, "because everyone has it. The Fuhrer and his generals know that if they used it, we would use ours three for one against them. Oh yes, we would. And it would be within hours. Very few people know this, but it is so. A threat against a threat. A threat in a war must be a horrible one indeed not to be used."

She was silent only a moment. "Then, why now? What is the difference in this and before?"

He felt his throat going tight. "It can only be that this—this disease, is far deadlier, much greater than anything before it. A disease is a living thing. It isn't like a bomb or a bullet, it can't be turned off or controlled like a cannon. Once it has started feeding its hunger, who would be safe? It can only be a last measure when the balance has fallen away. A madman's choice."

"Your friend thinks the Americans will come to our aid if the Russians are stricken."

"He is wrong. Too many Russians have died. The Americans know this. The people of my country would blame Germany for a crime they would not tolerate."

"But the leaders make the decisions, do they not? Like here?"

He stared at her a moment before answering. "Not like here. Not yet."

She kept walking. "I have heard many stories of things that have been done by the S.S.—things no one wants to believe. But I know now these things have happened. Klaus has told me of the things he has seen. Not rallies and marches as before, not wild acts of violence breaking out, but—camps." Her words stopped for a time as they walked, but she seemed unable to bear the silence and again tried to express the thing that was driving her on. "We have no dreams left. We only deny what we can see if we even dare to look for it. We no longer ask questions. What will happen to us when the war ends?"

He shook his head. "Some will have to pay. There will be a call for justice. There will be trials, I'm certain. But wars do not make justice. They only end. And then, there is a little place for life for a while. But, I don't know what will happen. I used to try and think about the effect of what was done—of the ultimate good that must come from the terrible things I did. I no longer treat myself to such illusions. I only know this weapon is a horrible thing and it must be stopped."

Clancey didn't like this conversation. It was a little late for the assassin to become a philosopher.

She nodded. "Yes. It is an evil thing. An evil thing will only make an evil end. Of course we must stop it."

Looking to the woods on her left, Reisa stopped walking and pointed. "This way. We can save time if we take this path. Rudi and I used to play along it when we were children."

Reaching the house, they had been surprised to see a pair of soldiers climbing aboard a motorcycle and sidecar. The two helmeted men had appeared bored and took a moment to light cigarettes before driving off down the road at an even pace. There was no other evidence of activity. The house seemed deserted and its windows were dark. Chris and Reisa circled the grounds carefully for a quarter of an hour before Clancey was satisfied. There was no sign of the servants or the dog.

Reisa led the way onto the back porch where a pair of bicycles had been kicked over and, in a few moments, they were pedaling off through the darkness toward the path that the girl indicated would lead them to their destination.

The winter night was cold and quiet. Gravel crunched a heavy wake beneath their tires as the man and the girl pedaled and coasted along the country lanes. Clancey would have enjoyed the exercise, the necessity of mindless action, as a momentary reprieve from violence; if the possible hazard of encountering a patrol had not demanded vigilance. He was becoming more and more intrigued by the Konnings girl. Her determination and resilience in the face of such overwhelming upheaval in her life contradicted the pattern he had prepared himself to encounter in an innocent idealist. Now, he wondered how far her idealism would carry her when she learned of her brother's death. He was surprised that he considered telling her. It would serve no purpose to his mission. Perhaps he resented her seemingly unshakable resolve. How could anyone living here, in the belly of the beast, retain a sense of purpose in such a war? He was tempted to kick open the ant hill of evil her country had become and show her the full light of day on the twisted, festering activity of the damned that had burrowed to the heart of Germany. Give her the full truth behind the rumors that proper Germans dared not hear. To what purpose? He caught himself. Anger? Resentment? He resented any mention of hope, yet he felt a growing sense of duty to something intangible. Certainly, not duty to the Colonel. He would not put a name to it, but he instinctively knew, even against the finely-chiseled instrument of his precise reasoning, that he would die in a moment to save this girl. And that was something he had not felt in a very long time.

CHAPTER 8

Geltman looked at the metal frame bed next to the concrete wall. He tapped the reading lamp on the hastily provided table that the sweating private had just set into place along with the extra quilting.

"Very good. Much better than our friends out there have this evening," he said, turning with a smile to face Shaeffer who stood in the doorway of the small compartment and was dismissing the young airman.

Shaeffer nodded. "As I said, Herr Geltman, there are no luxuries here, and this is a mark above the accommodations the dislodged tenant will have tonight as well."

Geltman sat down slowly on the mattress, his hands in the pockets of his dark overcoat. "He is providing his country an additional service by his sacrifice," he said. "Now, my good Shaeffer, go ahead and ask me what it is that disturbs you. Without doubt, it concerns your precious Klaus Reichmann?"

Shaeffer frowned. "You know I do not share your views as regards the loyalty of Captain Reichmann. However, that is not the issue at the moment. Obviously, in view of the attack on your headquarters in town, we are in danger of an attack of some sort here; and yet, I see no preparation out of the ordinary on your part to avoid it. If you have determined that Reichmann is a traitor, you have made no effort to restrain him."

Geltman held up a gloved hand. "Ahhh, but your own elaborate defenses should provide enough protection, should they not? And if anyone on the outside wishes to pursue further penetration, will they not most certainly attempt this through contact of some sort with our brave captain? Fear not, Shaeffer, my people are in place. I do not wish to close the trap merely on the mouse's whiskers, but to take his entire head." Here Geltman paused for a moment. "It is possible that we shall be visited by a party from Berlin quite soon, and I very much wish to provide them with a triumph. They do not care for excuses, Shaeffer. Neither mine nor yours."

Shaeffer straightened. So, the devil had his own worries, he thought. He would have been pleased if it had not meant that his personal demons would also be multiplied.

"What of the mission?" Shaeffer said, returning to the more pressing matters of his command.

Geltman closed his eyes. "I expect word at any hour. The science team assures me the weapons can be primed and loaded within twenty hours. We await the meteorologist's report and the latest reconnaissance. General Zhukov seems to be accommodating us. The main Russian armies are concentrated below Warsaw; they plan, no doubt, for a thrust west. Think of it, Shaeffer, three black birds appear in the sky, higher than their fighters can climb—just specks in the air—and then the invisible rain. Plague fleas. Think of the beautiful simplicity of it. We have the tiniest and deadliest warrior in history riding our wonderful new Big Geese. The greatest long range bomber in the world. There is no target beyond our scope, no wild rocket to land where it will, no misfiring ballistics."

Geltman stood up, his voice rising with growing enthusiasm as he painted the imagined event. "Within hours, the sickness begins. First the red faces, the retching, the writhing, and the fear, growing faster and faster. Dull-witted hordes of Cossacks, the superstitious peasant rabble—they will understand that their death is all around them. Within a day, there will be confused retreat, then wild rout as the deaths begin. Faster and faster will the rout become. They will abandon their guns and ammunition. The simple animal mind desperately seeks a futile hope. Home. Escape. Ahhh, it is wonderful, is it not? If there is time, more raids. The Big Geese can carry deeper and deeper, herding the frightened cattle before them, back to the Steppes. Then we can turn again to face the West. What will the Jew Roosevelt and the snorting bulldog Churchill do? They will declare peace, I tell you. They will say that a Germany that can turn the Red Tide is not all evil. We will be their bulwark against the communists. Their people will see this. And, in two years, Shaeffer, even a year, our scientists will have weapons for us that will make every power on Earth our friend or our slave." When he turned to face Shaeffer, Geltman was beaming as he waited for an expected affirmation of his vision.

Shaeffer felt sick. Impassioned speeches made him sick. The last years seemed to ring with one upon another. He could no longer listen to them. His mind now turned away. One day it would show. He wondered if it already did. He spoke to mask his disgust. "And our Imperial Oriental ally—a slave as well? What if our non-Aryan friends have plans of their own for this wonder weapon of theirs?"

Geltman nodded slowly. "It bothers you, Shaeffer, the Japanese? Yes, our little yellow friends have supplied the plan for the plague, and we, the means to deliver it. The Oriental mind is indeed devilish; much better to keep it on our leash. Do not worry my brave aviator; it is only kind fate that has given us the good fortune to pluck a single fruit of their labor for our own harvest. The time will come when we may have need of the Pacific; and with the rest of the world in our domain, it will be a simple matter to continue the purge of the world's lesser races. The Japanese agree with us. It is just that they start with the Chinese. A humorously misguided alignment of Destiny's Chosen. A quarrel between midgets."

Shaeffer remembered the pictures of the Japanese scientists' autopsies of the prisoners they had experimented on in China. The enlargements of the plague carriers had only inflamed his repugnance. "I cringe at the thought of those breeding tanks, Herr Geltman, just a few meters below the earth. The lice and vermin.

Crawling death. Why have the Japanese not used their weapon if it is so powerful? Why are we to use it first?"

"At the moment, it is fortunate that we have the greater need. For this will let the world see us as unconquerable. From the ashes of our defeats, we will rise more formidable than ever and the Emperor and all his yellow dwarves will know that Germany is not afraid to use the most horrible of swords. The Samurai respect such unflinching determination. Only those who are willing to use such power will have it, Shaeffer. Only those who can do such mighty deeds are worthy of the final victory." Geltman paused and smiled to finish with a calm statement. "The Earth shall be our throne."

Shaeffer's thoughts turned back at the final words of Geltman's tirade. He'd grown used to hiding inside his silence, enduring the ravings of fanatics in order to preserve the sanity of his command. It was all he could focus on now: the familiar discipline of his pilots and crews, the brotherhood of aviators. Before the war they had flown in air-shows, raced for records, even made friends with pilots from countries that flew against them now. Later, they fought duels over Britain and Europe, everywhere fighting the fight of eagles; first winning, now losing, but always fighting with honor. His mind's eye focused on the face of his son, Charles, named for Lindbergh, his own hero. The boy had turned thirteen, had been addressed in the huge stadium of Hitler Youth by the Fuhrer, himself. He remembered Charles telling him about it excitedly on his last leave home. He wanted to be an Eagle like his father, to fly in the Fuhrer's service. Hitler Youth. What had the Fuhrer said? They shall be fast as greyhounds, tough as leather, hard as Krupp steel. No intellectuals. Thinking would ruin his young men. Charles was being built into a man who would serve men like Geltman without the weakness of his father's doubts. Shaeffer felt a shudder run through him which he tried to suppress.

"What is it, Shaeffer? Are you ill?" Geltman rose to stare into Shaeffer's face, as if he might determine the thoughts behind the colonel's eyes.

Shaeffer shook his head. "No, Herr Geltman. It is just fatigue. I am perhaps more tired than I realized."

"Very true. We have been very busy these last days. We should enjoy our last days of secrecy. In two days, the world will know what we have known for weeks. It is important we be rested for the work that lies ahead. Good night, my colonel."

Shaeffer saluted and left the room. As he walked down the narrow hallway of the subterranean shelter—the "Warren" as it was known among the crews, he realized that he hated Geltman more than any enemy he had ever flown against. Even the Russian fighter pilot who had made his left eye useless. He would have prayed if he had hope in a God. God or not, he thought, the *Devil* seemed to be alive and well.

They had hidden the bicycles a hundred yards from the road and had moved quietly through the pines for perhaps twenty minutes before nearing the clearing. Chris could see the silhouette of what looked to be a simple farm fence; but as he approached the wooden rails, he became aware that it was much taller than it appeared—over eight feet. Strands of barbed wire ran between its wooden rails. Pausing to study this unusual barricade from the shelter of the trees, he realized it had been constructed to fool aerial photography. It would be difficult to judge the height of the fence unless a plane was very near tree-top height. Set this near to the trees, the shadows of the poles would be effectively masked.

"I am certain the gate is not far to our right," Reisa whispered, shivering in the cold night air. "But, there seems to be nothing here. Just a pasture. Yet, I know this was the road to the airdrome Klaus told me of."

Clancey nodded. "Their security seems well hidden, or they're risking a lot for invisibility." He looked overhead and gripped the lowest branch of the tree nearest him. He turned to Reisa and started to unbutton his heavy coat for more freedom. "I'll go up and have a look around. Don't call out if you hear something, just lay down. Keep your face hidden from the moonlight."

The girl watched quietly as he began to climb the straight trunk. In the dark, the sound of his boots scratching on the bark seemed loud to Chris, but he knew it would not carry far. And, if anyone were near enough to hear, the sound might be mistaken for movement of a hare or fox in the underbrush.

Now he'd reached a point where he could survey the near side of the long meadow. From here, it looked like any number of such fields he'd seen in the aerial photographs he'd studied before leaving England. His first thought was that the few trees dotted along the open meadow would preclude any safe use of the landscape by aircraft for a landing zone. And of course, the really large bombers would need a much harder surface to operate from than this field could provide. If not for the odd fence bordering the pasture, he would have been tempted to mark off the location as a mistake. It was then he noticed what appeared to be a pair of cows grazing beneath one of the trees in the pasture. Odd enough that a farmer would allow his cattle to roam in the night. But with no bombing since the night before, there was little chance of panic-driven strays. Pondering this discrepancy, he raised his small binoculars and focused on the still animal-shapes some hundred yards away.

A smile slid up the side of his face. There could indeed be pleasure in the hunt, he conceded. Chris Clancey appreciated clever deception and this was one to put right beside the rubber tanks and inflatable airplanes he'd seen used to create Patton's mythical pre-invasion army in southern England. These cows were not going to move without help. They stood upon wooden or plasticene legs, molded into models of bovine contentment. He had little doubt the solitary pines dotted about the meadow were of similar substance. From any altitude, photographs would confirm the benign nature of this dairy land.

Chris needed to see more. Surely there had to be a hard surface hidden somewhere. And where were the hangers? The fuel trucks? Not to mention the chemical storage areas. It all had to be underground and probably bomb-proofed like the submarine pens had been on the French coast. High altitude B-17's couldn't count on picking out such an invisible target and the low level B-24's hadn't worked out so well at Ploesti, he remembered. It could take a week or longer to be sure they'd knocked out the field. And they didn't have a week. Maybe not even days.

He didn't know how many fighter squadrons covered the area, but he suspected that only the smallest number of planes would be located here; only night fighters to keep any lucky reconnaissance planes from spotting the bombers during night training when the hangers would have to be opened. It had worked so far. Clancey rubbed his gloves together. The only thing that had given away the base was a traitor.

Chris sat in the crotch of the tree branch for perhaps ten minutes before he heard the sound. He twisted, then heard Reisa shifting below. He would have dropped down to be near her, but it was too late—the tell-tale steps of heavy boots marked the approach of the sentry just this side of the fence. Chris sat still, holding his knife behind the branch, shielding the bare blade from the moon as the too familiar outline of the soldier moved below him. He could see the tiny double lightening bolt patches on the jacket. The shoulder-strap submachine gun swayed gently in the soldier's hands and with his slower step attested to the state of alertness of the guard. Chris prayed the girl would stay hidden. After what she had been through, it was asking a lot. The sentry moved past them without stopping.

When he was certain the guard had gone, Chris leaned down and whispered loudly. "Reisa."

"Yes." The reply was almost a choke.

"Are you all right?"

There was a pause. "Do we go now?"

Clancey was about to climb down when he heard the truck. Off to his right about two hundred yards, he detected the slits of light from two masked headlamps at the edge of the tree line. The vehicle paused, perhaps at a checkpoint hidden in the shadows. The lights flickered as someone crossed in front of them. A few moments later the truck lumbered out onto the grassy field. It was a large transport and as it began moving with a crunch of gears, Chris brought his binoculars up and watched its progress across the wide pasture. Brake lights flashed and the truck stopped just before a low hillock. Several dark figures emerged from the shadows and approached the truck. A portion of the hillside seemed to darken. Then, a dull red glow lit the front of the transport and the profiles of the guards. The truck moved forward slowly, dissolving into the hill like an absurd version of Persephone entering the underworld. Then it was gone and the moonlight washed over a deserted meadow again.

As hard as he looked at the mound where the truck had disappeared, Clancey couldn't find an outward sign to give away the hidden structure. He knew he had found the base, but he had to see more. Something had to show. Something had to be visible. If he could just think what to look for. Then, it came to him. Air. They had to have air vents. He began to methodically comb the rolling meadow as best the moonlight would allow. Yes. There was a pattern of stumps repeated on various mounds of earth along the far edge of the pasture. He'd have to get much closer to be certain, but the German passion for detail, evidenced in the workmanship of these props, had apparently not overridden the tendency toward uniformity. The stumps seen alone were unremarkable, yet their constant width and repetitive patterning prompted Chris to visualize the general outline of buried bunker complexes.

He pulled back his sleeve and checked the radium dial of his watch. He still had time. He'd have to move closer to find the planes. Listening for more guards, he lowered himself from the branch and worked his way down the trunk, dropping at last to the pine straw below.

Reisa Konnings stood waiting. "You have seen it? There was a truck—"

"Yes. I watched it enter. I know this is the base."

"I was so frightened of the guard." He could hear her take a shaky breath.

"You were very good with the guard." Chris reached to touch her shoulder. "I have to go closer. You must go back to the bicycles and wait for me only another half-hour. If I have not returned by then, you must leave and tell Heidigger. Tell him the field is here, but it is not good for bombing. It will have to be done by a ground team with explosives. We will need more explosives than we have left. He should say this to our contact. We will require five times our amount of explosives and detonators. We will need commandoes—men. Twenty would be good. Forty would be better. You understand?"

She nodded.

Clancey looked at her. A single streak of moonlight lay across her nose and cheek. "Reisa, can you do this?"

"Yes."

"Tell it to me," he said.

He listened as the girl repeated his instructions. He unstrapped his watch and handed it to her. "Remember. Only half an hour."

Reisa touched his arm. "Be very careful," she said. "You must not be caught." Her hand tightened hard on his sleeve and Clancey realized she was shaking.

He smiled and patted her arm, then pulled her hand gently from his sleeve. "I am very careful. It will be all right."

She answered his smile with no more conviction than his own. "That is more than I can hope for."

He turned again and walked away, clearing his mind of the girl who watched him leave. He was grateful there was no snow. Crossing this open expanse with snow would be impossible. The tracks would be a sure sign to any sentry. His admiration for the complexity of the illusion only heightened his determination to uncover its deepest levels.

Clancey reached the fence and began searching for a way across. He couldn't be certain but there was a chance the fence was either electrified or contained a trip line that would set off a signal. In either case, it would not do to warn the enemy. He could only hope their eyes were trained on a larger field of search than their own front door. Looking at the barrier, he determined it was too tall for a man to vault and too far from the tree line to use a branch for help, either. The only feasible way was of cutting through. With somber resolve, Chris pulled the rubber-handled clippers from his pack and eyed the connecting wires playing through the wooden fence. He would have to snip two. He tapped both wires with the clippers to see if there was an electric current and was relieved to see no response. Careful prodding revealed no tripwire, but there might be mines just inside. This was the only way. He settled down to clip the two lines, then, using his parachute knife, slowly levered the bottom board free from the nearest post. Looking down the fence again, he slung his pack over the top. He waited, listening, then dropped onto his back and slid himself, pushing with his feet until his head and chest had passed beneath the fence. Gripping the dry grass with his hands, he pulled himself ahead, dragging his legs and feet through the opening. He rolled over and lay on his stomach for several seconds looking for any sign of activity, then, gripping his pack, began his slow crouch run toward the cows.

Reaching his target, Chris knelt down and rested for a moment, running a hand over the stiff form of the decoy. The earth felt hard beneath his boots, even harder than frozen ground should feel. He pulled his knife and began to cut at the short-cropped field. Even in the dark, beneath his gloves, he had been aware of a different consistency. Now, as he dug the point in, he felt an odd resiliency—firm, but stringy. Then the point scratched a hard layer a bare two inches down. He smiled. A very nice quilt. A rug over an airfield. Clancey wondered if it was pulled away before landings or if it was secured enough to take the friction of the wheels without skidding. Certainly it was an amazing undertaking, an engineering feat almost on a level with the development of the big bombers that must use it.

Sighting one of the stumps he believed to be masking ventilators, Chris had just determined to make his next move when he heard voices. Ducking down under the decoy, he strained to look for the source of the voices. A few dots of light were swinging at waist height moving out into the pasture much like the lightning bugs from his childhood summers. Electric-torches were playing over the ground in front of men sauntering across the frozen field. One light was swinging lazily in his direction as the voices grew louder.

CHAPTER 9

Klaus Reichmann took a slow drag on his cigarette and watched quietly as his new bombardier, Helmut Braun, nodded a salute and waited for a guard to open the door of the underground barracks and show him out. No one moved between sections now without permission and escort. Something was brewing. With Gestapo and S.S. officers multiplying everywhere, it was apparent sabotage was feared. This, Reichmann decided, was more than he could hope for. He must make his own destiny. As the door was closed after Braun's departure, Klaus pulled himself up from his bunk and walked to the center of the metal framed pallets, where he stopped and swept his eyes across the collection of veteran airmen. He felt a kinship with these men that he would never experience again. There had always been respect, sometimes affection, and ultimately, survival. They had survived together, not as seven individuals, but as one man. As a man depends on his eyes, his ears, his hands, they had depended on each other; each had saved the one life. Even the youngest had flown enough with them to share it. Over time, it dissolved all barriers. Quietly, as each man noticed his waiting presence standing above them, they all looked up at Reichmann. Detecting something unusual, their silence reflected an understanding of his temperament born of the long years of combat.

"I know what this mission is about," he paused for only an instant. "I do not intend to fly it."

The men of the crew looked at each other. Eyebrows raised. They waited for someone to speak.

"Captain," Willy Frankl, the youngest, spoke nervously, his eyes darting to the others. "You can not mean that. It is treason to refuse a mission."

"The *mission* is treason."

"What?" Frankl suddenly looked his nineteen years. "What do you mean, Captain?"

"It is treason against the human race. If we fly it, Willy, Germany will be a traitor to humanity. And, we will not be forgiven in this life or the next—if you believe in a next." He was looking directly at Frankl, but he was speaking to all of them.

Their eyes were wide now, but they were still watching him, waiting. So far, it was good. They still trusted him. They would hear their captain, even if he threatened to defy an order. He took another drag on the cigarette.

"This mission—what if it kills thousands, even hundreds of thousands, perhaps? What if the thing you start spreads, going on and on like a wild fire? What if there was no way to stop what we begin with this weapon?"

Von Tripps blinked. "What kind of energy are you speaking of, Klaus? What has this much power?"

The pilot's gaze slowly swept from one face to the next, forcing each man to lock eyes with him. "Plague," he said plainly, the word dropping before them with the heaviness of a lead bar.

There was a cold silence. It rolled over and around each man like the Russian winter had, submerging them in a deathly layer of fear and dread.

Lauda rose, reached over and took the cigarette from Klaus and lit his own from its glowing tip before handing it back. "A plague on both their houses, right?" his grin was as cynical as ever.

Klaus nodded. "The top men. They cannot surrender. They will consign us all to their deaths. Before they kill themselves, they will kill our souls."

Frankl seemed to be struggling against the cold. "Maybe they have a way to control it," he offered hopefully. "What if we could kill the Russians? Think of that. Maybe it could be contained."

Reichmann shook his head. "Can you imagine the bombing if we succeeded? Have you heard of the Dresden firestorm? Do you think the Allies will not use gas? What of the Russians themselves? Does Stalin care how many dead it will take to destroy us? No, the weapon that will destroy them will be our death as well. There is surrender at the end of a war, but murder is not forgiven with treaties."

Lauda looked at the others, then back at Reichmann. "Very well, Klaus. So perhaps *we* do not fly the mission. What of that? Someone will fly it, and we would be better off to take poison *now* than to refuse to fly."

Reichmann looked to the door. "Something is going on. All of you know about Reisa's brother. You know he disappeared. Well, he flew to the Americans. He knows of the mission. He has told them of the plague bombs. Something has happened here. I think we must be ready. But we must make up our minds now what we shall do if something begins. Right now, for me, these Gestapo and S.S. men—Geltman, Braun—these are not our superiors. These are our jailers. They are not the Germany I'm fighting for or am willing to die for."

He'd said it all now. All it would take would be one of them. One man in the crew who wanted the reward for turning in a traitor. One man who had been swayed by all the propaganda that had framed their every idle moment for ten years. His mother had often said he would have been a fine preacher. Well, Mama, he thought, I'm screwed. Here's my ninety-five articles nailed on the church door.

"What about the other crews?" Von Tripps asked. "Are any of the other pilots as enlightened as our captain?"

"You are the first I have spoken with. I doubt Schumacher or Prost even know what the mission is."

"Seems we're a little late to save the world," Reinhardt said.

Klaus bit his lip as he considered his next words. They were the final step to the gallows. "I think the Americans are here. That fire in town; that was no accident. They're penning us up in here so no one can get at us. There may come a moment when I will act. It may be suddenly. Is there a man here who stands against me?"

As he turned to look at them all again, the door to the barracks opened and a guard stepped inside. "There is a meeting of all crews in the main hanger in five minutes." He turned and walked out, securing the door behind him.

Reichmann felt the eyes of the others on him as he turned back to speak. "Say nothing. Trust me."

There was silence as the men stood and pulled on their heavy jackets. Klaus tried not to watch them as he picked up his clipboard and chart papers. "Trust me for what?" he asked himself, but his mind had shifted to Reisa Konnings. He'd not been able to see her or speak with her since Rudi's flight. She was seventeen and he had had to tell her the thing that was breaking him. Such a hero. Telling Reisa was telling Rudi. He knew they had no secrets. He knew they were as one. It should not have been Rudi, it should have been Klaus. Now he would have to do something. Now he was a traitor. Even if only his crew knew it. He could not go back now. Shaeffer had warned him to have nothing to do with Reisa, warned him of even appearing to have an interest in Rudi's disappearance at all. He had tried to bribe a call from a friend on the staff, but word had been given and no one could communicate with the outside now. He wished suddenly to get word to her of what he had done. Wished he could warn her. Of what? Klaus smiled bitterly. He could not warn Reisa from being Rudi's sister, could not warn her from being who she was. He could do nothing to protect her from danger. He knew it was already too late for that.

Chris Clancey had to be very careful to keep the cow between him and the two soldiers who walked toward him, talking. Fortunately, they seemed too absorbed in discussing the cold to notice a dark figure lying still in the artificial meadow grass twenty feet away. Had they been looking for him he could not have escaped the torchlight. He could hear them clearly as their breath came in frosty clouds.

"Curse this damned circus tent. It's bad enough we have to move the carpet for the Big Geese when they fly, but now we have to uncover for some prick from Berlin who wants to come nose around the place."

"You should be careful where you talk, Karl. These S.S. have no sense of humor. Come on, let's move the cow and find the eye."

"Ah yes." The first soldier bowed to the decoy Chris had inspected only moments before. "Greetings, Frau Milch Cow. Excuse me and my young friend. We are expecting company and must herd you to better grasses."

The men lifted the plasticene cow and carried it toward the fence, walking within fifteen feet of Chris who had rolled over and lay face down with his pistol beneath his stomach. Inching his face up, he watched, enthralled, as they returned puffing and panting. The torchlight dangled on a strap and its beam had passed haphazardly within inches of the spy. Still talking, the men paused and using the torch located a metal hoop that was anchored by heavy canvas fabric to the ground where the cow had stood.

Chris was aware of several crews of these men up and down the field and then saw that a series of trucks were driving from the shadow of the trees, moving slowly toward each of these teams. As the nearest truck arrived, he watched the two soldiers take their gloved hands from their coats again and reach to take up a large hook on the end of a cable from the back of the truck. This, they secured in the metal hoop they had uncovered.

Chris watched as the soldiers climbed into the truck which began reversing its course. The metal hook tightened, lifting the carpet edge of the artificial pasture back, rolling it along to reveal a concrete pavement beneath. He saw that the other teams were moving in concert, opening out a long, narrow grey ribbon of runway. He began to crawl backwards and edged to the side of another decoy cow, raising his binoculars to study the teams standing beside the trucks. He was aware of a low droning growing nearer and nearer. A moment later, several beams of intense light lanced upward from concealed covers along both sides of the landing strip and Clancey found the source of the droning motors. The Me 110 night fighter cut on its landing lights and dipped over the edge of the trees to the south. After a single pass, it banked, circled the strip at low altitude, and came in. Its wheels touched down twice as it bounced on contact with the cement.

As the plane braked and turned to taxi, a large section of the trees at the far end of the field shifted; then slid outward like a gate, revealing a glow of red lights inside a dark enclosure.

Chris was amazed at the ingenious design of the base. It had gone from a cow pasture to a landing strip and had retrieved a plane in less than ten minutes. The crews were already pulling the cables back, blanketing the hard grey pathway. The lights were off and the trees had rolled back into sentinel station, the red glow from the open hills no longer illuminating their trunks.

Time was running out. Clancey would have to hurry or miss giving the message over Joan Eleanor that he knew must be given. He wasn't sure if he trusted Heidigger entirely. It was just a feeling, a discomfort with the agent's attitude, but he knew the cost of ignoring subtle symptoms.

Michael Kitchens felt numb. Far below, he could see moonlight tracing over waterways, reflecting in short clips of movement as the tiny plane ghosted its way above the range of night fighters. Michael hated the feel of the oxygen mask, but, at least, it helped trap the warmth of his breathing against his face. The frigid night vigil was far longer than it had to be, but, the circuitous route was necessary in order that the Mosquito's destination would not appear obvious to any vigilant radar operator who marked their passing. Fortunately, the almost continuous bombing activity to the north was a distraction that drew away attention as well as the night fighter patrols and consigned their flickering presence to little more than a mild irritation. The planned variation of night hour contacts helped to disguise the actual target. Continuous circling of a false contact area to the east of Clancey's location made the flights excruciatingly tedious, but Michael remembered too well Clancey's report on the interrogation he was subjected to on his last mission—the mission that he alone had survived and spent most of last year recovering from. The unspoken rule was forty-eight hours. Hold out for forty-eight hours without contact and your team should know you've gone down and they are compromised. Forty-eight hours of sheer hell. Michael shuddered involuntarily at the thought. No, a few extra hours of cold and fatigue were a small price to pay for a man who held out when they roasted his hand.

CHAPTER 10

Klaus Reichmann walked in file, his shoulders hunched and his head tucked in behind the flap of his heavy jacket. His ears were cold in the rising night wind. As he stepped through the outer portal into the red glow of the blackout hall, he was conscious of the airmen gathered with him. Their backs reminded him of a string of crows resting on a telegraph line. Perhaps the eagles had been reduced to crows, he thought with despairing irony.

The outer blast door closed slowly behind them and the forward door was swung open to reveal the stark fluorescence of Hanger One. Reichmann trailed the group toward the three rows of metal chairs at the near end of the hanger where a podium had been placed. A hastily hung Nazi battle flag trailed from the beams overhead, making a backdrop for the small raised dais. Beside the scarlet banner hung a smaller field of white with a single red circle at its center. Reichmann marked this unusual display for he'd never actually seen a Japanese flag flown at any German military function. He wondered what occasioned its appearance there.

Behind them all, Reichmann's bomber stood alone. To Reichmann, it's thick, wide-spread wings called to mind the reaching arms of Atlas, stoically holding the world in silence above him. He smiled with nostalgic reflection at the colorful cartoon of the flying beer barrel that adorned the fuselage of his plane—and every plane he'd ever flown. It was the only touch of humor he could detect in the cavernous room.

Klaus knew the Beer Barrel's sister planes sat similarly poised in two other identical hangers nearby. The positioning of the buildings had been carefully planned to rule out the tell-tale pattern of a normal military establishment and further discourage attention in any aerial photographs taken of the region.

Everyone had filed into the rows by crews, nodding and muttering to each other and stamping their feet with the cold. The hangers were not heated in the same manner as the crew quarters.

Schumacher looked over his shoulder at Reichmann. "Well, Klaus, looks like they're sending in someone important to boost our morale or maybe, finally, someone really is going to tell us what the hell we're up to."

"Like Goering maybe?"

Schumacher grunted. "Ha! That's a good one." He added with a whisper, "It'd take one of our geese to fly that lard bucket here and back out."

"I'm not sure I wouldn't like a little mission like that for all of us."

Schumacher chuckled. "Hey, watch it. Your crew might hear you talking. Or, one of these S.S. boys. You can't even play with yourself in the shower around here without one of these little Berlin nose-pickers sniffing up your arse."

"Quiet, you two." Lauda hissed from beside Reichmann. "It's no laughing matter. Here comes trouble."

The door nearest them opened again. A soldier holding a submachine gun marched in, stamped to attention and waited as Geltman, Shaeffer, and another officer, who wore a black cape and the peaked cap of the high command, walked past. They were trailed onto the platform by a smaller figure clad in a light-colored fur coat. Colonel Shaeffer stepped forward to address the crews.

"Heil Hitler!" Shaeffer's arm came up stiffly in the perfunctory salute.

The crews responded with only the shortest delay, a few of the replies finished a full word behind the rest. Reichmann sighed. Perhaps their surprise at Shaeffer's greeting was the reason for this mild lapse. Shaeffer was well-liked among the base's Luftwaffe personnel and one of the reasons was his almost indifferent attitude toward formality. He usually left this to the junior officers, preferring instead, to let an air of serious professionalism substitute for the spit-shine façade that seemed such a source of arrogant enjoyment among the S.S.

After the greeting, Shaeffer placed his gloved hands in his coat pockets. The colonel's eyes played over the crews and Klaus detected something in Shaeffer's manner that he'd not noticed before. Standing between the crews and the odd threesome behind him, the base commander no longer appeared in control, seemed no longer the leader. The man who had directed their training and driven the crews at their tasks now appeared smaller, stiff. Another prisoner among the jailers. "Even Shaeffer," Klaus nodded to himself. He was realizing that when a man took off his blinders, he began to see more and more of the evil around him.

Shaeffer began to speak of their weeks of training, the work of the ground crews, leading up to this most secret of missions. The words were encouraging, dramatic, but there was no power behind them. Reichmann felt a sorrow for the Luftwaffe colonel now so obviously the puppet of the S.S.

His eyes moved to the men waiting behind Shaeffer. Geltman, he knew. The pompous, smirking face with the neatly-trimmed mustache and fashionably intense, wire-framed glasses was long familiar to him now. And, this other officer was unmistakably familiar as well. In the artificial light of the hanger, he, at first, seemed similar to Geltman in appearance, even to the round spectacles, yet his air was one of a quieter evil. Where Geltman seemed always in motion, on the brink of an outburst, this man appeared calm, almost bored—a vacuum. Yes, behind the spectacles were the dead eyes of a shark. Klaus quickly understood his frightening familiarity. Here was the model upon which the Geltmans based their grotesque lives. The newsreels had made this carrion bird a shadow of the Fuhrer himself. Heinrich Himmler. There were stories about him that even Klaus would not allow himself to think about. He knew that Himmler had recently been assigned a military command in the Eastern Front. Himmler, who had no military training, was ordering generals around as the Russians moved to the Oder. It was unthinkable, yet the pattern was growing clearer. The more important the command, the more fanatical one must be to claim it. The dark shadow that trailed the German army into every conquered land was now commanding it.

His eyes slid to the last member of this delegation. Most unusual of all was this small, fur-lined visitor. That was the only way that Reichmann could think of him. His obvious Oriental features could only be those of their vaunted ally in the East. Here was the first Japanese Klaus had ever encountered in the flesh. Fascinating that the Fuhrer could send soldiers to hunt down and murder German citizens who were indistinguishable from their neighbors if only their names had been more Aryan, yet embrace an alien race so different as to appear foreign not only from Germany, but from the Earth as well.

Shaeffer turned and presented Himmler. Oddly, Klaus found himself not watching the head of the Reich's secret police, but watching everyone else as Himmler spoke. This cold hanger was made even colder by the words of the chief Nazi. Klaus studied the faces of his crew. Not fifteen minutes ago they had listened to Klaus tell them to turn against the Reich. Now they would hear Himmler tell them their true duty. These were German airmen. He'd been a fool to have tried to persuade them.

Klaus had the curious sensation of accepting his own fate, and in choosing the manner of his death and its meaning, he also sensed a freedom he had long forgotten. As he listened, he wished only that he had made his decision sooner. In doing so, perhaps he might have found a way to save Reisa.

"German Airmen! The time has come for you. The time to deliver to the world the message that its new master will hold nothing back. Never will we allow the evil of the impure peoples to roll over our borders. You, glorious warriors, are to carry the greatest weapon ever devised. This weapon is a bomb that will rain down death on our mortal enemies. It will drive them back to the boundaries of their lairs where they will cower, awaiting our will. You bring them death. You bring them plague. Yes. The word is fearful to say. The word is mighty and it is ours. You have seen the scientists, the special bunkers, the midnight trucks, the large tanks. You have wondered at the heavy metal containers which mate with your great bombers. Now you will learn that all these have given us the final card to be played. You must be certain that your training has been no pointless game. You have been trained to release your bombs at certain altitudes. You have been trained to fly at night, to launch with rockets and enormous loads. You have wondered why. Now you will know.

"Today, we have proof of the great friendship between our Reich and the Empire of Japan. Today, you see before you the representative of the Japanese that have developed the weapon that we are to carry. This is Dr. Yakuro of His Majesty, the Imperial Emperor's Army. He is here to oversee the final stage of our operation. His courageous research has shown us the devastating effect this weapon will have on our enemies. Dr. Yakuro, you wish to address the crews?"

The Japanese smiled and responded with a slight bow which Himmler returned as he motioned him to the dais. Yakuro stepped forward and looked out over the men below.

"Soon you fly to victory. The seed we nurture in China, you will plant also in the West. The enemies of our peoples will soon see we are the masters of the earth. It is natural that this is so. We have no choice in our gifts, only the choice to use them or to sink to the level of the lesser ones. This shall not be. To victory! Banzai!"

Himmler shook gloved hands with Yakuro and then motioned for the cover of a large chart behind them to be drawn away. On the chart was a massive battle map of Europe. Red and blue arrows swarmed about it, indicating the positions of armies. It was clear that the broad red arrows to the east were the focus of the map and the western end was attached to a point that must be their base. The eastern end swept in a great southern curve which touched a point where three red arrows converged.

Himmler raised a pointer. "Now you will learn the destination of your raids. No doubt some of you have wondered where you were flying these 'New York' bombers. Don't worry; you'll see a lot of the world before our plans are finished. You see here that the Communists are massing for another push forward against us from Poland. Soon, if we do nothing, they will be at the doors of Berlin, herself. This, they imagine to be so. But then, just at morning light, your planes will fly above them and unleash their doom. There will be fighters massed to cover you from any planes they may have. And, after you return, there will be leaflet drops to explain to the victims below the nature of their plight. Within hours or days, the deaths will begin, the horror will spread, and panic will send these barbarians scrambling home in fear." Himmler paused and turned to Shaeffer. "Your commandant will give you the details of your flight plans."

Colonel Shaeffer took the pointer and slowly turned to look up at the big map. Before he could speak, a voice was raised from the audience.

"Colonel Shaeffer, sir. Permission to ask a question?"

Von Tripps was standing.

The Colonel turned back, surprised. He nodded. "Yes, Von Tripps, what is it?"

Reinhardt turned to face the Japanese scientist. "I would like to ask the distinguished Dr. Yakuro why Japan has not used these weapons against the British and Americans? Is he certain they will work?"

Shaeffer looked uncomfortably back to Himmler. The Nazi commander and chief of the secret police stepped forward slightly and smiled as he spoke.

"Who is this airman, Colonel? Do you ask permission of our men to give them their orders?"

Shaeffer was obviously unnerved and turned back to look at Von Tripps with an uncharacteristic anger that Klaus wasn't sure was for his co-pilot.

"Leutnant Reinhardt Von Tripps, sir," Von Tripps answered for Shaeffer. "I am a co-pilot on the plane behind us, sir. I merely wish to learn of the readiness of our weapon. We are all used to the work of our own war industry. We risk our lives gladly in the seats of Messerschmitts and Heinkels. But this bomb—well, it's sort of a borrowed business, isn't it, sir?"

Shaeffer turned back to Himmler. "My crews always follow their orders, Herr Himmler, but they do their best work when they best understand the full concept."

Himmler nodded. A smile had returned. "Very well. Let me assure Leutnant Von Tripps and any *other* Von Tripps among you, that the bombs are reliable. I have seen the successful result of their development."

Willy Frankl's hand was up. There was a long and uncomfortable silence. Then an apparently amused Himmler motioned the young airman up. Klaus was staggered. Reinhardt wasn't afraid to speak his mind anywhere, but Willy never interrupted a briefing, never questioned an order, much less an assembly of such importance as this one. He couldn't take his eyes off the radioman. Perhaps Frankl was about to denounce his pilot.

"Sir—I was wondering, sir. No doubt the weapon is as you say—devastating—but, sir, I was wondering. What about later? The effects when it is over. Could it spread? Poland is not so far— if it shifts west....."

Himmler had stepped up beside Shaeffer now and had laid a gloved hand on the colonel's shoulder. "Have no fear, airman...?" he paused to look inquisitively at the nervous young flyer.

"Frankl, sir. Feldwebel Willy Frankl, sir. Radioman."

"Well, Feldwebel," the smile flashed again, "let me say that we of the German Command have anticipated all eventualities. The moment the Communists are reeling back, dragging their rotting Cossack asses after them, we will send in our special teams. These sterilization units are fully equipped to deactivate the deadly germs." He laughed. "We are not crazy. We don't want to lose even *Poland* forever."

There was general laughter at this, Himmler having skillfully defused the tension. Klaus glanced at Yakuro. The Japanese scientist's eyes had only moved once, a slight look to the speaker when Himmler had mentioned the sterilization units. Klaus sighed to himself. *"No Willy, Uncle Adolf hasn't got a nice, clean miracle weapon for you. Or a clean-up crew."*

"I thought you had been caught," Reisa Konnings said, as they carefully walked their bicycles through the woods toward the gravel road. "I could not go without you."

Chris Clancey shook his head. "What if I had been caught? The longer you waited here, the more likely you would be caught, too. Reisa, I have to trust you to do what I tell you to do. If I can't trust you—"

"Yes, I know, I am no use to you. Well, I have done what I can do, now. Chris… I can't be caught again. If something happened, if we were to be taken—would you—"

He stopped the bike and reached over to grab her arm. "Don't talk like that. Don't think like that. I'm going to get you out of here. This bastard war is almost over. It's too near over to let anyone die who doesn't have to. I'm here to stop those bombs, and I'm here to get you out. I promised Rudi that before I left." He couldn't believe what he'd told her. He knew if the cards started falling, the only thing he could do was finish her first.

Reisa Konnings smiled. "Thank you, Chris. You make me think maybe God hears my prayers. One day, Rudi and I will thank you together."

He nodded and started pushing the bike. They would have to make good time to meet the radio contact.

Captain Yuri Gregor Karpov looped his gloved palms over the lowered barrel of his tank's main gun and, with a grunt, swung his bulk upwards to the metal deck of his T-34. Pushing himself upright and catching his balance, the tank commander paused to gaze along the moonlit flanks of the armored formation. As far as his eyes could discern were the dark shadows of his sister tanks. Rows of metal monsters waiting in silence. Every day the numbers grew. Like rising water against a dam, ton after ton of Russian steel weighted the spearhead for the final thrust. Soon, the dam would burst and the Russian resolve would pour on again. The captain looked down and could barely see the painted swastika markers on the turret; each marking the death of a Tiger tank. The Germans had fought hard, he conceded, harder, as they were pushed back toward their Fatherland. Still, soon they would wash over the last lines, drowning the enemy in a final flood of fire. Yes, it seemed certain. Even the British and Americans had pushed in now, squeezing the last life out of the enemy.

Karpov felt a sudden chill and rubbed his sleeves with his gloves, the friction doing little to warm his skin against the Polish night. Yet this was hardly cold compared to the white heart of winter he and his men had endured. He knew it was not the night that made his heart cold, but a sense of foreboding. The final step had not been taken. The Germans had seemed just as certain of their victory before Stalingrad. Then the world was turned upside down on them. Perhaps he should beware of thinking the end was finally here. Looking out at this massed sea of tanks and men, Karpov felt a nagging dread, a worried shadow passing over his heart like a cloud skidding past the moon. Might the Germans hold a final power? Could defeat roll back onto them yet? The captain looked up at the moon and its brightness washed over him like a spotlight. No, nothing but an act of God could turn back this metal tide, and surely God Himself, if Karpov's grandmother was right, could see that Hitler was the devil's own. With that thought, Yuri Karpov almost crossed himself in respect of his grandmother's religion but laughed at himself instead.

"What was that?" The voice was Private Pavlow's. Peering out from the starboard side of the tank, the young gunner was a less than vigilant sentry who had been startled to wakefulness by Karpov's laughter.

"Nothing, Pavlow. Lucky for you. I was just laughing."

Antoine Pavlow straightened and attempted to look alert, adjusting his cap as he stood. "Laughter, sir? At what?"

Karpov turned to grip the handle of the top hatch without looking back to Pavlow. "Moonshine, private. Just moonshine."

The barn appeared deserted as they approached. That was as it should be. Clancey motioned the girl to wait and laying his bicycle down, advanced along the edge of the road with one hand on his clicker and the other cradling his pistol.

Pausing in a moon shadow thrown by a pine, Chris raised the clicker and thumbed the little metal spring twice. He waited. A minute later, he gave the signal again. This time, a single click returned. A wave of relief washed over him despite his caution. He inched forward, watching the barn, aware that all was not as it should be. At last, he entered by the edge of the open doorway, pressed against the wood, making as small a silhouette as he could. The Luger was gripped against his leg, hidden in shadow. "Where's the woman?" he asked the darkness.

An electric torch clicked on, its beam shining up under Heidigger's features in ghostly fashion, accentuating his sardonic smile. "Dead."

Chris controlled his anger. "Why?"

The light moved onto the hay beside Heidigger and was joined by the electric lantern which illuminated the wider scene. He could see the feet of the woman agent behind a bale.

"She tried to escape. Tried to kill me. She didn't have anything left to bargain with anyway."

Chris walked over and looked down at the corpse. Her coat was unsnapped and blood trailed from the corner of her mouth. Her eyes were open.

"I see she tried to rape you first."

Heidigger started to laugh but grimaced with pain. "You should never waste anything in wartime, old boy."

Chris reached down and pulled the coat over the woman's face. "That's an order you disobeyed, Heidigger. You won't do it again."

"No, I won't. How'd you get along with little sister?"

Chris saw that Heidigger was nursing a shoulder. He put his flashlight on it. "So, she did attempt something?"

Heidigger sneered with pain. "First time I've ever been touched in this war, would you believe? Nasty job with a broken bottle our resourceful frau found in the corner."

"Before or after?"

"Now, Clancey, I don't ask you about your love life, do I?"

Chris pulled back Heidigger's coat. "Damn. She dug a good groove down your ribcage too."

"I got the bleeding stopped with the sulfur powder, but I need a little sewing, if you don't mind."

Chris walked back to the entrance and called to the girl who rushed to the doorway, then slowed to a stop when she saw Heidigger's face.

"What has happened?"

Chris took a breath. "The woman tried to kill him. He had to shoot her. Can you sew up his wounds? I've got to make a radio contact. The plane is due in less than five minutes."

Reisa Konnings started to move toward the corpse but Chris grabbed her arm and turned her to him.

"Please, Reisa. You can't help her. You've got to help Heidigger now. We might need to move at any minute. Our first-aid kit is right there beside him."

She looked over her shoulder at the feet of the corpse and then turned back, nodding slowly, to stare at Heidigger.

Clancey let her go and she moved to the wounded man. Chris crossed to the stall where the radio equipment waited. He lifted the canvas pouch and checked the battery connections. Pulling out the aerial, he stepped from the barn and turned his eyes to the sky. He hoped someone would be up there to hear him. He forced his eye and ears to the technical job of making contact while he marshaled his assessment of his situation.

Heidigger was even worse than he'd been before. Now he was injured, as well. The wounds were nasty and easily infected. He'd run high fever at the least. He knew not to be concerned about the dead woman, that would have had to happen sooner or later; and yet, he sensed a relief that he'd not had to make that decision.

Chris knew it was a bad sign when he wanted to avoid anything. He'd always pushed himself at things that frightened him. It was what had made him a pilot. It had made him a hero. It had finally made him a spy. It was a clear road to hell, but in stepping back from this inner drive, he felt a sense of diminished value in one more element of his identity.

The earplugs popped and Chris twisted the knob gently as he slowly pulled the magic voice down out of the ether. If the special team had designed prayer, it might work too, he thought.

CHAPTER 11

Chris Clancey sat huddled against the hay bail beside the Joan Eleanor kit. He absently watched the girl stitching up the wounds of the grimacing Heidigger. Heidigger's grunts and gasps irritated Clancey. He had no sympathy for the sufferings of his comrade which he reckoned were well deserved, but the added inconvenience the man had inflicted on them was a worry they didn't need. Heidigger's moans also reminded him of his own pains at the hands of the Gestapo. They'd used needles on him as well for a while. Watching Reisa Konnings, he wondered if her mind were occupied in similar fashion. She was too busy for that, he thought. That was the best antidote for reflection and fear. Just keep busy.

Well, they were going to have to stay very busy if they were going to survive this mission. He pulled the gloves off his hands, rubbed them together and breathed his hot breath into the cup of his palms and fingers. Even in the semi-dark of the barn, he could tell the difference in the two hands. The smooth scars of the new flesh and the supple familiarity of his other hand. He smiled. If my right hand knew what my left hand knew, it would never have let me out of the airplane. He looked up to see the girl coming over to kneel beside him.

"Did you order him to kill the woman?" she asked quietly.

"No."

"Would you have killed her?"

"I would probably have had to, sooner or later."

"So he was right to do it, you think?"

Clancey stared at her. "There isn't much right about Heidigger. He's just on my side, that's all."

She nodded.

"Look, Reisa, I don't like it. I don't like any of this. But you know what's at stake. You know what it means to you and what it—means to Rudi." He rubbed his face. "We've got to get a better place to hide. It's not going to take the Gestapo long to run into this place and we aren't going to have back-up for a while yet. Heidigger needs a place to rest and we need food and water. Foraging takes too long and I'm the only one who can do it. You're going to have to figure out someone we can turn to. Isn't there anyone you're close with? Some neighbor or friend you can trust? Just for food or a cellar?"

Reisa sat still and turned her head to look toward the entrance of the barn. "There is only one person I can think of."

Chris waited.

"Father Lott. Dieter Lott. He's the Catholic priest in the town."

Chris shook his head.

Heidigger's voice was cracked as he talked through his pain. "I don't think a priest who could stay a priest in Hitler's church would be a very good bet, fraulein."

Reisa turned her head. "You don't know Father Lott," she returned defensively. "He is a good man. He is a true priest."

Clancey reached over and took Reisa's hand as she turned back to face him. "I'm sorry, Reisa, but a priest who would not sell out to the Party would not still be a priest this late in the war. It's one thing to keep a secret about stealing or coveting thy neighbor's wife, but sheltering a pair of spies planning to bomb an airfield would probably enter a gray area for your Father Lott."

Reisa Konnings brought her other hand to cover Clancey's. "You must meet him for yourself. He was a friend of my mother. I would trust him with my life. You must trust him with yours."

Clancey stared into the girl's eyes. "He knew your mother was a Jew?"

Reisa's eyes stayed on his. "He knew her all her life."

Heidigger coughed. "Shit, it's cold. Hell, Chris. I can't hang around in here very long. I'll catch the damned pneumonia. Maybe we can tie up the old boy for a day or two anyway, at least until we can get a warm meal."

Clancey shook his head and snorted. "I haven't been in a church since I was eighteen. It looks like the Gestapo's going to do what my mother couldn't."

Reisa's eyes never left his. She didn't smile.

The Colonel hadn't been able to sleep. He'd known he needed his rest, but he'd not taken the pills. He had wanted to be clear-headed when the report from the plane came in. He'd hoped to be asleep when it came, but he wasn't. The knock was firm but not overly loud; still, he sat up quickly from the leather couch. With only the briefest pause to button his collar, he was moving to the door, calling to the adjutant.

"Is the plane in?"

"Yes sir. Just dropped down two minutes ago. Kitchens should be here soon, sir."

"Set up some tea and get the tape machine ready."

"Yes, sir."

The Colonel nodded as the adjutant moved to his tasks. The tape recording was a good idea for Joan Eleanor conversations. It made sure you got it right. Sometimes a plane couldn't stay in contact very long and you did well to have a record to play back when you returned. He wished he could eliminate the middle man entirely and again considered flying the next flight himself.

He was already drinking the hot tea when Michael Kitchens entered in his leather flying jacket, the briefcase in his gloved hands.

"Good contact?" the Colonel asked as Kitchens plopped down in the overstuffed chair by the fireplace.

"J.E. worked well enough. It's colder than hell tonight." Kitchens looked at the Colonel. "It's getting complicated, sir."

"More problems?"

"They've found the girl and located the field, but it's a tough job. He wants more explosives and men. And something else."

"What is it?"

Michael stared at the Colonel. "He says the bombs are for the Russians."

The Colonel stopped and then looked down at the tape. "You're sure?"

"Yes, sir. It's on the tape there, I'm certain."

The Colonel threaded the slick brown tape on the heavy metal machine and flicked a switch, rewinding the slowly whirling reels. He said nothing but, after a moment, cut the switch off and then on, listening intently as the recording played the thin but distinct voice of Chris Clancey against the droning of the twin De Havilland motors.

"...job requires ground attack. Multiple charges. Twenty man commando team minimum to be effective. Should have more. Attack must go in quickly, enemy believed to be aware of our presence in the area... time-table probably moving in accordance with this. Do you read?"

The Colonel listened to Mike's clearer, less tinny voice answering assurances.

"We have you, Horseman. Twenty-man team minimum. More explosives. Enemy aware of your presence. Over."

Chris came back with an odd note in his voice. "Enemy planes to attack Russians. Repeat... Russians, *not* west... *east*. Over."

The reply was almost as tenuous. "I read you, Horseman. Over."

The Colonel looked at Kitchens. "You were careful of your reply, Mike. That was wise. No sense telling the Brits everything when we're the ones running this little trip."

"Yes sir. What about it, sir? Do I start putting together a team? I'd like to go in on it. I could jump tomorrow. I'll get the requisitions ready."

"You're certain the Brits don't know the scope of the mission, Mike? They buy the simple story we fed them?"

"Yes, Colonel, they believe we've got a man monitoring night traffic, keeping us up on surprise moves in the southern corridor. They've heard the rumors of the shift to Austria. But what about Clancey, sir? Don't we need to get cracking on a team to go in? He seems ready to go."

The Colonel arched his brows and drummed his fingers on the desk top before dropping back in the leather chair. "Clancey certainly works fast, doesn't he, Mike?"

Kitchens looked at the Colonel quietly. "Yes, sir. He's excellent. Do I go in, sir?"

"I mean, he's hardly on the ground more than a day, really, and we know so much already. Almost *too* quickly. It makes you wonder."

Kitchens felt uneasy. "Wonder what, sir?"

The Colonel picked a fresh cigar from the box. He bit off the end and then looked quickly at Kitchens with the grin that he used to inculcate the image of unflappable craftiness to his staff. "I think poor Chris may be a casualty." He leaned back and held the cigar like a pointer. "They must have been waiting for him. I don't think we need to drop twenty more good men into a trap. Not yet. Not without a little more savvy."

Kitchens shifted on his feet. This was not what he had expected. He did not like this side of the Colonel. "Sir, Chris used his code name. He gave us information and a request. If we're not going to believe him, what was the point of dropping him in the first place?"

The Colonel looked over at the map before answering. "I need a little time to consider all the angles, Michael. That's all. I've been in this game a long time and I think I smell a red herring. We had trouble with that in Belgium and Holland, remember. I'll fly the next shift. Been meaning to fly one for a while now. Keep my hand in." He turned back to Kitchens. "You need a break, Mike. And the fewer men who know about this right now, the better."

Kitchens frowned. A growing discomfort gnawed at his tired mind as he listened to the Colonel. He hesitated before speaking. "Sir, this is—I mean, perhaps we might consult with someone in policy, sir. Shouldn't Colonel Donovan or even someone at SHAEF know the facts?"

"Of course, Mike, of course. Trouble is, Donovan's out of the country at the moment. You don't need to *know that*, of course. And, as far as the mother hens at SHAEF, well, it may well be that they will want to go in after I've laid out the facts. But, we'd better damn well be sure we know them first. To put something this big on the table, I'd need to fly over to Versailles or Reims, or wherever Ike is holding court today. It's still a mite premature to go knocking on his door. We'll just get a little more information before we make the case. Hate to rush in so fast we trip over our own feet, you know." The Colonel was facing the map again. "Remember, we put up a few good lies ourselves before Normandy."

"Things are happening very fast, sir. What about the men? What if they're needed?" Kitchens was aware he was on the edge of exhaustion yet sensed the most critical moment of the night was just before him.

The Colonel nodded and turned back around with a more personal smile. "Right. We'll be ready either way it swings, of course. You get Perkins to lay up plenty of plastique and line up a C-47, but keep it low key. I'll check on available Ranger units. We'll be ready at the drop of a hat. Don't worry, Mike. You've done a great job, son. Better hit the sack as quick as you can. I imagine you're going to need all your energy in the next day or two."

Kitchens wanted to speak but he was tired and not sure what to say. "Good night, sir." He closed the door behind him, leaving the Colonel staring up at the big map.

As the door closed behind Kitchens, the Colonel set down the unlit cigar. The Russians, huh? It certainly made sense. They'd been coming on like stink, mopping up whole German divisions. The Blitzkrieg in reverse. That's where he'd drop them all right. Even Smokin' Joe Stalin would have to slow down for a while if he got a kick in the face like that. It wouldn't be too hard to blow the works after the Krauts had run a mission or two. No bombs on our boys, anyway, and just a little *adjustment* to the post-war prize-picking. And if we could just manage to snag a few of the more prominent personnel before we burned it all down, well, you'd have to figure the country with the plague bombs would hold the trump card. It was definitely in the interest of the Big Picture to run this thing this way.

The Colonel's eyes moved to the framed pictures of Roosevelt and Eisenhower on the wall near the fireplace. What about Ike? Roosevelt was a politician, he'd appreciate not knowing about the moral choice until he didn't have one to make. But, what about Ike? Hard not to like Eisenhower. That D-Day job had been a real bitch. He knew the man had really put his head on the block with that call. Eisenhower wasn't crazy about the Russians either, but he was no Georgie Patton. He didn't talk about the Reds the way Patton did. Maybe Ike was a politician, too. The Colonel reached for the big black phone on the table that linked the office with SHAEF H.Q. while he looked at the portrait of Eisenhower. Then he knew what he would do and pulled his hand away.

Colonel Shaeffer looked up from the charts the young officer had brought in. "So you are certain the weather will open for two days?"

The meteorologist nodded. "Yes, sir. As of this morning, the report says clearing in forty-eight hours and holding, perhaps, another forty-eight. After that, or perhaps sooner, the front will move in and it may be some time before we are certain of as clear a window. It might be days or weeks."

Shaeffer looked up again at the battle maps on the wall of his office. His eyes were drawn to the point where several of the red markers rested on the Polish front.

Geltman stood next to the meteorologist and followed Shaeffer's eyes, then shook his head. "Intelligence cannot guarantee that Zhukov will wait much longer. This is the time for the strike, Shaeffer."

Shaeffer eyes did not rise from the map. "It will take at least a day for the science team to prepare the bombs, according to Yakuro. They can't be kept in storage indefinitely without losing potency. We can set up the diversionary bomber flights and have the leaflet planes ready within the same twenty-four hours." He turned back to the Luftwaffe meteorologist.

"You are dismissed, Stiller." He waited until the officer had left the room before turning back to Geltman. "What of your spies?

The saboteurs? Can you be certain we are safe to continue? It would not take many men to upset our plans. An air raid might stop us if it were perfectly run."

Geltman crossed his arms over his chest. "It is a difficult kind of war I fight, Shaeffer. Not your type at all. No clean attack with brave pilots jousting like knights in a romantic myth. No, I toil against an enemy whose greatest weapon is his mind. He is the fox. I must be the fox, also."

Geltman leaned back to rest against the desk top. "They have learned little, as yet, or at least, not enough. They have not called for a raid or help, for I have a dozen separate radio-transmission locater teams combing the sector. Yes, I have had these in place since the first work team arrived here last year. Nothing has gone out on wireless. If they have a transmitter, then it must be damaged or they have nothing yet to send." He punctuated his lecture for an instant with a mirthless chuckle. "Unless they have used the American Indian smoke signals?" Not waiting for a reply, Geltman continued. "No, they needed the girl. But she is not enough; they need more. There are not many of them. And since there are not many, they must come inside. They need more knowledge of the base and of the mission. The one person we know they want is Captain Reichmann. Reisa Konning's Reichmann. But we have him, and if we play him right, we can have them all as well."

Shaeffer stared at the Gestapo man. "So you are going to put Reichmann on a *gibbet* in the town square? Perhaps the spies have read *Robin Hood* as well, Herr Geltman. It seems a very long chance that spies would not expect a trap of some sort."

Geltman's smile unnerved Shaeffer as the Gestapo colonel answered him. "Not a hanging, Shaeffer. A celebration. We're going to give Reichmann and a few other heroes the medals they deserve. We'll have a nice little ceremony in the town square. A reception in the town hall. Everyone is invited. It's already being arranged. Leaflets will be delivered to all the local villages. It will be on radio. Unless these spies are not so good, they will know of it quickly; and they are certain to make a try at Reichmann whatever they suspect. It is impossible that they should not take such a chance."

"You know, you could be very wrong about Klaus Reichmann. He really does deserve a medal."

Geltman smiled again and shook his head. "No longer. One of his crew confided in us. He has told his men he will not fly the mission. He must have some confidence in the saboteurs to speak to them thus."

Shaeffer's head snapped up at Geltman's statement. "You are certain of this? That Reichmann has said this?"

Geltman grinned. "You might select a back-up pilot now."

Michael Kitchens was driven to the big country house near the airfield where the planes used on covert missions were maintained. The house was indeed grand, a private estate, fully stocked to give the agents preparing to depart a final place to rest in the greatest possible comfort. A fine place in which to be lodged and watched. For the first time, the idea of his being watched, of being studied, occurred to Michael. Was the Colonel having him observed? It would be understandable in a matter like this for the Colonel to take extreme measures, even measures that went against his own feelings. And certainly Michael had been pushing the edge of exhaustion since the beginning.

He had ridden with his eyes closed, yet something inside his mind was resisting the rational demand for the sleep his body craved. The little alarm—the tiny, insistent warning light was glowing in the corner of his mind's eye. He could choose to ignore it, but it would be a choice. Clancey had once warned him against ignoring the signal, especially where there was no clear reason behind it. "Your senses are smarter than you are, Mike," Chris had said, "pure logic can get you pure killed. I'd rather look stupid than dead."

Michael knew it was the Colonel. He didn't want it to be. He had served the Colonel since his last promotion. Hell, the Colonel had picked him. And from day one, Michael had been the closest thing to a confidant the man seemed to have. He'd made Michael feel more like a favored son than a subordinate. He'd pulled him in on matters he didn't have to. Michael knew a lot more of the "who and why" than a lot of higher-ranking officers outside the

Colonel's tight circle. That had been the way of it until now. Until the Konnings case. This was different. The Colonel had held onto this whole matter with an unmistakable suspicion of everyone, not just the Brits, but even his usual peers. Paranoia was sometimes warranted in this work, Michael granted, but no one owned the men who went into the dark alone.

After signing in at the desk, Michael made his way quietly to his room on the second floor and closed the carved oak door behind him. He sat on the quilted bedspread and began to slowly untie his bootlaces. In his tiredness, he watched his fingers as they absently moved through the routine seemingly undirected by his mind. His hands knew their simple duty, why couldn't he turn his mind free of its complex stirrings as well? Why not close the inner eye, assume the trust he had given unstintingly from the beginning? Why wouldn't his damned warning light fade off?

Michael dropped back on the bed, exhaustion flooding up through his body, shutting down his muscles, closing down his nerves. Still, his thoughts rang louder inside his head as they forced him to an unwanted focus. His sigh was one of surrender, not to the fatigue which he welcomed, but to the frightening demand for resolution.

It hadn't been right, not from the beginning when they'd sent that spooky Konnings kid over. From the start, the Colonel had seen something more than a simple deserter with a far-fetched story to buy clemency. There were plenty of those now: secret weapon stories, secret bases, hidden redoubts. *I can give you details—I served under Rommel*, or Kesselring, or Goering. The game was old and the sergeants who'd done the fieldwork had passed him back like an afterthought. But the Colonel had the gift of smelling the truth, sensing the man beneath the uniform. And he had caught something here that no one else had seen. Pure stuff, he'd said. Unfiltered and unrefined. Real intelligence was almost like a drug to some people. Michael thought of the Colonel's face as he'd listened to the tapes of Konnings' initial interrogation.

Sure, it was big. If it were true, it was the biggest thing they'd ever heard. And the Colonel had put it in his pocket without a sideway's look.

Michael could hear the Colonel's voice as clearly as the taped messages from Joan Eleanor. "Too big for the cousins, Mike. Too big for the next desk. We're going to work it ourselves. Run one team, hand to hand—only our best. Clancey's out of the hospital. He's the one to send. If it turns out to be true, we don't need to let all our new friends in on it, do we? Limeys and the Reds would love to go in and pick up the goodies and who needs that?" The Colonel had smiled off Michael's concerns. "My call, Mike. Don't worry. Any fall-out over procedure stops at my desk." As Michael listened in his mind, he felt again the fear and then awe as the Colonel looked over the transcripts. "This may be the next war," he'd whispered. "And maybe we can win it before it starts."

Michael did not want to see it, but there was really no diverting from it. If it hadn't been Clancey—if it hadn't been a man he admired—perhaps he *would* have been able to let it go. Still, somehow, flying over in the Mosquito, listening for that thin signal beam from the dark below—it was as if he'd held the end of a long rope over the abyss. A rope with Clancey on the other end. And now the Colonel was taking the rope out of his hands.

At last, the images played past. The voice faded. And with this final resolution, his eyes closed and the wave of sleep swept over him. The sleeping pill in the tea that they'd brought up at the Colonel's private command had insured the rest.

Below, near the foot of the stairs, a phone rang on the entry desk. Momentarily startled, the pretty WAAC sergeant lifted the handle. The men quartered in this house needed no interruptions in the night. The sergeant nodded as she listened to the voice on the other end of the line. "Yes, sir, he's sleeping now. Yes, sir, I understand. I have your orders."

Father Dieter Lott was splitting firewood at the back of the churchyard when he saw the woman entering the side door of the church. He called to her, but there was no response and the figure in the heavy shawl only glanced his way before hurriedly opening the door and going inside. Lott grimaced. He did not care to interrupt his chores unless it was an emergency, for the temperature would surely drop as soon as the dusk began to settle and his sweat would be cold when he returned to his task. At sixty-five, it was not good to risk such a chill. Still, the woman must have something very personal on her mind if she would not even approach him outside the church. He did not recognize the woman, though she seemed familiar. Of course, Lott was familiar with most of the inhabitants of the community no matter their church.

Pulling on his jacket and settling his axe against a stone grave marker, Lott bent to pick up a small load of firewood before proceeding toward the church. It had to be a confession, he thought as he neared the doorway. A physical emergency or need and the woman would have come directly to him and there would be no need for this sense of secrecy. Father Lott closed his eyes and mentally tried to change gears. It was growing increasingly hard to take proper notice of the small transgressions that a man or a woman might commit when the weight of a nation's crimes were bearing down more heavily every day on his soul. A part of his mind was always drawn to the great sermon, the denouncement that would clearly define the evil of the world they inhabited; yet he had chosen another way, or rather, it had chosen him. The martyr's path might come to him yet, he realized, but he had been given a charge he could not forsake, though it forced him to continue a routine that mocked his convictions. His thoughts were with Bonhoffer, the Lutheran, who'd spoken strongly and then done more than speak. He was in prison now with a gallows awaiting him for involvement in the assassination attempt on the Fuhrer. Lott did not envy Bonhoffer his very real martyrdom, he conceded, and an embarrassment at his pretended preference spoke of a spiritual pride he knew he would battle all the days of his life.

Shutting the door, he saw the curtain of the confessional close and bent to set down the firewood. The priest dusted off his coat and moved down the aisle toward the candlelit altar, bending before the crucifix as he tried still to let go of the business of his own life. He stepped into the confessor's booth and settled quietly onto the small wooden bench seat.

"Yes, my child?" he began the opening.

"Father Lott, it is Reisa Konnings."

Instantly, Dieter Lott sat bolt upright, all his previous thoughts abandoned.

"Reisa! What has happened? I was told the Gestapo had arrested you!"

"It is a long story, Father. It is a terrible story."

"You were released? I inquired of Adrian Vitt, but he said it was only a formality since there was a rumor your brother had deserted to the Americans. I tried to go to the hotel in town to speak with Herr Geltman on the matter, but—well, there was the fire. I was afraid you had been killed in the gas explosion. I could find no one to confirm anything today. I am so relieved. They seldom release—"

"I was not released, Father."

Lott realized he had been doing all the talking. Surely he knew to listen when one came with trouble. He grimaced and forced down his excitement. "Pardon me, child. I want to know everything. Please, tell me all that has happened. Perhaps I can do something."

Reisa Konnings began to tell the story of her brother, the plague bombs, and the spies.

Lott spoke when he realized the girl had reached the end of her tale. It was difficult to find the words; his mind was so full of her stunning account. He had believed that no new evil could catch him out. He'd learned of horrors and carried secrets no mortal man should have to keep, but now the devil seemed to have fashioned a capping stone for the pyramid of evil that towered over his country. To what purpose was a man exposed to such overwhelming knowledge? What was a simple priest to do? Petition for the end of the weapon? No, his meager strength was little use in such a work. He sighed and spoke to the girl.

"I can do little for you, Reisa. They are no doubt hunting for you and the men you spoke of. I can take you under my roof, but these men, these saboteurs; you, yourself, have seen they are ruthless killers."

Reisa Konnings leaned her head tiredly against the wall of the confessional. "Father, they are soldiers. At least, one of them is. What of that woman that hid the spies of the Hebrews in the Promised Land? Didn't God look favorably on her when they came back with their army?"

Lott chuckled sadly. "You are using the Bible on me, child? If they were found here, can you imagine what the Gestapo would do with us?"

Reisa was too tired to plead. "Father, what will you do if you do not help them? This is your chance, Father. I have listened to your sermons all my life. I have heard the spirit in your words even when you tried to mask it. This is your chance to—"

"To finally *do* something?" Lott finished for her. "Reisa, I am going to show you something. Something no one knows about. And then I will let you decide."

Stepping out of his side of the confessional, Lott was surprised to find two strange men sitting in the front pew of the church, not ten feet away. One wore a Luftwaffe Officer's uniform, the other wore a flight jacket with one arm in a sling and makeshift bandaging showing at the collar of the jacket. His skin was very pale. The one in the uniform was holding a pistol in his lap. It was a small weapon with a rounded extension on the end of the barrel. He knew in an instant that these were Reisa's spies.

"Sorry, Reisa, we could not wait," the officer began. "The good Father here is on our side whether he likes it or not."

Reisa stepped up to the priest. "Father, please. Help us."

"Just a few days," Clancey offered. "We'll be gone with nothing amiss. No one will ever know. Surely you've got a cellar or attic of some sort where we could tend to my friend here."

Lott looked back and forth between the trusting, earnest face of the girl, and the cold, tired face of the man with the pistol. It did not seem a visitation of angels.

"I must lock the doors first."

"We've taken care of that," the officer said.

Lott nodded. "There is little room. Come with me."

Clancey and Reisa followed the priest to the rail at the front of the altar and watched as Lott pulled back a worn rug and bent to knock his fist upon the boards three times. Reaching down with a slender pocket knife, he raised a short board up from its slot and then pulled at a recessed handle beneath it. Pausing only to take a firm grip, the priest lifted open a small trap door. Lott looked up at Clancey. "Please, sir, put away that weapon. Your uniform will frighten them enough already."

Chris almost smiled. The girl knew her men. She knew the strength of her brother. She was the conscience of the pilot, Reichmann. And she saw through the amiable village priest who had not damned the swastika but had quietly kept Jews hidden in the old crypt beneath his altar in the very heart of Nazi Germany.

CHAPTER 12

"Congratulations, Captain. I hear it's the diamond clusters to be added to your Knight's Cross."

Reichmann almost smiled at Willy Frankl. It felt mean to deprive the young airman of the joy of heroism and its trappings. He did not have the heart to tell Willy how little such medals meant to him; that the very idea of receiving awards for surviving the Russian winter was repugnant to him now.

"Well, it will be good to go into the village, again. These underground quarters make one crazy after a time."

"Here's to beer in the town." Von Tripps laughed, slapping Reichmann's shoulder. "You look too long-faced, Klaus. Airmen should never be so serious."

Lauda tapped his nose. "I don't know, Reinhart. They've walled us up in here for a week now and shut down all outside communications, even with censors. All this secrecy, and Himmler himself dropping by to cheer us up. Now this happy ceremony in the village with photographers and radio recordings. Something definitely feels wrong about it all."

Von Tripps shook his head. "Perhaps they're trying to freshen us up for the missions. Remind us what we're supposed to be flying for."

They had not spoken of Klaus' announced intention to refuse the mission since the briefing. It was as if it had never happened. He could almost convince himself he'd dreamed it except that he was aware the men were sneaking furtive glances at him and each other when he passed them. Had someone spoken? Had someone informed the commander that his captain had gone mad? And now this business of a medal. Reichmann didn't like it either, except that it got him out. And maybe somehow he could make contact with Reisa. If he could just know that she was safe.

"…Josef Zimmer," the pale-faced youth answered Chris Clancey's query as they sat with the others near the altar. "And my brother is Ricard. We have been with Father Lott for fifteen months. Before that, we were in a house with twelve others in Ulm. It was raided, but we escaped. We were traveling at night when Ricard got sick. I had to try to find help. The first bicycle I encountered was Father's. We asked for directions to a doctor, but he saw through our story and brought us here."

"So you've been living under the church for all these months?" Reisa was incredulous. "It's unbelievable."

"The times are unbelievable, fraulein," Josef replied. "And so is Father Lott."

Clancey shook his head. "I could not stand it."

The younger brother, who Clancey guessed was about fifteen, answered with a soft, high voice. "You stand more than you think you can, if you have to."

Josef nodded. "It has been very hard for Ricard. He has been ill, but Father has done wonders. And we get out inside the church at night, sometimes even outside."

Heidigger grinned. "And these are the lucky ones, Clancey, if the stories are true."

Dieter Lott frowned. "Tell me, sir, what is the news? Is the end near? Is your army coming soon?"

Clancey looked at the two boys. "Not soon enough. If this mission fails. I don't know. It might be longer. Much longer."

Reisa looked at Clancey. "You must not fail."

Heidigger sighed, leaning his head back on the wooden pew. "You're down to one, Chris. I don't think I'm going to do much more than use the radio and the bathroom for a while. I can't move the way I need to, to give you much backup."

Chris raised a resigned eyebrow. "Maybe you won't have to. I'm counting on the Colonel to send in a full team with everything it takes to blow this place away. We'll need to get Joan Eleanor up. There should be a plane due in another three hours. A day flight for a change up. The bell tower could be an excellent position, Father, if you don't mind."

The priest nodded. "Yes. Now we must do all we can. The time to wait is past. This thing must be stopped."

Clancey patted the edge of the briefcase and looked at the two brothers. "If they look for us, they might find you."

Josef Zimmer turned to his brother. Ricard nodded and coughed. Josef turned back to Clancey. "The story of the bombs is too awful to run from, sir. If nothing is done, no one will have anywhere left to hide. If you will give us a gun, we will not run again."

"Shit. These boys don't know anything about guns, Chris."

Clancey ignored Heidigger. "Show me the way up to the bell tower, would you, Josef?"

Heidigger grimmaced. "You better hope they sweep wide, Chris. We're a good five miles south of the last fix."

Chris started for the front of the church. "They're supposed to sweep a ten mile zone. They know we might have to move around. Don't worry. Kitchens is a good man."

Michael Kitchen's eyes slid open slowly. The room was dark but the thin sliver of light that outlined the window shades told him the day had started. He rolled over on his side and looked at his watch on the bedside table. The glowing dial came into focus and he was aware he'd slept two hours past his usual five o'clock rising time. It was deeply ingrained in him, even rousing him after hard nights of field maneuvers. It wasn't right. For an instant, he considered collapsing onto the luxurious sheets, but he thought with a sudden urgency of his conflict with the Colonel.

The Colonel. Where was he? Michael rose on unsteady feet and moved to the window, pulled the blinds open and stared out over the countryside beyond the house. It was almost seven. The

Colonel had said he would fly the next mission. The plane would already be heading for the French field. Madness. He could send other men. Then Michael realized with clarity why the Colonel had insisted on going. He did not want anyone else to know the order he was sending Clancey. Not yet. Maybe never.

His thoughts were interrupted by a tap on his door. The pretty WAAC sergeant walked in with a full tray of breakfast. She smiled and apologized for the intrusion.

"I hope you don't mind, sir, but I was told to bring you breakfast whenever you woke. You're to take the day off here and that's an order." She laughed as she concluded, "An order I wouldn't mind getting."

Kitchens smiled. "I'd prefer to check in with my headquarters. There are a few matters I'd like to discuss with my superior."

The sergeant smiled apologetically. "I'm really very sorry, Lieutenant, but the orders were quite specific. It's really for your own good, you know. I'm certain whatever it is can wait."

Michael took a reluctant breath. "Yes. Perhaps you're right, sergeant. Maybe, instead, an afternoon in London would do me good. If there's a car available, that is."

"Well, I don't know if that's possible, sir, but you'll probably want a shave and a change of clothes, no matter." The sergeant eyed Kitchen's wrinkled uniform in an obviously critical manner.

Michael rubbed his face. "I suppose I *was* a little careless about pajamas last night."

"You must have had a long day, sir." The WAAC set down the tray next to the bed and picked up one of the pillows that had dropped to the floor, fluffing it and setting it back in place as she spoke.

"Two long days and one very long night. You're sure there's no way into town?"

"I'm afraid the orders were for you to be our guest here, sir."

"How about a phone call?" He grinned. "Maybe one to my lawyer, at least?"

The sergeant shared his grin. "Oh, I'm afraid the lines are all tied up just now, sir. They've been trying to straighten it up all morning. Word is that the buzz bombs have made a mess of communications. I'll let you know as soon as a line is open. Why don't you just relax here and have a nice breakfast and a good cup of coffee to steady you up?"

"Why not?" Michael wondered aloud as he stretched his arms and rolled his head on his shoulders to flex the muscles in his neck. He wondered exactly what kind of orders they'd been given here. He wouldn't be able to find out, that was certain. They were used to looking after odd fish for any number of reasons. They wouldn't find it at all out of the ordinary if someone wanted to keep a man who'd obviously just flown in from the continent under close observation or even house arrest. No, they kept a nice, comfortable cage here. And, of course, the Colonel could always say he was just enforcing a good rest on an overworked subordinate. He'd had to do it before with at least one hyperactive agent who'd gone around the bend and damn near killed off his whole team. The truth was, Michael concluded, even if he got a chance to make a call, he'd very likely substantiate whatever story the Colonel might be using to keep him tucked away.

"There are cigarettes in the side drawer over there if you want them." The sergeant left him with a smile as she backed out the door. "Just hit the button on the table there if you want anything else."

Michael watched his attractive jailer close the door behind her. He looked down at the tray and reached instinctively for the coffee mug. As the aroma of the warm brew touched his nose, he paused. He'd slept like he was drugged and suddenly was sure he had been. Sleeping pill for his own good, no doubt. He could almost hear the Colonel's voice. *"Boy needed a day of sleep—been up for almost three, hadn't he? Didn't know what was good for him."*

He set the coffee down and then he picked it up again. He walked to the bathroom and carefully poured it down the sink, washing away the errant drops of brown liquid. He proceeded to shave and change into the fresh uniform provided for him. When dressed, he set the empty coffee cup on the bedside table, tapped the button, and lay back on the bed, leaving his hand next to the buzzer and rolling his head peacefully to the side. His eyes closed the instant he heard the doorknob turning.

The clouds to the west glowed with the hidden sun and Colonel Shaeffer raised his mug of coffee to his lips with a thankful salute. Maybe it was best. The plague. Fuck the Russians. Maybe when the war was over. Maybe then things would be right. No one would stand for the type of men who commanded such things now, not in peace time. No, there was always a price for a better day and this must be it. His eyes drifted to his son's picture on the corner of the desk. He thought again of his last letter. Hitler Youth. His son was Hitler's son. Just a boy, and ready to die for the Fuhrer. Shaeffer felt the heaviness which he had been fighting closing over him. He could not live in a world that took away a man's son. Christ. If it would just end now. Quickly, for all of them.

The jangle of the phone jarred him so that he slopped the coffee onto the desk top. His voice was hard when he lifted the receiver. An enemy plane had been sighted above the sector. Fighters were being scrambled from the next field and would intercept within five minutes. Not a bomber. Probably reconnaissance. Mosquito. He called his adjutant and commanded all personnel to stay inside the bunkers. No external movement. Probably nothing to do with us, he thought. The damned Allies had so many planes they didn't know what to do with them so they photographed everything in Germany over and over, nailing it all down: trains, troops, airfields, factories. They were like vultures looking for prey. Everything had to be moved at night.

No reason to be paranoid about it, but even as he thought it, he smiled at the idea of Geltman's doubtless reaction to any such flight. No reason for *both* of them to be paranoid, he corrected himself.

"I repeat, Horseman. No action. Cancel all action. Coffee brewing." The Colonel held down the sending key.

The answer was back in a flash. "Not understood, Top Fox. Situation urgent. I repeat, action is imminent."

The Colonel frowned. "Horseman. This is a direct order. Withdraw. Coffee brewing."

There was no answer for several seconds. "Top Fox. Is there another team?"

The Colonel bent down the key. "Coffee brewing. You are out. Horseman. You are out."

Suddenly, the Mosquito tacked hard and the Colonel cursed as he braced himself against the bulkhead.

"Sorry, sir." the British voice cracked on the headset. "Jerry is after us. Pair of 190's in pursuit. We're ducking out. Hold on."

The Colonel grimaced and shouted his last message. "Damn it, Horseman! Get out! Get out, Chris!"

Wilhelm Shuppan bit his lip and cursed as he watched the twin-engined shape pulling away from him. His race to bring his Focke-Wulf up to attack range was futile. Damned Mosquito made a Spitfire look slow. In anger, he fired the rounds of his cannons and watched the tracers falling helplessly away at the departing enemy. He knew it was a waste. If only his plane were a jet. They'd been promised Me 262's. The dates kept changing. As always, he fought down his frustration and fear at the impotence of his fighter against the long bomber streams and high flying reconnaissance planes by imagining the day when he could feel the screaming whine of the twin turbines under his wings. Surely they must triumph. Had not every great invention of the war been theirs? The jets? The rockets? They just needed time to cancel out the massive numbers of bombers that flowed in from the west. Well, one Mosquito would make no difference. Shuppan only wished he could find a Mustang or any other fighter to tangle with.

The single electric bulb cast sharp shadows from all their heads as Heidigger grinned from the dark corner of the crypt. "So, it's like I thought. They've decided to let the Russians get a taste of the plague before they shut down the deal. Can't say I blame them."

Josef Zimmer stared at Heidigger. "I do not understand. The Russians are your allies, are they not?"

Heidigger laughed and then squirmed with pain. "Shit. The Russians have served their purpose. They've occupied the bulk of German strength for three years now. Pretty soon they'll be a bigger problem for us than even your Third Reich. In fact, we might even need your Reich to help control them."

Zimmer eyed Heidigger coldly. "It is not *our* Reich."

Reisa looked worriedly to Clancey. "What will you do?"

Clancey said nothing.

Heidigger answered for him. "What will he do? He'll do what any soldier would do. He'll obey his orders. Just like every man in this war on either side. That's the only way a war can be fought. So much for your noble crusade, Chris. Sorry you had to be here when the masks came off, fraulein."

Josef Zimmer looked back to Heidigger. "What do *you* fight for, Mr. Heidigger?"

Heidigger was silent for only a moment. "I fight to feel alive, Mr. Zimmer. Each time I am not killed, I feel very alive."

Zimmer stared at the wounded spy. "You are a good soldier?"

Heidigger winced. "I follow orders. Just like Clancey."

Everyone turned to look at Clancey who slowly shook his head. "No. Not any more."

Heidigger raised an eyebrow and laughed. "Oh, shit."

There was a rapping on the panel above them and a moment later Father Dieter Lott was peering down at them. He frowned at Heidigger's raised pistol.

"I have some very interesting news."

"Something's happened?" Chris asked, straightening.

Lott lowered himself carefully into the crypt then slid the trap door back into place above his head. Dropping down onto a wooden crate, he rubbed his arms and looked from face to face.

"There's to be a special celebration in the village tomorrow. It seems your friend, Reichmann, will be awarded an important medal, Reisa. They're inviting everyone for beer and a concert by the military band. They stress that everyone should attend."

"Hardly the traitor we hoped, eh fraulein?" Heidigger said through a cynical smile.

"I don't like it," Father Lott said, scratching his chin. "Why now, suddenly? Especially since they've gone to so much trouble to keep the air base more or less a secret."

"Because they're using Reichmann for a trap to get at us. They know all about his feelings for Reisa and the mission. They've come to think there's a connection between Reichmann and the explosion. They want to pull us out so the planes will be safe.

They're getting ready to take off and they can't take any chance on us catching them." Chris looked at Heidigger. "Without a real team, we've got to have Reichmann to move. They're dangling him like bait."

"And you're going to bite, aren't you? You stupid bastard." Heidigger growled, frowning against a sudden twist of pain.

Ricard Zimmer stared at Clancey. "What if Reichmann has changed his mind? He's a hero, you know. Maybe getting this medal—can you trust him?"

Chris looked at Reisa Konnings. Her eyes met his own. He smiled and turned back to Zimmer. "You can trust him, son."

"Father," Chris Clancey leaned toward the priest. "I need you to draw off this town, then weasel any scrap of information you can out of your friends about this special occasion."

Ricard put a hand on his brother's arm and spoke softly. "Now, Josef. Now we are going to do something about it all."

Father Lott sighed. "I'm sorry, boys. I'm sorry you are here for this."

Josef smiled widely. "Don't be, Father. I'm glad we're here. Maybe we were put here for this."

Heidigger sank back against the wall and muttered. "Shit."

CHAPTER 13

Sitting with the other airmen in the rear of the covered truck, Klaus Reichmann felt a peculiar dreamlike sense of disembodiment as he watched the road rolling away behind them. It was as if they were running backwards, rewinding their lives from the present; reversing the days to the moment when they had first arrived here. They sat in their starched uniforms, smoking and laughing, facing each other across the bed of the truck as they rode to the village.

The tree-lined lane gave way to bricked pavement, reassuring curbs and familiar storefronts. Banners and bunting adorned the streetlamps and doorways. Here was a crowd of civilians and eager children—many had been sent here to live away from the Allied bombing, he'd been told. And the old people. His generation was missing. A few uniformed Hitler Youth and the prerequisite middle-aged officials were the closest links in the broken chain.

The trucks stopped and Klaus climbed out among cheers and fervently waved swastikas. Young girls brought flowers to the airmen as they moved to a decaying bandstand across from the town hall. Klaus' eyes searched furtively for any sign of Reisa. It seemed as if everyone in the region had been summoned for this grand occasion. He was being tugged along by Willy Frankl who moved nervously beside him.

"What's the matter, Willy?" he asked, without looking at the young airman. "You should be enjoying this. You may be seeing the last such celebration of the Luftwaffe."

He was chilled by Willy's anxious whisper as the two of them stepped onto the wooden platform.

"Klaus. They know about you—I told them."

Despite his accepted sense of fatalism, Klaus turned quickly to stare in Frankl's face. "What?"

Willy swallowed, his eyes dropping. "They were asking questions and they tricked it out of me. I told them. Forgive me!"

Reichmann took a deep steadying breath and then, smiling broadly, reached into his pocket and offered Willy a cigarette. "Take it, Willy. Now, do the others know? Von Tripps? Lauda?"

Frankl shook his head. "No. I wanted to tell you this morning, but I couldn't. Then when I heard of the medal, I thought maybe they had not believed me."

There it was. Klaus blew out the cigarette smoke in a long stream. "I should have a blindfold with this." He gave Frankl a quick grin as he continued calmly. "Thank you for telling me, Willy. Will you help me get away?"

Willy had no chance to reply as Colonel Shaeffer signaled for everyone to be seated. The ceremony began. Shaeffer gave over to the mayor who began to read a speech about the defense of the Reich and the modern knights of the air. Reichmann scanned their surroundings carefully trying to decide at what moment he should attempt to escape his captors. His one advantage was that they did not know he had learned of Willy's betrayal. Then, he realized exactly why he was here. They were looking for the saboteurs. It was all about Reisa. She was either dead or with the saboteurs. It was all that made sense. That crazy bastard, Rudi. It must be true. He had reached the Americans. Klaus' mind raced with possibilities.

Colonel Shaeffer was standing again and calling forth the pilots of the group. Schumacher, Prost, and Reichmann. They stood together awaiting the medals which Shaeffer took from a case held by an adjutant. Reichmann's eyes were on the colonel, who paused a long moment as he presented the diamond clusters.

"This award is for gallantry against the Communist forces in the valiant winter campaign," Shaeffer intoned, staring fiercely into Klaus' eyes. "They are for a hero of the Luftwaffe. One who would sacrifice *all* for his country without question. Wear them with pride, Reichmann."

Klaus saluted, wondering what to make of the obvious emotion in the colonel's gruff voice.

Now a trio of young women in peasant costume presented beautifully adorned victory wreaths for each of the pilots. They were followed with loud applause by members of the Hitler Youth who shook the pilots' hands as a photographer recorded the greetings between the heroes and their worshipful admirers. As Klaus shook hands with one particularly sallow young man, he was surprised to feel a wad of paper pressed into his palm. The boy paused an instant to whisper a single word. "Reisa."

Klaus almost gasped and brought his hand quickly to his pocket—a move he felt must have been obvious to everyone there. Thankfully, the eyes of his captors were trained on the crowd and paid scant attention to the boys in the starched brown shirts.

Returning to the rows of chairs again and edging in next to Frankl, Klaus carefully brought the scrap of paper out as he lit another cigarette. Its message was short.

"Go to the church—R"

Klaus leaned back and took another long drag on the cigarette. He could see the steeple of the church beyond the square. He had been to Mass once with Reisa. He tried to remember the surrounding streets. He plotted his path if he could get free. It was perhaps three hundred meters. A thousand possibilities between here and there, he thought. The band was drawing light applause as its leader bowed for the crowd and turned for the next number.

Klaus put an arm over the back of Willy's chair in a casual manner, tapping his knee to the music as he spoke close to Frankl's ear.

"Willy. Will you help me?"

Frankl's neck and ear were red. "Yes," was the hissed reply.

"Good. When we leave, I want you to stay seated a moment, until I am clear of the platform. Then, I want you to trip against this rail. It is rotten and it will break. You must fall off the bandstand and onto those women. Make a scene. I need a few moments of confusion. You can save my life, Willy, and maybe Germany's."

There was a long silence. "Yes, Klaus. I will do it."

Hans Geltman moved nervously behind the line of parked trucks, chewing his inner cheek, taking small bites of the skin to grind in his teeth. His mouth often hurt from ulcers he inflicted on himself, but his excitement drove his habitual behaviors while his mind raced to control every moment of the event. He had managed this well, he told himself. He had covered every possibility. His men had all been shown pictures of Reisa Konnings and had heard the descriptions of the men with her by the old frau who'd seen them. Disguises would be easily seen through. There were few men in the crowd whose profiles could mask the physiques of these commandoes. The spies would make their move shortly and he would have them. Or, they would stay away and thus admit their impotence. The planes would fly tomorrow in either case and Klaus Reichmann would live just long enough to see it, Geltman promised himself. And that damned Shaeffer would give the order for the execution. He would see to that.

He heard the band finish and the crowd applauding as Shaeffer thanked the townspeople. The crews were filing down from their seats. Geltman had turned to study the edges of the crowd again when he heard a sudden crash. Wood splintering. Something had happened back on the bandstand. People were crying out and guards were rushing forward.

He pulled his Luger from his coat and sprinted through the crowd, shoving old men and young boys to the side. Reaching the stage he was disappointed to see several of his men helping Feldwebel Willy Frankl from the crowd. An old woman cried in pain and several people were pressing in, trying to assess the damage and offer aid.

"It was the rail," Frankl apologized to the woman. "The wood is rotten. I tripped and fell against it. Can I help you?"

Geltman was furious at the distraction. "Get him on the truck," he ordered and, giving no thought to the moaning woman, turned to scan the rest of the square. All the other airmen were loading back onto the trucks. No. One was forcing his way toward him from their ranks. It was the bombardier on Reichmann's crew.

"What is it?" Geltman felt his anger rising at the disorderly events.

"Reichmann's gone."

"Gott in heaven!" The Gestapo officer spun around, barking his orders to the gathering circle of soldiers. "Find him. Find Reichmann or I'll have your balls."

Klaus moved through the crowd swiftly with his cap off. He forced himself not to run. He needed something to shield the uniform, but more important still, he must appear to know where he was going and what he was about or someone in the crowd would notice him. He pressed on with an officious frown, weaving his way through old men until he abruptly reached a break in the throng. A twenty meter clear walk to a corner. To avoid this would mean time. To take it meant trusting against fear of discovery. He was well into the road when he heard the shouting. Geltman had discovered his absence. He hoped Frankl wasn't punished for his contribution. He did not quicken his pace as he walked, though he felt conspicuous in the clearing. He must be spotted at any moment. Reaching the curb, he stepped deliberately around the corner and into an alley between two shops before bursting into a sprinter's run. Now it was hard boots on the pavement. His own breath burst loudly from his lungs as he called on every ounce of strength in his body to gain the freedom he had hardly dared hope for until the note was pressed in his hand. Ahead, visible across the next street over a low stone wall, was the steeple of the church. Amidst shouts and whistles, he could hear boots running far away. The search was spreading out. If he did not reach his destination in the next few seconds, he would never reach it. Reichmann could not wait. He threw himself onto the wall, scaling it; only pausing atop it for a moment as he swung his legs up and over. In that instant, he glanced behind him and down the alley.

At the far end, he saw a grey-coated soldier stepping into view. The helmeted head swept left, then right. The next sweep would bring the eyes to Reichmann's perch. In that frigid instant of fate, as he dropped backwards, a part of his mind wondered if gravity or vigilance would win the race. Klaus heard the air rush from his own lungs with a jolting gasp as he landed on his back inside the churchyard wall.

He lay stunned. The pain in his ribcage warning against sudden movement. Klaus could not wait. He forced himself up on his arms and turned to look past the gravestones at the faded grey back of the church. A paneled door with peeling paint opened and a dark figure, its cloak flowing back like an angel of death, rushed toward him between the stone crosses. The angel did not wait for him to speak but gripped him solidly by the shoulders, pulled him to his feet, and taking the airman's arm over a broad neck, lead him, stumbling along, toward the open door.

Once inside, the priest did not rest from his labor but pulled the door closed and latched the bolt while still supporting Reichmann. Without speaking he led Klaus into the sanctuary. Waiting inside were three others: a tall, slim-faced man of his own age whom he knew instinctively to be in command and two young boys, one of whom still wore the uniform of the Hitler Youth.

"Go in," the leader spoke to him in German, pointing to an open hatchway near the altar. Prison or hiding place, Klaus wondered for only an instant, as he saw the reassuring face of Reisa Konnings in the waiting aperture. Her arms went up for him and, asking no questions, he rapidly lowered himself into the crypt.

Inside, Reichmann's eyes were blinded by the darkness. He heard the other men dropping into the hole behind them. Only when the hatchway closed with a soft thud did he perceive his new surroundings. Someone had turned on a small electric lamp and the harsh reality of his new quarters revealed their unflinching confinement. He wondered if this crypt, which was hardly tall enough to stand in and wide enough for only perhaps three bodies to be laid to rest, had ever been used. He sat down on the stone floor next to Reisa Konnings who hugged him firmly, her fingers gripping his shoulders as if she must convince herself of his presence. Beyond her lay a cold-eyed, grinning phantom on an old scouting cot. The phantom's left arm and upper chest were bandaged tightly; his chest rose and fell with labored breaths that confirmed his mortality. The light, no doubt, heightened the man's ghoulish appearance but could not have created it. Reichmann's eyes turned to the two boys standing across from him and the leader who was watching him quietly. Klaus started to speak but the man raised a finger to warn him to silence. The priest was missing.

Geltman pointed to the row of houses on his left. "Take those, Leutnant. I want each one searched. We are going to catch this fellow."

"Javol!" The S.S. officer replied with a snapped salute and resumed his running. A pair of guards followed on his heels.

Geltman turned to Shaeffer, who stood behind him. A grim smile had returned to the Gestapo colonel's lips. "Don't worry, Shaeffer. The rats are *in* the trap. It is only that we must not let them out of it."

The Luftwaffe colonel looked down the streets where men and women were being ordered out of their lodgings while soldiers furiously searched through them. "These people are loyal German citizens, Geltman. They are the Germany we are sworn to defend."

Geltman snorted, pulling out his handkerchief to polish his wire framed glasses again. "These are the old Germany, Shaeffer. Their days are numbered with or without a little excitement. I would spend less time worrying about them than about the security of the mission, if I were you."

Shaeffer did not reply. His eyes had turned to the steeple of the church behind them.

Geltman laughed. "Perhaps you wish to go have a prayer for our search? That is well. Perhaps it's time to visit the good father and see if Heaven can offer us some help."

Shaeffer was not a deeply religious man, yet he felt a sense of what could only be revulsion and shame as Geltman roughly pushed open the doors of the church and led him inside. Striding quickly down the aisle between the pews, his eyes scanning their rows, Geltman was all business again. Shaeffer viewed the surroundings with the skepticism of his generation. Still, he considered, if the *new* German god was the truth, it offered him little reason to embrace it after serving it as faithfully as any medieval crusader. Yes, the Fuhrer's gospel had only one angel. The death angel.

At the altar, the priest rose slowly from his knees as Geltman approached him. The priest's eyes were distant--as if he were viewing, not men, but creatures from another world. He did not seem alarmed, only mildly disturbed at their aggressive arrival.

"Yes? What do you seek?" The priest's robe and peasant-carved crucifix contrasted sharply with the rumpled overcoat of the Gestapo officer. The sinister uniform that had become an informal intimidation for even the most stolid soldiers. Shaeffer was impressed with the size of the priest, whose admirable bulk towered over the sharp-edged little official. He'd only met him once in passing, but Shaeffer decided that Dieter Lott was immune to the acid tongue and evil eye Geltman normally used to impose tyranny over any individual he addressed. Shaeffer envied him his calm.

Geltman looked hard at the priest, then turned his gaze left and right. "I seek a traitor, Father. A Judas to our cause. I have personally examined your record and have no reason to believe you have any confusion about harboring such a fugitive under some pretext of misguided sanctuary, do I not?"

Father Lott stared back into the contemptuous eyes of the Gestapo agent. He saw himself reflected in the rimless glasses and spoke slowly, surprising himself at the truth of this calm. "I have given you no reason to fear me, Herr Geltman, have I? Have you heard a word from this pulpit that would bring such a charge against me?"

Geltman hesitated. He did not like this priest. He did not care for any priest, but this man's manner was singularly irritating. He had hoped to spark a resistant response. Instead, his vitriolic inquiries met a disturbing calm that swallowed up his insults; much like a quiet pond would swallow a fistful of pebbles with only the hint of ripples to acknowledge their entry.

"It is unfortunate that I have not had the privilege of attending your sermons, Father," Geltman replied. "The war does not provide some of us with a day off. Perhaps I *should* attend and listen *closely*."

Staring into his reflection in Geltman's glasses brought to Lott's mind the sudden idea that he saw himself as perhaps the Devil saw him. That, perhaps, he was face to face with something almost as old as the God he worshipped. A part of him began to grow dizzy. No, Dieter, you should not focus on yourself. Look only for Christ in any man… no matter the man. The prayer was only an instant, yet it sank into his heart to remain long after most of his sermons had departed.

"The door is open for all, Herr Geltman."

Geltman did not reply. He walked past the priest and threw open the curtain of the confessional. His eyes quickly scanned the small booth. He tapped his gloved hands against the wooden panel. "If only these walls could talk, right, Shaeffer?"

At Geltman's crude joke, Colonel Shaeffer looked at Father Lott; but seeing the priest staring at the floor beside him, shifted his gaze and started. There, unmistakably, resting on the worn carpet was a German Cross with a diamond cluster. His eyes rose to meet those of the priest. Silence passed between them. Then, as Geltman turned back to face them, Shaeffer took a step forward. His boot covered the medal as he adjusted his stance.

Geltman sighed. "Well, Shaeffer, I have found little comfort for my spirit here. If you are ready, let us return to the world of the living." Without acknowledging the priest, the Gestapo man stalked quickly back up the aisle past the waiting Luftwaffe Colonel.

Shaeffer looked back at Father Lott but said nothing as Geltman departed. A moment later, he inclined his head in a brief nod and turned to leave. *All right, Klaus…we're done. Find your silly girl and go far away. Live through this damned fire and raise a child that the madmen can't touch. Leave the damned to bury the damned.*

Dieter Lott watched the door of the church close then bent to pick up the medal. Yes, he thought, Look for Christ in every man, Dieter. Sometimes he looks back.

CHAPTER 14

Klaus Reichmann held the rough drawing of the airfield Chris Clancey had sketched the night he had scouted the hidden installation.

"There are two other underground bunkers here and here. This one is the top of the special laboratory. It is the chemical magazine. No Luftwaffe personnel are allowed there." He looked up at Clancey. "The bunkers are steel-reinforced concrete several meters thick. You have seen the Kriegsmarine submarine pens on the French coast?"

Clancey nodded. "Yes, almost indestructible from the air. So, the hard landing field is the only vulnerable air target and it's so well hidden with the fake trees and animals that it's virtually impossible to verify from above. That's why an air raid is out of the question. Not that it matters now. We have to do it ourselves."

Klaus tapped his finger on the crude map. "Of course, now everything is closed up tight. They must know you are here somewhere. And we were placed on mission alert."

Clancey ran his eyes to the guard posts Reichmann had drawn in. "You are certain the mission is on?"

"Yes, yes. It will be within forty-eight hours. They can't have the bombs ready much faster than a day, as I understand it." Reichmann felt the girl's fingers tighten reassuringly around his arm again. Reisa had said little after the hurried and awkward introductions at his arrival, but her continued presence at his side confirmed again Klaus' decision to break free.

Dieter Lott shook his head. "So soon. What can be done? You've little explosive, as you say, and without assistance from the Americans, even now it would be too late."

"It can be done, but I cannot do it alone and anyone who helps me must make up his mind to death. To hope for more that that will make a man a coward."

Reisa shook her head. "No. You cannot mean there is no hope. You can't ask anyone to give that up."

Father Lott spoke, his words measured and heavy with the sense of futility. "I have hidden these boys so they may live, Captain, not to be killed in the last of this war."

Clancey looked to Klaus.

Reichmann said nothing but nodded slowly.

Reisa's voice was almost pleading. "Call for help, Captain. Tell them they must send help. They must."

Clancey lifted the Luftwaffe medal from the crate at his side, absent-mindedly studying the Germanic cross. "We are all here now because of you, Reichmann. Men and women have died. We will probably die. You knew you couldn't fly those bombs. It's gone too far. You're like me. You've dried up. You thought everything was over. When you've lost every slice of your heart— any reason to fight for—then you see the devil. That uniform you're wearing is a lie. You're naked now. No uniforms, no countries. I can't do it without you. Are you going with me?"

Reichmann stared into the hollow eyes of the American. Never had he seen fate so clearly written on the face of a man. He took a sharp breath. "Unlike you, Herr Captain, I do have something to live for," he turned to Reisa, "and that is why I will go with you."

"That is where you are wrong, mein Herr." The voice was ragged but strong with anger as Heidigger raised his pistol to point at the pilot. "All *you* are going to do is die."

Reisa Konnings' cry came seconds after the side of Heidigger's skull exploded against the wall. Clancey's silencer smothered the report of his gun as Klaus Reichmann's hand moved to smother the girl's scream. They all sat in the resonating silence of the crypt. Reichmann held the sobbing Reisa in his arms, her face pressed against his blood spattered chest. Josef Zimmer looked to his brother, Ricard, who was gasping for air and wiping a piece of Heidigger's brain off his arm. After several terrible, stunned seconds, Dieter Lott crossed himself and moved to lay a blanket over the blood soaked cot where Heidigger's body lay. Chris Clancey still held the smoking pistol and considered how quickly the madness of Heidigger had disappeared. Chris knew that wherever Heidigger had gone, no doubt, he now waited for him.

Clancey turned his head to face Reichmann and Reisa. He set the pistol down on the floor next to him. "You decide. There are no more decisions for me."

Reichmann at last spoke as he held the girl. "Yes, Captain. Not for any of us."

As the Mosquito banked around the outside perimeter of the French airfield saluting the P-47 air cover, the Colonel grimaced at his full bladder and was glad for the fuel stopover before the sprint back to England. Donovan was right, he conceded, this was a young man's game. He had hated having to pull Michael Kitchens out of it for this one, but one day he'd understand. Kitchens still didn't see the 'big picture,' still didn't understand the cost that ultimate victory sometimes demanded of good men. Well, it was done. Clancey wasn't fool enough to try and pull off a full commando raid alone and, if he was, there was no way he could succeed. A bad feeling to have to depend on a man failing, especially a man he really liked. Still, he'd have that full raid go in soon enough to make sure the next bombs didn't fly against the West. When the plague bombs were in the right hands even Michael would see the Colonel's decision was the only sane one. He'd drive over to check on Michael when he got back to England this evening. Just a few hours delay and the prize would fall our way. No one would ever thank him for this, he knew. They need never know of it. Kitchens was the only one who would and he'd come to understand it in time.

When the wheels of the plane slapped down on the air strip, the Colonel cursed his bladder again and peeled off his leather flying helmet. As the Mosquito taxied around the end of the field, he tapped his fingers on the slick leather briefcase that held the recordings of his Joan Eleanor conversation with Clancey. He watched impatiently as a bored-looking airman walked them into a space near a dirt-streaked P-47 Anticipating the reprieve from the confinement of the slender fuselage, the Colonel unbelted and started down the hatch the moment the motors stopped. He carefully guided his feet to keep from taking a spill from the tall airframe and braced himself as he dropped to the ground with the briefcase tucked under his arm. Stepping from beneath the airplane, he saw three men waiting for him by a jeep. He was astonished when he recognized the young lieutenant standing between the two military policemen. The Colonel straightened instinctively and returned his aide's salute.

"Michael. What's all this? How the hell did you get over here? I told you to get a day's rest. I specifically ordered—"

Kitchens cut him off. "I am here on the orders of the Supreme Commander, sir. It is my duty to inform you that you are under arrest and that I am to have any information you may have gathered on this flight."

The Colonel froze. He stared first at Kitchens and then at the sergeants behind him. "You went over my head? To Eisenhower? Do you know what you've done, son?"

Kitchens was ramrod straight. His eyes never left the Colonel's face. "Yes, sir. And I know what *you've* done."

The Colonel rocked forward on the balls of his feet, his hands tightening to fists at his side. Neither Kitchens nor any member of his staff had ever seen him like this. "You impertinent, self-important little bastard. You can't imagine what you've done. I'll break you for this, Michael. You've betrayed your country."

Kitchens stared back evenly. "You betrayed Chris Clancey, Colonel, and that's when you stopped being my country. Guards, take him to the jeep."

At the mention of Clancey, the Colonel seemed to sag; his shoulders lost their height; his face, its color. At last, a sigh escaped his lips and he shook his head as the M.P.s stepped up beside him. "Anyway, Michael, it's too late for Clancey's raid. I guess I've had my moment in history. Let those who follow judge us both."

Michael Kitchens reached out and took the briefcase from the Colonel. "I've been putting that team together we talked about before, sir. The one you didn't intend to use. All I could get my hands on was a patched up parachute unit down south, but they're there, Colonel, waiting on me to drop in with the word. I'm turning this Mosquito around now for a J.E. contact with Chris, if he's still alive, to see if he has a plan. From there, I'm winging straight back to the paratroopers at Base Forward. The weather reports say this thing is going off fast. It may be too late already, but I'm going to find out. These gentlemen will see you to your destination. You'll forgive me, but I'm in a hurry."

As the M.P.s started to move with the Colonel toward the jeep, Kitchens turned again and stopped them with a raised hand. Reaching into the prisoner's flying jacket he pulled out a fresh cigar and crammed it into his pocket.

"One thing I learned from you, Colonel, and from Clancey. Don't quit until you're finished. I'm not finished yet. Not by a damn sight."

END OF PART I

THE TRAITORS

PART II

CHAPTER 15

Reisa Konnings sat across from the priest in the low light of the crypt. They were alone except for the naked bodies of two young men that lay between them. Reisa had watched as Father Lott administered the Last Rites and now he began to cover the stark white faces, pale in the low light of the electric bulb. She saw him pause to look down on one face and slowly touch the man's temple with a gentle finger.

"I knew this boy, Reisa," he said quietly. "He was at mass often. I heard his confession. And today, I have helped his killers. May God have mercy on our souls. This war I have joined is murder upon murder. There are no more quiet places to hide."

Reisa took the cover from the priest's hand and finished pulling it over the face. "When a rock falls from a mountain, it carries many with it, Father. You told me that years ago. We are at the foot of the mountain."

The priest looked up at the girl, a tear shaking on the edge of his nose, as his words choked out. "Would to God we had had the courage to grab that first rock before it fell. Would that we had stood against the evil men when it would have mattered. I would have my tongue ripped from me now if only I had used it to call down the evil when it seduced our nation."

Reisa took the priest's hands in hers. Her words were for herself as well as for Lott. "Father, you must forgive your sin as you pray for the sins of others. I remember once you preached about the thief on the cross. You said the final turning is sweet to God because it can have no pride; only despairing of self to offer all that is left, even if it is only the final word of praise. Father, we are all thieves on a cross."

The priest began to sob. "God, protect them... protect my boys."

"And Klaus," Reisa whispered. "God be with them all." How strange to pray for the killing they must do. Yet she must, for Reisa knew that the evil was far from done and to despair now would only continue the horrible slide of the avalanche that rumbled onward, gaining momentum toward an end beyond nightmare.

Doctor Gerhardt Jost stepped out of the safety shower stall and unzipped the rubber hood from his suit. Smiling with satisfaction, he addressed Professor Yakuro, who had observed his work through the double windows of the laboratory. "They are loaded, Professor. All of the projectiles are primed. The sterilization barriers are intact and the loading carts can be brought in. The clock is running. Our bombers can be ready by midnight."

Yakuro's response, in halting German, though more restrained, was as obviously sincere in its intensity. "Most impressive, Doctor. Teutonic engineering has long been the envy of all industrialized nations. You must take great pride in the design of these shells. The operational construction multiplies the effect of our weapon many times. The saturation ranges should produce a devastating effect on our enemy."

Jost tugged off his rubber boots, dropping them into a chemically laced pail. "It seems we are destined to work together, Professor. Each of us has so much to offer the other. Now we shall turn the world on its head and confound our enemies in a single morning."

The Japanese scientist bowed. "May it be so."

A light over the door at the top of the metal stairway behind them blinked red and the two S.S. guards brought their machine

guns to bear as the metal hatchway slid open. Geltman's arrival
was no surprise to the scientists.

Jost saluted with a boyish energy, his smile jubilant at the
approach of his superior whose shoes clattered down the metal
steps toward them. "Heil Hitler."

Geltman returned the salute irritably. "Are the bombs ready?"
Geltman's response to tension was anger and his tension was now
nearing an apex.

Jost nodded. "Primed for loading, Herr Geltman. We can have
them on the planes in less than an hour with no interruptions."

Geltman grunted. "I am working to see that nothing interrupts
us, Jost. Have them loaded at once. The security patrols are
doubled. Nothing moves within a mile of our gates without—"

The black telephone on the wall near the stairway rang loudly.
Its clamorous alarm stopped Geltman in mid-sentence and his
breath caught like a spike. Without a word, he turned on his heel to
grab the receiver offered by one of the guards.

"Geltman here."

"This is post three, sir."

Geltman gripped the instrument tightly to silence the sudden
icy shiver of dread that moved through his chest.

"What is your report?"

Jost and Yakuro watched the Gestapo colonel as he listened to
the voice on the other end of the line. They each noted with
relieved curiosity that the thin smile of arrogance that marked his
confidence had returned.

Geltman barked an order into the receiver. "Keep them at the
post. Make certain they are unarmed. I will be there in fifteen
minutes." He shoved the phone roughly at the waiting guard before
turning back to the scientists.

"As I said, gentlemen, you have little reason to fear
interruptions. I have just received word that one of the spies has
been killed by our men and two others captured. In a moment, I
will have all the assurance I require to establish the complete
security of our base. Indeed, it seems that nothing stands between
us and our moment of destiny." He paused and looked through the
laboratory windows at the long, flattened cylindrical shapes resting
in the core room of the biological magazine. It was obvious he

savored the words he spoke next. "In seven hours, when we know those bombs have been dropped, I will make a call to Berlin, Professor. The Fuhrer himself will be awake and awaiting that call. It will be news he has been awaiting for over two years. The beginning of the final victory."

It had worked so far, Josef Zimmer thought. Against the taut muscles of his arms, he held the submachine gun steady and in line with the back of Chris Clancey's head as he waited for the coming moment. The plan had gone amazingly well, he reflected; not believing that in this very instant of complete tension, his mind would somehow review the events of the evening though he knew he must be completely focused on the present. Yet he had no more control of his leaping thoughts than he had had on his heart when he had lured the two-man patrol into the alley earlier that day. It had been so easy. Everyone trusted Hitler Youth. Hitler's Boy Scouts. Even killing the two soldiers had been easier than Josef had imagined. The American had been as ruthless as a tiger, yet completely without emotion. He had killed silently and fast, not for mercy, though perhaps the surprise and shock had masked the fleeting moment of pain. The twist that snapped the neck had saved the uniform Josef now wore, along with the oversized boots filled out with rags. Reichmann, the German pilot, had had more difficulty with his man. He was not used to killing men with his hands—only blasting them to pieces so far below that they could not be seen. He had used the American's pistol with the silenced muzzle, close up, in the back of his victim. They had had to hold his man down in his death throes, holding his mouth closed until he was still. Reichmann had turned white and Josef had wanted to be sick. He was glad Ricard had been the watch-out.

"Javol." The German sergeant hung up the phone in the hut, jarring Josef's reflection. Josef fought to stay calm as the ring of six guards shifted around them, uneasy at the presence of the two captives who knelt on the floor before them; their hands on the backs of their necks. Josef's eyes moved to the grotesque figure which lay just to the left of Clancey's knees. Heidigger's ruined half-head stared like a gruesome   cyclops   at the roof of the guardhouse. Sticky, black-red blood puddled thickly in the corner of his remaining ear.

Moments before, Josef and Ricard had forced Clancey and Reichmann ahead of them, struggling with weight of the bloody uniformed corpse they carried between them. As the captives stumbled into the spotlight of the post, the guards were distracted by the gore of Heidigger's mutilation. Clancey and Reichmann were pinned to the floor and searched as the rest of the guards rushed in, shouting and cursing with excitement. This would get them all a pass to Berlin.

Standing here, blood hammering in his chest, gun in hand, Josef felt an unexpected sense of freedom he could not remember in the sixteen years of his life. His earliest memories were of evil signs painted on his father's store, armbands for his mother and sister, and fights with gangs of boys—Hitler Youth. And then, they had taken his family. He and Ricard had seen it happen. Helmeted men in uniforms, like the one he now wore, forced his parents and sister into the back of a truck. He ran. He and Ricard had been running for five years. Running and hiding were all he knew. But no more. Not now. Even if it was to be his last day. They would not take him off in a truck, sitting cowed and afraid.

The sergeant stepped away from the phone, looking down contemptuously at the two kneeling captives. "Search them again, Karl. Don't be shy. If they have knives up their asses, I want them. Take off your boots, shithead." He kicked at Clancey's knee and the American fell forward and looked up in feigned confusion at his captors.

Josef was ready now. The moment was here. Clancey had gone over it with them again and again. Clancey and Reichmann were sitting now, tugging off their boots. The next few seconds meant everything. He and Ricard must not worry about the guards behind them. There were two. They must not even turn to glance at them.

"Your pants, swine."

Reichmann and Clancey slowly stood, unbelting their pants and began pulling down their trousers amid the laughter of the six guards.

Now.

"Rouse," Josef grunted. He stepped forward, slapping Clancey roughly with the side of the submachine gun as if he had seen some move that angered him.

Clancey, trapped by his trousers, stumbled onto the bloody corpse on the floor to the cruel delight of the laughing guards. The nearest of them kicked him as he started to rise. They had not seen his hand enter the blood-soaked, torn uniform of the dead spy.

Josef started with the guard on his left. The submachine gun made an odd burping sound as he swung it in a rapid arc, his hands gripping it so tightly that he was surprised how little it recoiled. The three soldiers before him all sprawled backwards with shouts of surprise. As he turned, he saw his brother finishing his own bloody sweep. Before them lay five dead men. The brothers' eyes met briefly. Ricard nodded.

Josef remembered to breathe again and turned to look behind him. The two other guards were still there. They lay in the awkward unconcern of their sudden deaths. A small, red dot marked each face: the nearest, above one eye, the other, just below it.

"Mein Gott." Reichmann said as he stood up, belting his trousers.

Josef felt a steadying hand on his shoulder and turned to face Chris Clancey, his pistol smoking in the cold of the hut.

"You did well, Josef. But it's just the start. We've got to keep going. All right?"

Josef swallowed. He had never felt so dry. "Yes Sir."

Hans Geltman tapped his gloved fists on his knees as the Mercedes jolted along the path toward the distant guard post, the car's partially masked headlights reflecting a nervous progress through the frigid night. Perhaps now he would, at last, rid himself of the overpowering sense of dread he had felt since the burning of the hotel and the loss of the prisoner Reisa Konnings. It seemed everything had been against him from the start. What should have been the jewel in his crown, the highest moment of his service, threatened now at every instant to turn to ashes. Again chewing the soft sore skin of his inner cheek, he reminded himself that he had

had to work alone to save the mission which would ultimately save the Reich. With only token aid from the Luftwaffe, he had matched his cunning against the hated saboteurs who had invaded his small command. Indeed, the Luftwaffe had proven almost as great a problem as the Allies. The traitor Konnings had flown to the enemy and the great hero Reichmann had joined them. He had been the very one to pass the secret out. And Colonel Shaeffer, the ass, was a lost fool; a hollow shell of an airman who had apparently grown so soft and affectionately attached to his dear pilots, that he understood nothing beyond the ends of his airstrip. Geltman had tried to inspire the colonel into sharing the glory of their mission, but saw now that it had been a waste of energy as the man had no wit for inspiration and was too dull to threaten. He was chaff that would be blown away in good time. For now, he would fill a purpose until better men were available.

Geltman chided himself as he impatiently watched the far tree line, just visible in the moonlight, growing larger. When the vehicle turned a curve in the gravel, the sudden light of the guard post marked his prize. Perhaps he had been too clever, he admitted, too creative in his attempts to bring them to the surface. Had he followed his instincts earlier and crushed Reichmann and killed the Konnings girl, the whole adventure would have fallen apart. But now the fates seemed to be moving with him again. Perhaps the astrologers in Berlin were right, nothing could destroy the Reich, no matter how bleak the day grew. In an hour, the bombs would be on their way. In an hour, it would not matter if the spies were alive or dead. He smiled. The ones who lived would wish they had not and they would pay for every moment of his fear. He would bury it with them.

The car's headlights reflected on the wooden panels of the guard post. An instinct born of years of practiced suspicion gripped him.

"Stop the car, Ulli."

The Mercedes slid to a bouncing halt some forty meters from the post. The following truckload of guards from the inner barracks slowed to a stop behind them.

"The field glasses, Ulli," Geltman commanded. He lifted the heavy lenses to his eyes and thought of a great shark circling its prey. No matter its power, it must first watch and touch the victim. The bite would wait for certainty. He promised himself he would take no chances now, not after all that had gone before. Focusing on the wooden structure, he was perplexed at the lack of activity from the post itself. Perhaps, everyone was inside keeping close guard on the prisoners in accordance with his instructions on the phone. It was then that Geltman's lens found the broken glass from the windows and his tightening focus showed the pattern of round holes that swept along the thin walls of the structure. Even as the smile of bitter pride in his cunning narrowed his lips, he inhaled the cold air and felt the spear point of fear return its pressure inside his chest. He was jarred by the ringing of the field phone beside him on the seat and lifted the receiver before his aide could reach it. Geltman listened for just a moment, then turned to face the approaching platoon leader from the truck parked behind him.

"Sergeant. The nearest patrols report automatic weapons fire in this area within the last five minutes. Surround the post and approach in full readiness. It may be we are nearing a trap."

The sergeant saluted and yelled instructions to the black-uniformed soldiers leaping out of the transport. Geltman pulled off his gloves and plunged a hand into his jacket's inner pocket near his heart. The heart pills would hold off the pressure. A few more hours and then it would all be gone. As he pulled out the small bottle, he noticed the silver skull's-head ring on his left hand. It had been a present from Himmler two years earlier. He remembered it had been something of a grim joke between them for the signet of esteem held a small cyanide tablet within. "*A string on the finger, Hans. Just a reminder.*" Himmler had grinned.

Geltman placed his glycerin tablet under his tongue and waited for the medicine to fight down his rebellious pulse. Yes, a reminder, Hans. A reminder that death is preferable to failure in the court we serve.

Father Lott pulled out the watch chain again and read the time. "Another ten minutes, my child," he said with a sad smile to the questioning Reisa Konnings. "You know it is most probable that there will not be another plane. The last message was an order to withdraw."

Reisa nodded. "He said we must check every hour from sunset until morning, every twenty minutes past for five minutes. The codename is Horseman. Ask for Geronimo." Her eyes rose to meet Lott's. "It may be nothing. But it is what we can do."

The priest lifted the Joan Eleanor from its pouch and wrapped the earplug wires around his hand. Reisa handed him the antenna as he turned to the ladder of the bell tower. The radio transmitter was no burden compared to the weight he carried in his heart for the girl. Clancey had left him a greater burden. One which he wished he could withhold from Reisa.

"Hang on to your arse, sir." the British co-pilot's voice rang tinnily in Michael Kitchens' headphone as the Mosquito banked hard to port, the black horizon swinging vertically, the moonlit streams below them the only visual witness to their wild maneuver.

Kitchens braced hard against the wooden bulkhead behind him and felt his stomach shift as he heard the distant crackle of machine gun fire.

"Night fighter sneakin' up on us, sir." the cheerful monologue from the cockpit continued as the Mosquito rocked to starboard, flipping the horizon again. "Jesus, Sippy. I swallowed my bleedin' cud."

Kitchens braced his feet against the opposite bulkhead and pulled his sleeve back to see his illuminated watch. Two minutes to transmission. He pressed his throat microphone button. "Any chance of getting through?"

"We are, sir. Not a 110 made can climb our stairs. Sippy says we did carry a few souvenirs with us, though."

Michael touched the mic. "Say again?"

"Termites, sir. Bullets. Jerry took a few bites out of the port wingtip. No problem. We'll plug 'em up with chewin' gum and sawdust. No flies on our Rita."

Kitchens smiled in spite of the cold cramped quarters. It felt good to fly with boys like this. Pilots, killing at a distance, could keep the war clean. That wasn't Clancey's war anymore. He remembered something Chris had told him once. In this job you didn't have to imagine what Death would be like when you met him. You walked side by side. You saw him in every mirror.

Geltman stood beside the car; one gloved hand on the doorsill, one shoe on the running board. His full concentration was on the guard post where the small platoon of soldiers at last moved to the inside in a series of strategic lunges. The men were throwing themselves in the doorways with guns at the ready, crouching and flinching, as if for a blow that did not come. After several seconds, the sergeant reappeared and signaled to him that all was clear.

As Geltman began to walk toward the tower, he felt his shoes break through the thin ice of a puddle in the gravel road, his feet sinking slightly into the new mud below. The cold would not last. Had the thaw begun? When the ice melted and the mud dried, the tanks would roll on again. Thousands of Russian T-34s. Only his mission stood against them and the Fatherland. If this mission succeeded, even the Fuhrer would hold him in his debt. His attention was drawn again to the guard post as he approached the waiting sergeant who snapped a relieved salute.

"All dead here, sir. Only one commando. The phone is cut and the bicycles are missing."

Geltman did not return the salute but pulled himself wearily up the two wooden steps and entered the bullet-riddled structure. His eyes ran carefully over the oval ring of corpses as he quietly stepped over the sprawled, lifeless limbs. Two of the soldiers were bending close over the hideous figure of Heidigger. They had set down their guns, preparing to turn the body over for the Gestapo officer's inspection when Geltman shouted, jumping forward to stop them.

"Idiots. Do not move him."

The men stood up quickly, confused embarrassment on their faces as they glanced at each other and to their sergeant.

Geltman bent down and pulled the glove off his right hand, running it gently over the corpse's sides. He nodded with satisfaction and grinned up at the sergeant.

"Perhaps you should teach your men something of booby traps, Sergeant. There is a thin line attached to this man's belt which leads directly beneath a bent nail on the floor and then to his pack. I am more than certain you will find explosives there, waiting for the tug of the witless fish on the other end of that line."

The sergeant glared at the two soldiers standing uneasily beside the corpse. "These men will personally disengage the trap, Herr Geltman."

Geltman shook his head. "No, Sergeant. They will not. We shall vacate this post and then we shall pull a line attached to this one. Our commandoes may be waiting to hear the explosion and we shall not disappoint them. This little trap was meant for me. Very well, let them think the Gestapo is beaten."

Kitchens rubbed his eyes again and looked at the tape recorder beside him in the plane. It was a good thing they used these recorders; that way, no one could accuse him of making it up. So Clancey had started without them, had taken the chance. How? With what? He didn't have enough firepower to destroy the field. They couldn't hope to overpower the number of guards that this kind of target would have. Who was helping him now that Heidigger was dead? The German pilot and a couple of other men? Who were they? The bombers must be going now or Clancey would have waited. Or had he figured out what the Colonel was doing? Well, if Clancey thought it was worth a 'do or die' mission, Michael was sure as hell going to try and get the bastard done. If only there was time. A few more hours. If Clancey could just screw up the works for a few more hours.

Kitchens frowned. He was too much of a realist not to consider the odds of failure. And then what would the Russians do? Germany was not going to be able to stop the war, but what form might it take? Would they all be using the bombs? Who would draw the line? Michael felt a gnawing sense of dread. He'd stopped the Colonel, but what if the Colonel wasn't the only one who thought that way? What about Donovan? He and the Colonel had been close enough, even if the Colonel had resented Donovan's unorthodox manner. Well, he hadn't had time to take a chance after escaping from the country house. He had had to put all his eggs in one basket and risk everything on one play. It meant calling in favors in a hurry. First, the black-market blackmail to hitch an unauthorized lift to France in a C-47 with a cargo load of blankets and boots. Then, a short hop to Versailles on a forged order form as a replacement Piper Cub pilot for SHAEF staff. The airfield was within twenty miles of Versailles. It was time to take the plunge. Time was running out. The Colonel was probably flying out of England by now. Straightening his flight jacket, he had walked over to a pair of M.P.s drinking coffee in their parked jeep.

"Sergeant," Michael said, saluting as he stepped to the driver's side of the vehicle, "I need you to take me to SHAEF H.Q. immediately. I've got information that General Eisenhower has to have."

The driver looked at Michael and straightened up slowly as he swung out from behind the wheel, frowning as he saluted the bedraggled Kitchens. "Excuse me, soldier. What makes you think we'd do that? For that matter, what makes you think SHAEF H.Q. is any fucking where near here?"

Kitchens kept his eyes on the man's face. "I know. I'm with O.S.S. I can give you code words out the ass, sergeant, but I'm not telling anyone, short of the Supreme Commander, what I know. Now you can arrest me or whatever, but you've got to get me through to the General and you need to do it fast, because what I know could be the difference in thousands of lives and it will probably be too late tomorrow, if it isn't already too late right now."

The sergeant looked back to the other M.P. "You think this guy's for real?"

The other sergeant, who still held his coffee cup, shook his head. "I think he's nuts, or maybe a spy. Either way, we better keep him under the gun."

Kitchens nodded. "Right. I'd do the same thing. Search me, but get me to somebody who can get a message straight through. You can run a flashlight up my ass, if you think you need to, but if you fuck around and I don't get hold of Eisenhower, you will both be spending a long time in somebody's freezer, I promise you."

The M.P. stared at Michael hard for a minute and then picked up a radio from the jeep. "This is Turnip Three to Mudflap. Mudflap, we got a crazy here, but I'm bringing him in to the front desk at the hotel. Tell them they might want somebody important from SHAEF to come over and listen to him. I'll be there in half an hour."

It hadn't been easy to get to Eisenhower. He knew that Ike believed in the chain of command and he'd taken out about a half-mile's worth of links. He also knew the Supreme Commander admired courage and apparently had a passion for the common soldier. He had prayed that wasn't all press corps horseshit. If he weren't willing to go to the wall—see the Colonel broken or be broken—he wouldn't have had a chance. He'd had only one card to play when he finally got to a SHAEF desk. It would be the end of him if he played it to anyone but Eisenhower. It might be, anyway. He had prayed that the phone call the corporal at the desk made would relay to the Supreme Commander in time. He knew, at any moment, there might be an alert for him and he could be dragged off without a whisper. If they got him first, he'd be lucky if they even bothered to carry him back to the safe house. At the hotel, he had looked the skeptically-inquiring corporal in the eye as the man held the phone, asking for more information before continuing his petition.

"Tell the Commander that only he can stop 'Toledo'."

The corporal had seemed doubtful at the odd message and even more surprised when he finally received a return call ten minutes later.

"Sir, you are to wait here. They are sending someone for you."

Half an hour later, he had been ushered onto a country estate of which the only resemblance to an army post were the crisply-uniformed guards standing at attention at the entrance.

Eisenhower had seen him alone. There was no hint of the famous grin.

"Lieutenant, I trust you know your use of the codeword 'Toledo' is a serious breach of our rules of communication. The very rumor that biological warfare is being spoken of in our chain of command could lead to dreadful consequences for our alliance. I trust, also, that you realize that your superiors in intelligence will be notified of all your actions. Now, realizing all this, let's hear your story."

The meeting lasted twenty minutes and Ike made three phone calls during it. Michael realized, after one minute, that he had the entire attention of the SHAEF commander. In ten minutes, he knew he had his confidence. In fifteen minutes, he realized, without being exactly sure how, that the horrible secret and the weight of his fear, had passed from his shoulders to the balding, four-star general tapping his fingers on the black telephone receiver and frowning at the big map of Europe on the wall. When Eisenhower called on the M.P.s to escort the Colonel, Michael swallowed, almost hating to add the weight of needed action to the terrible choices.

"Sir? What do I do if Clancey's still alive? What do we do?"

Dwight Eisenhower turned back to him and stood straight. His hands rose to his hips, spreading his unbuttoned jacket. The blue eyes narrowed. "Well, Lieutenant Kitchens, I suggest you 'run out your bunt'."

Afterwards, on the flight back, Kitchens shook his head at the memory. 'Run out your bunt.' That was West Point for 'shit or get off the pot'. The only thing here was, if you get thrown out, you don't get to go to the dugout for another inning. Game's over. Maybe for everybody. Well, they hadn't given him General Spatz and a flight of B-17s, hadn't taken it off his shoulders with a pat on the back and given it to General Patton, or even to Donovan. They'd handed it back to Mike. Ike put it in his hands. No matter how they'd looked at it, there just wasn't enough time for anything else. Maybe it was enough. Whatever happened, he wasn't sure if he was in more trouble leading a team into Germany or flying back to Versailles. Sure, 'run out your bunt'. Kitchens snorted and then with surprise at his own strange relief, he laughed. "Yeah, Mike. Run out your poor, old, motherless-bastard bunt."

Up forward in the cockpit of the Mosquito, the co-pilot leaned close to the pilot. "Sippy, I think the lad back there's gone a bit bonkers. He's laughing like a drunk lord on boat race night."

The pilot nodded, his eyes never leaving the moonlit horizon. "We're all mad, lad. Mad as 'atters, every mother's son of us."

CHAPTER 16

"That was the grenade," Clancey said as the four men stopped their bicycles at the sound of the explosion behind them. They had taken the bikes from the guard post and were slowly working their way just inside the tree line bordering the southern pasture that masked the lower approach to the hidden airfield. The filtered moonlight was their only guide among the shadows of the woods. "If we're lucky, we might have killed your Geltman," Clancey said, looking at the dark figure of Reichmann standing to his right.

The pilot nodded. "That is one killing I would not regret."

There was coughing behind them and Clancey turned to the two brothers who were resting against their handlebars. Ricard was coughing, trying to smother the sound in his throat.

"Are you all right, boys?"

"Yes sir," Josef answered quickly. "Ricard is winded. He will be ready in a moment."

Reichmann leaned closer to Clancey. "I don't like that cough, Captain. Soon, we will be near the warren. If we are heard—"

Clancey nodded and turned back again. "Ricard, we need someone to cover us. You wait here. We should be back in an hour. If the bombers fly, then crawl out through these woods. Go due east. Get to the church and tell Father Lott we are lost and to keep reporting it until it is acknowledged."

Ricard cleared his throat and his hoarse whisper answered Clancey. "I will not return without you, Captain. If you are lost, I will use the grenades to stop them."

"Don't disobey an order, son," Clancey said sternly. "You getting killed by yourself won't stop the bombs. You do as you are ordered."

"He is right, Ricard. He is the leader." Josef placed a hand on his brother's shoulder. "He knows how to fight. He has given us the chance."

Ricard coughed again and, with a sharp nod, looked away.

Klaus Reichmann pulled off his pilot's scarf and clamped a hand on the boy's arm, handing the silk piece to him with a nod. He turned back to Clancey. "Well, Captain, it's downhill from here on, as we say when the propellers stop."

Clancey grunted. "Lead on, Reichmann. I just hope you are right about your crew, or about enough of them."

Klaus Reichmann hoped so, too. He hoped they wouldn't have to kill any of his team. It was one thing to turn against the Gestapo, the S.S., even against the Luftwaffe and the High Command. Those were "powers without souls," as Reisa would put it; but men he knew, men he had saved and had saved him—that was a different matter. Klaus sighed as he pushed the bike forward on the pine needles. God grant it did not come to that. Just don't let it come to that. If you're any kind of God at all, don't let me have to kill my friends.

In the bell tower of the church, Reisa Konnings sat looking out at the dark sky, the big moon and the stars that flirted with the passing clouds. She shivered, whether from the cold or sudden foreboding, she was not certain. She started to move back from the large window to the dark opening and narrow stairs of the tower when she heard movement below her.

"Don't be afraid, my dear. It is just me."

Reisa let out a tense sigh and looked out over the village as Father Lott joined her.

"It is too cold out here at night. You should come back down. I can warm some milk. You are doing them no good up here on watch, you know."

"Yes. I'm not doing them much good at all."

"We made the contact. Now it's beyond us. We must only follow our orders, and it is not yet time."

Reisa nodded. "I wonder what they make of it, the Americans. I have a difficult time understanding them. Clancey. Heidigger."

"Not because they are Americans, dear. Indeed, the captain is perhaps not much more welcomed by his leaders than your pilot is by the Luftwaffe. If anything is certain in all this terrible business, it is not for any country's glory that they are doing this thing tonight. If they were, I could not allow it."

Reisa put a hand on the priest's arm. "You're worried about the brothers. Father, you can not blame yourself that they felt they must do this. They had to go just as Rudi did. Klaus and Clancey need them."

Lott sat down beside the girl and she was aware that he was studying her, uncertain, perhaps waiting for something.

"What is it, Father?"

The priest spoke quietly. "I have been waiting to tell you something, Reisa. I could not speak of it before."

"Yes?" The evening chill began to sift inside her.

"Captain Clancey told me something he wished for you to know. Something he could not say to you."

Reisa waited.

"It's about your brother, Rudi."

"No." Thoughts tumbled through her mind rising like the sudden wind. It must not be. Not Rudi. He was free. He was safe. They might kill them all, but Rudi had lived. *Would* live.

"Rudi died before they reached us."

There it was. She tried to grasp it, but her hold was slipping. Everything had been a balance, a gamble, a holding out for hope. They had planned it together. They had known it was death, but they were too young to truly believe in their own mortality. She had fought it all. The Gestapo questions, the drugs, the fear, the killing. Everything had hinged on a tomorrow, an ending where it would all be right again, but that tomorrow was gone now. The fierce hope had not mattered. She was alone. The night seemed to rush into her like an evil wave through a broken dam. She felt herself falling, as in a dream. She could not move to save herself. She had no heart to save herself.

Dieter Lott gripped the girl, chiding himself for his own grief when this child had born his as well as her own. It had been a weakness to wait until now, until *he* was ready. Cradling Reisa in his arms, he felt her begin to shake with sobs from deep inside. He stroked her hair and spoke softly.

"I am sorry, daughter. He was a wonderful boy. The captain said he was the bravest man he had ever met. He said he would not have kept on with the mission if it were not for Rudi and you. He said you were the only reason he could find to fight for anything now." The priest remembered Clancey's quiet conversation. "He said that it was the first time he had ever been afraid to tell anyone anything. He made me promise to tell you, that no matter how many lies he has told, this was true."

"Sign." The guard called out in challenge at the rap on the barracks door.

"I've got special codes for Radioman Frankl," was the shivering reply. "They didn't give me the stupid sign. Take the damn things yourself."

"Frankl, are you to be given special codes?" the inner guard called, turning from the entrance to face the airman who sat on his bunk tugging on his fur-lined flying boots.

Willy, puzzled at the message, looked up, then froze as the door crashed open and the automatic black-out switch cut off the light. In the momentary darkness, he heard the sound of the guard's body crumpling to the floor, his helmet and pistol clattering on the cement. Before anyone could respond, the door closed and the light came on. A tall Luftwaffe officer swung over the unconscious body of the guard and stood in a crouch, holding a pistol at arms length and locking all of the air crew in their places.

"Place your hands on top of your heads and move away from the bunks."

It seemed to Willy that the madman was pointing the weapon directly at him, yet each one responded as if he alone were the target of the threat. Willy stood, one boot on and one boot off, and stepped to rejoin the small line of nervous men who glanced at each other as they waited, hands on their heads. Some were wearing only their underclothing. This could only be one of the spies Reichmann had spoken of. He wished Klaus were here now. Klaus had been their heart and Willy had nearly killed him. He swallowed and steadied himself. "What do you intend to do with us?" he heard himself ask, his voice much louder than he intended.

The answer came, not from the commando, who reached over to control the light switch; but from the next man who entered. Klaus Reichmann.

"I need you, Willy. I need you all."

"Klaus!" Several voices, some angry, all surprised, answered Reichmann's entrance.

"Yes. I've come back with these men to stop the bombs. They can not be dropped."

The crew was uncertain of how to respond. The first man still held the gun firmly trained on them. A second stranger entered, a young soldier holding a submachine gun. He immediately set about dragging the fallen guard toward the bunks and threw the body roughly onto the first of the low beds. Quickly, he moved back to the entrance and trained his attention on the passageway.

Von Tripps brought his hands down very slowly. "It is the Gestapo who give us orders. You are asking us to risk more than death, Klaus."

Reichmann turned to the man beside him and motioned him to put away the gun. The commando nodded and drew back the pistol; yet still held it upright, his finger inside the trigger ring. Klaus moved toward them.

"I am asking you to be men. To be German. Not slaves to the Gestapo and SS. The war for Germany is over. You know that, Reinhardt. And you, Lauda?"

The navigator looked to the others and nodded soberly. "Yes, and we are just trying to stay alive until it ends, Klaus. You have two men and two guns? Do you think you can capture the whole air base? Are you going to crack the head of every poor bastard here like that stupid guard?" Lauda motioned to the unconscious soldier lying on the bunk.

Klaus shook his head. "There are three planes. Without these planes, the plague won't be unleashed. It won't take an army to destroy the bombers. It will take you."

"We're fliers, not commandoes," Von Tripps said, crossing him arms and assuming his usual casual stance. His eyes never left the American.

"That's what we need," Klaus continued. "We take our plane. We use the guns to disable the other two planes and we fly out. We spend the rest of the war in Switzerland. The Allies will be here before anyone can modify any other planes to carry the bombs even short distances."

"They are that close?" Frankl was stunned.

The American answered, "The next tanks you see enter the village will be American."

"Or Russian," Paul Hoffman snorted. "Don't forget the Cossacks."

The other gunner, Peter Kroft, nodded.

Reichmann turned to the gunner. "The bombs will only slow them down, Paul. Do you think they won't take revenge for that?"

"They will want revenge for the whole war," Heinrich Lauda agreed. He paused and added, "And for the camps. They will have plenty of reasons to hate us." He looked at the others, "We know that."

Klaus shook his head. "There's a difference, Heinreich. We didn't build the damned camps."

Frankl noticed the young guard's head turn to them at the mention of the concentration camps. He saw something in the soldier's eyes that sent a shiver through him. He'd heard whispered stories about those places from this crew. Something they'd seen once before he'd joined them. He hadn't wanted to believe them but the eyes of the guard seemed to turn those wishes to dust. Willy was thankful when the soldier turned back to the passageway.

Reichmann was continuing. "We are not murderers. We are the Luftwaffe. The plague bombs will not fall if we do not carry them. It ought to matter to us. And it might matter to the Russians as well."

Reinhart Von Tripps carefully pulled out a cigarette and lit it. "Very well, Klaus. Perhaps some of us might go along with you. What about those who don't?"

The American stepped forward. "We aren't here to beg. Who goes with us?"

Klaus held a hand out. "You won't be killed. You must decide now."

Von Tripps turned to look around the four other crewmen. "If the others go—"

Frankl stepped forward. "I'll go. I'll go with you, Klaus."

Reichmann smiled. "I knew you would, Willy." He turned to the gunners. "I need you, Paul. We've got to knock out the other planes before the crews board them. I need my gunners."

Hoffman nodded.

"Peter?"

Kroft shook his head. "I am sorry, Klaus. Maybe this thing you do is right. It is hard to know. But I can not leave my wife. I don't know what they would do to her if I go with you. Do what you have to do but I can't leave."

Reichmann nodded. He turned to the navigator. "Heinrich?"

Lauda rolled his eyes. "Shit. Shit, yes. Someone's going to kill poor Heinreich. Perhaps it should be for not doing something terrible instead of all the terrible things I have done."

Klaus turned back to the American. "This is enough, Captain. We will fly."

The American stepped over to the nervous Peter Kroft who had chosen to remain behind. The commando motioned for him to turn around. The moment Kroft complied, Clancey brought the butt of his gun down fiercely on the airman's head.

Willy Frankl gasped at the force of the blow but saw that the commando had caught the falling figure of his crewmate and now lowered his unconscious weight onto the nearest bunk. The bruise that would soon ripen would testify to his innocence. An innocence Willy had chosen to abandon.

Now Reichmann was hurrying them. "Get on your gear. We've got to get into our plane before the others." He turned around. "Where is Braun? I had forgotten about him."

Lauda was pulling on his heavy flight jacket. "The warden? He's over at the bomb magazine with the other bombardiers. Apparently, there are a lot of tricks to these bombs. They told us to be ready to board in a half-hour. It takes some time to set up the equipment in each plane. We are to meet him on the hanger grid for our final instructions."

Clancey stuck the pistol into its holster, moved to an open locker and began to hunt through the stored gear. He spoke as he pulled out a set of gloves and goggles. "Is your plane the first to be armed?"

Von Tripps shook his head. "Last. We're still waiting for the replacement pilot for Klaus, actually the replacement co-pilot. I'm to pilot in Klaus' place."

"Congratulations," Clancey said without looking up.

"Your German is quite good. What are we to call you?" Von Tripps asked as he zipped up his pants.

"Captain, will do. If this falls through, the less you know about me, the better for you."

Von Tripps nodded. "If this falls through, I will save the Gestapo any pains they might take in discussing the matter with me on an intimate level," the tall co-pilot observed with a final tug of his zipper.

"Someone is coming." Josef Zimmer whispered loudly, gripping the machine gun tightly and bracing himself for the confrontation.

Reichmann turned to Reinhardt Von Tripps. "What's the sign and countersign?"

Von Tripps shook his head then stammered, "Uh—Bismarck. And—"

Zimmer straightened at the rapping on the door to the room. "Sign?" he called, steadying himself as he mentally rehearsed again the killing he'd been taught.

"Bismarck." Josef heard the guard outside slapping his gloved hands together and then call out, "Countersign?"

Josef steadied himself as he waited on Von Tripps who was frantically looking to the other men.

"Prince Eugen," Willy Frankly hissed loudly, finishing for the co-pilot, who nodded gratefully.

"Countersign, Ernst, you lazy bastard." the voice repeated angrily from outside. "You want us to freeze?"

"Prince Eugen," Josef answered, pulling his collar up over his cheek and stepping to the side so that his face would be shielded as the door opened.

"Replacement for you," the outside guard said casually as he stepped inside. The light shut off for the opening of the door and clicked on again as it closed.

Now, two men stood inside. One, the heavily-cloaked outer guard rubbed his face and turned to the small wood stove near the door, while the second man, wearing the heavy flight suit of the Luftwaffe, stood beside him and nodded to the silent crew sitting on the bunks.

Without looking up, the guard said, "This is Hauptman Ziffle. He's just come in from the commandant's office. These are the crew of bomber three, sir. Well, I'll be heading back to the hut, Ernst. Word has it we've all got leave after these boys get back."

Josef Zimmer was staring at the back of the guard, trying to decide what he should do when Von Tripps stepped forward, saluting the new aviator.

"Welcome to bomber crew number three, Hauptman. I am Lieutenant Reinhardt Von Tripps and the rest of the boys will be happy to introduce themselves. We've got a couple of lazy lads among us. Hangovers, I'm afraid, but a shot of oxygen will have them ready in a moment," Von Tripps laughed with good spirit. He turned to the guard who was looking over the airman's shoulder at the two figures in the bunks behind him, the covers thrown over their bodies.

Lauda caught the guard's sleeve. "Sergeant. You seem very loose with your talk about our mission. I suggest you keep your gossip to yourself. I wouldn't want to report such slackness to Herr Geltman."

The soldier straightened reflexively and glared at the airman but only swallowed and nodded. "Javol." he said with a tight-lipped frown. Shouldering the machine gun which hung at his hip, he turned to open the door again. When the light returned, the guard had vanished and Josef could hear his boots crunching the frozen ground outside as he retreated to his post.

Clancey turned around slowly and held up his pistol. "Hauptman, I will have that flight jacket, if you don't mind."

CHAPTER 17

The Mercedes sawed through the crunching gravel of the path and came to a shuddering stop at the foot of a prominent earthen mound. In the moonlight, two sentries stood stiffly erect facing the steaming automobile, their breath frosting in twin clouds. The Gestapo officer stalked past them, ignoring their parallel salutes. At his harsh command, a moonshadow opened in the hillside.

As the leather-coated figure disappeared into the square black cave, the driver of the Mercedes was reminded of his grandmother's stories of wizards and warlocks. Ulli Kleski frowned as he watched his "wizard" vanish into the earth. A moment later, the door closed, sealing the hidden entrance as completely as any magic spell. Perhaps his childhood nightmares had been prophecies of these days. The evil phantoms the old woman had warned him against had now become less fantastic as he sensed a great web of events contracting around him. Kleski knew well the fear the very name of the Gestapo elicited from all who heard it. No man-eating troll he'd imagined at Nina's knee had been more fearsome than Herr Geltman.

Colonel Shaeffer noted something different in Geltman's manner. Something he had never quite seen before. The Gestapo official bent over his desk now, pulling off the black leather gloves he fancied, as he filled in Shaeffer on the night's proceedings. It was a mixture of hunger and fear, Shaeffer decided, and above all else, obsession. He had seen it once before in a squadron leader he had grounded. There was no grounding Geltman. No stopping any of the Geltmans, Shaeffer concluded. They seemed to be everywhere now, demanding everything, threatening everyone, and coming from everywhere in a hurry like foxes routed in a hunt. Their eyes were wild. There was nothing they would not do. And they were always behind you, on the end of every line. Berlin seemed to be nothing but madmen and boys—his boy. At this moment, some bastard like Geltman was, no doubt, giving asinine commands to the only ones left to hear them. The old men and the children. No man he still respected remained in the chain of command, Shaeffer realized. All that remained was the chain. And the chain was tightening. He also realized he must listen to Geltman. It was still important to survive. He must survive for his son.

"It is all very close now, Colonel. Your Captain Reichmann has led the spies right onto the base. They are moving in on us even now. No, I will not sound the alarm. They must not be run off, but taken. I have informed all units to be on the alert and to show no laxness in their rounds."

Shaeffer rose and moved to take his field coat from the stand in the corner of his office. "The bombs? Surely they are the target?"

"No, I do not think they will attempt to attack the magazine. They can be only a few and even Reichmann knows that it is triple-guarded and built to withstand the shock of a thousand-pound bomb. No, the one vulnerable point is the planes. I have sent double guard squads to hide in the dark along the walkways and hangers. Even the ground crews will be double checked. Anyone attempting to get near a plane without the proper checks will be killed outright. We are within minutes of success. I have just sent the reserves down both sides of the runway. Any attempt to fire on the planes will be immediately dealt with. I have the dogs looking for Reichmann. Fortunately, he left us quite a lot of laundry to familiarize them with." Geltman's train of thought seemed to change tracks, the look of evil humor vanishing in an instant to a cold detachment as he suddenly held up his wristwatch. "It is time we went to the tower to observe operations." He turned rapidly and started for the door but paused to confront Shaeffer again as the colonel moved to follow him. His mood again shifted; a somber, almost visionary, look filtered his eyes as he spoke. "I will be remembered not only as the man who defeated the Russians; but also as the man who caught the traitors. Rise to this occasion, Shaeffer, and some of the glory will rub off onto you."

Shaeffer did not smile. "May you receive all you are due, Herr Geltman. Not a mark less."

Geltman stared back at Shaeffer for an instant before speaking. "You must see that the planes fly on their exact schedule times. Everything must be perfect. The fighter cover is alerted?"

Shaeffer nodded. "The fighter squadrons are overlapped. The diversionary attacks will be launched on time. Everything is underway as according to the plan."

Geltman grinned. "I knew I could depend on the Luftwaffe." He turned before Shaeffer could reply.

Ricard Zimmer crouched in the wood. He felt the cold in his chest, digging again like a barbed spike. The cold he knew he could never lose was tightening around his heart like a rope. He remembered his mother's concern for his colds as a child. No, that was not a thought for now. He shut it from his mind and fought against the pain that answered his every breath of air. He pulled the soldier's coat sleeve back to again examine the glowing wristwatch the American had given him. It would be an hour very soon. What would he do if nothing happened? There should be one plane. That was all. They should be on that one plane and it would wag its wings. More planes would mean the mission was on. If there were more than one plane, how should he know which to fire on? Reichmann had told him of the flying beer barrel cartoon on the side of the cockpit. Would he see it? He wondered about the priest. He would have liked to have said something special when they left, but he hadn't been able to. Lott had been like family. He pitied the man. He did not understand the faith, but he could see the grinding doubt in the priest. Ricard had wanted to comfort him. All he had was the Star of David from his childhood. It would be better to give it away than to be captured with it. He remembered that he had smiled when his brother had taken the priest's hand and joked that, "All God's heroes were martyrs." He did not smile now. He did not feel like a hero. He did not wish to be a martyr. Soon, he thought. Soon, it would end. It was then he heard the dogs.

Clancey walked directly behind Reichmann, who was just behind Von Tripps and Lauda; the two officers were feigning a casual conversation, laughing at some dark joke. Chris felt the heady sense of power and freedom he alone of the team was experiencing. His trained mind efficiently directed the pulsing adrenalin to heighten his senses without emotion. He was calm within himself. He worked from within the eye of a storm. He knew this advantage was the difference in life and death. It was one thing to overcome fear. It was another to be so familiar with its attributes that only its physiological impact was considered. It was like having another set of trained muscles where other men had only desperation.

Chris considered the small team following them while they walked in the forced rhythm of careless routine. These were ordinary men, whose fear might erupt at any moment, puncturing the pretense of normality that was their only shield. They walked between sets of S.S. troops, machine guns at the ready, only dark faces on either side of the pathway. Their attention was set on the perimeter of their watch like Trojan sentinels protecting the entry of the wooden horse. Chris' gloved hands swung loosely at his sides. He purposefully turned to look at the guards that showed interest in the crew, even giving a slight nod of greeting to dilute any stirred curiosity. Chris knew it was this capability to invert his emotional self that let him do the killing he had done and would do again. He knew this very ability gnawed away at his real self. The self that knew these acts to be horrific could not remain; it must rebel at some point or cease to be. It was a final damnation.

Training for this mission—even this day when he had lain in wait for the guards to follow Josef into the trap—he had believed that that self had died. But he knew it was not so. The girl had brought it back. Reisa and her brother had pulled back the thick curtain of his heart. For the life of thousands to matter, the life of

one must matter. He had wished he could care for the thousands as
had the girl and her brother. They had given him the focus, the life
worth saving. He would give all for that. He knew he had no life
left to offer, only his death. Chris Clancey knew with sudden
surety that, ultimately, there were but two states of being. Love and
fear. He had lost one and denied the other. Was his denial ending,
or only his life? To be thinking such things as he walked into the
heart of the Nazi base heightened the sense of detachment he now
moved within. Yet, the smile he felt crease his lips seemed
incongruously genuine. Perhaps, he considered, it was his own
goodbye kiss.

They stopped at the entry to the third hanger and Chris could
hear the crunch of gravel as the other crews arrived at their hangers
beyond them. Ahead of him, Von Tripps spoke and the doorway
opened. They followed inside, only to stop once again. The outer
door closed behind them. Close above their heads, a hooded, red
light flicked on and cast their faces in exaggerated shadows of red
and black. A company of demons at the gates of hell, Chris
observed dryly, as they waited for the inner door to open.

The bright lights of the hanger interior stabbed into their eyes
as the inner door slid open. They moved into the vast room and
Clancey saw the big bomber for the first time. It sat, squat and low.
Its tricycle landing gear gave it a lower nose attitude than the B-
17s that reared back on their tail wheels, pointing their noses
skyward as if eager to bound off into the air. Chris noted that the
cigar shape fuselage had no raised cockpit but was fared in with
the forward bombardier/ gunner enclosure. The whole plane had
obviously been designed to reduce drag as much as possible. It
seemed certain to Clancey that only the advice of an astrologer
could have swayed the Fuhrer from pursuing the manufacture of
such an obviously potent weapon. What Germany might have done
with squadrons of these bombers was incalculable. Nearing the
plane, Clancey noticed several white-robed technicians working at
the centerline, clearly tending a large, rounded slab-shape attached
to the bottom of the plane nestled in close with no light separating
it from the fuselage. The appendage seemed to reach within a foot
of the cement floor of the hanger. The plague bomb. Other flight

line personnel were busily pulling away fueling carts and trays of tools.

The crew stopped at a nod from Von Tripps and began hitching up their parachutes, pulling on gloves and zipping up flight suits. Clancey felt a hand on his arm and turned to face Reichmann whose face glowed palely, even in the harsh electric light of the metal cavern.

"Here comes Braun."

"Right."

Clancey glanced down the line of the crew. The others moved about nervously, taking more than ordinary interest in their zippers and cinches. Josef Zimmer seemed lost in the study of his parachute pack. If Braun counted the crewmen, he would know something was wrong. Clancey looked up coolly at the approaching bombardier. This was it. Be close in the clinches. Stay in the blind spot between the eyes.

Von Tripps stepped forward to answer Braun's salute, shielding Reichmann from the bombardier's casual inspection. "You are ready, Braun? All is in order?"

"Yes, yes, we are on schedule, but we need to be certain to be off rapidly. There is a rumor of commando activity on the base. I had to personally clear everyone on the ground crew before they could come near the plane. I understand a night fighter ring is picketed in a wide sweep of the field, ready for any surprise attack. We must be ready to be off within the next ten minutes. Has the replacement arrived?"

Chris Clancey stepped up and saluted Braun. "Here, Herr Braun. Hauptman Ziffle. I flew the first prototypes back in '42. It's good to put these big birds to use at last."

Von Tripps grunted. "We shared a barracks in Rosieres-en-Santerre back in '40, during the English campaign."

Braun smiled. "Well, it seems we have a much improved team, Hauptman. No long faces for this mission now. A few hours and we'll show the Russian sons of bitches what German air power is."

Clancey laughed. "Javol."

Von Tripps nodded.

Clancey clapped his gloved hands together. "Can we board? I want to get a feel for the old girl's tits."

Braun snorted at the joke. "Ja, it's time to board up." He turned and waved to the technicians moving away from the plane, then led the crew forward under the shadow of the wide port wing. The curved hatch of the cockpit was low to the ground and made mounting much easier than that of the bombers Clancey had known before.

Waiting at the end of the short crew line, Josef Zimmer felt his fear growing exponentially as each member of the team entered the plane ahead of him. Each second he stood exposed in the line seemed certain to hold the shock of discovery. It was as if he were waiting to be pulled into a lifeboat from a shark-infested sea but must wait until the last man had climbed aboard. He almost shouted at the sound of a shrill whistle and the sudden clattering of boots rushing across the floor of the hanger. He fought to keep from dashing ahead, shouldering his way past the others into the recesses of the airplane. Something was happening. Somewhere, he heard muffled explosions and gunfire. His mind exulted in relief for only the briefest instant as he saw the soldiers rushing not toward the plane, but to the entrances of the hanger. Then he realized that it could only be Ricard. He stood rooted at the open hatchway. His brother was out there fighting for his life. Josef started to turn when he was jerked forward, lifted by his shoulder straps into the plane. He stared into the hard face of Chris Clancey and for the first time, he saw sadness.

The tower had been designed to appear as a wooden silo from the air. Its greater height was not noticeable from a high-flying reconnaissance flight and the dilapidated barn nearby confirmed its domestic quality. Now in the dark of night, it came alive with flight control activity. The unearthly red glow of the interior lights appealed to Hans Geltman's desire for the dramatic. With his shoes ringing on the grating, he neared the top level of the winding metal stairwell. Geltman observed the faces of the tower personnel turning to him from their stations, awaiting his command, and indulged himself in a moment of dramatic silence before dismissing their attention.

The men turned back to their duties and Geltman moved to stand beside the tower director. He spoke, without looking at the man, as he scanned the dark horizon spread before them in the moonlight. "Have the crews boarded their planes, Hauptman Klein?"

"Javol, Herr Geltman. Each of the bombers is loaded and standing by for the command."

Geltman crossed his arms. He was about to speak when a flash of light several hundred meters away caught his breath. A muffled explosive shock thumped against the glass pane before him.

"Commandoes." the tower director shouted.

Geltman felt the spearpoint lance into his heart. "Shit." Shuddering with rage, he shouted for the telephone. He gripped the receiver tightly as he spat orders to the command post.

There were the sounds of machine gun fire and other explosions. Obviously grenades. Geltman felt his control returning and his pulse dropping from the sudden spike. After all, this was what he had expected. Now they could be dealt with. It had been a mistake to go after them. In the field, the fox is a match for the hounds. Waiting here, patiently, for the inevitable attack had proven the wiser course. The spies could not win the waiting game. And indeed, they had lost it after all. Had he not been right? They had been trying to reach the planes. Still, he could not be careless. It could be a diversion. The spies had proved resourceful but he knew the one resource they did not have was men. No, a handful of spies or commandoes could not expend the members of their small team so carelessly as these did. Each violent action drained their strength. And he had the strength to overmatch them in every encounter at all points.

Renewed confidence flickered along Geltman's lips. The tower controller saw it from the corner of his eye and felt a tremor ripple through his own chest at the unnerving quality of the expression. He straightened and turned as Colonel Shaeffer stepped from the stair behind them.

"Hauptman, what is the status of the crews?"

"Ready, Colonel. It is time for the runway to be uncovered. Shall I give the command?"

Shaeffer turned to Geltman. "Have the commandoes been captured? The way cleared?"

Geltman shrugged. "The firing is over. No doubt the extra patrols have reached their positions by now. It is time to light the field. Their moment has passed, Colonel. We have succeeded. It is time."

"You would risk the planes?"

"It is time, Shaeffer. We control the perimeter of the field. The attack was far from a critical position. The traitors and spies have lost their chance. The planes are ready. We cannot wait. We will commence."

Shaeffer nodded. "Very well. Send the trucks, Hauptman. I am going to the hangers to see the crews off." He paused and turned to Geltman. "You don't need me here?"

Geltman glanced out the window of the tower as the lights of the field flickered on and the cover crews drove out to the open pastures to begin sliding the artificial cover off the hard field. "Yes, see your heroes off, by all means, Shaeffer. I shall ride down to meet with the patrols along the left perimeter of the runway. I imagine there will be prisoners or bodies to be examined. Who knows? Perhaps your wayward bomber pilot among them." Casually lighting a fresh cigarette, he walked confidently past Shaeffer and started down the metal stairs.

Shaeffer was still staring after the smug Gestapo officer when Sergeant Rheaman stepped up to him, coughing for his attention. Shaeffer turned to face the young radioman. "Yes, sergeant?"

Rheaman cleared his throat before answering. "Sir, there is a private message for you."

In the bomber, Chris Clancey sat in the co-pilot's seat to the right of Von Tripps and could just see the top of Braun's head forward and below them beneath the rounded lattice work of Perspex panes. Behind him in the shadows of the fuselage's interior, Klaus Reichmann sat out of sight just past Willy Frankl. The radioman nervously glanced at Clancey and attempted a quick smile which Clancey did not return. Chris turned to look out through the nose of the bomber and saw the big doors of the hanger crack apart and slowly spread aside as the ground crew pulled them along their metal tracks. Outside, the field had become a chilling pool of blue light as marker beacons bathed the open runway in a polar haze. Above the field, Chris noticed a star moving across the sky. Night fighters. The microphones crackled with a clear command to start motors.

Clancey watched Von Tripps glance out an open rectangle of Perspex beside him and shout "Port two." A flight crew mechanic stood in front of the plane watching the propeller of the inner port motor begin to rotate; the whine of the magnetos answering the switch the pilot had snapped upward on the forward panel. Clancey heard the familiar cough and bark of waking mechanical life as the big motor fired its initial breath of fuel. Then, as Reinhardt cracked the throttle, it began to bellow its dizzying song of power. Clancey saw the mechanic nodding and pointing to the starboard wing. Von Tripps did not shout over the resonating hum of the port motor but simply nodded and flipped the shiny metal toggle. For a brief instant, Clancey could hear the starboard three motor coughing spasmodically to life, then joining its cry to its sister's. Von Tripps closed the window again and gave a thumbs up to the mechanic who now pointed to the far port engine. This motor answered readily, merging its cadence with the others. Clancey looked out past the hanger doors again. So far, it was all working better than he could have hoped. It was not part of Clancey's pattern to pin much on hope. He turned back to Reichmann.

"The guns are ready?"

Klaus nodded. "Yes. The boys know what to do. They're going to be aiming at the motors and tires, Captain."

Chris Clancey looked across at Willy Frankl and spoke quietly to Reichmann, mindful of Braun ahead of them in the nose. "Your crew is a remarkable team. I would not have counted on them to do this."

Klaus kept his voice low. "We have seen more of the S.S. and the Gestapo than even you, Captain. I would not have done this six months ago and neither would they. Frankl hasn't been one of us long, but the rest of us crash- landed our Heinkel near a camp after an encounter with some Russian fighters in December. The camp was a place called Dachau. They brought us in and fed us. Treated us as heroes. I couldn't keep that supper down, Captain. A man can only disbelieve a thing so long. At Dachau, you don't have to open your eyes. You can smell the truth."

"Shit."

Clancey jerked back to stare at Von Tripps who was shaking his head and waving a hand at the mechanic out front. The pilot spoke angrily as he gestured to starboard. "We've got a problem with starboard four. Damn bitch is acting up. Can't get it to fire." He gripped his microphone. "Crew, we're having a little motor trouble with four. Stay ready. They're getting on it right away."

"Herr Geltman! Herr Geltman!" The S.S. sergeant was shouting as he ran, holding his machine gun away from his body, his boots clicking on the hard surface of the path leading from the hidden barracks.

Geltman felt his heart freeze like a stopwatch as he waited for the guard's report.

The sergeant's black helmet bobbed with his gasps as he barked out his message. "Barracks three, sir. The guard has been overcome and two members of the crew are unconscious as well."

"What? Explain yourself."

"Sir. I reported to change posts and found no one on duty. Inside, I found three unconscious men. The guard I was to relieve and two airmen. There has been a struggle. It must be commandoes, sir."

Geltman turned instinctively to glare back at the tower. "Shaeffer's damned pilot has come for his crew and his plane."

The sergeant blinked. "He can't have done it. A whole crew? Where can they have gone?"

"Don't you see, fool? He's stealing his plane. He's turned them all to traitors. I'll see them all in hell."

Geltman watched as the first of the bombers moved out of its hanger, its engine suddenly drowning conversation. The black giant rolled past them with its brakes screeching as Shumacher taxied it onto the runway.

"We must stop the take-offs." The sergeant started for the tower.

"No." Geltman grabbed the soldier's arm and shouted to be heard over the motors. "We stay on schedule. We only stop the third plane. We stop Reichmann. Take three squads and seal hanger three."

CHAPTER 18

Three of the tachometer needles vibrated methodically at their idle settings, but Chris Clancey's eyes were fixed with trance-like intensity on the fourth needle. It lay slack against the tiny metal peg of its gauge, registering only the silent vacuum of the impotent motor. He had taken them this far on skill and luck. Perhaps that luck had run its course. With cold acceptance, he realized that every second they were immobile was a second of hope lost. The window of chance was beginning to slide shut. Even now, he could see the other bombers beyond the hanger doors. The first plane was taxiing out of sight while the second was executing a slow pivot in front of its hanger. Chris pulled his pistol from its holster inside the flight jacket and laid it gently in his lap. In a moment, things would begin to come apart. The thin layer of surface tension that they had walked upon would break and they would sink.

The radio buzzed as the controller's voice crackled in the headphones that lay loose around Von Tripps' neck. Reinhardt looked at Clancey as he listened to the command.

"They want the pilot and co-pilot to come out for a final map check," Von Tripps said, nodding slowly to Clancey.

"Of course," Clancey replied. "Tell them we are coming." He flexed his fingers slowly on the pistol. A rap on the canopy behind him brought Chris' head around sharply. He was looking directly into the eyes of a grinning flight crew mechanic who indicated the window latch on Clancey's side of the windscreen. Chris released his fingers from the pistol in his lap and snapped open the small transparent rectangle. The mechanic was shouting over the milling drone of the motors echoing in the hanger around them.

"It was a fuel pump, sir. We have it correct. Try again."

Clancey saw the quick swallow of relief in Von Tripps' throat as the pilot closed his eyes before reaching up to throw the switches to starboard four. He listened with renewed tension as the now familiar magneto whine signaled the opening note of the motor's prelude. The long, fat blades of the propeller had just begun their lazy, hesitant rotation when Clancey felt Reichmann's hand clutch his shoulder. He turned to stare where the pilot pointed. The hanger doors were moving again, this time reversing their tracks. The crews were pulling them back. Beyond them, at least a dozen black-coated S.S. guards were rushing in from the contracting opening.

"What is this?" Braun's cry was part confusion and part anger. Clancey could see the bombardier's head rising from the nose seat before him and turning to stare over the bulkhead between them into the darkened interior of the cockpit. It was obvious, in that moment, that he had seen Reichmann behind the pilots, a lighted gauge illuminating Klaus' face.

Clancey's shot was muffled by the sudden burst of power from number four motor and Von Tripps' shout of elation was transmuted into a cry of shock at the sight of the bombardier's head snapping back against the clear nose of the plane from the impact of the bullet. Braun's blood streaked the canopy in an even scarlet stroke as the dead man slid downward, his hair serving as a grotesque brush.

"Go." Clancey shouted dropping down through the narrow passage to the bombardier's seat. He was aware that behind him, Klaus Reichmann was climbing into the seat he had vacated. Swinging into the forward station, Clancey grabbed at the handles of the mounted, heavy-caliber machine gun which was secured in a locked position alongside the bombardier's aiming tripod. As he used his feet to shove Braun's body away from the ball mount on the muzzle of the weapon, he drew back the bolt and gripped the trigger. He felt the plane vibrating as the motors revved toward peak rpm and the brakes squealed in protest. Before him, he saw the approaching guards suddenly slowing at the slicing menace of the propellers and the forward movement of the bomber. Their orders obviously required the capture of the crew, but, doing this without damaging the airplane or risking the detonation of the deadly cargo, must have added to their reluctance. Chris did not wait for them to decide on their next course of action. The big machine gun fired, its raw destructive force heralded by the overpowering echo of the hanger. The forward line of guards was blown back like leaves in a cyclone. Helmets, guns and even boots seemed to launch themselves with the horrific energy of the gun's blast. The entire building was swarming with bodies now. The flight crew was fighting to get away from the monster they had tended only moments ago. S.S. guards attempted to move to safe positions from which to attack while the ground crew continued to tug at the huge metal doors. Clancey turned a stream of lethal lead onto the men manning the doors as he shouted for Reichmann and Von Tripps to clear the hanger.

"It's no use." Von Tripps shouted. "The doors are too far in. We'll never clear."

Clancey let go of the trigger to lean forward, peering through the blood smeared Perspex to look. Quiet rolled over them as the guns quit firing, though the motors still churned their power. Clancey could see Von Tripps was right. He could also see the first bomber lifting off outside, its lights floating upward silently in the distance. "Ram it." he shouted. "No choice. We may get away with a shaved wingtip."

"No. I'll go."

Clancey turned to look past the pilots at Josef Zimmer turning the handle of the side entrance hatch. "You can't do it, Josef. It's too heavy." He was starting back through the metal passage when he heard Frankl.

"I'm with you."

The Jew paused in the hatchway only a second as the young radioman moved to join him. With a short nod, he moved on, leaving the airman to follow him through the opening.

Before he could drop back into the forward station, Chris heard the top turret guns firing. Looking outside, he saw a pair of S.S. guards falling away from a metal dock railing. He wondered how Lauda felt shooting Germans, but knew in an instant that the caustic navigator was saving his crewmate. Willy Frankl had crossed the final Rubicon for all of them. Hell or high water, they would not have to be watched now, only led.

Klaus Reichmann felt the muscles on the backs of his hands knotting as he held the throttles. His feet pressed hard on the brakes as he watched the two young men sprint across the body-strewn concrete to gain the right-hand hanger door track. The guns above kept barking. He heard the jingle of the brass ammunition jackets between the bursts as Lauda attempted to pin down the guards along the left side dock. He fought to keep from screaming; his stomach twisted with dread as he watched Frankl and the young saboteur straining at the metal handles of the door. It was impossible. They would never be able to do it. Where was the S.S.? Surely, the next instant they would be dead. Christ. It was moving. One foot—another—just a few more. Come on, you bastard, move. It must be now. "NOW," he screamed and felt the whole airframe shake as the brakes relaxed and the moment of inertia shifted with the conflict of energy and mass.

They were rolling forward now and Klaus felt power seeping into him with each rising pound of momentum. He could barely stand to watch the two struggling men who still heaved against the metal barrier as the bomber neared them. He heard the rear gunner firing and prayed the low fuselage would afford protection for the pair as they attempted to return to the plane. The night was opening before them, the cockpit filling with the welcome darkness as they nosed out of the hanger. Klaus was braking again and trying to keep his mind on the wingtip he was teasing past the metal door, but his eyes were drawn to the two figures waiting just outside the hanger.

Josef Zimmer was first, running hard, bending low. He was almost to the slowly moving hatch when the shooting started again. Josef threw himself the last few feet to the opening. With unbelieving relief, he felt the reassuring slap of strong hands gripping his forearms and looked up with surprise to see anguish on his savior's face. Looking beyond him, Von Tripps shouted, "Willy."

Josef looked over his shoulder. Behind him, stumbling onto his knees was the young radioman. A bloody gash of white bone and meat at the knee attested to the marksmanship of the S.S. guards. Josef did not make a decision. He knew, as he dropped back from the embrace of Von Tripps to the cement, that he could choose no other way. Reaching the wounded airman, he bent down to hook his arms under Frankl's shoulders. Over the gasping moans of the young German, Josef drew the man upright onto his tottering feet. Then, bracing himself, dropped him across his back, lifting him clear of the ground and turning to run after the slowly rolling plane.

Josef could see that the plane had stopped again clear of the hanger. The tail gun was flashing, sending tracers into the white glow of the hanger behind them. The pop of the guns at their back seemed inconsequential in reply. He felt his breath turning to fire as he forced his heavy legs on. Just as he neared the hatchway, he felt the razor-hot stinging along his side. There was a sudden loss of control as his body betrayed his will. His legs seemed to be running as before, yet everything was tumbling over and losing color. A part of his mind was aware of his dying, for this was not like anything else. Yet, there was too much to do to believe that. The pain seemed far away, as if waiting for everything to end before approaching. He opened his eyes and saw that the world had tilted. He realized he was lying on his side, his face was resting against the ground though he could not feel it. He could see the wheels of the airplane rolling upward on the vertical plane of the cement apron. He seemed to be looking down a dark tunnel and he wasn't able to move his eyes. He couldn't see anything now, but he could hear the moans of the young aviator lying near him and the motors of the plane as it moved away.

"They've had it," Chris Clancey said, pulling Von Tripps back from the hatch where the co-pilot stood staring at the two prone figures receding behind them. "We can't help them. Reichmann needs you."

Von Tripps swallowed the knot in his throat and pushing away
Clancey's hand, angrily forced himself back to the co-pilot's chair.

Guns chattered behind them again and Chris turned to watch
the S.S. troops taking up their chase apparently resolved to stop
them at all costs. He heard Hoffman firing from the rear gun
position and, from the long bursts, sensed that the gunner was
unleashing his own anger now.

"There's Prost." Reichmann was all business now as Clancey
moved past the pilot's station. "They're making their pivot to enter
the runway. We won't get much closer. He'll start his run in a
moment."

Clancey slid down the tunnel, calling over his shoulder, "Go
after them. Full revs. Close as you can get. Tell the gunners to
switch everything onto them. Hit the engines, the wheels. Watch
out for the bomb."

Arriving at the nose gun again, Chris braced his feet in the
stirrups and slewed the heavy machine gun around on its perfectly
balanced fulcrum. He was aware for the briefest instant of Braun's
dead face staring accusingly from the corner of the cramped floor,
a grim witness to his violence. Braun and Heidigger. New
phantoms to haunt his way. He wondered, for just a moment, if
only the eyes of the dead truly saw him. And then, in that same
instant, he was again reminded of the girl. Had she seen what she
wanted to see in his face? Or had she seen something he no longer
dared to think was a part of him? Maybe it was there now.
Whatever the case, Clancey had resolved to be whatever Reisa saw
in him for these last hours. True or not. If the girl needed to believe
in him, as Rudi had, then he would be that to the end.

He watched the other bomber begin rolling forward, pulling
slightly away from them. But now their plane surged ahead, its
motors screaming louder than ever and he wished he had had time
to pull on his earphones. He gritted his teeth and lined up the long
perforated barrel of the gun with the inside starboard motor of
bomber two. He could see the flashes of exhaust fire from the
motor framing a perfect target and now he followed his tracers,
walking the streaking projectiles up from the tarmac to hit into the
pod of the motor. He was aware of the top gunner's aim sliding
across the port wing, taking the outer motor, the farthest from the

fuselage; where the stunned crew no doubt twisted in their straps to watch in disbelief as their sister plane destroyed them. The shock of fratricide lasted several seconds before the rear gunner of the targeted plane took up a desperate defense. As Clancey turned to bring his gun to bear on this threat, he saw that the top gunner had already marked the new target and was slamming the paired fifties into the manned nodule at the tail of the plane. Closing on their victim, he watched shards of metal and glass tearing away from the rear gunner station as its guns fell silent. Now the starboard motor was afire and bomber two veered to port, rolling off the runway onto the soft earth, dipping as the landing gear cleared the hard surface. Clancey saw dark figures leaping out of the belly of the plane. Their shadows flickered against the illumination of the burning wing. They were passing the plane now, rolling by the stricken ship and its crew of forsaken comrades. He looked over his shoulder to see Von Tripps staring out the side of the canopy while Reichmann's eyes focused straight ahead—his face lit from below by the glow of the instrument panel, an impassive mask of determination.

"It's Prost, Klaus. He's screaming at us." Von Tripps banged a gloved hand on the canopy as he answered the shouts. "Shut up, you bastards! Shut up!" He dropped back in his seat, gasping, "My God. What have we done, Klaus? What have we done?"

"We've killed our friends," Reichmann replied, his eyes dropping to meet Clancey's.

Clancey saw Von Tripps turn to stare at the pilot.

Reichmann brought his eyes back to the field ahead of them and added, "And we are not yet finished."

Turning back to his station, Clancey saw movement in the distant blue lights. "They're moving trucks onto the far end of the field. Can we make it?"

Von Tripps cleared his throat. "Not with this weight. Not even with rocket assist."

The earphone crackled again. "Captain, there is a truck coming out from the hanger. I don't know how long I can hold them off."

Clancey looked down at the belt of armor piercing shells feeding into his gun. They'd already used more than half their supply of ammunition and weren't even airborne. "We've got to try. Throw out everything that isn't bolted in. Unclip the guns."

"No." It was Reichmann. "Captain Clancey, the bombardier controls on your left. Do you understand them?"

Chris glanced at the illuminated dials and levers. "Not the bombsight. It would take too long to dismount."

"The bomb. Drop the bomb." Reichmann's voice was calm.

Von Tripps started to object then stopped.

Clancey smiled in spite of their danger. It was brilliant. The bomb was unarmed. It hung, on an even level, only a few feet from the runway below them. It was flat-bottomed and built to withstand the torque of hard maneuvering, designed to break apart only when the charges unleashed the contents of its internal canisters. They had no tail wheel to catch on the weapon as they moved away from it. The only drawback was the lack of a shield. Without the bomb to screen them from the more devastating attack of the night fighters that must be circling above, they would become easy prey. But that was later. The way before them was obvious.

The whole airframe shuddered with the release of the massive weight when Clancey pulled the lever. The loud crash of the five-ton load hitting the cement below them—skidding and screeching on its metal hull—made every man wince. Clancey heard Hoffman's shout over the earphones he had finally connected. The upward rebound of the landing gear shock absorbers nearly twisted the ship out of control. Freed from their monstrous shackle, the powerful motors immediately surged with excess energy and began to hurl the mammoth plane down the runway at a pace far more suited to the anxious hopes of its straining passengers.

Clancey could see a soldier running from the parked trucks six hundred yards ahead of them and saw soldiers rising from the bent postures of riflemen to run from the strip. It was obvious to all that the behemoth could not clear the barrier of parked vehicles clogging the final third of the airstrip. He could do nothing now but tighten the seat constraints and brace his feet for whatever the next ten seconds would bring. They were in Reichmann's hands now.

Klaus Reichmann pushed the wheel forward, reducing the wandering pull of the tires, as the mighty torque of the motors tried to twist off energy through the spinning tires below them. Klaus knew he must anticipate, not resist, every suggestion of yawing rotation; for resistance burned energy and every ounce was needed to lift them into the air in the next six hundred yards. There was no sense looking at the airspeed indicator; it meant nothing now. No brakes could stop them short of the trucks. The decision had been made. He must not waste a single motion. Flat. Keep it flat, Klaus. He felt the drumming as the big craft began to rise on the tires. He felt Von Tripps' eyes on him waiting for the command for ATO rocket fire. Not yet. He must keep her ready for a single bound. To lift gently, as she was trying now, would produce a fatally flat angle that would drift them into the trucks. Klaus did not think of the trucks. He thought of nothing. He became the airframe, felt himself feeding into the very aluminum and steel below his hands and feet, becoming the spreading wings, pulling like the arms of a rower digging his muscle into the water to pull his slip forward. Now. He pulled back with all his strength and lifted the heavy airframe, pivoting on its main gear. "Now." The word was barely out of his mouth before Von Tripps triggered the six rockets tethered beneath the wide spread wings.

Klaus felt the black giant slowly heaving its massive bulk upward, shuddering at the mad barrage of demon flames as the ATO rockets scorched the pavement, exploding the air. Thick smoke bellowed out behind them, cloaking their still earthbound tail assembly like the wake of a swordfish throwing back a wide spray as it twisted free of the surface. Reichmann was that creature now, his nerve and muscle no longer discernable from the tearing energy he commanded into the waiting air. He became the great digging blades as they cut handholds in the sky. The earth and cement and trucks and men below fell away from him in an impossible downward swell as he rode the invisible wave of air that threatened to drive the crew out of their straps.

Von Tripps' hoarse whisper was audible in Clancey's earphones. "Jesus Christ, Klaus."

But Chris Clancey was a pilot and knew it wasn't over. The steep angle and the dropped flaps, the momentary surge of the rockets—these had given them the immediate thrust to bound above the trucks. But now they were falling off that angle. A stumble and they would take their full fuel tanks into the trees below. In the silence of the spent rockets, his ears strained for the faintest sign of a stalling motor. He could hear the air screaming around them as they nosed over again, not fighting the pull of the ground, but using it, taking on the added speed and praying they could change it into the critical lift they must have. Chris smiled around his clinched jaw in full admiration of the German's skill and force of will. This was gripping the sky—fighting it with bare hands. Some men flew airplanes. Klaus Reichman was a pilot.

CHAPTER 19

Hans Geltman trembled as the distant lights of bomber three rose from the tree line against the moonlit sky. His gloved fists tightened at his sides. The men standing near him kept their silence in fear of his simmering anger. Only one man ignored him.

Colonel Shaeffer crouched, resting on one knee, while he bent over the young airman bleeding to death before him. His right hand was beneath the blond head, shielding it from the tarmac. Shaeffer was trying not to see his son's face in the dying boy's. He made himself listen to the whispers from the pale lips. He grimaced as he sensed the arrival of Geltman at his side.

"Well, Shaeffer. Here is one of your Luftwaffe heroes. What does the traitor say? We need something to put on his grave."

Shaeffer leaned closer to the boy. He found his own voice strangely hoarse. "Frankl… why? Why did you all do it? What made you turn against Germany?" Staring into the flickering eyes of the airman, Shaeffer saw the last thing he expected. As Willy Frankl's gaze shifted to the Gestapo officer standing above them, a thin smile etched his dying lips. A smile of assurance that floated away with his last words.

Geltman grunted as the colonel carefully set Frankl's head back on the pavement and stood up. "Well? What did the dog say?"

"He said, 'We are not Germany.' "

Geltman glared at Shaeffer and then at the corpse. Breaking the silence with a furious shout, he kicked the body, knocking the legs into an awkward sprawl, like a discarded doll. Spitting out orders, determined to force order into the spinning chaos of the night by the sheer power of his voice and shivering with unrequited fury, Geltman turned back to Shaeffer.

"We still have one bomber on the mission. It must arrive. Call the fighter groups. Order the night fighters to shoot down Reichman."

Shaeffer looked at Frankl's body as the guards lifted it to remove it along with the corpse of the other saboteur. "Yes, I see what must be done," he replied. "Come." He turned and made for the main blockhouse.

Geltman barked orders to the S.S. squads as he followed the colonel on the path. "Secure the bomb. Have the science team out here with the crane. Remove the wreck. Have the bomber crew report to their barracks for a full report. I want total security at every point—and bring me the bodies of the commandoes from the wood."

Shaeffer kept his hurried pace without looking back; but once in the blockhouse, he turned to make certain Geltman was following him. "Come, Herr Geltman. We must make our official report from my office. We must make plans."

Geltman ignored the saluting guard as he stalked through the entrance and moved down the red glow of the hallway. Storming into the office past the door that Shaeffer held open for him, he moved immediately to Shaeffer's desk and picked up the phone. With the receiver at his ear, he turned to face the colonel who was locking the door behind them.

"You must call the fighter group immediately and demand all available units of night fighters to intercept them. What good are the damned night fighters, if they can't bring down one plane?"

Shaeffer walked forward and took the phone from Geltman's hand and moving past him to the desk, ripped the phone wire from its socket.

Incredulous, Hans Geltman stared at the impassive Luftwaffe colonel. "What the hell are you doing, Shaeffer? Have you gone mad?"

Johan Shaeffer took off his officer's peaked cap and dropped it on the desk. He began to unbutton his coat and calmly answered the glowering Gestapo officer.

"Tell me, Herr Geltman… have you ever killed a man with your bare hands?"

His comprehension dawning, Geltman could hardly speak as he stared at the Luftwaffe colonel before him. When he attempted to regain command, he felt his bluff voice failing into a pleading whisper. "Shaeffer, you must get hold of yourself, man. You are a German officer."

As he dropped his coat over a chair, ignoring the feeble response, Shaeffer continued. "I ask that, Geltman, because it occurs to me that every Gestapo man should have done that once or, at least tried to do it." He moved a step closer to Geltman who shifted backwards reflexively. "You are going to have your chance, Geltman, because you will have to do it to stop me from killing you. Don't be so surprised, surely Himmler's supermen are up to that. You see, I promised myself I was going to do this one day and now, that's the only thing I have left."

Reisa Konnings heard the hammering on the church door and, despite Dieter Lott's insistence that she take cover in the crypt, hid in the confession booth. Peering past the curtain edge, she watched as the priest moved to the door of the church. He hesitated as he pulled his nightrobe over his clothes and glanced back toward her before calling out to his would-be visitor.

"It is late. Is this an emergency?"

Reisa could not hear the answer but saw the priest throwing back the bolts and pulling the door open to take the shivering form of Ricard Zimmer into his arms. She raced from her hiding place to join them.

"What has happened?" Father Lott asked as he gently laid the limping youth on a cushion Reisa pulled from a pew and propped behind his back against the wall of the vestibule. Lott motioned for

Reisa to close the door which she bolted before crouching beside them.

Ricard coughed and started to shake. Wiping his mouth, he noticed a trace of blood mixed with his spit. His eyes turned to Lott, who nodded and reached for a handkerchief. Ricard swallowed and, in a harsh whisper, tried to speak again, pausing for breath between phrases.

"I don't know what has happened... one bomber was destroyed. Two others took off. There was a lot of fighting. The last bomber... the guards were shooting at it."

"You are certain? They were shooting at it?" Lott was trying to stay calm.

"Yes."

Reisa closed her eyes. "Klaus. He is flying after them—the other plane that got away."

Ricard coughed again.

Reisa looked at his leg and saw blood stains along his pants. "Have you been shot?"

"No, it is from the barbed wire. They were after me with the dogs—" He coughed again before continuing with painful but rising enthusiasm. "Then I remembered that Klaus had given me his scarf. I knew they had his clothes for scent—I hid the scarf in a thicket and climbed a tree and waited." Ricard stopped to swallow while Reisa and the priest waited for him to continue. "The dogs came and tore into the thicket. I yelled and shouted as they fought over the scarf below me. The guards came running. I waited with the grenade until they had all come—I killed them all. And the dogs." He coughed hard again; then, taking a breath, took up the story once more. "I heard a lot of firing after that, but no one came. I waited. I could just see the fire and the planes taking off. I had not realized I was cut until I was well along. I'm afraid it is my lungs—I can barely breath."

Lott rubbed a hand over his face. "You must rest, Ricard. I have to monitor the radio."

Zimmer raised his eyes. "There has been contact? Something is being done—something is happening?"

Lott nodded. "Yes. Something is to happen. God grant us it will happen well."

Reisa took Ricard's hand. "What of Josef, Ricard? What has become of Captain Clancey and of Klaus? You must tell us everything." Her face was hard. "I know about Rudi."

Ricard Zimmer nodded his understanding. "I was left to cover their path. If they lived, I do not know. I know only that your pilot must have flown that last plane. He could not do that by himself. Your Reichmann is a brave man, fraulein. He will not be—" Ricard paused and smiled. "He will not die easily, I think."

The girl raised Ricard's hand to her lips. "Thank you, Ricard," she whispered.

"Come, Reisa; help me get him to the crypt. You should make hot tea, and we will see to those cuts." Father Lott took Richard's arm. "We will need your courage again tonight, my son."

CHAPTER 20

"What is the damage?" Klaus Reichmann asked as Heinrich Lauda entered the dark cabin, bracing himself with a hand on each pilot chair.

"Not so bad as I thought, Klaus," Lauda replied. "No vital hits. No fluid loss. There's a loose wire slapping around from the radio mast that could be a problem but Paul is cutting it free. The receiving unit is still able to pick up course beams and the short scan radar seems to be working properly, but apparently our radio transmitter is dead."

"We have no one to talk to, anyway," Von Tripps said.

Lauda continued. "Hoffman says we've used up more than half of our ammunition. If we meet any opposition, we may not be able to keep them off very long."

"We can use the ammunition from the waist guns," Klaus said. "We don't have enough crew left to man them."

"That's not much of a solution," Lauda replied. The navigator looked at Reichmann. "No bomb, low guns, not much crew. What the hell do we do now, Klaus?"

Before Reichmann could reply, Chris Clancey answered, "We finish the mission." The spy pulled himself up from the cramped bombardier's nose bubble and settled himself against the airframe near the pilot's feet.

"Which is now what?" Lauda was angry. "Yes, we got Prost, we ditched our bomb, but every night fighter in the Reich will be after us tonight. We did what we could. The Swiss border is less than an hour from here. Haven't we done enough for you, Captain?"

Von Tripps reached up and gripped the front of Lauda's flight jacket. "I'm not flying the mission for this crazy American bastard, Heinrich," he hissed. "You know, we always laughed at Willy. He wanted so badly to be one of us. He'd have followed any of us to hell, but I'll tell you something, Heinrich," he tightened his grip on Lauda. "It's me that's going to follow *him* and I will throw anyone out of this airplane who tries to stop me."

No one spoke for a moment as the four Daimler Benz motors droned relentlessly outside the tiny pocket of life that slipped like a secret through the cold German sky.

Lauda shrugged as Von Tripps unclasped his jacket. "Good. Good then. We have quite a chase to catch the Black Arrow."

"I suggest you see if you can compute a course of interception, Heinrich," Reichmann said. "Speed and a deviation from our flight path would be helpful. Right now, we're following a ribbon on a map in Shaeffer's office. We're a pretty big fish in a barrel." He turned to glance at the navigator. "Let's see if we can make it a bigger barrel."

Lauda made his way down the fuselage to his equipment and maps.

Reichmann looked down at Clancey. "Well, Captain, you're the commando. Do you have any plans for getting us through the night fighters?"

Clancey grunted. "We should have been dead ten minutes ago. So, I'd say we're pretty much along for the full ride now. They won't be sure for a while if we plan to follow Schumacher or turn and head for Switzerland. That cuts the odds back a little. If Lauda changes the route, that trims some more off. We're flying light. We have a smaller crew and no bomb load. If God's awake tonight, we might have a crack at catching them. But there's another problem."

"Another problem," Von Tripps stared at Clancey in the dark. "We don't have enough?"

Clancey nodded. "The other plane. If we bring it down, even if they haven't armed the bomb yet, I wouldn't count on it not breaking up in a crash."

"Damn." Von Tripps slammed a fist on the control panel. "You hear that, Klaus? What can we do?"

Klaus Reichmann didn't look at either of the two men. He answered cautiously. "There is a way—if we're very, very lucky."

"Well, that's us," Von Tripps laughed. "We're so damned lucky we might live long enough for Geltman to hang us."

Clancey was studying the pilot. "What is it? What's your idea?"

Reichmann didn't answer but pressed his throat microphone. "Navigator."

"I'm busy as hell back here, Klaus."

"Shut up, Heinrich. Listen. You've got to lay our course to intercept exactly where I tell you."

Michael Kitchens frowned as the last man filed into the tent. Twenty men didn't look like much of an army, even if they were paratroops. But these were the cards on the table. Each man volunteered and volunteers always scared him. Well, no time to figure out these people and no time to run a psychological profile. Just hope their motivations didn't lean toward the death wish side of heroics and that they were as interested in coming back as going. He nodded to the sergeant at the entrance who nodded back as he pulled the tent flap closed. Michael stepped up on an empty ammunition crate he had chosen for a podium to address the semicircle that had formed around him.

"All right, men," he gave a quick smile, "you have five seconds to change your minds before I tell you the situation you are volunteering for. I will say it is extremely dangerous and I don't like it at all. It's been planned in the last four hours and it's got to go off in the next couple. Who's out?"

Nobody moved. Michael grinned, in spite of himself. "Shit for brains," he remembered his own parachute instructor's appraisal of the "Screaming Eagles" of the 101st Airborne. He turned his eyes back to the chart he'd hung from the center pole. He flipped over the front cover and tapped the enlarged black and white photograph of what appeared to be a patchwork of woods and pastures. He could tell the men were searching for something to identify as an objective.

"This, gentlemen, is what your objective looks like from 2,500 feet as of 0:900 this morning. You'll notice that there appears to be nothing here but a few common farm buildings and a scattering of dairy cattle."

Someone shuffled his boots. "Hell, Lieutenant, if we're russlin' cattle, we could get in a passel o' trouble." The Texas drawl was accompanied by a few subdued laughs.

"Shut it, McCoy. You yap when I tell you to." A hard, southern accent cut against the westerner's comment as a sergeant eyed down the private.

Kitchens continued. "Relax, Texas; we won't be russlin' cattle, but that's the only good news." He tapped the photo again. "This pasture is a rug. It covers a hard landing strip built to take the weight of three secret bombers bigger than anything they've ever had. They're hidden in disguised hangers you can't see. The planes are secret, but the big secret is what they're carrying." He looked at the men. "What I'm about to tell you now is so secret that if you speak about it outside of this tent or after the mission, we'll lock you up for treason. Now and forever amen. Got that?"

There was a grunt of assent and Kitchens proceeded. "All right. The weapons that are assembled below ground here in a bomb-proof laboratory and primed when they are ready to be used are biological weapons."

"Shit."

"McCoy."

"Damn it, Sarge. He's talkin' goddamned germ warfare. Ain't you, sir?"

Kitchens nodded. "That's it."

"Holy shit—sir."

The Georgia accent rasped harder than before, whether to squelch the private's interruption or to gain self-control, Kitchens wasn't sure. "So, McCoy, you goin' with us or is your butt in the damn dungeon?"

"Guess my ass is in the damn saddle now, Sarge."

Michael turned to look at them all. "The plan is simple. We've got a contact on the ground. We're going to do a low level jump in a field near here. The contact will guide us to the target and we will attack. Our mission is to burn out that laboratory and kill or capture anyone who might have any connection to the biological team. We want to destroy any planes and disable that airstrip."

The sergeant had a question now. "Sir, what kind of defenses does this base have?"

Kitchens looked at the photographs. "Our reports are sketchy. We know that, though it's a Luftwaffe field, the operation is run through the S.S. The guards are all S.S. We think that this is as much for suppressing any possible desertions as for protection from outside threats. They were hit by a small raid tonight. We don't know how successful it was, but it wasn't aimed at destruction, only delay. Perhaps that attempt will put them off their guard for a stronger action." Michael hated having to suggest such an unlikely hope to these men. He noticed they didn't even bother to refute him. They'd jumped at Normandy. From what he'd heard, this wouldn't be worse than St. Mere Eglise. "We get a little help. A flight of P-47s are scheduled to strafe the guard posts at first light. We hit right on top of that. That ought to put the odds more in our favor."

"Sir?" It was the Texan.

"Yes, Private?"

"Sir, I count twenty of us. I reckon we're maybe the meanest sons of bitches in the whole damn army, but I don't imagine you think we can hold this little ole farm 'til General Patton comes, do you?"

Michael didn't want to like this boy any more than he already did. "Private, the plan is to get the job done. If we do, a pair of C-47s with a P-51 cover will come in and scoop us all out of there as quick as damit. Right now, nothing runs on German roads unless our fighters aren't around. They don't have tanks to spare and my guess is that their main defensive effort is concerned with bombing raids, not commandoes. Most of the German army is elsewhere, thanks to our Russian friends and you boys." Michael turned to face the men whose faces were long in the hooded light. "Any more questions?"

Predictably, McCoy raised his hand. Michael noted that the Texan had come to serve as the unofficial voice of the young veterans.

"Sir? Just one more thing. If we get some of these germs—if a man gets this stuff on him or in him or whatever—can we do something for him?"

Sergeant Tucker stepped forward with a look from Kitchens and turned to face the group behind McCoy as he spoke. He drew his service revolver out and held it up. "The only known cure."

There was quiet as McCoy nodded. "Well. I asked."

"…but to steal the doctor's car." Dieter Lott protested.

"Is there another in the village?" Ricard asked.

"No. No, there is no longer another vehicle that has not been appropriated, and petrol is even rarer. But, Ricard, even the S.S. have understood we must have—"

"Ricard is right, Father." Reisa Konnings said as she looked over the crude map of the base that Klaus Reichmann had sketched that afternoon. "This is the best use of the car. And if we steal it, no one can blame Herr Ritter for helping the saboteurs."

The priest frowned but nodded. "Yes. You are right, of course. It is just difficult to take such measures. Of course, it is a small thing compared to what we have already done."

The girl put her hands to her face to stretch the tired muscles. "That is perhaps why it is so difficult. All the things we have done have been acts of war and the enemy has always been in a hated S.S. uniform. It is now necessary to do more. To stop now is wrong. Everything we do or don't do affects everyone. You know that. You always preach that—"

"You will use my words against me forever, Reisa." the priest replied. "Come, Ricard, I will lead you to the car. Ritter keeps it garaged in a stable behind his house. We must be very careful not to wake him."

Reisa folded the map and tucked it into her coat. "I will take the radio transmitter. I will wait just beyond the bridge. I won't come out until you stop. The moon is bright. Do not use the lights."

Ricard nodded. "Be ready. We will be in a great hurry."

Shaeffer leaned forward in the swivel chair and opened his
bottom desk drawer then fished out the shot glass and the bottle of
Napoleon brandy his squadron had presented him with at the end
of the last war. He'd kept it for a reunion that never occurred.
There weren't many of them left. In 1939, he'd promised himself
he'd open it at the end of this war. Wiping off the dusty label, he
looked through the swelling under his eye to the prone shape of the
Gestapo officer crumpled on the floor of the disheveled office. He
raised his glass.

"Well, here's to you, Herr Geltman. You put up more of a
fight than I would have thought you capable. If you had had the
right training, your fear might have made you dangerous. I have
not killed you, quite, but that is no favor, for you have failed," he
licked his lip. "And as you bully boys always tell us pasteboard
heroes of the Luftwaffe, failure is worse than death. Well, perhaps
you'll be able to measure that theory for yourself along with some
help from your colleagues. I don't know if you can hear me right
now, Geltman, but if you could, I know what you'd be saying
whenever you got past your curses." Shaeffer laughed before
pouring the brandy into the small glass. "You'd swear vengeance
on me and my family," he took a drink. "Swear we'd regret ever
being born. Well, the only thing I regret is waiting so long to do
this. You see, Geltman, I received a notice this evening that my
son... my son had died... heroically defending the Fatherland."
Shaeffer paused and then raised his voice, growling out the words
in mocking anger. *"Heroically defending the Fatherland."* He
brought his hand down on the table, splashing the drink across the
papers. "He was fifteen-years-old. He was defending a diseased
maniac and his court of parasites from what's coming to them. He
died for the likes of you, Geltman. He was all I had left to fight for.
All I had left."

Shaeffer reached into the desk again, laid his Luger on the
desk top and refilled his glass. He was very tired. The glass seemed
to weigh as much as the Luger. He raised the potent liquid in a
silent toast and drank it off in one long swallow. He set down the
glass and lifted the pistol. Without looking away from the picture

of his son on the table, he bid Geltman farewell. "I leave you to your friends. I go to be with mine."

S.S. Sergeant Bruno Buckholz, standing guard at the end of the hall, turned slightly. Had that been a shot? The doors were thick, built to withstand shock waves. Still, the sound was undeniable. Quickly, he moved to the door of the colonel's office and knocked. There was no answer, yet he had seen both the colonel and Herr Geltman pass inside several minutes before. He attempted to open the door and finding it locked, braced himself and kicked at the lock. The door was unyielding. He drew his whistle and called for help. Clattering boot steps from down the hall signaled the arrival of comrades. Smashing their weight against the door, the team was able to splinter the wood at last and force the broken door open. Entering the room, Buckholz stood stunned by the scene that lay before him.

The gun that had brought him to the room lay cradled in the lifeless hand of the dead colonel. Shaeffer's head lay flat on the green blotter of the desk, spilling his deep-red blood from the neat round hole in his temple.

The sergeant's attention was drawn from the desk to the floor of the wrecked room where another body lay behind an overturned chair. A shaking hand groped for one of the chair legs and a hoarse whisper brought the sergeant rushing to the side of the stricken Gestapo officer.

"Help me," Geltman gasped.

"You see the system is quite efficient, Captain," Klaus Reichmann said as Clancey squatted behind the pilot seats, leaning forward to listen to the pilot's explanation of their navigation. "It is the basic system we used in much of the English raids. There is an electronic signal beam pointing along a chosen corridor of space. The planes find the invisible beacon and follow it until they reach another beacon signal intersecting it that pinpoints another turn heading for the raid. It works very well unless there are a lot of the jamming strips about, but as we are following a deceptive route, there is little danger of such a thing."

"Won't they just switch the beacon off?" Von Tripps said, thumping a sticking temperature gauge. "We could hardly hope to pinpoint Schumacher without it."

Clancey shook his head. "I doubt it. It would mean postponing the entire mission. A delay now might mean no more opportunities before the Russians smash on out of position. Besides, they know the Allies know about the mission now. They can't be counting on getting away without a B-17 or B-25 pasting. I imagine, by now, they're probably trying to decide where to relocate the most critical equipment. God willing, they won't get enough time to try using it again."

"But if we ride the beam, they'll know where we are," Von Tripps objected.

"We can cut in and out, do a little zig-zagging. But we're going to have to do more than follow Schumacher. According to Lauda, we've got to overtake him in about two hours." Klaus said.

Clancey rubbed his chin. "I didn't think we were that far from Poland."

"We're not. But the raid is not going in straight." Reichmann's eyes searched the dark horizon, his face a pale red from the glow of the instrument lights. "The Russians have learned how to fly and they have more planes than brains. Our course hooks south and follows the Carpathian Mountains on the border of Yugoslavia. We hold a southeastern course until we come in behind the main defenses. There will be a series of diversion attacks to the north that will hold their attention. We will come in with the dawn light from the south and east. The drop will not require the precision of a normal bomb attack. The bombs are designed to rip apart at 760 meters and release canisters of the infected vermin in a wide scattering range."

"What is our plan then?" Clancey wished he had one of the Colonel's cigars. He wondered what the Colonel was doing right now. Was he sitting behind his desk, waiting for the German bombers to fulfill his wishes?

"Our plan—" Klaus Reichmann turned to face Clancey. "Our plan is to catch Schumacher in the mountains and bring his ass down. Hopefully, a little higher up than 760 meters."

Von Tripps laughed. "This is nice. We thread a needle in the dark, catch a fully-armed bomber, and bring him down on precisely the right spot. And not too hard, mind you. Very nice. What a good cinema this would be."

Clancey smiled. "*You* think we're going to do it, don't you?" It made it more hopeful to speak loud enough to cover the hum of the motors, he realized.

Reichmann leaned back. "It is all that is left to do. It is what remains, isn't it?"

Chris nodded in the dark. "All that remains."

Von Tripps slowly shook his head. "It is hard to believe we do all this to stop one bomb. We don't know if the damned thing will even work."

Klaus rubbed his knees with a gloved hand. "One bomb is certainly less than was planned, Reinhardt, but if it is able to infect even a small body of men, the fear will run rampant. The Russians might falter, but only for a time. What would happen to Germany then, would make the sack of Carthage seem no more than a beer putsch."

The intercom crackled with Lauda's voice. "Klaus, we must bring our speed up. Assuming Schumacher's speed to be the mission setting, we must make 385 kph."

"Can your engines hold that?" Clancey asked. "For two hours?"

"*That*, we will soon learn, Captain." Reichmann's hands inched the throttles forward, the tachometer needles dancing closer to the red quadrant of their gauges.

Geltman's head felt as if it were split open. He sat in the tower listening to the reports of various S.S. patrols and duty crews as they attempted to re-secure the field and clear wreckage of the broken second bomber. Both the bombs had been successfully returned to the magazine and work was now in progress to re-mask the field from above. Geltman's thoughts rushed from first one course of action to another. Which? He must tell everything to Berlin—Berlin must know nothing. Himmler must know all. He stopped himself. His eyes fell to the silver ring with the secret cyanide capsule. No, not everything. That was clearly impossible.

After all, he himself did not yet know all. He must first have a course of action to assure him of his own survival. He must have a scapegoat. Fortunately, he had one. Shaeffer had tried to kill him, had clearly plotted to sabotage the entire mission from the beginning. Thank God for that. He, Geltman, had discovered the plot just in time to save one crew and send it on its way to deliver the bomb. The failed assassination attempt on the Fuhrer in June and the ring of high traitors would make his own situation plausible. After all, if the Fuhrer himself had been fooled by these career soldiers—nearly murdered by them—of course they must accept this thwarted coup as evidence of his own unswerving devotion to the hard course. Had he not saved the mission?

What of Reichmann's bomber? Already in Switzerland? No report had indicated such activity. If only he had been able to call the night fighters in on the second plane as Reichmann took off. What had those fools thought was going on down here anyway? Of course, a commando attack had been transmitted to them. They had come in low, looking for enemy paratroops or even enemy bombers. They had lost contact with the big planes even as the fool Shaeffer had been attacking him. Wherever Reichman's crew had flown at least they didn't have the bomb. That had been the most frightening part of the whole business—recovering the bomb from the field where it had dropped. Jost had managed to get his people to do it, but Geltman wondered if they would have managed that if his S.S. had not been behind them.

He looked around the tiny office at the other staff members. A few Luftwaffe flanked by his own guards. He still had control. His men would silence the others if need arose. There were less than fifty Luftwaffe personnel on the base. There were sixty five S.S. at his immediate command. Geltman again considered the possibilities: if Schumacher's bomb was dropped on target successfully, if the commandoes are all killed, if the remaining bombs and equipment could be removed and Schumacher's plane recovered. He smiled. After all, it was impossible that the cursed Reichmann could do anything to stop the other bomber even if he had chosen to pursue it. Schumacher had a full fifteen minute head start on them and Reichmann's crew had clearly used up most of their ammunition in fighting their way out. Everything hinged on

Schumacher getting through. He would only make certain there was fighter protection waiting for Schumacher when he neared the front.

He surveyed the room again. There were not many Luftwaffe personnel who knew what had really happened here. Few who fully understood the mistakes he had made. The escape of Reichmann at the ceremony, the baiting of the trap with the false Konnings girl; these had been his decisions, calculated risks demanded by events unfortunately falling against him again and again. Still, if it were only a coup, if no American or English agents were actually involved, it might just be possible to overcome all the damage to both the mission and his standing. Well, if it was an American raid, it was sure to be followed up by bombers. Hours had passed with no reports of air activity against them. Still, the Americans only bombed in daylight, unlike the English. Geltman knew Berlin. This would be their thinking, also. If he could withstand the next day without attack, then, all was well. A simple traitorous mutiny put down. If the Americans came—he would be held accountable, regardless. He ran a pencil over the figures of personnel on the paper before him. If it came to it, the fewer witnesses to his mistakes, the better his odds. Those Luftwaffe officers who knew too much would never be interviewed in Berlin. They would be casualties of the "underground" raid like poor Colonel Shaeffer. A smile flickered on Geltman's lips. Or, perhaps, there might be an unfortunate accident when removing the bombs from the biochemical magazine. That would serve nicely. He could still be the hero. He had been betrayed like the Fuhrer, but he still held command.

As Geltman tried to convince himself of his impregnability, he knew there was one other possibility. "And one must have a plan for every possibility" he remembered Himmler telling him once. A smile grew as Geltman considered this new thought, but the broken skin of his lip split again and he grimaced in pain as his wound opened. He summoned a black-coated guard who moved to his side and bent to hear his hoarse command.

"Bring Dr. Yakuro and Professor Jost."

CHAPTER 21

"The one thing we have in our favor," Lauda's voice buzzed over the headphones, "is Schumacher. He's such a damned perfectionist. He took off on time and he follows the schedule like a monk. If nothing interferes, he will put his bomb on Zhukov's tea tray for breakfast."

Clancey was sitting on a parachute pack just back of Reichmann. In the cockpit dimly lit by the red and orange glow of instruments he watched the silhouetted pilot nod and turn sideways to speak to him over the motors. "He's right about that. I've seen Schumacher hold course when every other bomber dropped back when the fighters came in. He could throw that Heinkel around like a Focke-Wulf when he had to. A good pilot."

"Not one I'd fly with." Von Tripps added with a cynical chuckle from the co-pilot's chair beside Klaus. "They don't need a big graveyard for fools like Schumacher. The pieces are so small you can bury them in a cigar box."

"Okay," Clancey said, "we can figure on Schumacher, but that doesn't do us much good unless we're sure where we are. A minute's as good as a miss."

Reichmann tugged his collar tighter around his neck. "Yes, but when we hit the second beam, Heinrich will know exactly where we are. We'll be able to calculate his position then and he should be on the zag back from the south. We'll cross over and try to catch him from ahead."

"Cutting ourselves a little closer to the front," Clancey replied. "There may be a few Russian dawn patrols flying the mountains."

Reichman nodded. "Maybe. If Lott got word back that we are coming, there might be a lot of patrols. Let's hope they find Schumacher first."

Von Tripps rubbed his left sleeve with his gloved right hand trying to encourage the circulation in the cold altitude. "I don't think they'd listen to our story even if our radio did work. It will be light soon, and we're heading into the sunrise."

"That's it." Lauda's voice was dead serious in the earphones.

"What?" Clancey asked.

"The second beacon. We have reached the far turn, Captain," Reichmann said. "Now we trust ourselves to God, Schumacher, and Heinrich Lauda."

"Some kind of a bombing attack from the west or south? What kind of a balls-up report is that, Comrade?" Major Peter Ilyoshenko stubbed the crooked cigarette into his mouth as he ran his fingers though his anthracite-black hair and stumbled around the damp room looking for his boots.

"Yes, Major; it is less than nothing, but it is something. If the Americans say the Germans plan some sort of surprise weapon attack, it may mean that they only wish for us to slow our advance so that the capitalist nations may catch up with the greater prize of Germany while we wait listening to lies—"

"Shut up, Nikita," the major said wearily, dropping to the bed with his flying boots in his hands.

"Yes, my major."

"My head hurts. My back hurts. These Polish beds and Polish whores are killing me at night and these German flak guns are killing me in the day. I do not have to listen to you talking political shit before I have my cigarette lit, do I?"

"Here, my major." The sergeant held a match in front of Ilyoshenko's flinching eyes.

The major took a long drag on the cigarette and exhaled the smoke in a powerful stream above him. "Ah, Nikita, whatever duty this day brings, whatever glorious acts I must perform, I hope the fuck you get me a new pack of cigarettes before I return."

"Yes, Major."

"And so I am to take a patrol south? Well, if there is anything south of nowhere, then I am flying to see it. The Germans don't even have a plane that could make that circuit. Is it a zeppelin attack? Are we looking for the Hindenburg? For three days, I can't even bait the bastards into sending up a Focke-Wulf when I strafe their kitchens. Now, suddenly, we're supposed to brace ourselves for some wonder weapon. I'll tell you the wonder, Nikita. It's a wonder I don't shoot myself for being stupid enough to volunteer for this glorious role as a winged avenger of the revolution. I could be in Volgograd, working in a factory, side by side with Oxana, rolling brass shell jackets through a hopper, contributing something real to the great war effort.   Instead, I am puttering around the south of Poland waiting for some German propaganda phantom plane and wondering which sorry factory manager is trying to get up my wife's skirt."

Michael Kitchens looked at his watch as the mud-brown C-47 battled through the night. The backwash of its twin propellers beat at the treetops of the dark pines only a few hundred feet below him. The glowing radium hands of the time piece seemed to Michael like some speedometer of accelerating fate, a metronome out of control, measuring his headlong rush toward an unknown destiny. He almost smiled. It was Clancey who'd called him a poet and warned him against the romantic flaw in his character, accusing him of playing at war. Clancey had taken him around to McAndoe's burn hospital to get him over that. It had worked.

Michael looked at the rows of men lining the fuselage of the airplane. They sat sprawled against the rounded walls, their belly packs distending before them, their net covered helmets pressed down over their faces, shielding their eyes from the moonlight. Kitchens thought of the over-armored Tweedle Dum and Tweedle Dee from his childhood storybook. He wondered if Lewis Carroll had foreseen the timeless men waiting before him now. Eternal caricatures of the nonsense tale of war.

He became aware of an intermittent ratcheting sound from portside and moved close to the covered window. The small rounded viewport cut down light and discouraged ground fire. For a few moments, he caught the slash of tracer and knew the Black Widows guarding them above had encountered German night fighters. Again there were streaks, farther away, but no shots worked through the droning of the big motors. He swallowed, grateful at another hurdle crossed and turned to face the barely discernable figures of the paratroops.

It was at this precise instant that the red light flicked on above him. The men pushed up to stand in a single ragged file, each soldier snapping his metal clip onto the long cable down the center of the plane. The men were a study in black and red. Even the white Eagle patch seemed to take on a devilish tone. Kitchens wondered if anyone who ever saw a man in this light—wearing the black war paint, the severe helmet, and the fierce set of the eyes—could ever see him again without some ghostly echo of the moment, no matter how many years might pass. Some of these boys might be grandfathers one day and their grandsons would never know this about them, never really know this part of them. It could not be told, only lived.

Michael felt the plane rising, pulling up for a clean jump. There had been a great stink after Normandy about these low level night jumps. Some of the planes had gone too low and men had jumped to the earth without their chutes opening, leaving a string of broken bodies in the fields behind them.

He looked at Sergeant Tucker next to the door, which was open now—the wind kicking up the sandy grit from the dried mud they'd tracked aboard an hour ago. They were waiting for the green light. He knew the crew up front was waiting for the car lights—the three times on and off message that would signal the rendezvous. It was time. It had to be time by now. The light stayed red. Kitchens began to think of all that might have happened to the woman he'd heard on the Joan Eleanor. Perhaps no one waited for them below. Perhaps, the S.S. waited. Maybe the Colonel was right and Clancey had been captured on landing. He might be worse than a fool and leading these men to certain death. They could have made the wrong turn and might be miles from their intended target.

The green light switched on and every thought that had gone before vanished. There was a calming quality to that light, he thought, the release of the starting gun, the release of physical action that freed man from introspection and doubt. They were going out now in one-second intervals, whirling past him until the sergeant turned to him and nodded before ducking out, leaving Kitchens as the last man. Michael surged out the open rectangle thinking, "The last leaf down the grate."

Reisa Konnings leaned against the door of the old Horscht sedan, drawing the collar of the outsized uniform jacket close as she looked up again at the moonlit sky above the field. She wondered where Klaus and Clancey were now. Dead in some distant countryside like this? Perhaps captured as she had been, awaiting death at the hands of the S.S.? Or, somehow still pursuing their mad quest? When would it end? Had it ended already? She shivered, but not with the cold alone.

"You should rest in the car, Reisa." Father Lott looked larger in the darkness. To the girl, he seemed to have taken on a quieter, stronger presence in the last hour. Perhaps he had passed some invisible marker. No longer did he protest the dangers they faced.

"We must be ready," she answered. "You are the one who should be resting, Father."

"Soon, perhaps."

She smiled. "Then pray for us, Father. Pray for them."

The priest's answer had an almost ironic humor in its tone. "I have been doing nothing else. Perhaps I have at last learned to pray without ceasing."

She closed her eyes. "I have the words, but my heart sinks."

The priest's voice was soft. "I believe, Lord. Help my unbelief."

Reisa raised the watch to the electric torch. "It is time. We should see them."

As she waited in the darkness, a strange feeling fell upon her. The silent moments slipped past and the life line of hope slid away. There was a lightness, a lifting of weight from her shoulders.

What was this betrayal of concern? Was it the strength of the priest—of someone else to take the weight? It was not hers to do now. She had had to let Klaus go. She had held on to one thing only, Rudi. Though she knew he was dead, perhaps she held on to him even more. Now she was letting loose of it all. She could not solve or control it. In the darkness, she could sense it best; the denial of the world she lived in had ended and the dreaded challenge had come at last to her. She had met it and though a part of her had died, she was free. The crushing weight must be someone else's now.

"There they are." Ricard shouted from farther down the gravel roadway. "I hear them."

"Yes." Father Lott pulled open the door of the car. He leaned in to grip the light switch and flash the signal that Kitchens had radioed down to them at the last contact.

Reisa Konnings watched the western horizon above the black treetops as the faint hum of motors grew from a rumor to a pulsing echo of power. Through her tears, she saw the moving shadow against the stars.

CHAPTER 22

"So we will be closing on each other at a combined airspeed of over six hundred and forty kilometers per hour?" Klaus Reichmann felt the return of adrenalin as Heinrich informed them of the approaching confrontation.

"Yes."

"That's a very quick pass," Von Tripps commented hoarsely. "We might not see them even if we are on the right track."

Clancey licked his dry lips as he listened to the crew behind him over his headset. Outside his clear-bubble cabin, the night passed like the deep of the ocean. He touched his microphone button. "It will be light at this altitude in less than twenty minutes."

"That is our window," Lauda called over the headphone. "I calculated the approach for as much light as we could have. Any later and we'd have a devil to make the turn and we'd run out of mountains. That's what I understood—"

"Yes, Heinrich. Thank you," Reichmann replied. "You should be able to pick Schumacher up on your radar set?"

Lauda's voice was still irritated. "We can't attack by radar, not with these mountains if he's flying low. We don't know if the radar is functioning properly, anyway, after all that shooting. You know the forward radio mast was next to it."

Reichmann closed his eyes and rubbed them. The hours of tense flight had numbed him to the danger of the encounter he sensed approaching. It was as if he had begun this flight in a dream and now was waking to find himself uncertain in the reality of the breaking dawn. He looked across at Von Tripps who grimly held the other control yoke. He felt a sudden resentment at the unblinking trust his crew held for him. The very thing he had counted as the great bond of their success now seemed an unfair weight. He had used that bond to bring them into this. Had he not used his heroic front to inspire young Frankl to martyrdom? He was Reichmann, the man who had rebelled at the monomaniacal authority that commanded them. Yet had he not elected to play God Himself? He no longer felt the comfort of his men. Now, he saw in himself the same lonely banishment that Clancey lived within. The American had drawn him into the god game. Well, the game was ending soon. The sky was changing. The stars were fading. So were the dreams.

"I'm taking her up to 6,000 meters," Reichmann said. "We'll need the altitude to make a move on Schumacher and help our own radar. Get your oxygen masks ready."

Clancey could see Braun's dried blood on the nose glass now as the sky reappeared. The blood was the only reminder of the corpse that had spiraled away from the hatch as they had lightened the bomber, jettisoning any unnecessary cargo. Was he like that? Clancey wondered. Had he stripped his soul of all the unnecessary cargo? Or, perhaps thrown away something so necessary that to continue his journey was pointless?

The peaks of the Carpathians began to grow into rumpled shadows like the bunched-up blankets he'd used for mountains with his train set on the floor of his bedroom in Iowa. The wind-up train. Chris had been ten. The little wind-up key, the way the tracks fit together and the taste of the metal. It all came back in an unexpected rush of image and sensation. A strange thing to think of now. His mind wanted to go home. To be anywhere but here. He was bothered. This wasn't his pattern. His mind was shifting away from the equation like a sailboat cut adrift from the dock. His thoughts were moving on a wind he did not control. Would it betray him now when he most needed the focus of his training? The great wall—the dam he had built—had shifted. Clancey sensed a hidden fissure working through the foundation. With the next uninvited push, it could all break up. Or, had it already started?

"Going to oxygen," Von Tripps' voice intoned over the headphones.

Clancey pulled his mask flap into place and snapped the clips together. Slowly, he turned the valve and tasted the thin breeze of life flowing through the long rubber hose. They were rising now, reaching up for the roof of the sky. Clancey had always enjoyed threading this fine edge. This separation from the Earth. "The cold monastery of flight," someone had said. Was it St. Exupéry? Chris had wanted to meet the poet/flier but the Frenchman had disappeared; taken up in his P-38, perhaps to a garret in that monastery? Chris closed his eyes. No, the enchantment of separation, the temptation of the silence, was wrong, and to mask his fear with false romance was the real damnation. Worse than the denial of Heaven was the masking of hell as paradise. Chris closed his eyes. Was he getting too much oxygen? For so long, his mind had had the virtue of silence—the single focus, the disregard of rival thought—discipline so clean his concentration had had the efficiency of a bullet. Now, he no longer fought the swell of memories that tumbled freely through his consciousness. There was no remaining sanctuary from the self. The part of him he most feared losing was now a painful accuser. The life-giver was no passive spirit to be silenced but a forceful voice determined to speak through every cranny of his character. What was the demand? Couldn't this mad martyrdom at least be lived out with some sort of dignity? Jesus. Did he have to have a hope for salvation? No. No more hopes to lose. That was what he wanted; just to end it, without fear. There was no getting around it, the fear was there. For the first time in three years, he was afraid of losing something. He had returned to the kingdom of life.

Geltman listened carefully to the voice on the other end of the telephone connection. It was important to listen carefully, to know when to speak and how to say what he needed to say. One must present the plan so that it was obvious. They must see that his actions were the only actions that could have been taken. His logic must be air-tight from one end to the other. There must be no doubt in his voice. Doubt was the blood sign, the mark of the wounded— the one to be cut from the pack.

As he listened, Geltman's mind frantically structured his truth to encompass the spoken and unspoken commands of his superior. One truth was certain always; there must be a clear answer for failure and someone responsible for it. He had learned this. If you were uncertain where to draw the line of responsibility, then they would draw it behind you. They must always be given success, even when they must be given a failure. What Geltman gave them now, he was not sure of.

"Of course, Commandant," Geltman's eyelids narrowed reflexively to assume the caricature of confidence he was attempting to convey. "We have followed our procedures for such an attack. The saboteurs have been hunted down and destroyed." He shook his head. "Their identity is sketchy, but I have reason to believe they were a small cell of the Jewish/communist underground. There is little evidence that this was a planned Allied commando raid, especially as it seems to have been so poorly supported. As we have long suspected, our true enemies are within. That is why the work of the Gestapo and S.S. is so important now."

Geltman instinctively toned it down. His last harangue had become more emotional than he should have liked. It was important to be in control and to exude control. The commandant was taking stock now. The questions had changed. Geltman must change smoothly as well.

"Yes, Commandant, I agree, it could have been much worse. It is only due to the efficiency of our S.S. guard that we have recovered the bomb the saboteurs attempted to steal. In spite of all their efforts, we have not lost a single biological weapon."

Good, the more technical the questions, the better. "No, the Luftwaffe personnel assure me that the second bomber is not too badly damaged for repairs," Geltman lied. "They are certain that, with the right support, it should be operational again in a short time." Well, he thought, with the right encouragement, they will repair it, anyway.

Geltman squinted. There was no avoiding the one thing that could not be ignored. "No, my Commandant, the lost bomber has not been located. We believe it has either crashed or been heavily damaged. It is doubtful it could have been flown to Switzerland. The western radar net has shown no activity since the bomber raid to the north an hour ago. Before that, there was no activity that could possibly be the flight of the 264."

His lip twitched from a stab of pain at the corner of his mouth where a blow from Shaeffer had broken a tooth. The commandant was reminding him of the importance of keeping the bomber from contact with the Allies. Didn't the fool know he understood this? He felt the twinge again at his instinctive smile on answering his inquisitor.

"The routes south and east, of course, are less thoroughly covered, since the large radar are along the other fronts. However, should they attempt to escape south, they would find no airfields available and our perimeter flights have been alerted to shoot down any unauthorized craft." He paused for the question. "No. There is, of course, no mention of the mission. All is still secret. The eastern route would prove foolish as well. Assuming they might gain the Russian front in a direct path, the Russians would undoubtedly bring down a bomber such as this and our fighter cover will be waiting to escort the number one bomber when it arrives in the bomb run zone. They would make small work of the traitors. In fact, I have instructed one squadron to extend their interdiction farther east than previously charted at the recommendation of my Luftwaffe advisor. This should make certain that any suicidal attempt by these traitors to track down our lead bomber would be dealt with shortly."

He sensed he had been talking too much and paused. The silence was uncomfortable, but he must proceed as if he were waiting for nothing.

"We have a cover of night fighters to screen for any sign of incursion. Though I believe the field is secure, I am having the most sensitive materials prepared for removal. The damage from the attack is being controlled. We are monitoring progress of the mission through coded signals with Schumacher. Such signals have, of course, ceased until the weapon has been delivered. On return of the bomber, I suggest a transfer of equipment might be practical in case the underground has been able to get any information out. I would request transport for the biological magazine and science team to a more secure location until we are certain of our success."

The line was quiet for a moment. Good. They were thinking. A fast answer meant they had already decided. He was still part of the solution, not the problem. If his hunches were all right. He'd always managed to stay near the front of the pack. He had gone from strength to strength. Perhaps, this was the final hurdle. Perhaps, he would run at the front soon.

"No, of course, I am glad to have any assistance you wish to send. An inspection of the base could only aid me as I concentrate on the recovery of the strike team. Not at all, mein Herr. I would insist on such an inspection had you not suggested it. Tomorrow afternoon, then?"

Geltman set the receiver on its cradle with a pensive click. Damn. The old bastard didn't trust him altogether. Well, it would all depend on who they sent. He must be certain that he knew everything there was to know before they arrived. Surprise was a thing they never tolerated. Surprise meant incompetence.

"Herr Geltman," the sergeant saluted as he stepped into the office.

"Yes, sergeant?" Geltman forced his eyes to assume the assurance of command again. No one, not even the lowest soldier, must ever suspect him of less than total control. He realized that this was his religion—the litany of the orthodox. To exude control proved one's right to it.

"The bomber's gunner we found unconscious in the barracks, sir, is able to speak now, the doctor reports."

Geltman frowned. "And he will." Geltman moved past the guard, drawing on his gloves determinedly as he started for the infirmary. This Kroft might be a victim of the saboteurs but they hadn't killed him. And now he was going to tell Geltman who 'they' were.

"We can be there in two hours," Michael Kitchens said into the microphone of the Jane Eleanor set beside the Hortsch. His eyes were on a map spread on the hood and illuminated by a small pocket torch held by Sergeant Tucker. He looked up to see the grim-faced teenager with the German machine gun on his shoulder nodding to affirm his remark. Michael was impressed with the work this little band had done. The girl and the priest had been precise in their contacts, and the car they had stolen would make carrying the explosives and light mortars a much simpler job. He turned to survey the squad of paratroopers gathered along the side of the road resting quietly as he continued. "You bring in the P-47s with the rockets at exactly 0600. Make sure they hit the points on the photos I showed you. The targets don't look like much, but they're not supposed to. We'll be moving on the barracks and the biological magazine. We'll either have the field taken in fifteen minutes, or we'll be screwed. Anyway, make sure the pickup is ready for touch down on the red flare. Halfback over."

He set down the microphone, switched off the set and sensed the last link with his army slipping away with the invisible Mosquito three miles overhead. He saw the questioning face of the priest as a thin profile in the electric torch light.

"There are so few of you. You are certain you can do this attack?" The man's English was better than Kitchen's German. They'd conversed in Kitchen's language since their first meeting.

Michael tried a reassuring nod. "We have precision air support, Father. We have only got to knock out the guard and destroy the armory. It is clearly marked. We will be gone before they know what has happened here. You understand?"

The priest smiled. "I understand that you are brave, my son."

Kitchens looked over at the girl standing next to the young saboteur. "Do they understand, Father?"

Dieter nodded again. "Yes." He put a hand on the officer's arm. "I must ask you a favor, Lieutenant."

Michael waited.

"When you leave, you must take them with you. Both of them. The boy is Jewish. I have hidden him for many months. The girl has no one here now."

"Yes, Father, I promise. And you?"

"No," Lott said quickly. Then he spoke again, smiling, "No. I have my orders, too. My war will not end so soon as yours, Lieutenant."

Michael looked at the girl. "I'm sorry about her brother," he said. "I heard about him. She has no one else?"

Lott frowned. "Only God knows that answer."

Kitchens looked at his watch. "Yeah, well, here's hoping He's listening."

"It is close," Von Tripps was saying. "You think we could have missed him?"

"Lauda's radar set should have picked him up by now," Reichmann agreed. "In a few minutes, we will be past hope."

The morning sun was breaking over the cloud cover; the tops of the Carpathians poking up through the slow-moving channels of white mist below them. If the reports were right, the cover would be breaking up.

Clancey grew sick of the rubber mask, the sounds of his breathing in his own ears and the unbroken uncertainty of their path. He pulled off his gloves to rub his hands together to fight the unrelenting cold that pressed constantly against him. He watched the sunlight shifting across his hands. The shadow lines of the canopy sliding like zebra stripes on his skin. His skin—yes, it was the skin of a professional assassin; but, he knew now that it was also the skin of the ten-year-old on the Iowa farm. He was the teenager who'd hitched a train to meet Wiley Post, the young man who'd traveled Europe flying everything he could talk himself into. He was the volunteer in London who'd fallen in love with Anne and lost her and his heart in the Blitz. He was the captain who led his crew out of the prison camp and entered the dark world of the spy. He was the man who'd unsuspectingly glimpsed himself again in the eyes of Rudi Konnings and given himself to the faith of Reisa. And now—here in the light-filled cockpit—was given himself again. Clancey closed his eyes. He had been given his life again, just in time to die.

Peter Kroft's eyes hurt. The blow from the pistol had given him a convincing alibi and an enormous headache. Bandaged, he lay propped against the pillows of the infirmary bed and tried to dismiss his friendship with Klaus Reichmann from his mind as the Gestapo officer stared down at him. Peter noticed the gloved hands gripping the metal railing and could see that the knuckles under the black leather were straining as Geltman fought to keep an appearance of cool, penetrating calm. He could tell by the damage on Geltman's face that someone had had a time with the Gestapo man as well, and he hoped it was one of the crew.

"No, Herr Geltman. I'm not sure how many of them there were. It was all so fast. They were on us and we had no time to even call for help."

Geltman nodded. "Perhaps you were surprised that they were led by your pilot friend, Klaus Reichmann?"

Peter licked his lips. "I… was shocked. I could hardly believe my ears when he told us of the plan to steal the bomber. It was fantastic."

"And the others? They thought it was fantastic, too?"

"Yes. I am sure of it, though—"

"Though what?"

Kroft wondered what point there would be in trying to pretend that any of them had truly resisted. What point in making the argument that their leaders had gone mad, that they were joining their only real leader in resisting the madness around them. He must not sympathize with those who could turn from their duty. "I was stunned. Horrified. I begged them to resist, but Reichmann said they would be well paid. A fortune for each man."

"What fortune?" Geltman scoffed. "How could Captain Reichmann produce a fortune?"

Kroft swallowed. "It was the leader with him, the one who seemed in command. He must have been the commando chief. He was so sure of himself. A true killer. I thought he would shoot me when I resisted."

"And why do you think this commando did not shoot you, Kroft?"

Peter felt his mouth drying up. "I don't know, sir."

Geltman took a deep breath and let out an impatient sigh. "Just why do you think this man was not a traitor like Reichmann,

Kroft? Perhaps he was a Jewish underground leader. What do you think? Isn't it very likely?"

Kroft tried to think carefully as he spoke. "Perhaps, sir. I think he was an American—something about his voice. Just different."

Geltman's hands had stopped moving as he stared at the wounded airman. There was silence as Kroft wondered what raced behind the cold blue eyes.

"Thank you, airman. Remember that this is a secret matter. A Gestapo matter. You are not to speak of it with anyone else without my permission. Is that understood?"

Kroft straightened instinctively and pain shot through his skull. "Yes, sir."

Geltman turned and left the room.

Outside, in the cold between the buildings, Geltman felt the frozen dagger dig deeper into his bones. So, it was commandoes. Then, it was not over. Headquarters would want to know that. They would find it out. It would change everything. He paused and looked up at the starry sky. Perhaps, it had already changed. Perhaps, it would be best to think of greater possibilities. He still had time to come up with new ideas. There had been no follow-up bombing raid on the field. Perhaps there was a way for this to end quite well for Hans Geltman after all.

CHAPTER 23

"Mein Gott! Captain!" Lauda's voice rang over Reichmann's earphones so loudly that he grabbed the headset.

"What is it, Heinrich?"

"The radar, Klaus. There are several headings. It has to be Schumacher, but there are *more*."

Clancey's voice was cold. "Fighter escort?"

"Shaeffer must have figured our course and pushed a unit further east to meet us," Reichmann answered.

"Where are they?" Hoffman, the tail gunner, was asking.

Everyone was trying to get through to Lauda. Reichmann called for silence. "This is the pilot! Everyone keep your eyes open and listen. This will be hard, but we *will* get the bomber. Conserve your ammunition."

Lauda's voice was the professional again. "Captain, there are three sets of headings. All from different points. I think they must be fighters."

There was silence as Clancey listened for Reichmann's response. Whatever excitement the sightings had brought, this crew was all business now.

"Heading for the bomber, Navigator?"

"Starboard 80 degrees, Captain. He's going to cross our nose if he does not alter his course. Range is three kilometers and closing. Fighter plots are port 10 degrees and port 70 degrees. Both are better than five kilometers and closing."

"There's Schumacher. Two o'clock, running low." It was Von Tripps. "Six hundred meters below us."

"I have him. Full throttle. We're going in." Reichmann's doubts were forgotten as he set the big plane into a tuck for speed.

Von Tripps shook his head. "I'm glad our radio is out. I'd hate to hear what he's calling us."

Clancey called over his throat mic, "He's seen us. He's banking away." His hands, gloved again, pulled absently on the bolt, unlocking the heavy machine gun on his right. His braced his feet as he freed the muzzle of the cold weapon. He could see the end of the ammunition belt trailing onto the floor below him. He had maybe seven seconds of firepower left. It would have to be enough.

Lauda's voice was tight in Chris' headset. "All groups converging, Captain."

"Get off the radar, navigator, and get up in the turret." Reichmann, the pilot, was in total command; the cold air of the cockpit again charged with his energy as he bent the plane and its crew to his purpose.

Chris could see the wide-winged black bomber below them. It grew inextricably larger as they dropped down; their dive overmatching the belated surge of Schumacher's motors. Chris' eyes were drawn to the dots sliding from impossibly high above them—the all too familiar Focke-Wulfes dropping in even faster dives than their own. The fighters must be using belly tanks to have come so far, he decided. Idly, he wondered if they held any hopes of a return to their home fields. He could hear Hoffman and Lauda shouting from the rear of the plane as they fired their guns at the on-coming escort. Now he saw that Schumacher was making a hard turn to port, forcing Reichmann to pull the big plane over in a murderous bank that threw them against their straps. It was maddening to see the target slipping out of his sights just as they were nearing range.

There was a sudden, passing shadow and a quick slap of rival noise against the whine of their own straining motors as the 190s screamed past them and the staccato bursts of machine gun fire raked over their port wing. Clancey had instinctively pivoted his gun to follow the broad-nosed profiles as they shot past above his head. His grip tightened and he felt the bursts of power as the gun threw a futile train of metal after them. He cursed himself and vowed to keep from wasting his few shots on the fighters. He must trust Reichmann to get them close for the kill. He must not save himself. The fighters were the end of that option. Again, he brought his eyes to their dark twin now descending closer to the mountains below, ducking between clouds of mists. Schumacher was using all his skill to throw them off their attacking dive.

Again Clancey heard Lauda's warning and braced his nerves for the assault of the Focke-Wulfes as Reichmann pulled still closer to the heavily loaded bomber below them. Less than a thousand yards were melting away, and now tracer fire was streaming back at them. A shell hit the clear nose with a resounding slap and streaks ran across his vision, yet the heavy canopy held against the shot. Where were the fighters? They should be on them by now. If only Reichmann could keep them alive just a little longer.

"By God, you are right, Yuri. They *are* Focke-Wulfes. And they are mixing with some poor bastards down there. Take them in pairs, boys." Major Peter Ilyoshenko glanced at his wingman in the heavy YAK off his starboard side and threw the throttle full forward. The YAK was not a high altitude fighter and the 190s would have the advantage if the Germans climbed. But, perhaps, his mother's prayers were working for him in spite of the red stars on his wings. Ilyoshenko grinned as he saw the German fighters lining up for another pass at the mysterious plane in the distance, apparently, they were oblivious to his patrol. Despite his delight in the exposed vulnerability of his natural prey, his eyes were caught by the large planes the fighters were angling for. For an instant, he was struck with confusion. This was no Russian plane, or any Allied model which he knew.

It was big. They were big. Two of them. They seemed, for all the world, to move against each other in a wild weaving pattern— far too low to be a planned formation. They were a mystery except for the large Luftwaffe crosses on their wings and that meant enemy. Why were these fighters running an attack on their own bombers? Something was very wrong here and Ilyoshenko did not like things that puzzled him. There was a choice. Concentrate on the fighters or take the bombers. Necessity was the great General that Major Peter Ilyoshenko had always followed. Now, he realized that his advantage on the turning Focke-Wulfes would last no longer if he chose to seek the big planes first. They must wait. His smile returned as he pushed the long nose of the YAK into the blind spot of the 190 ahead of him; its pilot intent on the lumbering giants below. Ilyoshenko's cannon shells, which had broken up Panzer tanks around the Don that winter, now slammed into the soft, white underbelly of the German fighter. The major shouted with frightened exuberance as the pieces of the exploding fighter rattled off the heavy armor of his YAK. The yellow-orange ball of burning gasoline surrounded him for an instant as he flashed through a hole in the air that had contained his victim only a moment before.

"Two coming in at eleven o'clock." It was Lauda.

"Keep them off.   I have to close on Schumacher." Reichmann's voice was pure ice water—a surgeon focused on the tip of his scalpel.

"Got one. Wait. That wasn't me. It's—Russians!" Lauda's surprise overrode the fear in his voice. "It's a miracle."

"Straight from the devil," Von Tripps called back to the gunners. "They're *all* against us."

Chris knew the truth of Von Tripps' call; but he would take a miracle now and wonder at its source later—if there were to be a later. Taking a deep breath, he brought his eyes to sight the gun barrel protruding through his cracked canopy and fought to keep his attention on the weaving bomber ahead. Amazed, he watched as the big plane dropped closer and closer to the mountain ridges below. Schumacher was trying to use the peaks and cloud banks to throw off the pursuit of his squadron leader.

Chris heard Von Tripps' nervous shout to Reichmann. "Has he armed the bomb?"

Klaus reply was even toned. "If he has, he's just 240 meters above detonation."

Chris swallowed and again braced against a shift as he sensed
their entry into the level of the mountain peaks. It was as if they
had dived from their eagle's track in the sun into a dark sea of
dangerous shapes and shadows. Rock and ice shot below them
throwing up cushions of dangerous updrafts and shearing
undercurrents. He was certain they'd tagged a wing when the
explosion of a fighter above them rocked the mountain air.

Klaus heard the gasp over his headset. He could not discern
the shells breaking into his plane in any objective manner, only the
faint sense of a disruptive vibration fighting against all the
thousand other resonances working up his arms, feet, and spine.
The hit was bad. There was no scream of agony, no cursing—the
hopeful herald of a less than vital hit. Only the gasping silence
over the headset. "Lauda."

"Here, Captain."

"Clancey?"

"Here, Reichmann."

"Hoffman?" He waited.

"Hoffman." Von Tripps repeated over his microphone. He
glanced at Reichmann and shouted, "I'll take his gun, Klaus."

"No. There's not time. I need you here. Help me hold her in
the banks. It's getting hard."

Reinhardt Von Tripps nodded. His hands were sweating as the
two men worked in concert; he followed the lead pressure of his
captain in an almost simultaneous response. He had never seen
anyone fly a bomber as Schumacher and his captain were doing
now. He would never have believed it could be done. Again and
again, his nerves had screamed inside him as he watched the plane
ahead floating just over and around the rock ridges like a giant
stingray rippling through a coral reef. It was as if Klaus and
Schumacher were conducting some intricate ballet that they, alone,
understood and might execute. Schumacher had the advantage of
turning with the terrain while Klaus must react with even greater
reflexes, drawing the line between them closer and closer while
anticipating each of his quarry's moves before they were made.
Reinhardt wondered in a part of his consciousness if Klaus were
watching the control surfaces of their rival rather than the moves

that followed. If that were true, he did not wish to know it. He was afraid to look closely at anything near to hand, afraid to let his concentration stray for an instant lest his muscular grip hold a flash too long and freeze the unhesitating flow of Klaus' lead. Often, over beer, he had boasted that he would fly into hell with Klaus Reichmann. And now he began to think he might fly out of hell with him as well.

Lauda called from above. "I'm out. Lost them. Bastards are off chasing themselves."

At that moment, Klaus saw it. The inevitable bobble as Schumacher corrected a mistake. His plane lurched away from a threatening wall of rock. Klaus' right hand crushed the throttles forward, surging them into the slipstream of the first plane and moved them in. He called for the kill.

"Clancey."

Chris Clancey pulled the trigger back on the machine gun as the tail of the target bomber swam into full range. The gun bucked reassuringly and he guided the tracer in a quick arc that laced into the rear gunner's station and across the inside port motor. He was surprised at how quickly the stream of smoke broke from the black plane. All at once, an unexpected, ringing silence severed his concentration like an amputation. Desperate, he searched wildly for the source of this disaster. Several rounds hung from the breech. With a curse, he slammed the bolt again. It was no use.

"Jammed." Chris called up to Reichmann. "I got one motor."

Lauda was down, hugging the back of Von Tripps' chair. "Pull up, Klaus. For God's sake, get us out of this now. Schumacher's hit. He won't make it."

Clancey pulled himself up on his straps and looked back at the pilot's face. There was silence for only a moment. It seemed to drown out the roar of the motors shaking against the tortured air around them. Reichmann's eyes never turned to his, but Chris knew that he saw him—saw everything—perhaps even Reisa.

Klaus Reichmann's hand on the throttles slid forward. "No. It is not enough. Brace."

Clancey had heard of fighters ramming bombers. It was a wild gamble. A chance to cut away a control surface and pray you had enough propeller left to get back on. He had never imagined a bomber attempting such a maneuver. The plane ahead was slowing; its stricken motor was causing some problems. Schumacher seemed to be looking for a chance to let his top turret gunner have a burst at them. There was another slapping echo as a volley ran across the nose of the plane. Now, Klaus swept them up, cresting a wave of frigid air, hanging them an agonizingly eternal instant directly above the massive black craft below. They plunged downward.

Clancey's stomach turned over at the endless drop. His grip on the straps slipped as he felt the portside propellers biting into the starboard rear fin, tearing out chunks of metal. They plummeted in a terrifying spiral that sent him crashing into the bottom of the canopy. His face smashed against the glass in a violent impact that promised to be the last moment of his consciousness. Blindly, he pulled himself up against the wild forces of the plane's next hard bank. Through the blur of his streaming eyes he was only vaguely aware that the other plane was crashing into the snow-covered side of a ridge below them. Then, Reichmann was sweeping them up, clawing to the surface of this cloud world.

"Nothing, Major. They have vanished."

Ilyoshenko grunted, bewildered. "Crashed? Turned? What the hell were they, Yuri?"

"I don't know, Major."

Peter felt the blood in his chest receding again. The fight was over. The 190s had been blown apart. Three German fighters this far east and south. To do what? It didn't make any sense. It had been easy. They'd hit them with complete surprise. It had taken only a minute. Everyone had come through all right, even Petrovich. He was always amused when the woman came back. She showed too much aggression.

"We'll make another sweep. Keep your eyes open. Form on my port wing." Banking the YAK slowly he watched the other fighters sliding into formation and frowned at the low cloud cover along the mountains below. If they could hide in that, they were too brave for him, anyway.

"Major. Our fuel is running low."

"Yes, Yuri—Babushka. We'll turn back." He shook his head as they eased back around, pulled up, rose away from the mountains and headed back for the flat, open stretches of Poland to the north. His thoughts were still on the mysterious shadows twisting through the mists he'd watched. Whoever you were, you got away this time. But what the hell were you playing at? Wonder weapons? Nobody tries to shoot down their secret weapons. Maybe the Germans were deserting. An airplane would be a good way to do it, but not here. "Flying the wrong way to surrender, boys."

Chris pulled himself back onto the bombardier's chair and peered through the cracked canopy. He noticed a smear of his own blood on his pants leg. His face throbbed from his impact on the canopy. They had been fortunate. The clouds were shielding them but now they masked the peaks below from their inspection.

He heard Von Tripps above him. "We'll never find them, Klaus. Let it go."

Clancey knew by now that this pilot would turn back from no portion of his mission, even this final, useless search. He was about to say this when the co-pilot's voice broke against his thoughts.

"There. It's Schumacher."

Clancey leaned forward and, in a quick moment of clear air, saw the broken bomber pinned against the snow-covered ridge. Black smoke boiled away in the mountain updrafts obscuring their vision as Reichmann swept low. In the next instant Clancey saw the flattened cylindrical shape of the plague bomb a hundred yards ahead of the plane, half-buried in the snow. A deep furrow traced its slide over the ridge among the rocks.

"Altitude?" Clancey asked.

Von Tripps' answer was a hollow whisper. "790 meters, more or less."

Lauda's voice broke over Clancey's thoughts as the wreckage and bomb disappeared behind them in the mist. "Klaus. Paul is dead."

There was silence.

Von Tripps cleared his throat. "It is done, Klaus. For good or evil, we're done. What do we do now?"

Clancey waited for the answer.

Reichmann's voice was very tired. "We go home."

Lauda's reply echoed coldly in the earphones. "We haven't got one."

Chris Clancey was surprised by Klaus Reichmann's answer, for he realized it was also his own. "Yes we do, Heinrich. Now, we do."

CHAPTER 24

Michael Kitchens ducked his helmet into the cold earth to shield his face from the spinning shrapnel. An orange ball of flame signaled the detonation of the blockhouse a bare second before the shock wave of sound roared over him and the six men lying near him.

"Satchel charge cleaned them out, sir," Sergeant Tucker assured him, rising from the ground on his left. "McCoy's squad will be ready for any stragglers trying to make the hangers over there."

Michael turned as his retinas tried to readjust to the morning darkness from the spear of light the explosives had stabbed into them. "What about the halftrack? I haven't heard anything from there."

Tucker shook his head. "They'll wait on the guards to come out for it. Cross is good."

Kitchens believed that. This bunch was all he could have hoped for. They worked in the dark better than any team he'd had and the sentries had gone down without a hitch. Even in the early light, the P-47s had hit the field right on the button. Their rockets had smashed the hidden sheds and huts that Reichmann had indicated to Clancey were guard posts. In and out and gone. A few German fighters had tried to block the 47s but they hadn't lasted.

Michael would have touched wood, as the English said, but he didn't dare to think of luck as a factor in anything.

There were short bursts of automatic weapons fire and cries along the line of the woods. He could see figures falling in the grass. McCoy's squad had caught the stragglers.

"These bastards were off guard," Tucker said, as they moved forward to the smoking rubble of the blockhouse. "Looks like they had just finished cleaning up after that wrecked bomber and pulling it off the field. I guess they figured the fireworks were all over. But it's damned odd that they wouldn't be any more set for a raid. S.S. too, most of 'em. Whoever was in charge must be some fucking general's dumb-ass son-in-law."

Kitchens tried to accept the relative ease of the attack, the swift thrust of the paratroops. They had hit in four squads, textbook fashion. They'd had a pretty good plan of the base from Reichmann's hand-drawn map, pinpointing the guardhouse and bunker, the command post, hangers, and barracks. The telling factor was that the field had been built for concealment, not for defense. Hitting the command post, destroying the transmitter and cutting the cables had been simultaneous with the P-47 rocket run. If they were as lucky as it seemed, then there would have been no call for aid. They might have an hour before the situation was realized anywhere else. The beauty of an isolated base like this was that it was also far from military strongpoints. The sudden loss of communication might easily be attributed to the bombing run to the north. It was a fortunate coincidence that had, no doubt, drawn off some of the night fighter protection this sector had been assigned. Kitchens could allow himself little hope that all would go as well as it had to this point. The sky was growing lighter every moment. The morning star had already disappeared. He wondered if they would live to see it again.

As he walked beside the sergeant, moving up the side of the field from the burning blockhouse, he saw figures filing out of a doorway of what looked like a small hill. The men were clasping their hands on the backs of their heads, elbows high and wide and obviously assuring their captors of their peaceful surrender. He could see the dark, field outfits of his paratroopers now; their machine gun barrels pointed like accusing fingers as the prisoners moved past them in the awkward, accommodating shuffle of confusion and fear he'd seen so often in the last few weeks. From their walk alone, Kitchens could tell these were Luftwaffe, not S.S. troops. The pop of gunfire, further ahead, alerted him that not all the defenders had been captured and that these last few would no doubt be the hard core ones. The S.S. always demanded their pound of flesh. Michael was determined they would have as little as could be offered. He prayed they were not in the one structure he knew would be hardest to breach. Passing a seated line of shivering prisoners under the watch of a lone guard, he saw a dark figure loping toward them in the now familiar gait of the lanky Texan.

"Sir," McCoy nodded a salute as he met them. "We got the rest of them penned up, but they got themselves pretty well set."

Tucker grunted. "Casualties?"

The Texan nodded. "Five, I know of, sir. Potts and Bullock are dead. Davis, Wilber and Feinstein are hurt pretty bad. Feinstein may be gone already."

Kitchens frowned. "Did we capture the biological magazine?"

"No, sir. We hit the command post, all right. Transmitter down and radio shed shot to hell along with half the crew. But, we think they got maybe a dozen or so down into the magazine. They weren't all uniformed, either. Probably some of the scientist crew you were talking about."

"Damn it." Tucker rubbed his eyes, "That's just stinking great. Well, we got any more hot spots?"

McCoy lifted his helmet and wiped his close-shaved head. "We just snuffed out the last one, if nobody else comes rolling up the road, that is. We can't hold it too long if they do. Not without those P-47s. We're close to shootin' our wad."

Tucker nodded. "Good thing the Krauts decided to build this thing so far from anywhere else to hide it. It's the only favor they did us."

That was, indeed, the only hope their mission had been able to count on, Kitchens conceded; but the Germans had paratroops too. Damned good ones. And secret base or not, they couldn't hope for much more time before someone in the chain of command decided something was very wrong. The sky belonged firmly to the morning now. Even without glancing at his watch, Michael knew the C-47s would be flying down in an hour, looking for a chance to land if the flares were burning. The fighters that would come with them could hold a cap for maybe fifteen minutes. It wasn't much time if they were under attack. It was going to be tight.

"How many prisoners so far? Officers?" Kitchens asked.

McCoy smiled. "Got better than forty prisoners, most of 'em pinned up in a barracks past the wood there. Lots of ground crew but several S.S. guards too. Just three of our boys guarding 'em. We can seal the entrance when we leave. Oh yeah, the damndest thing was a corpse of a Luftwaffe colonel laid out with a sheet over him. Shot in the temple. Looked like a suicide. Think he's been dead a few hours though. Stiffening up pretty rigid. Of course, you get rigid right fast in this weather. In fact, there was a good eight cold S.S. laid out in a row in one of the hangers. Hell of a shoot-out in there a while before we got here. That'd be your team I guess."

Kitchens didn't have much hope but he asked anyway. "Anybody that looks like a scientist? Anybody that maybe worked on the bombs?"

McCoy shrugged. "I'm not Dick Tracy, sir. They just look like a bunch of scared guys to me. I think your lab boys got down in that bitch of a fortress over there. That's most likely where I'd hide 'em if I were in charge, anyway."

"What about it, Lieutenant? We're losing time." Tucker was looking across the clearing in front of an empty hanger to the small copse of trees that marked the round top of the heavily fortified magazine.

Kitchens lifted his binoculars and focused in on the shadows along the base of the mound. The fighting had blown away the camouflage on a pair of large iron doors that were the obvious access for the bombs. Fresh tracks led to it and the body of an S.S. soldier lay across it. A few openings might be ventilators or observation portals. Probably any venting would be through pipes in the artificial copse. Kitchens reflected on his orders. He must capture any personnel who could provide information on the bacteria or technology and destroy any capability of the enemy to produce more biological weapons. That meant taking that damned anthill. He had to make sure that every ember of this hellfire was stamped out cold, and he didn't have long.

"Bring the car with all the heavy stuff and the charges. I think we're going to have to burn these bastards out, if I know my fanatics."

Tucker watched as McCoy started off in a crouched run.

Hans Geltman rubbed his sweating brow with his sleeve and turned from the periscope. Through the haze of the glowing red lamps, he looked at the scene around him. Two distinct parties made up his remaining command. A half-dozen S.S. guards stood in battle-ready positions, grim-faced and intent on the narrow gunslits ranged around the circular chamber. Inside this ring of hardened defenders, stood an inner circle of scientists and laboratory workers, huddled in a tense, murmuring clump around their leader, Doctor Jost and the singularly imperturbable Professor Yakuro. The science team was gathered on the raised elevator platform normally used to bring up the plague bombs from the depths of the magazine below, passing through multiple sealed barriers as they ascended.

Geltman knew that each floor of the structure was built in reinforced concrete. Not even the English Blockbuster bomb would be likely to penetrate the complex defenses unless it could be dropped with an accuracy beyond the capability of any air corps in the world. The commandoes could be fought and held off for hours. Perhaps, they would break in the first level, but to take all four would be a problem that would take much too long. They must know this. Which meant that the Allied raid would ultimately fail. The commandoes must decide to leave or be captured.

Time. That was the problem for him as well. Yes, he'd been right. He had realized that he alone knew the absolute truth of the entire situation. The mission against the Russians might be a success, but there could be no more such missions from this base. It would now be a constant target for the Allied bomber command. He had suspected this from the beginning, from the moment he had learned of the destruction of the hotel in the village. He knew this could not have been any local uprising or Jewish conspiracy. Such

things only existed in the propaganda. He had known it was
nothing less than an Allied commando team.

It would take weeks to set up another appropriate chemical
support base capable of servicing the plague bombs. Modifying
smaller planes to replace the lost bombers would take far too long
and would restrict the target zone almost to their own doorstep.
The threat to the heartland of the Allies was lost. To switch to the
unpredictable rocket team might bring a weapon in time for the
next war but this one was clearly ending. Geltman knew this now.
Without the plague bombs to force the Russians and the Americans
to negotiations, they would be at the gates of Berlin in a matter of
weeks or even days. And where would he be then? He knew that
he had been right not to send an alarm to Berlin when the second
attack had started. His own bullet had shattered the emergency
radio transmitter when the first explosions alerted him to the
commando raid. He smiled. There was always a place for the
Geltmans in this world.

Except for heading changes from Lauda, the crew hadn't
spoken in the last hour. Chris Clancey moved back through the
plane to get a bandage for his forehead. His scalp had been sliced
by a corner of the bomb-sight tripod as he was thrown against the
canopy in the collision with the other plane. The bleeding had
finally stopped and the blood clotted the white gauze crown that
Von Tripps had wrapped around his head. The sulphur had cut
back the pain to a dull throb now and Chris sat sideways behind
the pilot and co-pilot, his back resting on a parachute pack propped
against the curved interior of the fuselage. The vibration of the four
motors hummed though him like a second pulse. He felt a tiredness
working into him and though his survival might depend on his
alertness in the next minutes, he was having difficulty caring very
much about it. Only the girl remained. What they could do for
Reisa, he did not know. The war was washing over them and he
knew that the only thing he and Klaus Reichmann had left was this
idea—this attempt to protect her. What Von Tripps and Lauda had
left to them, Clancey could not determine.

They were flying in the stark daylight now. A single plane
moving across the empty sky of Germany like a fly trapped in a

bottle. Soon, they must settle. Surely German fighters would intercept them. There must have been a frenzy of communications from Geltman and Shaeffer to all Luftwaffe units to find them. Except for one simple factor. They were doing the one thing they should *not* be doing—returning to Halburg at full cruising speed a scant hundred feet above the trees to hide from radar eyes. Vaguely, Chris wondered if the command was aware that the other bomber had been downed. The more he thought of it, the more certain he was that they must be. There were supposed to be fighter units along the Polish front that would have been ready and waiting to escort the returning Black Arrow. Pilots, who wouldn't know why, would be ordered up to meet a small formation of unusual planes. They wouldn't question it. When none appeared, they would know that something was wrong. Clancey's mind washed back to the village. By now, Geltman would have launched another intensive manhunt for the remaining conspirators. He would know that Reisa Konnings was somewhere near at hand. His only hope at redemption with his superiors would be to produce any traitor he could lay his hands on.

Traitors. No doubt, the Colonel considered him a traitor now. If he should manage to reach his own lines, Chris could hardly expect much better treatment than Geltman would receive from his superiors in Berlin. Disobeying orders was viewed with a singularly nonpartisan vehemence by all warring peoples, including his own.

Clancey watched as Lauda crawled through the rounded portal from the navigator's cabin to move behind the two pilots. The navigator put a hand on Reichmann's shoulder and waited for the pilot to acknowledge him before speaking. "Klaus, I have been thinking. I know what you want to do. Maybe you can do something for the girl. Maybe not. I don't know. Probably, she will be caught soon. Even if you should somehow find her, you cannot hope to fight your way out of Germany. I say this as your friend. Give up. Turn south. We can almost certainly make Switzerland. It is the border we do not defend. What can you do for her? You have done all she asked and more."

Clancey waited quietly for Reichmann's reply. He saw that Von Tripps was waiting, also.

"Heinrich, I cannot leave. It will be as we decided. The American and I are going to parachute outside the town. You and Reinhardt can still make the border." The pilot smiled suddenly, as if he had just remembered how to smile. "God willing, we shall meet in Berne in a few weeks."

Lauda looked to Von Tripps who only nodded with little enthusiasm. "Yes. Well, we're about sixteen kilometers out. You had better strap on your pack, Captain."

Chris was slipping the straps of his parachute over his shoulders when he heard Von Tripps' warning shout.

"Christ. Fighters. P-51s."

Clancey leaned forward, staring out of the glass of the pilot's canopy. There, far to starboard—high and falling toward them—a pair of American fighters, the sun glistening off their polished aluminum wings. Chris was ready for the sudden tug of inertia as Reichmann threw the big plane into a bank to spoil the trajectory of the speeding attackers. Then he caught sight of a black smoke trail etching up from the ground directly ahead. It had to be the base.

"Look." Now Lauda was shouting. "C-47s."

"It's a raid." Clancey slapped Lauda's shoulder. "It's a goddamned pickup. They changed their minds. They sent in the troops."

Von Tripps was shoving Lauda back. "Get on a gun. These fighters are going to tear us apart."

As if in answer to the co-pilot's cry, there was a loud, ripping hail as a silver shape sped past them from the portside.

"That's the number three motor," Klaus grunted. "Lock it, Reinhardt." He rocked the big plane into another defensive bank.

Lauda's fist slammed into the back of the co-pilot's seat. "Damn. I knew it."

Von Tripps turned back to Lauda. "We're better off going in, Heinrich, with three motors and a bent blade. Make the choice, now."

The navigator glared at Clancey, then nodded quickly. "Yes. Take her in." He turned back to face Clancey and gritted his teeth. "I promise you one thing, Captain. If we do not survive, neither will you."

Clancey didn't smile. "I wouldn't worry about that."

CHAPTER 25

Reisa Konnings sat inside the car beside Ricard. The shivering boy was wrapped in a blanket and the girl kept an arm around him, trying to warm him from the cold that seemed to have lodged in him like a solid thing. The youth had done wonders that night, Reisa marveled. Somehow, he had shoved aside the cold illness of his lungs to take his place at his brother's side and then had managed to rendezvous with the Americans. But now, his strength had collapsed and little remained to summon against this consumptive siege. Stroking his head, Reisa prayed silently for Ricard and his brother but a great uneasiness distracted her as she gazed with foreboding at the men across the wet field.

While the fighting of the dark morning had been frightening, the quiet calm that encompassed them now seemed to hold an even more sinister quality. Reisa felt herself shudder involuntarily at the sight of the Gestapo officer talking with the American lieutenant and the priest. The small group was halfway between the crouched paratroopers, who lined the edge of the trees, and the deceptively peaceful-looking mound beyond them. Father Lott had tried to keep her informed of events as he listened to the men around them in the last hours. But when the white flag had appeared from the hidden fortress fifteen minutes ago, the lanky private had come to get Lott to act as an interpreter. Reisa had had only her vision of events to interpret.

She remembered the Gestapo officer well. His face was etched in her mind. He had had an arrogant, hateful glee—a mocking voice of dominance as she had lain restrained. She had watched the injections and waited as she felt the drugs working through her body; first, turning her own muscles to relaxed treason and then, her thoughts themselves to witless collaborators. She remembered the losing fight, the slow failing, until only a sense of despair had remained to help her fight. Yes, it was an edge of desperate defiance that had seized on the one lie that had been allowed to fall through unchecked. She shuddered again at the nearness of that total defeat. Yet she had always believed miracles start with such small unreasoned acts... keys that unlocked the chains of the mighty. Reisa sought comfort in this thought but could not overcome the knot that grew in her stomach and the chill the sight of the figure in the black overcoat seemed to emit even here in the safety of the car. Beneath the banner of truce, the man still seemed triumphant. For all of their efforts and all their sacrifices, was this to be the moment of victory? For *this* had Klaus, Rudi, and Clancey, been swallowed up by the sky?

The Gestapo officer turned and walked back toward the hidden bunker. Kitchens and Father Lott were returning. The lieutenant stopped to talk with the gruff paratroop sergeant, but the priest continued to the car. Stepping inside, he quickly closed the door to the cold. He was obviously distracted but spoke to Reisa. "Ricard sleeps?"

"Between coughs," she said. "What has happened?"

Dieter Lott bit his lip before answering. "A truce. A bargain, perhaps."

Reisa searched his face, uncertain of his thoughts. "They will surrender?"

"Yes. Geltman has agreed to bring them out."

"What of the bombs? The danger?"

Lott looked out the window, pondering the full consequences of the meeting with the Gestapo officer. "He says there is a system to destroy the germs; a fire to burn them out. It will be done."

Reisa followed his gaze out the window, looking toward the lieutenant and the sergeant. "In return for what? What does he want?" A sick feeling, like an internal imbalance, began to weight her senses.

The priest drew a breath before answering. "He wants to be taken prisoner with the scientists. There are two men who understand the bombs. He will bring them out only if he is promised no prosecution for his position as Gestapo head of this operation."

Reisa trembled. "I do not understand. Can this be done?"

Lott nodded. "Yes. Geltman wants to be taken along with these great prizes. He will be treated no differently than a common soldier. He fears reprisal when the war is over. He will not face prosecution as a war criminal. He is demanding a written order to be signed by the lieutenant assuring him of this condition."

Reisa swallowed but the knot in her throat was not eased. "The Americans will do this? The lieutenant will allow this? You know what he has done. What he *is*. The murders, tortures…"

Lott took Reisa's hand firmly in his. He waited for her to gather herself before answering. "Child, what would you have the lieutenant do? We have so little time. It would take a great battle to break through the defense of that bunker in order to destroy what is inside. It would cost the lives of many of these brave men who have already risked so much this day. It might cost all our lives. Is justice for one evil man worth the lives of all these?"

Reisa stared at the priest in quiet protest. At last, she closed her eyes and answered. "You are right, Father. It is only when I think of Rudi and Klaus and Clancey." She bit her lip.

Lott touched her face. "And, you. And, doubtless, many others he has broken. Yes. I think of them, too, Reisa. I won't pretend I do not hate him. I hate him as I have hated no man in my life. I cannot deal with that now. That is not the purpose of this day. The bombs will be stopped. That is why Rudi and the others have given so much. Think only of that."

As he spoke, the priest looked at the rounded hill of the copse and saw the thick metal doors opening. Some of the Americans were moving into the field with their rifles and machine guns at the ready, spreading out to cover the opening with a wide angle of fire.

A few empty seconds passed before several German soldiers came out in a single file, hands above their heads, weapons left behind.

There was a tapping on the window of the car. Lott opened it to listen to the paratrooper who waited outside.

"Father, the lieutenant needs you again, sir."

Lott looked at Reisa and let go of her hand, leaving a rosary in her fingers. Shutting the door firmly behind him, he turned to follow the soldier to rejoin Lieutenant Kitchens in the field.

Reisa watched as the eight German soldiers paused and waited for the wide circle of paratroopers to move up to them. They were marching past the car; grim-faced and tense in front of a single American paratrooper who held a machine gun pointed toward them and walked with a confident saunter, chewing a wad of some material which distended his left cheek in a peculiar manner. Reisa wondered vaguely if it were perhaps some salve for an injury. Looking back to the copse she saw another smaller group of men were coming out of the hill. There were five with Geltman leading them. These were not soldiers but were dressed in overcoats and parkas. Trailing below the border of one of the overcoats like a hastily gathered slip was the white hem of a laboratory coat. These were the scientists, the men who had concocted the horror that was burning below ground if what Geltman had said was true. The Gestapo officer was waiting with these men for the lieutenant, Father Lott, and two paratroopers to meet them.

The awkward sequence of surrender was interrupted in an instant as Reisa saw all the men freeze and turn as one to stare at something behind and above her field of vision inside the car. Before she could understand their surprised actions, there was a drumming roar that shook the car and a flash of shadow and bright silver directly overhead. It was a plane, rising to clear the hillock, its roiling wake whipping the trees of the copse wildly as the men crouched. Then, like excited children, the paratroopers were cheering and waving as the silver plane rose tightly upward bearing its white stars and blue bars like a proud bird. The tail was painted a bright red with flashes of black. It was the American fighters. The transports would arrive for them now.

The sight of the gleaming, aluminum planes tearing over the fields from all points of the compass and pulling up in wing-wagging salutes made Reisa feel a sense of awesome power so great it dwarfed the smug evil of even the Gestapo officer into insignificance. These dashing, roaring fighter planes seemed a vision of an avenging host of heaven. Reisa sensed movement at her side and turned to see Ricard staring out at the twisting fighters. Quietly watching the glinting quicksilver in the morning sun, a thin smile slowly creased his pale face. "Father Lott's angels," he whispered and closed his eyes, settling back again to rest.

As she watched the boy leaning back onto the seat, Reisa caught a sudden light in the mirror of the car, followed instantly by an audible thump. She turned to watch a bright green flare shooting over the end of the field. She could see that the men were pointing toward something in the distance. She opened the car door and stepped out, pulling herself up and against the top of the door frame to peer beyond the tree line. Now, she could see them: a pair of large dirty-brown airplanes. One of them was banking slightly and moving down toward them. Its wheels were extended. It was their transport. It was the way out.

It all seemed to be drawing to a close. She turned to look in the car at the resting Ricard Zimmer. She opened the door wider and leaned in to wake him again. "Ricard. The transport plane is here. We will be going now."

Zimmer's eyes opened and he smiled.   Suddenly, a harsh chattering drew his head up. The sudden sound of machine gun fire commanded their complete attention. What had happened? What had gone wrong?

Reisa was staring, frozen to the door of the car, as Lott and McCoy reached her on the run.

"Get down, ma'am," the Texan was shouting.

"Come, child." Lott was grabbing her arm, pulling her away from the car as the sound of the guns drew nearer.

"What is it, Father?" Reisa cried, but turned to see for herself. The big black shape of a bomber plunged down toward them, smoke trailing from the wing, a single wheel down, and the fighters raking it with fire.   Instantly, she knew that it was Reichmann.

"Klaus!" she cried. "My God. Klaus!" Now Reisa was running forward, tearing away from Lott and the soldier, running toward the field as the Americans were dropping down, raising their weapons to fire on the German plane.

Lying beside the Gestapo officer and Tucker, watching the insane approach of the crippled bomber, Michael Kitchens saw the girl rushing, stumbling from the car toward the field as the guns around him were firing. In a flash, he knew. "Hold your fire, men! Hold your fire!" He yelled, leaping to his feet and waving his hands. "Jesus H. God. It's Clancey!"

Lieutenant Johnson barked orders to his wingman over his radio microphone. "Lay off 'em, Oscar! They're the guys the troopers are here for! Just got a call from the ground leader. Go check the road for any traffic. I'll check the ceiling." With a nod from his partner, Marcus pulled the big P-51 Mustang up to sweep the sky over the field. This cover job had been called in at the last minute and he'd hardly known what to expect. Jets and rocket planes? The Krauts were full of surprises. He glanced back down at the crashed bomber at the edge of the trees. They should have told him what to look out for. The 100th fighter squadron was an aggressive bunch and they'd had no warning about this plane. He and the five other red-tails that scrambled for this trip were supposed to suppress anything approaching the field. Nothing was going to keep those Dakotas from taking off, but he hoped they got on with it. They didn't have their biggest fuel tanks and it was a long way home.

Chris Clancey was clawing for life, tearing at the straps that bound him even before his mind had cleared from the brain-rattling impact. The big plane had hooked around on the single wheel and skidded into the tree-line where it had shattered itself into a broken mass of metal and rubber. Chris could not remember the handful of seconds that encompassed the arrest of their fatal inertia. More than anything, he was aware of a surreal stillness. A deafening quiet seemed to cover his instinctive struggle for survival. It was as if he were watching a different self, his own body fighting to free itself from the smoking metal fuselage with an urgency his spirit

could not seem to muster. Now, from above, he saw a hand
descending, its wide-spread fingers and palm brightly lit in the
shadows of the dying craft. It was a vision of Messianic proportion
he thought in cynical disappointment with what must be the last
desires of his desperate heart. Now the reaching hand broke free of
his supposed hallucination and gripped his forearm with a force
that threatened to crack the bones. He felt himself pulled to a
growing awareness of reality like a drowning man hauled to the
surface of a dark sea. His head swam with light and new pain as he
looked into the face of an incredulous Michael Kitchens.

"You're not dead yet, you bastard."

Clancey croaked and nodded.

"McCoy, Kirby! Get this man out of here! This whole plane's
gonna' blow!"

Clancey began helping the men who were lowering him down
from the broken opening in the fuselage. As his feet reached the
ground, he was able to make his way with only the arm of Private
McCoy for support. After several seconds of a stumbling run
across the grassy field, the men stopped and Clancey dropped to
his hands and knees to take long, deep breaths of the cold air into
his smoke-filled lungs. His vision was clearing and his hearing had
returned. He could hear the crackle of flames and the sound of
aircraft motors nearby. He sat up on his knees and looked at the
people gathered around him. Kitchens was smiling like a Boy
Scout. He recognized Father Lott who was anxiously watching as a
medic bent down beside him and began pulling away the remains
of the bandage that Lauda had wrapped for him.

"The others?" Chris choked.

Lott bent down beside him on his knees to speak over the
sounds of the fire. "Klaus and the navigator are all right. The co-
pilot was killed in the crash."

Kitchens knelt down. "Clancey, what about the raid? The
other bomber, the one that got away? What happened?"

Clancey shook his head. "We stopped them. They're all dead."

The priest crossed himself as Kitchens leaned closer.

"No bombs?" Michael asked.

"No bombs," Clancey reassured him wearily. "There won't be
a plague." He turned his head toward the hillock where the bombs

had been prepared. "What about this place? You burn the stuff? Get rid of it all?"

"It's cooking right now. We even got the top men. Couple of scientists and a Gestapo officer to boot. He was ready to deal."

Clancey stood slowly, steadying himself against the medic. "Deal what?"

Sergeant Tucker stepped into the group and with a brusque nod interrupted Clancey's query. "Lieutenant. We got to get going. This fighter cap can't wait. There'll be somebody on us any time now if we don't clear this field."

"Deal *what*, Michael?" Clancey repeated. He hadn't moved and his eyes were locked on Kitchens' face.

Michael frowned. "You know. The scientists, the germ plans, for considerations. Look, Chris, it's not pretty. I don't like it either, but we've stopped the Nazis. Come on."

The group of men started to make their way across the field toward the waiting C-47s. Clancey saw Reisa Konnings standing beside Klaus Reichmann and Heinrich Lauda at the ladder to the nearest transport. Reichmann's left arm was in a sling and Reisa turned from the pilot to face Chris as he followed the small party toward them. He could see Reichmann's face was hard. Chris followed his cold stare to a small cluster of figures a dozen feet from them.

Under the watchful eye of a sentry with a machine gun held loosely on them, the party of prisoners waited to board one of the transport planes. Clancey had never seen Geltman, but the uniform of the devil was clear enough. Beside the Gestapo officer stood three uneasy figures in various jackets pulled over the tell-tale lab coats of technicians and a tightly-bundled oriental gentleman with them could only be the Japanese scientist described to Chris by Reichmann.

Clancey stopped in front of Reichmann and the girl as a pair of paratroopers carefully lifted a wounded man into the wide double doors to his left.

The German pilot spoke quietly to Chris. "Reinhardt died."

Clancey nodded. "Yes."

"So…" Klaus paused and his eyes moved tiredly to the prisoners as he finished. "Now, *you* have the bombs."

Reisa said nothing but looked at Clancey. He could read the sadness and pity in her face.

Chris saw that the other transport had wound up its motors and was taxiing away. Turning further, he could see Kitchens helping Ricard Zimmer from the car. Father Lott was beside him, taking an arm over his shoulder as Kitchens brought the boy upright. Speaking German again, Chris turned back to Reichmann and Reisa and uttered a quiet, "Nein." Then he moved to his right.

The flat of Clancey's hand on the young sentry's neck fell with the perfect force to render him unconscious. As he pulled the machine gun from the hands of the dropping paratrooper, Clancey was aware of the shouts behind him. Bringing up the barrel of the weapon as he crouched over the stricken sentry, he saw the sudden fear etched on the faces of the five prisoners. He felt the bullet strike his back, just below the right shoulder in the moment after he had depressed the trigger. Chris held the firing machine gun on his targets even while he sagged to the earth. He saw all of them fall. Before the new pain could blank his mind, he felt the weapon being twisted from his hands and rolled onto his back, looking up at the face of Reisa Konnings who was bending down near to him.

Clancey heard someone reporting loudly from beyond the circle of faces over him. "They've had it, sir. All five of 'em." Kitchens was crouching over him again, grim-faced and shouting orders.

"Tucker. Get these people loaded. No, the priest stays." Kitchens turned back to Chris. "Damn it, Clancey. Damn it."

Chris winced as he felt the paratroop medic pulling him to a sitting position with Reichmann's help. He coughed and felt fluid pooling in his lungs.

"He'll live, sir. If we can get him back fast enough."

They were all shouting now over the growing drone of the transport motors. The medic's report seemed more optimistic than Chris felt. The soldier motioned to the sentry Clancey had attacked who was being helped up the ladder.

"Clemmons will have a sore neck for a week, but it isn't broken."

Kitchens grit his teeth. "Get Clancey's ass on the plane." He stood up and helped the medic escort Clancey to the wide door where the soldiers took him up. Michael stood back and looked around him. The other plane was clearing the field. His gaze fell on the five dead men in the grass just ten feet away. The priest was standing over them; the motors of the C-47 washing his grey hair around in whipping strands over his bare head. He looked up to meet Kitchens' eyes. The motors were too loud for him to hear anything the old man might say, but he saw the priest raise his hand in a somber blessing and Michael nodded an uneasy salute as he took the hand of the airman in the doorway of the plane and pulled himself aboard.

Dieter Lott walked alone in the stillness of the deserted airfield; the only sound now, the crackling of fires and his boots on the frozen ground as he moved among the stranded bodies of the dead left behind by the conflict. The Americans had taken their own with them on the planes. The retreating Germans had not returned from their rout. Near the open cave that had been a hanger for the great secret planes, he found the one he had been searching for. He bent down to close the open eyes and gently stroked the fine stubble on the young face. Josef had been his favorite. "Hear oh Israel, the Lord our God is one," he whispered as he prayed. Surely, Christ knew his own, even if they did not, Dieter told himself as he lifted the boy's body in his arms.

"Lieutenant, we're over our lines." The airman had carefully worked his way down the fuselage from the cockpit to report.

"Thanks." Kitchens turned to look across the narrow aisle of the transport at the girl and the Luftwaffe pilot. He wished he spoke German. These two must know the whole story. He could only imagine what dangers they had faced, what risks they'd run. These were not traitors, not turn-coats like the dead men on the airstrip who held no honor higher than survival. In the eyes of the pilot, he saw a hero like Clancey. The man on the stretcher between them stirred and the medic who tended the plasma bag that ran to the needle in Clancey's arm leaned forward.

"He's coming back around, sir."

Kitchens saw Reisa Konnings squeezing the German pilot's hand as they watched Clancey's eyes open. He saw the moment the spy's eyes met the girl's and the smile. It was the first real smile he had seen on Clancey's face in all the time he'd known him. The girl shifted forward and reached down to take Clancey's hand in hers.

Clancey rolled his head to the side and looked up at Kitchens. He was still smiling.

"You shot me?" Clancey's voice was faint above the drum of the motors.

Kitchens bent down to answer. "Hell, yes," he said.

"Piss poor job."

"Waste of a bullet," Michael replied. He shook his head. "Why, Chris? Why did you do it? We had them."

Clancey closed his eyes for a second and swallowed before he answered with obvious difficulty. "You were right... We stopped the Nazis." He paused to gather his strength. "But, who's going to stop *us*?"

Kitchens sat looking into Clancey's face for a moment and wondered, indeed, if anyone could ever close Pandora's box. He felt a sad empathy for this man who had tried. He saw Clancey was trying to speak again over the motors.

"This crew... these Germans... they're heroes, Mike. You've got to take good care of them." The words were hard work.

"It's done," Kitchens assured him.

Clancey let a hard breath out. "Throw my ass to the Colonel." The smile had returned.

Kitchens shook his head. "We already threw his ass to SHAEF."

Clancey's eyes opened wider. "Who did?"

"I did."

Clancey blinked and nodded his approval.

Michael chuckled mirthlessly. "Yeah, they sent me on this little soiree to save the Russians, and get my hands on the bombs. Well, I guess I got you, instead."

"They're gonna' be disappointed, Mike—" Clancey coughed hard.

Michael Kitchens turned to the sergeant sitting next to him leaning tiredly on his field pack. "Tucker?"

"Yes, Lieutenant?"

"You will remind your men that any discussion of what happened today—any loose talk at all—is punishable by—"

"Don't worry, sir. This whole damn mess is so top secret I've already forgotten it myself. You just take your man home. And if I were you, I wouldn't lose any sleep over dead Gestapo."

Michael looked past the sergeant at the paratroopers resting down both sides of the fuselage. Though they had heard little of the talk, the nearest faces nodded their agreement with their leader and Michael knew he had ample reason to trust these young men. He turned back to Clancey who still held Reisa Konnings' hand.

You could never know if the victories were worth the costs, he considered. And, maybe he couldn't stop wars and the evil that men do to each other. But there was one thing he could do and that was send Chris Clancey home. Maybe the Colonel was right. Sometimes, you had to play God.

THE END

6265482R0

Made in the USA
Charleston, SC
04 October 2010